An Anthology of Fetish Fiction
Edited and with an Introduction by John Yau

An Anthology of Fetish Fiction

Edited and with an Introduction by John Yau

FOUR WALLS EIGHT WINDOWS
NEW YORK / LONDON

INTRODUCTION © 1998 JOHN YAU
ANTHOLOGY SELECTION © 1998 JOHN YAU

PUBLISHED IN THE UNITED STATES BY:
FOUR WALLS EIGHT WINDOWS
39 WEST 14TH STREET, ROOM 503
NEW YORK, N.Y., 10011

U.K. OFFICES:
FOUR WALLS EIGHT WINDOWS/TURNAROUND
UNIT 3, OLYMPIA TRADING ESTATE
COBURG ROAD, WOOD GREEN
LONDON N22 6TZ, ENGLAND

VISIT OUR WEBSITE AT HTTP://WWW.FOURWALLSEIGHTWINDOWS.COM

FIRST PRINTING OCTOBER 1998.

LIBRARY OF CONGRESS CATALOGING-IN-PUBLICATION DATA:
YAU, JOHN.
FETISH: AN ANTHOLOGY/EDITED AND WITH AN INTRODUCTION
BY JOHN YAU.
P. CM.
ISBN 1-56858-117-3
1. FETISHISM—FICTION. 2. FETISHISM (SEXUAL BEHAVIOR)—FICTION. 3.
PSYCHOLOGICAL FICTION, AMERICAN. 4. EROTIC STORIES, AMERICAN.
PS648.F43F48 1998
813'.0108353—DC21   98-36710
CIP
10 9 8 7 6 5 4 3 2 1

TEXT DESIGN BY MORGAN BRILLIANT
PRINTED IN THE UNITED STATES

IN MEMORY:

KATHY ACKER
DONALD BARTHELME
CHARLES BUKOWSKI
WILLIAM BURROUGHS
ANGELA CARTER
ALLEN GINSBERG
JOHN HAWKES

TABLE OF CONTENTS

III. Us-Them

INTRODUCTION
John Yau

We live in an age of anthologies, perhaps because the world is—
both the end of the "Cold War" and Rodney King's plea not with-
standing—still divided into the tribal pronoun clusters of "us" and
"them." And because, whenever I go to a bookstore, there seems to be
an anthology for every kind of "us" or "them" (depending on whether
you are a writer or a reader)—*Emerging Poets of the Great Chalk
Basin*; *Children Who Have Written Monster* (or is it *Monstrous) Stories*; *Men Who Have Written About Neither Their Mothers Nor Fathers Nor Anything Else Having to Do with Relationships, Planetary
or Otherwise*—that exists, I began wondering if there also existed an
anthology that transcended the categories I kept seeing displayed
prominently. In short, I started fetishizing about what this anthology
might be, began wondering what this imaginary object might contain
in order to satisfy my desire for an anthology that would neither rep-
licate previous anthologies nor settle for an already defined category.

Freud, Marx, Picasso—our century started with fetish, with ana-
lyzing as well as incorporating what was deemed forbidden, desirable, exotic. Fetish was (and is) the idol, the manifestation of the
distant and unobtainable and therefore worshipped; it is the sleek
new car that someone can never afford, the colored contact lens one
needs to become perfect, the diapers, gloves, hat, mask, fur, whip or
teeth one needs to have present in sexual love, the African gods that
Picasso learned from, as well as incorporated into his art.

In integrating the abstract patterning and flattening of African
religious sculpture with the images of prostitutes in his
groundbreaking painting *Les Demoiselles d'Avignon*, Picasso joined
together the exotic and the forbidden for the delectation of all. Is the
size of the audience the difference between the artist and the thief,
or am I falling back again into that tribal pronoun usage of "us" and
"them"? Don't both artist and thief worship Mercury, the messenger god? Thus, we might recall that in *Les Demoiselles d'Avignon*,
one of the women has just pulled back the curtain, showing us—
the client and viewer—what is for sale.

Recently, in the newspaper, I read about a man who had been accused of terrorizing a mother and four daughters. It seems he (it was assumed to be a "he") kept stealing their underwear off the clothesline. The frightened mother called the police, who began staking out her backyard. After they caught the culprit on videotape, the police arrested him. It struck me that in videotaping the man in the act of swiping the women's underwear off the clothesline, the policemen became voyeurs. There is the illegal theft and the sanctioned voyeurism. Isn't reading a kind of voyeurism? Isn't this one of its delicious and guilty pleasures? Isn't this why we leaf through certain glossy tell-all magazines while standing at the supermarket checkout line? We want to know what others worship. Is it only something as boring as money? Or is it something only money can buy?

In thinking about, as well as putting together, this anthology, I tried to define a different kind of "us," one that was infinitely open, one that didn't derive its admission standard from a category based on a style of writing, on race, gender, or sexual preference. One writer, however, refused to have her story reprinted, because, as her agent told me, she didn't want to be typecast. Still, it seems to me fetish, that which is unobtainable and/or that which becomes emblematic of our desires, is a constant; it plays a role in all our lives, and it is a trace of our precivilized past, our days of living in caves and worshipping idols. Who among us does not fetishize? as Rilke might have called out, but didn't. We want to know more about what others among us worship, desire, need. We are voyeurs peeking through the windows of someone else's world, which is, of course, ours.

The reader of this anthology is someone looking across the airshaft, yard, room, or time. On the other side is a bed rigged with a strange contraption, an apartment in which the past (in the form of an ex-lover) clings to one's body, a dream of flying, a dimension in which numbers and things blend together. A train crosses a landscape, a car circles a neighborhood, a sphere arrives from another dimension, a woman hears the steps of her husband in the hall and begins hiding the tell-tale evidence.

Is it "I" looking at "you"? Is it "I" seeing "myself"? Or am "I" finally alone with "it"? Open this book, read, find out, and enjoy.

NOTE

In putting together this anthology, I solicited authors who had been influential on my own writing, authors who had been in classes I taught, and authors whose work I admired. Still others heard about the anthology through word of mouth and sent me work. In nearly every case, the writing I received had either never previously been published or had only a fugitive life, appearing in a magazine or in a foreign publication. One story, "Baker Betterlaugh Today" by A. G. Rizzoli (1896–1981), was written in 1934, but was never published during the author's lifetime. This is the first time his fiction has been published.

Many people helped me by providing addresses and phone numbers, as well as suggesting authors whose work had slipped my attention. I would like to thank Mary Jo Bang, Garrett Caples, Lynn Crawford, Guy Davenport, Brian Evenson, Jonathan Lethem, Albert Mobilio, Laura Mullen, and Eileen Myles for their advice, friendship, and encouragement. I would also like to thank John Martin, publisher of Black Sparrow Press, and John Oakes of Four Walls Eight Windows.

—J.Y.

I

I-You

CALL AND NO RESPONSE
Lynne Tillman

"Spending my days, thinking 'bout you . . ." Phone doesn't ring. "Can't explain myself." Hate this. "Are you still . . ." Fucking phone. "Let me know . . ." Phone rings once, dies. "I'm gonna call your name." Hate him. "I've got something to say." Love's ugly. "Never let me down." Love should be embarrassed. "Something's going wrong." Love's sick. "Love and happiness." Grab the receiver. "Someone's on the phone, three o'clock in the morning." Open wound. "Be good to me." Bleeding. "Love'll make you do wrong." Wordless, hang up. "Love is." Over. "Baby, won't you hold my hand." Need something sweet. "Nighttime find me." Fetal position. "There's a whole lot of crying you and I could do." Remember. "What about the way you love me?" No, no. "All you have to do is call me." Mouth, neck, skin, mouth. "Won't you talk to me." Remote, cold. "Life goes on." Infinite replays. "This world keeps on turning." Nausea. "Be glad we had this time together." Time's shit. "Place your head on my pillow." Numb despair. "Make believe you love me one more time." Sleepless, TV. "For the good times." Dumb regret. "But now the day has come." Daybreak, day's broken. "But these things don't come overnight." Life's a grave. "Baby." Monster. "Look what you done to me." Water, mirror. "The price you have to pay." Swollen face, emptiness. "One of these days I'm gonna call you." Hollow waiting. "I'm still in love with you."

3

WAIT UNTIL DARK
Kevin Killian

On either side of the trailer park a patch of wild native flowers billows and whispers, kind of eerie. I'm stepping through it, on tiptoe. The moon is up, a white ring of neon in a black, black sky. Seems like a good night to look for Gary Radley. I want to know if his trailer's been sighted anywhere in Gavet. To wade through these flowers I take off my shoes, ditch them in my little blue bag. I'm quiet, like the moon, and I'm watching his space.

I stand stock still and let the various scents of the flowers rise from the ground and climb up my nostrils. Lovely, lovely! Reminds me of the flower market in Covent Garden where Audrey Hepburn, in Cecil Beaton rags, slaves all night with that bad Cockney accent, black soot smeared on her cheekbones. Everyone always asks me, what *is* it with you and Audrey? Dunno. She's so reserved and valiant. Did you know she was the youngest member of the Dutch resistance? Tell you the truth, I don't really know what the "Dutch resistance" means. But the people who buy my autographed photos of Audrey don't seem to care either. They just know, by looking into her eyes, that she was young, thin, brave as Hell. So there I am, cruising the violets and the Dutchman's Breeches—those pale, mushroom looking unhealthy flowers ... at night they look particularly pallid, in moonlight—when I saw his trailer. His trailer come back. I could feel my heart quickening and banging inside my chest like a cage filled with hamsters as I approached its dark silvery hulk and began to knock my fists into its side. "Gary!" But no one was home, no matter how hard I knocked I couldn't make him *be* home if he wasn't home. "Come back!" I repeated, out loud on my way back to my house, kicking the pebbles and the tinsel that littered my path. It was days before I got the nerve to go back and knock like a man.

The moon grew smaller, no longer a ring, more like a piece of something bitten off and chewed. One night I had this idea of surprising Gary Radley, after watching a tape of Audrey in *Wait Until Dark*. If you haven't seen this movie, it *is so scary and she's blind!*

I picked my way to his trailer, stepped in, tentatively I held out my two hands. "Since you went away," I began, "I went blind."

"Did you?" said Gary Parker Radley.

He's a mystery man who appeared in our town a few months back, won my heart, then up and left me. He's 37 according to court documents. Tall, sharp-featured *mensch* kind of guy. Don't know what he does now, but it can't be legal. Not with all those tattoos and the air of violent crime that surrounds him like a cloud of perfume. I had only "dated" him two or three times before he asked me to speak to his parole officer on his behalf. That's not a good sign, or is it? I thought, *he's trying to make something out of himself.* Then he disappeared and I had to do a lot of fast talking. Mostly to myself. So when I stepped into his trailer I thought, *if I'm blind he won't leave me. He'll know he's needed.*

His trailer's not big but when you can't see a space, oh does it stretch out! I kept thinking, it's terrible to be so blind. I could feel the cool air on my wrists. It was night but—how did I know?

I turned over my hands so that my palms hung down. Again the cool air. "Yes, and everyone's been wonderful. Just wonderful, Gary. The only thing is—I try to be brave."

A woman in the far end of the room began to speak. "I'd better go," said she in cultivated accents like she's from Bryn Mawr like Grace Kelly.

I jumped up a little and darted my closed eyelids every which way to show surprise. "We're not alone?" I gasped.

"No," said Radley. "I have a girlfriend here. She's soft and pretty."

I moved a step here, a step there, as though confused. Confusion wasn't hard to feign. Actually I felt confused as hell. "Is there anyone there?" said I. Ugh, then I stepped on something that felt like a stuffed animal.

Gary snickered.

Just that one snicker. This should have taught me right there, don't get involved with a straight man. Because you never know when they'll have *girls* over their trailer, especially if you don't call first. The girl pulled on her gloves (I heard this kind of *woolen* sound) as though she really were going someplace. "Oh no," said I, "don't leave on my account. I'm the intruder: you're the guest."

But people have this social training, and I guess especially at Bryn Mawr, that makes them bend over backwards to be nice to the blind, so the girl rose up a little bit and again she said, "I'd better go," to Gary Parker Radley—and in her voice a series of tiny trills and bumps alerted me to this kind of romantic passion she had for him—maybe? Because he was seductive. I couldn't stay away from him no matter how hard I tried. At work I couldn't pay attention to my new orders, back orders, stock orders, sales slips. Once I found myself throwing away a wonderful sepia print of Ruby Keeler—and I pulled back, sat down, put a wet washcloth to my throbbing temples.

A narrow escape since I already had a buyer for my Ruby.

Anyhow we got it sorted out and Girlfriend stayed where she was. Where exactly that was I couldn't tell. She was just this cold austere wedge of silence seated patiently in the trailer space. I could feel her presence like a chill in the air. When you get involved with a man out of the state penitentiary, I reminded myself, don't be surprised at anything he does. Just let him be him! I felt disapproval moving back and forth between me and Girlfriend like radar blips in *Ice Station Zebra*. I didn't like her and she didn't like me. Or maybe she had a prejudice against *all blind people?* But Gary's trailer was pretty spooky, I had to admit. He had a mask of human skin pinned up to one wall, and an umbrella stand filled with human bones jammed into a corner. Wouldn't a *seeing* girl get the picture and make her excuses?

On the table before me, I felt some lumps and grit that must be drugs, I thought, remembering Audrey Hepburn's terror in *Wait Until Dark*, when she realizes what the evil gang members want—that little doll—but she racks her brains, why? Why? Why all this violence for a doll! Oh Audrey how could you guess—it's stuffed with heroin. In the movies drugs have this evil value placed on them that I agree with while the movie's in progress. It's like I looked into her skull and saw an adorable, brave blind girl who abhorred heroin by nature, like me while I watch the picture, but after I turn if off I'm okay with crack like anyone else. When I touched that crack my fingers shriveled up like wet water, but where was my rival?

The more I thought about it the surer I was that she was sitting on the bed. Ever try to go somewhere with your eyes shut, somewhere you've been only once or twice *drunk?* Muy duro trabajo! One thing is, your fingers have to prop you up from place to place, and fingers aren't very strong.

"Geoff here sells autographs," said Gary Radley. "He's got his own mail order business."

"Isn't that something," said the girl. Grace her name was, just like Grace Kelly, is it a law?

"Least he did until he went blind," Gary interrupted. What a comedian, imagine if I really was blind?

"I have a trustworthy assistant," I replied. "I would count on him against all odds. He's honest as the day is long."

"I'd be tempted," said Radley. "Ever so tempted. You got a nice picture of Clark Gable, your assistant, he says, 'Oh that's not Gable that's'—who's some no-account nothing star?"

"Like Andrew Dice Clay?" said the girl politely.

"The Diceman, yeah, and you go, oh shit, sell *that* one for one dollar, and your assistant, he takes the buck out of his wallet and who's the wiser, not you for sure, eh Geoff?"

"What iniquity there is in the world," I said with a little shudder. "However Ricky is not that kind of guy. He's straight," I said. I touched with my fingers the greasy salt and pepper shakers on the table and trembled them up and down as though to tell the world, I'm shaky, how about a drink? And then Gary Parker Radley opened the top off a bottle, elsewhere, and the smell of bourbon filled the hot space between his bottle and my nose. I had to smile. He knew me so well. When that happens it makes you feel invincible. It makes you cocky. "He's straight and clean. Like a line of Pindar's."

"You're lucky," said the girl softly. Then she giggled and I realized what was up and why.

It gave me some insight into the reasons why a woman like Audrey Hepburn would choose to play a blind woman at the time she did (1965). She was turning a blind eye to the troubles in her marriage to that awful Mel Ferrer. She could have played any part in the world, but she chose, due to the divine instinct with which she took a role, to go symbolically blind. I could tell they were fucking on the bed. They were only about four feet—tops—from where I sat, patient, attentive. "But what does he think we're doing?" she whispered. Her high calves made these slick sucking sounds on his ribcage. "Geoff," he called out for her benefit, "we're making the bed, you just—rest, okay?"

⸺

"It was nice meeting you," Grace said. "You're very brave and good God, do you know a lot about Hollywood!" She told me I should go on TV or do a CD-ROM whatever that is. I gave her my card. After she left, he came to me and sat me on his lap and asked about how I was feeling. "How do you think," I snapped.

He wheedled. "Hey, I'm the one who got locked up for eight to ten," he kept saying. Kept holding me tight on his lap, his big bare arms like pythons around my shoulders and chest.

A little bit later his hand was under my shirt rubbing my nipple, some warm unguent melting on his fingertips. "That tickles." "How you feeling, huh?" "Good," I told him. "You feeling good? Open your pants a little, then? For me?" Yeah, I opened my pants a little, for him, and he dragged my shirt down from my ribs, I heard it slither onto the trailer floor. Then he began to touch me with another hand, grasping my dick firmly, this no-nonsense touch you might believe came from Clark Gable or someone that stalwart. "How you feeling now?" "Good," I said more carefully, trying not to rub against his legs, trying to sit perfectly still in his lap. My eyes still shut.

"Grind down on my knob," he said. "Put your whole ass into it, Geoffrey Crane, make me hard."

A pearl button got torn off my boxers. It fell down somewhere among the chicken bones and the pop tops on the trailer floor. The hair along my arms stood up like electrification. Once a scientist came to Gavet Junior High and put his finger on a big brass ball in the center of the gym. Then all the students brave enough to approach touched it but I refused, digging in my heels on the free throw line. I didn't want my hair sticking up like Diana Ross when they let her out of detox in *Lady Sings the Blues,* no way. Around my balls I felt his greasy hand sinking deeper, until it paused, as though the heat were fatiguing it, the low heat I didn't want to produce. It paused and he said, "How you feeling, Geoffrey Crane?"

and blindly I turned to him and felt for his mouth with my fingers. "Good," I told him, in sign language, spelling out the "G" on his throat, the two "O's" on his throat, the "D" on his throat.

He laughed. "I'm giving that babe a good college education," he said. "But you are still my number one meat boy."

In the seat of my boxer shorts he turned over his greasy hand and rubbed me in circles. Along his forearm my dick was like this wet hot ruler it felt like, gasping like a cartoon thing, and then one of his thumbs slipped into me. I wonder if any of you reading this have ever been involved with a man like Gary Radley—a man with big strong biceps and a tattoo of a snake that's speckled and metallic, a snake that crawls all across the stainy musculature of his hipbone and disappears, daringly, into the crack of his ass. So that you want to pry his cheeks apart and find out, does it have a head or has his asshole swallowed it up, tighter than a drum. Wonder if he sticks his hand down under your balls and pries open your butt with two fingers, each greasier than the last, while he's biting and twisting your nipples, to get you to come without touching your prick. While you're pretending you can't see anything, but only to increase the erotic tension, that feeling of danger and carelessness you get with a really wild stud card. Involuntarily your knees jump up so he can feel the slick dime size hole he's questioning with his finger, you're spreading your legs like you need him, and he's breathing very easily, quite naturally, as if this wasn't sex per se but something calm like examining one's stamp collection. Leisurely.

A man who takes his time. Something he learned at San Quentin I guess, sitting there, marking the days off the wall with a burnt stick.

He whispered some love words into my ear.

All the time my dick was standing straight up alongside his arm. I knew if I opened my eyes and wasn't "blind" any more I'd see it, ready to explode, humping his arm like a dog's dick humping your leg.

I could feel the heat rising out of his groin while I sat on his bumpy cock, humping up and down, trying to soak it up into me through his pants and through what remained of my underwear. The chair was hopping, the floor of the trailer clattering, my feet twined behind his ankles and his heavy muscular calves. "Hey," he mumbled, "you're getting me hot now, boy . . ."

"Take that big bone, Gary, fuck me with it," I said—the words coming bubbling out of my mouth like fog. I saw the look on his face, too late.

Then Gary Radley put this wild potion across my nose on a rag. Period. Full stop.

It took me awhile, after I came to, just to figure out what went down. And where I was. I lay outside his trailer, in a patch of grass under some maple trees, and the moonlight was vivid, showing me every flower and blade. And I could see the whole length of my naked body, outlined like a corpse's in a crime scene. The after-sex feeling, like sweat, swirling around my body like the fudge swirl in a pint of mocha fudge. Wouldn't settle down and rest. It kept spinning around as though hesitant to land in any one place and reveal itself. But finally it stopped and then it told me its name and serial number. Well great, I told myself. Goddamn great!

I seemed to be covered with grease, and violets, slimed with grease and flowers . . . And one or two cigarette butts clung to the skin of my bare stomach, I was like the little mermaid, covered with barnacles. Lying in a field of flowers, the patch of low violets hugging the ground. Their poisonous blue, all the blue in the world, with a film of darkness squeezing each petal. In the middle distance the silver trailer buzzed with noise, the seventies metal of Jethro Tull. I paused and sunk to my knees. Violets aren't always blue, some are yellow, some white, like the bees they attract, the bees that flip out over the dark charm of violets. At night violets glow like radioactive elements out of Satan's laboratory, and I kept asking them, what would Audrey Hepburn have done? While I huddled, a big hedge protected me from most of the wind, cold for May, I smelled the funny smell of cherry cough drops, or syrup, that means you've stumbled into a chokecherry bush.

I took one of my hands and just as I figured, something had been thrust up me, while I was "out."

I called out his name.

Oh, it was a human bone, human he said. "What's the problem, bud," Gary said. "It's straight and clean as a line of fucking Pindar's."

I sat there in a garland of garlic mustard flowers, bemoaning my fate, and through the red pine branches above the stars peeked down like when Audrey starts singing, "E'll take good care of me," and all the old dustmen agree, wouldn't it be loverly? Gary stood there, licking his lips, his big full lips, and I could feel the soft silkiness of my own semen sinking into the earth like rain.

"That's my boner," he said, with a broad wink.

"Thanks," I said. "You are one unexpected stud, Gary Radley." The bone lay in the grass beside me, a foot long or more, like the inside of someone's arm, I wondered whose.

"I can see again," I said.

He sank to his knees and snickered. "Bet you're wondering why I took our scene outdoors. It was just more—picturesque I guess."

He kissed me then. "I know," I said, brooding about it. "33When you're cooped up from eight to ten—"

"Not *from* eight to ten," he interrupted. He patted my butt. "It's not a time, it's a sentence."

"I never was fucked by an arm before," I told him honestly. I was considering if this meant he cared for me. He told me he didn't do it a lot, but I had such a hot ass he couldn't resist.

"You didn't have to knock me out," I complained.

"Oh yes I did, bro," he said. "I'd of shot my wad if you was awake."

HER FIRST BRA
Cris Mazza

There was one more card from Millard in November, a Thanksgiving card that said *hope to see you again ... someday ... somewhere.* Dale picked it up from the floor under the kitchen table and said, "Who's this from, your mother?"

"Yuckity yuk." Loralee was slicing hot dogs to go into canned beans. Dale ate lunch at about 10 AM when he got home from delivering tortillas to restaurants.

"Well, who is it?"

"It's a photographer I did a session for. I guess he liked me. Whose mother should we visit for Thanksgiving?"

"A session? What's that mean? You're working as a model? Since when?"

"About six months."

"Why didn't you tell me?"

"I thought I did." She put a plate of tepid frank-n-beans in front of him and then started sorting through the mail, putting the utility and credit card bills in one pile for Dale to pay from his checking account. The rent and food came from hers. She had a session that afternoon. The guy on the phone yesterday had asked how old she was and she'd answered *I'm VERY bold, why'd you ask?* then the guy digressed to something else, the color of her hair and eyes, how tall she was, her measurements. She'd changed her ad again. It said *Young, versatile female model for private photo sessions with imaginative photographers, you won't believe what your camera can do.*

"How much have you made?" Dale asked.

"Not much. The rent went up, remember?"

"Well let's make out a budget or something, maybe we don't have to sell anything to buy grass. Or Christmas presents for that matter."

"Sessions aren't predictable, Dale. We can't *budget* for them. I thought you were *off* grass, anyway."

"Well they use it for cancer patients, don't they? Maybe it'll help."

"Help *what*. God, what a hypochondriac, it really gets old."

"I'm getting this shortness of breath all the fucking time, dammit, I'm hot then cold, I start sweating my fucking ass off. What would *you* call it?"

"Maybe it's menopause."

"Har-de-fucking-har." He put three huge spoonfuls into his mouth in rapid succession before chewing and swallowing. "So you wanna go away for Christmas this year?"

"No, not now."

"Then when."

She picked up the empty plate and put it with the dirty pan beside the sink. "Dale, I tried to tell you what'll probably happen, but you wouldn't believe me. That's fine, you can pretend. Sure, everything *normal*, right?" She boosted herself onto the counter and swung her feet into the sink to shave her legs. "Luckily I don't think you'll even miss me."

Three more jobs popped up right away in December. The first just wanted her feet—feet walking, feet splashing puddles, feet showing over the side of a pick-up truck, feet on gas pedals, feet kicking a ball, feet in high heels. He said he'd done sessions with guys and older people and little kids, and some animals. When he took her out for lunch after the session, she touched his leg with her bare toes under the table, but nothing happened, so the *Feet!* exhibit he said he was working on must've been real. The second wanted her to hang laundry on a line—just white sheets and towels—on a very windy day, wearing a light cotton dress and bare feet, but the photographer was a woman and, as a matter of fact, almost didn't want Loralee at all when she saw her short hair. The third worked out a little better because he said from the start he wanted a nude, but he also made her sign a form promising she was over 18. Still, he liked her newly shaved pussy and fucked her afterwards, but only gave her $20 for cab fare when she asked, although she was parked around the corner from his house.

The photographer handed her two fifties before she came through the door. The session was at his house—he had his living room furniture pushed to one side and a corner converted into a set resembling a dressing room in a fancy department store. A three-sided mirror and stool, clothes with tags draped over accordion partitions, big umbrella photography lamps preventing anything from showing a shadow anywhere.

"Okay, listen to this," the guy said. He had long hair parted in the middle, the kind that either looks dirty or, if it's clean, is so fine it's like baby hair that was never cut. He also had one of those halfway mustaches that usually only 16-year-old boys can grow, more baby hair. "Okay, listen," he repeated, "it's like you're shopping, it's a big day because . . . you've come to the store without your mother—"

"My *mother*?"

"Yeah, listen, you've come shopping, you took a bus or rode your bike, but you came to this upscale store where you get one of those personal shoppers. You see, you're here to get your first . . . training bra." Suddenly he ducked his head and looked through a camera on a tripod. She wasn't even on the set yet.

"Does anyone even *use* training bras anymore."

"Sure they do, and listen, you're all excited, this is a big day for you, a milestone, know what I mean? Today you become a woman . . . and all that." He stood up but continued to look at the set, not at Loralee.

"And I suppose my dressing room has a hidden camera or two-way mirror. And then what, my personal shopper is a man?"

"Maybe," he said slowly. "We'll see. The importance of this is— this is such a big day for a girl. It makes her feel like . . . anything can happen. Um, hang your old clothes on the hook there, like you would in a dressing room. And here you go, try these on." He pulled a plastic Sears shopping bag from behind one of the partitions.

"I doubt Sears has personal shoppers," she said, looking inside. There were three or four practically cupless bras and matching underwear, one set white with purple flowers, one baby blue, one with pink polkadots, and one set basic white with lace. The bras were just stretchy material with elastic straps and a hook in back.

"You can have them when you're finished," he said. "Do you have any that nice?"

"No I can't say that I have any like these. In fact, I don't have a bra."

"You don't?" His face and sad brown eyes and repulsive

mustache seemed to leap at her, but he hadn't moved closer, just was looking at her. "Oh god, that's great. Perfect. Like . . . this's *real*, isn't it? Your first bra."

"Yeah, whatever. Where should I change?"

"Well . . . the dressing room, of course."

She looked back at him for a moment while he touched his limp hair then touched his moustache then put three fingers over his lips and dropped his eyes.

"Of course, silly me."

He dragged another stool over so he was sitting behind the camera. After her jeans and t-shirt were hung on the hook and her socks were stuffed into her shoes (he said leave them under the stool, and let one sock come trailing out of the shoe a little), she glanced at the camera while putting on the flowered bra and underwear with her back to him, but of course she showed in the mirror, tits and trimmed bush. "Your first bra," he murmured, the camera clicking, zipping to the next frame and clicking again. "How does it feel?"

She turned to hide a laugh as a small burp. The bra actually fit her but the underwear was not bikini style. The high waisted underwear made her tits look even smaller, the bra like an elastic headband around her waist.

"Oh god," he moaned, "god-in-heaven." The camera clicking and clicking. Something in her gut popped, drilled through, leaving behind a vibrating jello-y place in her middle. She turned slowly back and forth in front of the mirror, stretching to check her ass over each shoulder which also stretched the bra.

"*Oops!*" One tit popped out when the bra rode up. "Where's my personal shopper, I need to know if this one fits."

The guy was huddled on his stool, his face almost to his lap, no longer clicking, sort of whimpering.

"Come on, please, mister? It's my big day, help me pick one that fits."

He slid off the stool onto his knees and shuffled toward her. His head came up to her stomach. His eyes were murky and glistening, sweat on his upper lip had dampened the disgusting little mustache. He held her around the waist with one hand, pulling the flowered underwear tight against her chest, bending her knees slightly and throwing her off balance so she had to hold onto his shoulders and lean backwards slightly. With two fingers he eased the bra back over the exposed tit.

"There, it fits like that," he breathed.

"Are you sure?"

He moved his hands slowly up her body until he was holding her around the ribcage, a thumb on each nipple. He moved the thumbs back and forth, hardening the nipples under the stretchy purple-flowered material. His face tilted up. His two watery eyes right behind each thumb. "Yes, this is how it goes. Like this. Like this."

"I know, um, 16 is sort of late for my first bra, but my mother still thinks I'm not old enough," she said, making her voice airy and higher. The flowered underwear was wet between her legs. She tried to grind her twat against his chest but zingers of adrenaline were zapping her almost continuously and she was in danger of falling over backwards.

"It's O.K.," he whispered, "maybe you were 15 just yesterday. But you had to be ready. You knew you were ready."

"I'm ready."

"Today you were ready. Today was the day. Oh, but if only your little titties wouldn't grow anymore," he sobbed, "so impatient for this day, but now they'll be ruined." He slid his hands to her back and pulled her stomach against his face, blubbering against the skin below the bra.

"Hey, mister," she breathed softly. "Today's not over yet." She touched a bald spot on his crown with a single finger. "Remember, today's my big day. And there's still a half hour of it left."

He lurched to his feet with her in his arms. "Like a baby," he smiled through his tears down into her face. He bent and kissed her gently, touching her lips with the awful mustache, while carrying her out of the set and down a hall. The room they went into was dim, but after placing her on the bed, he turned on the night stand lamp and she could see the white lace canopy, the matching white lace lampshade and bedspread and curtains, antique-looking dolls in white or peach or baby-blue satin dresses lined up on a shelf, plus little troll dolls and glass princesses, horses and china puppies, a brush and comb set on the dresser, a life-sized white teddy bear sitting in a corner.

"This isn't your room is it?" Loralee asked, propping herself up on her elbows. He was kneeling again, beside the bed.

"No . . . it's yours."

"Huh? *Oh* . . . ," she lay back slowly. "It's the room my mother doesn't know I left to go buy my first bra, right?"

"That's right." He took off his shirt. He was as skinny as Dale but not a single hair on him, except his armpits. "Just touch them against mine while they're still little, while it's still the big day." He got on top of her. She couldn't see or feel any hard-on inside his baggy green army-surplus pants, but his hips were below hers, on the mattress between her knees, so she wouldn't've felt it anyway. He pressed his gaunt chest against hers, his head down against her neck, then without raising his body eased the bra up so her bare breasts were against his chest. He rocked slightly so their nipples brushed back and forth. And he started to tremble. She could feel his heart like a fist on a windowpane, banging to get out. His swaying continued for five or ten minutes.

Loralee's buzz was long gone. She checked her watch by raising one arm in the air behind his shoulders.

Then he was easing the bra back over her, with his chest still pressed to hers. "Okay," he whispered in her ear. "I didn't hurt you." He backed off of her and stood beside the bed. "I'll leave you in your pretty room, with your bears and dolls." He clicked off the light and retreated toward the door.

"Hey!" A crude voice blasting through the room. Loralee sat up. "I *would* like a doll like one of them. Where could I get one?"

"A doll shop." He was a shadowy form by the door, putting his shirt on.

"How much would it cost?"

"Some of them are as much as $200."

"I could just get a *fifty* dollar one, though . . . couldn't I?"

He didn't answer, buttoning his shirt, then he looked up, but she couldn't see his eyes. It was too dark.

"A girl should have a doll like that before she gets too old . . . don't you think?"

He slowly reached for the door knob. "Too old?"

"Yeah, like . . . before she's . . . say, *eighteen* . . . don't you think?

He opened the door and a crack of light lay on the floor between him and the bed. I . . . guess so." Then he went out and closed the door.

She lay back on the bed with a suddenly thudding pulse, but not the same thing as the earlier neon bolt of adrenaline. The waves of nauseous weakness passed, a feeling that almost stunk, and she thought about the symptoms Dale described, then she got off the bed. Her clothes were folded on the sofa in the living room with exactly $100 in cash placed on top, a fifty, two twenties, a five and five ones.

— —

January was a slow time for both student photographers and sickos. Loralee got her hair cut into a pixie style and used some of her savings for white jeans, a white jean jacket, and several new tank tops. She had her ears pierced and wore just the two pearl studs that came with the piercing. She let Dale pay for the piercing and call it her Christmas present, but he also bought her a corduroy skirt and jacket set that was one size too big, so she exchanged it for a denim mini and peasant-style top with sequins, both from the girls department. Dale said she looked like a baby pop star in *Teen Beat* magazine.

"That'll work," she answered. "Maybe I'll add some cheap jewelry like the girls on my bus."

"Whadda you talking about?"

"Oh . . . I don't know. If I want to start a real modeling career, I hafta have an angle, you know? My own shtick. Like, go for the junior high market."

"You can't start a real modeling career just because you get a few new clothes and *say* you want to be a model."

"You don't know anything about it. I've had some gigs. How many gigs have *you* had lately?"

Dale stared at the TV screen. It wasn't even on. He still had hair down to his collar, except where he didn't have any hair at all, and it looked wet even when it wasn't. The flattened cushions in the chair that had come with the apartment had stains now where his head rested. Sometimes he still tapped a drumstick on the coffee table while he sat there. It seemed the drumstick appeared and disappeared by magic, but she'd found it once, by accident, stashed under the seat cushion.

Loralee loaded some celery sticks with peanut butter, wrapped them in a paper towel and placed them on Dale's lap on her way to the sofa. "Dale, can we talk?"

"About me being a failure."

"No, but *we* are. You know? It's only been, what, three and a half years. We could just call it one of those things. We're both very young, we could . . . you know, still be like our ages."

"Instead of old married farts."

"Speak for yourself, but I guess that's the general idea."

The drumstick appeared, but he didn't start tapping. He held it up and placed the tip against his lips like a long finger saying *Shhhhh.* "No."

"No? That's it, just *no?*"

He took a bite of celery then replaced the tip of the drumstick against his mouth while he chewed. It sounded like a horse chewing corn. It sounded kind of nice.

"It wouldn't be like we hate each other's guts and go to court to fight over the car and stereo. And it doesn't have to be now, we could do it when we're both ready, when we can both afford it, you know?"

"We can barely afford this shit *together.*"

"I know, but I'm working on a plan."

"You mean becoming a famous cover girl by next week."

"There's lots of types of modeling, Dale, and maybe I've found my niche, and I can even capitalize on it, expand the potential."

"Now you sound like a yuppie businessman." He swallowed what looked like a hard lump.

"I'm just saying I've discovered a way to make what I do more lucrative, and when I make enough of a stash, how about I share it with you and we, you know, go our separate ways?"

"What if I want to stay with you?"

He was just sitting there looking down into his lap like an imbecile who watches himself pee, holding a celery stick with gobs of peanut butter in one hand and the drumstick in the other.

"Please, don't turn into Karen Carpenter on me." Loralee stayed on the sofa only a few seconds longer, then went into the bathroom, shook her short hair and watched it fall back into place. For the first time in her life she was glad for the strip of freckles across her nose. She wondered how much colored contact lenses would cost, because some pure green eyes would really complete the package.

LOVE FOR $17.50
Charles Bukowski

Robert's first desire—when he began thinking of such things—was to sneak into the Wax Museum some night and make love to the wax ladies. However, that seemed too dangerous. He limited himself to making love to statues and mannequins in his sex fantasy and lived in his fantasy world.

One day while stopped at a red light he looked into the doorway of a shop. It was one of those shops that sold everything—records, sofas, books, trivia, junk. He saw her standing there in a long red dress. She wore rimless glasses, was well-shaped; dignified and sexy the way they used to be. A real class broad. Then the signal changed and he was forced to drive on.

Robert parked a block away and walked back to the shop. He stood outside at the newspaper rack and looked in at her. Even the eyes looked real, and the mouth was very impulsive, pouting just a bit.

Robert went inside and looked at the record rack. He was closer to her then and sneaked glances. No, they didn't make them like that anymore. She even had on high heels.

The girl in the shop walked up. "Can I help you sir?"

"Just browsing, miss."

"If there's anything you want, just let me know."

"Surely."

Robert moved over to the mannequin. There wasn't a price tag. He wondered if she were for sale. He walked back to the record rack, picked up a cheap album and purchased it from the girl.

The next time he visited the shop the mannequin was still there. Robert browsed a bit, bought an ashtray that was molded to imitate a coiled snake, then walked out.

The third time he was there he asked the girl: "Is the mannequin for sale?"

"The mannequin?"

"Yes, the mannequin."

23

"You want to buy it?"

"Yes, you sell things, don't you? Is the mannequin for sale?"

"Just a moment, sir."

The girl went to the back of the shop. A curtain parted and an old Jewish man came out. The bottom two buttons of his shirt were missing and you could see his hairy belly. He seemed friendly enough.

"You want the mannequin, sir?"

"Yes, is she for sale?"

"Well, not really. You see, it's kind of a display piece, a joke."

"I want to buy her."

"Well, let's see . . ." The old Jew went over and began touching the mannequin, touching the dress, the arms. "Let's see . . . I think I can let you have this . . . thing . . . for $17.50."

"I'll take her." Robert pulled out a twenty. The storekeeper counted out the change.

"I'm going to miss it," he said, "sometimes it seems almost real. Should I wrap it?"

"No, I'll take her the way she is."

Robert picked up the mannequin and carried her to his car. He laid her down in the back seat. Then he got in and drove off to his place. When he got there, luckily, there didn't seem to be anybody about and he got her into the doorway unseen. He stood her in the center of the room and looked at her.

"Stella," he said, "Stella, bitch."

He walked up and slapped her across the face. Then he grabbed the head and kissed it. It was a good kiss. His penis began to harden when the phone rang. "Hello," he answered.

"Robert?"

"Yeah. Sure."

"This is Harry."

"How you doing, Harry?"

"O.K., what you doing?"

"Nothing."

"I thought I'd come over. Bring a couple of beers."

"O.K."

Robert hung up, picked up the mannequin and carried her to the closet. He pushed her in the corner of the closet and closed the door.

Harry didn't really have much to say. He sat there with his beer can. "How's Laura?" he asked.

"Oh," said Robert, "it's all over between me and Laura."

"What happened?"

"The eternal vamp bit. Always on stage. She was relentless. She'd turn on for guys everywhere—at the grocery store, on the street, in cafes, everywhere and to anybody. It didn't matter who it was as long as it was a man. She even turned on for a guy who dialed a wrong number. I couldn't go it anymore."

"You alone now?"

"No, I've got another one. Brenda. You've met her."

"Oh yeah, Brenda. She's all right."

Harry sat there drinking beer. Harry never had a woman but he was always talking about them. There was something sickening about Harry. Robert didn't encourage the conversation and Harry soon left. Robert went to the closet and brought Stella out.

"You god damned whore!" he said. "You've been cheating on me, haven't you?"

Stella didn't answer. She stood there looking so cool and prim. He slapped her a good one. It'd be a long day in the sun before any woman got away with cheating on Bob Wilkenson. He slapped her another good one.

"Cunt! You'd fuck a four-year old boy if he could get his pecker up, wouldn't you?"

He slapped her again, then grabbed her and kissed her. He kissed her again and again. Then he ran his hands up her dress. She was well-shaped, very well-shaped. Stella reminded him of an algebra teacher he'd had in high school. Stella didn't have on panties.

"Whore," he said, "who got your panties?"

Then his penis was pressed against the front of her. There was no opening. But Robert was in a tremendous passion. He inserted it between the upper thighs. It was smooth and tight. He worked away. For just a moment he felt extremely foolish, then his passion took over and he began kissing her along the neck as he worked.

Robert washed Stella down with a dishrag, placed her in the closet behind an overcoat, closed the door and still managed to get in the last quarter of the Detroit Lions vs. L.A. Rams game on T.V.

It was quite nice for Robert as time went on. He made certain adjustments. He bought Stella several pairs of underpants, a garter belt, sheer long stockings, an ankle bracelet.

He bought her earrings too, and was quite shocked to learn that his love didn't have any ears. Under all that hair, the ears were missing. He put the earrings on anyhow with adhesive tape. But there were advantages—he didn't have to take her to dinner, to parties, to dull movies; all those mundane things that meant so much to the average woman. And there were arguments. There would always be arguments, even with a mannequin. She wasn't talkative but he was sure she told him once, "You're the greatest lover of them all. That old Jew was a dull lover. You love with soul, Robert."

Yes, there were advantages. She wasn't like all the other women he had known. She didn't want him to make love at inconvenient moments. He could choose the time. And she didn't have periods. And he went down on her. He cut some hair from her head and pasted it between her thighs.

The affair was sexual to begin with but gradually he was falling in love with her. He considered going to a psychiatrist, then decided not to. After all, was it necessary to love a real human being? It never lasted long. There were too many differences between the species, and what started as love too often ended up as war.

Then too, he didn't have to lie in bed with Stella and listen to her talk about all her past lovers. How Karl had such a big thing, but Karl wouldn't go down. And how Louie danced so well, Louie could have made it in ballet instead of selling insurance. And how Marty could really kiss. He had a way of locking tongues. So on. So forth. What shit. Of course, Stella had mentioned the old Jew. But just that once.

Robert had been with Stella about two weeks when Brenda phoned.

"Yes, Brenda?" he answered.

"Robert, you haven't phoned me."

"I've been terribly busy, Brenda. I've been promoted to district manager and I've had to realign things down at the office."

"Is that so?"

"Yes."

"Robert, something's wrong . . ."

"What do you mean?"

"I can tell by your voice. Something's wrong. What the hell's wrong, Robert? Is there another woman?"

"Not exactly."

"What do you mean, not exactly?"

"Oh, Christ!"

"What is it? What is it? Robert, something's wrong. I'm coming over to see you."

"There's nothing wrong, Brenda."

"You son of a bitch, you're holding out on me! Something's going on. I'm coming to see you! Now!"

Brenda hung up and Robert walked over and picked up Stella and put her in the closet, well back in one corner. He took the overcoat off the hanger and hung it over Stella. Then he came back, sat down and waited.

Brenda opened the door and rushed in. "All right, what the hell's wrong? What is it?"

"Listen, kid," he said, "it's O.K. Calm down."

Brenda was nicely built. Her breasts sagged a bit, but she had fine legs and a beautiful ass. Her eyes always had a frantic, lost look. He could never cure her eyes of that. Sometimes after love-making a temporary calm would fill her eyes but it never lasted.

"You haven't even kissed me yet!"

Robert got up from his chair and kissed Brenda.

"Christ, that was no kiss. What is it?" she asked. "What's wrong!"

"It's nothing, nothing at all . . ."

"If you don't tell me, I'm going to scream!"

"I tell you, it's nothing."

Brenda screamed. She walked to the window and screamed. You could hear her all over the neighborhood. Then she stopped.

"God, Brenda, don't do that again! Please, please!"

"I'll do it again! I'll do it again! Tell me what's wrong, Robert, or I'll do it again."

"All right," he said, "wait."

Robert went to the closet, took the overcoat off Stella and lifted her out of the closet.

"What's that?" asked Brenda, "what's that?"

"A mannequin."

"A mannequin? You mean? . . ."

"I mean, I'm in love with her."

"Oh, my god! You mean? That thing? That *thing*?"

"Yes."

"You love that *thing* more than me? That hunk of celluloid, or whatever the shit she's made of? You mean you love that *thing* more than me?"

"Yes."

"I suppose you take it to bed with you? I suppose you do things to . . . with that *thing*?"

"Yes."

"Oh . . ."

Then Brenda really screamed. She just stood there and screamed. Robert thought she would never stop. Then she leaped at the mannequin and started to claw and beat at it. The mannequin toppled and fell against the wall. Brenda ran out the door, got in her car and drove off wildly. She crashed into one side of a parked car, glanced off, drove on.

Robert walked over to Stella. The head had broken off and rolled under a chair. There were spurts of chalky material on the floor. One arm hung loosely, broken, two wires protruding. Robert sat down in a chair. He just sat there. Then he got up and went into the bathroom, stood there a minute, and came back out. He stood in the hallway and could see the head under the chair. He remembered how he had buried his mother and his father. But this was different. This was different. He just stood in the hallway, sobbing and waiting. Both of Stella's eyes were open and cool and beautiful. They stared at him.

SOLOW

for Chris and George Tysh

Lynn Crawford

I was immediately attracted to the public speaker; his pressed slacks, his rounded shoulders, his straight gait. He spoke of birds and aviation. While I myself do not fly, it is true my aspirations have always run along those lines.

We met on a warm day. My dress wrinkled at the waist, his whiskers curled in ringlets. I'd gone shopping, then to the library, so was carrying a lot. After his talk I questioned him about being a stewardess and joining the Air Force. He kindly outlined each career, eyed my big bags and offered me a ride home. True I lived within one block of the auditorium. But as I just mentioned I was loaded with packages and books.

Making an enormous circle (it took ten minutes), he drove while relating anecdotes of life in his field. Once we reached home it was his turn to wait. I arranged the objects in my room—piles of clothing, jars of cream, matchboxes—before we entered it. The speaker removed his hat from his head, then closed the door behind him. Leaning down he kissed me and grew affectionate, sensuous and wholly irrational. Our bed became a wild sea, and we vessels bobbing to her movement. While he moved easily in the darkness, my own motions were sober, efficient. I've already mentioned I cannot fly, though I always had special feelings toward the sky.

He later took a cigarette tipped with lipstick from between my fingers. "You only die once," he said.

People have described me as birdlike, and I've sometimes thought of planes carrying my wishes on board.

In the morning we had boiled eggs and toast. The public speaker drank his coffee black, and encouraged me to do the same, saying eating light helped with any form of flying one might do. I had shopping to complete, among other things to do, so he suggested I keep the car, dropping him off and picking him up at his speaking engagement, which promised to be a long one.

Shopping was easy, but concentration proved difficult. My

thoughts were on the public speaker, his hands, his shoulders, and on a possible air profession. At this point everything had turned out well that could have turned out badly. Still I began to feel lonely for him even before he went away.

1.

I am happy to have the public speaker here; I do not want to think about him ever going away. Still I prepare for the departure I feel must come.

I use my room as a site to construct a contraption. At the base of my bed sits a platform on which stand two stirrups. Attached high up on the facing wall are two adjustable pulleys, each having an airplane for a handle. Slipping my feet into the stirrups—ducks—and holding onto the pulleys—planes—I am able to lift myself and let myself down.

Two suspended strings, each tied to the quill of an exquisitely slender feather, are separated by a distance equaling that between my nipples. If I make proper use of the contraption, the tips of the feathers graze my breasts with a perfect amount of pressure. From a third suspended string, the longest, hangs a fairly small globe which can be inserted into my vagina.

Globe inserted, I grip a plane in each hand, and fit my feet into the slippers (ducks). I lift myself gently then vigorously to a point when you would call the movement violent. Having reached a lifted position, I straighten until the strain is gone and I'm left holding the slack pulleys in each hand.

I practice daily. If I do not keep at work and to a schedule I may lose any safety I've just begun to build.

2.

When the day to hear the public speaker for a second time came I felt happy, too happy, maybe, for the occasion. In a dress and light stockings I asked for a table near the podium, and was prepared to refuse any other. The room was full: people with pressed suits, people with wrinkled ones, people with frayed jackets, ballooning skirts, trousers.

The chair I'd been given teetered on the edge of a raised section of the floor, or it may have been because its legs were unequal.

The day on which he spoke was warm, sunny, the auditorium a

robin's-egg blue. The speaker entered the hall, doors swung behind him. A hand held his hat, another ran through his hair. "It's almost as blue in here as it is out there," he said.

I hoped the two of us could travel to North Africa where some Arab tribes use mud to build entire cities, or even visit some of those aviation clubs they have in Paris.

I later saw the public speaker in the wings. It was as if he were looking into somewhere far away, perhaps in the south, perhaps in the past, the sky maybe. Making sure my seat was saved I walked from the front of the room to the back, and then from side to side— I also went up to the balcony—keeping the figure of the speaker in my view. He looked different from different angles, and different again if you scanned his top or looked into him fully. For a long time he held his forefingers on each side of his nose as if to straighten the bones. Finally he lifted his head; blood was rushing to his face. I caught his two eyes and for a while could not take my own away.

3.

It was later that evening when we reached a new state, removing what we learned were imaginary borderlines. We began in silence; his shoulder grazed my rib, hip then kneecap. I could hear my heart inside his body. At times the pauses in his breathing were of great length, at times they were short, staccato. We trekked from lowland winter pastures to high and cooling altitudes. We encountered birds; birds ejecting over gulfs, turning and twisting high above land, adrift amid a sea of thunderclouds, and some skimming eastward, eastward. Then, as if having given into one another's forces, we arrived at that place where any influence seemed to end.

I feared the pauses in the public speaker's appearance would become agonizing in their length, and told him so, then fell silent. The public speaker fell silent too, tracing the lines of the table with his finger. "Think of me located somewhere in your heart and not somewhere on the globe," he said.

Imagine, learning to carry him with me. If I'm here the public speaker is here, if I'm there the public speaker is there too. If I go out the public speaker goes out, and so on.

I grew unhappy, like I wasn't before. First I was happy because the public speaker was there, then unhappy because he was. "You can't turn happiness into unhappiness as simple as that," he said.

I began to understand the urge I felt not as one to relieve my plain suffering, but one to relieve my sense of him absent.

4.

Relieve my sense of him absent. I was not behind in my preparations, I simply had more to do.

Increasing the number of suspended feathers from two to thirty (the original two remained the longest, allowing me to use them for localized nipple sensation), I can raise myself higher, allowing belly and upper thighs to graze the soft and dangling stimulators.

A pliant and thick band attaches the nose to the body of each plane (handle). When I want to drive I hold each handle. When I'm in the mood to ride I stretch the nose from my body, wrapping the bands around my wrists.

Before I had foam-filled pillows, now I have ones with down lining.

Facing the problem of my speed, which is accelerated, I take measures I hope will allow me to enjoy a more moderate pace. I arrange for a projector; shadows break across my ceiling. One: a clip of the public speaker and a machine designed to provide the loftiest view ever of the universe. He dangles from its fifty foot mechanical arm. Two: a clip of the public speaker climbing up a plane where, once inside, he's about to orate. He enters the cockpit, puts a cap on his head, then shuts the door behind him.

The addition of visual became all-engrossing. I had a contraption that was not only useful but a pleasure to look at. Still, on so many days I meant to begin work at four o'clock and it suddenly became five.

5.

There is a speech that conveys a manner the speaker expects in return (greetings, good-byes, pleasantries), but the public speech is designed to affect behavior (bring listeners to a point of view, maybe prod them toward some action).

Some people find themselves in flight and owe it to historical experience. I have not located that event in my life. I recall crouching, listening, but it's a thought that spreads into so many places.

To say the public speaker found himself in flight would not describe it; he lost nothing to begin with. Still he used the themes of birds, and ones of aviation, to really impact his expression, both bombarding listeners with sensations and shooting them discreetly.

6.

The sun became closer, the wind blew harder, and my focus shifted between ground operations and lofting myself into space. The public speaker would be leaving soon—he said not for long— to oversee an engineering project on a flight of outboard aircraft.

From the moment he mentioned going away I thought of nothing but him coming back. I felt a stab at the chance sight of his hat lying on a shelf one day; pain stood there strong, yet increasingly I viewed it as an appliance to prepare me for the future.

Undoubtedly we had a type of thing, and he addressed it with this story: a spacecraft, designed to lock onto a specific large and bright star (which, in turn, would guide it), drifting from its chosen body and locking onto a nearby slightly dimmer one. It was a change that caused the craft to lose its orientation, to become misguided. Now it's floating up there in that sea.

Out loud I recalled once gazing into a sky of bodies; bare, luminous, no color; wanting to view each stellar object on the one hand, feeling dizzy at the size of that project on the other.

The speaker placed two hands on my shoulders. "Linkage," he said, "is a question of focus. It's like wanting to get a plane. If thoughts veer to upholstery and heat you never want to get it. So you say 'I want to get a plane.'"

I quarried what I could from his example, then returned to my contraption.

7.

In constructing my contraption I attain materials, then employ them with passionate mechanics. I cannot take such care when I'm obliged to meet a deadline.

My bed, a rectangle of fragrant Oriental wood amid organic and industrial machinery, is now a nest I get both into and outside of. If the contraption pens in the area geographically, that thing removes so many demarcations.

Imagine being launched into space; at times piecemeal, at times as a single unit.

The machinery's anatomy is hardly unimportant, blasting off requires considerable stabilization. In general it withstands contractions of my body, still I'm faced with problems. A good launch can bring me to a point when I feel my torso sway away like the wing of a great bird. That sway commands my (suspended) limbs to counteract enormous motion. But often they in turn— fragile, sometimes jittery—only add their own vibrations.

8.

As the public speaker's (temporary) absence drew closer, his speaking engagements dribbled to a near halt, the work being picked up by others who were capable but in no way fascinating.

Soon before his departure, we made last contact in a spacious but low-ceilinged room. Clothing was discarded; my blue shorts, his striped ones; my stockings, his hat. The encounter included tones ranging from deeply muscular to lightly embroidered. In the past we'd enjoyed many long drawn-out moments, but on this occasion settled for a short and quickly organized one.

I expressed agitation at the separation about to come, wondering out loud what we'd grow into. Two comets like smears trailing away from each others as points of light being focused on? Two radio telescopes located far apart, operating in unison? Would we view each other with sharpness, clarity, or with a myriad of fractured distortions?

The speaker took my chin in his hand. "We will be defining some of our linkage," he said. "We are not losing any of our linkage, we are deferring some of it."

I sank into the cushion of his body.

9.

The speaker phones. He's keeping one eye on possible hydrogen leaks within fleet systems, another on the weather, and caught a lucky glimpse of an uncommon form of lightning: flash between cloud top and sky above it. His voice emits an enormous amount of energy, and I'm able—even from this distance—to mine great feeling. Allowing for an interval of silence I describe to him a piece of what I imagine; him amid air and amid water; him on a wild green sea beneath a wide blue sky, and I reveal my hope to see him soon. The speaker's voice blows the receiver like a cosmic wind. "You can do a lot of good speaking but you have to look closer to home than I had been planning," he says.

If nothing goes wrong mechanically, or with the activity of the wind or precipitation, he expects to be home before next Friday.

METEMPSYCHOSIS
Garrett Caples

Near the top of the doorframe on either side are screwed two thick metal bolts to which her wrists are attached by means of two equally metal pairs of handcuffs. Her legs are spread the width of the frame by what is known as a *spreaderbar*. But I am not looking at either of these, nor am I looking at her yellow callused heels, the back of her knees, her shoulderblades nor shoulders. I am looking instead at the white thickness of the diaper stretched across her ass and pulled tightly around her hips. And I am looking at it, I confess, with an obscene and nearviolent engorgement of penis, which, by and by, I intend to insert (nay shove) into the asshole quivering within. It all sounds distasteful, I know. And I know too that when I tell you that that same asshole has been recent recipient of a rather powerful suppository—with an eye towards filling the seat of the diaper with an unspeakable riot of bodily filth—I cannot expect your approbation, though I do ask your forbearance, however brief, while I indicate something of what went into our present positions. I can't say I expect to convince you of the decorum or sense of this, and, frankly, I don't much care to. While, like the deviant throngs before me (the women, the gays, the Jews, etc.), I sometimes cloak my motives in the guise of social equality, when it comes right down to it, I'm a bit of an exhibitionist. And exhibitionism is not without its cost; I may, for example, lose my float in next year's St. Patrick's parade. But, though Irish Catholic by birth if not behavior, I doubt I would have attended. I never have fun in straight lines, and besides, the only green diapers I know of (Depend) are not to my taste. I prefer, of course, the white, such as the fine specimen currently enveloping the hipsasscunt of the present damselindistress.

On the kitchen counter—it's a oneroom apartment, so don't sweat the details—on the kitchen counter, next to a pack of cigarettes, an unwrapped yetrolled condom waves its reservoirtip gaily. It's been there for some time now, unused, and whether it shall remain so much longer, I couldn't possibly say. (I heard some crinkling a few minutes ago, but determined it to be some flexing of the asscheeks brought on by fatigue.) While I can make legitimate claim to being the greatest novelist of the coming century, I confess to little knowledge of either medicine or augury. And I confess to not caring. The event will take place, and I can stay hard like this all day if need be, my bathrobe (torn, terry) providing easy access for a quick supplementary stroke. I may strike you as an indifferent fellow, I'm afraid, with my pissing on parades, my utter disregard for your delicate sensibilities, but what's a poor boy to do? And think of the poor girl, her lovely vertebrae just visible above the diaper's elastic waist, like a set of knuckles on a desperately clenched fist. Look at her poor neck, the signs of stress in the shoulders, the would be shift of arms prevented by a lack of slack between bolt and handcuff, handcuff and hand. It only took Christ three hours to die in such a position. (And, if our standard plastic, plaster, and wood depictions are at all historically accurate, we may note too that our Lord and Savior was similarly diaperclad on that occasion. Perhaps he was; the Romans knew a thing or two about execution with its attendant releases of urine and feces, and it may be they took precautions, much as, to his final dismay, the grizzled, hardened, deathrow inmate is handed an adultsized Huggies right before his march to the chair, thus releasing his hold on life in the same attire in which he first embraced it.) Be that as it may, I seriously doubt we have three hours ahead of us, and even if we did, she's a great deal more hale than JC probably was after being smacked around by Pilate's boys for a few days. And—though this you'll never believe, for who could believe such a thing about a beautiful, young, potentially paradegoing woman?—I ask, would it make any difference if I said that the young lady was in this position at least in part because she wanted to be, that her fantasies were of kidnap and torture, and worse? I didn't think so. In any case, we can wait, for the event will occur in its own sweet inevitable time.

I am torn, I confess, between desires, not the least of which are the desire to smoke and the desire to shave. I have always considered it good form for a man to shave before having sex, having once been admonished during youthful cunnilingus, and my face is in dire need. But, I wonder, have I time enough for a full and luxurious shave before the unfortunate shits herself? I suppose the luxury of controlling time—in addition to discharge—is what diapers are for, and I am confident that the brand I have chosen (Attends) is equal to the task of confining indefinitely the most fluid of bowel movements. You may accuse me of a certain lack of spontaneity in my sexual exploits—and this would be true to a point—but even the necrophile, waiting patiently bedside for weeks perhaps before her future lover exhales his last, even the necrophile likes her corpse warm. And what has all my infinite care and labor—down to befriending and bribing a pharmacy student in order to obtain a suppository of such illegal potency—what has all this patience and deliberation been in the service of, if not the spontaneous loss of sphincter control? For, though I have hosted a virtual olympics of excretory events, the one which I most desire to witness is, alas, one of the more challenging to effect—the truly non-volitional act, to wit, *the accident.* That it takes rather advanced notice to realize such flitting phantoms of the fetishist in corporeal form is a fact I will not dispute, knowing fullwell it flies in the face of our nation's ethos. But fuck this ethos (or rather don't), this image of frenzy and fumbling which leaves the one facedown snoring and the other wideeyed in the dark, in eternal unsatisfaction. This we term "passion." I will take instead the agonized delay, the tedium, the penis flaccid with boredom and waiting before I'll return to the exhausted three minutes of Jack Splat. I cultivate here exquisite sensations, and I'll not be hurried down shortcuts through which I'll not be able to bring them forth, fullblown and fullbloomed like a noxious brown rose of painstaking hybridization. It's late in the century, I know, but that only increases my methodological patience and my glacial deliberation.

Forgive me for getting into a bit of a lather just now, but I *am* shaving, though I can't say it hasn't come about without some effort. For if I live in a oneroom apartment, the only realistically available doorframe in which to bolt my almost incontinent friend is, of course, that leading into the bathroom. My neighbors might object to my using the front door for such activities and, let's face it, one wants to be in fairly close proximity to the bathroom when engaging in matters of excretory sex. Blocking the entrance to this

needful chamber mightn't be the wisest of ideas, even for such as
myself, but, stripping off my robe, I managed to find just enough
room between her spread legs, between the anklehigh spreaderbar
and the outpuffing thickness of diaper to slip myself through, all
without even lightly brushing against her or banging my head on
the sink. It was important not to touch her, for her sake more than
mine, but I am sufficiently vain that I like to do my job well and
it would have been unconscionable to touch her with any but the
most composed, deliberate gestures. Ideally, she should not even
know I've passed through her legs, but this I have no way of
knowing. Her face is impossible to read, and, as I brush lather on
my face and absently stroke my penis, the droop of her head
reminds me of those curiously faceless dolls in Hans Bellmer
photographs, if you've ever seen them. Her silver rectangle of
mouth (duct-taped), her eyes invisible behind a strip of black cloth,
she appears almost lifeless save for an occasional nostrilflare, a slight
heave in her smallbreasted chest. I open my razor and, ruminating,
begin to strop it on the leather belt I keep nailed to the bathroom
windowsill. An idea slowly takes shape in my mind. I run the spigot
as hot as it goes, and run the hot water over the open blade of the
razor until it faintly steams upon removal. I bring the razor near her
throat.

But I realize I've forgotten to tell you why I'm to be the greatest
novelist of the coming century. Such a statement no doubt appeared
more untoward than my admission of uncontrollable arousal at the
prospect of the bound woman before me shitting herself. That the
two propositions are as intimately related to one another as cause
and effect might strike you as odd, indeed madness itself, but, at the
risk of overextending an already thin line of credibility, I am forced
to admit that such is the case. Perhaps my sole saving grace as
holder of this position is the utter and almost saintlike humility it
entails, for I stake such claims not on the basis of my own talents,
considerable as those are, but rather on my humble capacity for and
selfless acceptance of the role. Having realized early that I am the
reincarnation of James Joyce, while bringing me a certain prestige
based on my future greatness, has furnished me with no small
amount of awe and even horror as I consider the vast achievement

of *Ulysses* and *Finnegans Wake*. Imagine, if you will, the feelings of an Egyptian slave brought to visit a pyramid, only to be told that he must build another. Well I know why such as he were paid in beer, for, on evenings of less optimistic cast, I have been known to down glass after glass of that same beverage as I contemplate the monumental labor ahead. Such moments are rare, or rather, not usually provoked by despair, for generally speaking, I find myself charmed by the role that, in its impersonal logic, History has deigned to offer, and indeed feel I would display the most unpardonable arrogance not to accept it. There's a certain Grecian elegance in the immortality available to the most writtenon writer of a century, and this will no doubt atone for whatever hardships and privations I may endure in the coming years as I trudge towards my inexorable destiny.

I should mention here that my feelings, on first ascertaining that I was indeed James Joyce in a more recent incarnation, were primarily those of relief, for it explained a great deal my interest in women relieving themselves. Joyce's more-than-passing interest in waste is, of course, well known; from the young girl Stephen Dedalus catches "midstream" in *A Portrait of the Artist as a Young Man*, to Molly Bloom's memory of wetting a complicated pair of drawers in *Ulysses*, his work is fairly ringing with women in the excretory act, and it's only natural that I, his spirit reembodied, should share this taste. Believe it or not, before my discovery, I used to find my fascination morbid, not to say shameful, and for some time I searched in vain for a door at which to lay responsibility. My mother's cancer, for example, evidenced a corruption deep within, as if our decaying line were gorging itself on its own entrails like a black snake on its tail. Too, my father's everwillingness to tilt a glass of Bushmills provided me with further grist, so that it seemed I was a mere misshapen product shat forth from boozy, exhausted loins. Neither did it augur well that my birth occurred late century, when monstrous perversions are likely to flower; my time spent incubating—for, I admit, this one time I was premature—perhaps yielded an unnatural bloom in which corruption was latent. But these improvised shelters for my miserable soul were quickly swamped by the flood of realization that I was Joyce. Even my early Freudian researches could not withstand its epiphantic rush, for what was, say, seeing poor Mina Kennedy piss her pants in kindergarten, compared with the knowledge that I was embarked on a course of artistic genius? Simply unfathomable.

I want to place the heated razorblade flat against her throat, and this is trickier than it sounds as she hasn't been touched for an hour or more. She's sure to flinch, from both the heat and the surprise of sudden pressure in an unexpected place. It's thus best to tilt the blade almost imperceptibly towards the butt so any sudden movement leaves the throat intact. As such, we get all the terror and none of the mess, though "none" might be too strong a word, for I'd be lying if I said I didn't half hope the resulting terror would cause a sudden and violent ejection of the contents of her bowels. Not that I'm rushing things, mind you, for I remain stony in patience and erection alike. I'm just intoxicated by the possibilities here, by the barest chance of grammar to take on sudden substance, for though we're frequently assured that, in times of crisis, someone nearly "shit her pants," we seldom witness such an occurrence. Imagine a brief brush of art's lips against those of life before returning to separate orbits. I'm not saying this is likely or ultimately even desirable. But a rush of adrenaline—its tensing and relaxing of muscles—coupled with an assful of suppository might very well produce such a discharge, and should it do so I need be prepared to rinse off my face and get down to business quickly. (And you say I lack spontaneity! I may need forgo my shave!) What most interests me, then, as I actually apply the steaming razor at an angle of approximately .5 degrees from the plane of her throat are the two muscles on each inner thigh which materialize suddenly like spokes on a braking wheel. The severity of the movement suggests to me that my passage between her legs went undetected. I remove the razor quickly, leaving its reddening shadow behind, and contemplate its effects: an increase in breathing rate; flared nostrils; an increase in shoulder tension; brief rattle of chains. Nothing more. I feel somewhat dissatisfied with the overall result. Something seems out of proportion, the design threatened, the terror not thick enough, and as these events occur in time, I realize precious seconds are slipping by as I hover in indecision. Then I receive a sudden, zenlike flash of illumination, and I know exactly what to do, but must time it exactly right. I wait, an agonized delay of perhaps two seconds, as her startled breathing just begins to turn towards regulation, then I reach around and slap her hard across the face, then pause to observe my handiwork.

When immersed in a scene of your own creation, the easiest thing to lose is perspective, and one need step back from time to time to assess its overall design. And, I must say, from this Olympian vantage, I am pleased now with the result of my recent additions. The larger, more openended imprint of my hand on her left cheek is balanced quite nicely by the slim red rectangle left by my razor on the right side of her throat. Her cheeks are puffed with breath that can't escape the tape across her mouth, and the increase blows wetly through her snotringed nose and heaves her small adorable breasts like a pair of wayward citrons bobbing gently on the sea. The snot isn't entirely to my taste, but I appreciate its color, its contribution to the composition at large, and such considerations must override the artist's personal whim. Those of you without a head for abstract art will probably find this ludicrous, but concerns such as color and balance must dominate the artist's attention. Their interpretation I leave to others, and, ignoring for the moment the uncharitable conclusions you've undoubtedly already drawn, I must confess that I don't even know what they carry for her. She's told me, of course, some fantasies, some things she'd like to have done in exchange for the loan of her bowels, but as for the exact effect of each act of mine on whatever inner drama she entertains, your guess is as good as mine. I provide simply the skeleton of torture for her to flesh out; for all I know, we might be acting out the latest issue of *Captured by Pirates*. I'm merely exhibiting structure here, and I can't be responsible for the ways people choose to inhabit or inhibit it.

Prrprr.

But wait. Is it?

Fff! Has she? *Rrprr . . . ?*

No.

Her asshole has just sent forth a volley of farts, but nothing more, no noise of ripping bowels or sign of filling seat. Still, I gather the

bouquet of this lateblooming harvest for appraisal. There is a whole
language of flatulence for those with the nose and ear, and Joyce
himself could be somewhat longwinded on the subject of his
expertise. In letters to his wife Nora, he sketched out various criteria
for their classification, "big fat fellows, long windy ones, quick little
merry cracks," and so on, being so bold as to declare he "could pick
hers out in a roomful of farting women." Like everything else, I
have inherited this faculty from the man, and have even so far
elaborated on it as to make it a sort of augury. In the present
instance, certain ambiguities make their interpretation difficult.
They haven't, say, the effervescence of a chance wind born of soda,
nor the epigrammatic quality of a selfcontained blast of beans. Their
stench is such that I know them to be some deep and weighty
missive from the colon, harbingers of future attack, yet they retain
a slight superficial air as if not fully committed. They haven't quite
the corpselike effluence of enemas I've administered. They caution
prudence, yet promise grandeur, and their whispered endearments
have sent me stroking to such a degree that, I realize, a few clear
drops have drooled from the mouth of my urethra. I halt even this
idle caressing for the moment and turn my back on her, resting my
penis on the cold porcelain of the sink and beginning to shave with
a steady hand. The asshole's language of flatulence is, I confess, a
dangerous one, because it appeals to senses other than the
intelligence. An orgasm right now would greatly threaten the design,
as I've hereto conceived it, but my intoxication with her opiate
fumes nearly sent me past the brink. No wonder it took Joyce
anywhere from seven to seventeen years to write a book; the hand
of Onan no doubt often stayed his pen. Is this not evident from his
letters, which frequently break midsentence as Jim pulls jet after jet
of jism into his trousers? Fortunately the novel form allowed him
to conceal these Coleridgean lapses, though, again, at the cost of no
small amount of time. In the present medium in which I work, time
is much more a factor, and despite the intoxicating odors breathed
forth from her quivering anus, I will touch myself no more. And I
will touch her no more until the event takes place, for you'll note
that in such matters I have an almost classical restraint, which
undergirds even those moments of apparent heedless debauch. This

will be essential to my art, I'm convinced, when it achieves its full flower sometime next century.

Provided her sphincter holds out, or in, I can complete this leisurely, straightrazor shave, which, being a fairskinned Irishman, I should be able to stretch into two days with propriety. You mightn't think such as we of this soiled and sodden brotherhood would be concerned with outward respectabilities, but a fastidious sheen is of utmost importance to our appearances. When, for example, in photographs, have you ever seen Joyce outfitted, to the extent his means would permit, in anything less than a coat and tie? Similarly, the sheer grandeur of his instructions as to the design of Nora's drawers would expose the deepest of Victoria's secrets as so much common knowledge. Much of the draw for the excremental fetishist inheres in elaborate furtiveness, in contrast between outside and in, and we might even posit that the degree of attention Joyce devoted to the white exterior of Nora's drawers—"all frills and lace and ribbons"—is in direct proportion to the angle of his "great cockstand" at the prospect of her shitting in them. You could think of this as simply dictated by logic, for without the concept of the "clean" there can be little prospect for the "dirty," and you can be sure that the most lurid wallower in filth by night is the most impeccable dandy by day, that the necrophile sheds real tears at funerals and the coprophile always brushes his teeth. Even my bound friend here carries pepperspray in real life, and has bars on her apartment windows.

I, of course, am no stranger to the inside/outside game, and it thus came as no surprise when, on first perusing Joyce's *Selected Letters*, I found, mere pages after his instructions on her drawers, the following more sinister design: "You say you will shit your drawers, dear, and let me fuck you then. I would like to hear you shit them, dear, first, and then fuck you. Some night when we are somewhere in the dark and talking dirty and you feel your shite ready to fall put your arms around my neck and shit it down softly." Though no surprise, I confess my pleasure on first coming across this passage was such that I immediately jacked off in my pants. Lo and behold, so did Joyce, for before he completes another sentence, he must break off, only to resume "No use continuing! You can

guess why!" And it was in the endorphin ebbing aftermoment of
this orgasm, or oracle, I first received communication that I, in fact,
was also Joyce. Had we not come together, as it were, in a moment
of communion over the same passage of grammar? Did we not at
that moment both speak with the same tongue? At that moment,
between contracted lids I seemed to see the kitchen table at 44
Fontenoy Street hover dimly before me, and a hand that was both
my own and someone else's scrawl black ink across a page. The
heavy tread of the ticketpuncher quickly recalled me to the fact that
I was actually on Amtrak between New York and Boston, but not
before the vision took on some assurance, and I knew quite before
we finished passing through the tunnel that affinities once vaguely
sensed between myself and Joyce were more than merely superficial.

Having finished my shave, I passed through the legs of my friend
to the other side—for there is where I'll need to be when the event
occurs—only to notice a faint yet discernible yellow stain on the
crotch of the diaper otherwise white. This observation occasioned
two further supplementary strokes of such startling degrees of
wetness that I dare not hazard a third for fear of jinxing the entire
show. It seems my friend has pissed herself, and, though I'd like to
think this occurred with the application of razor to throat,
realistically, and like Joyce I have a strong streak of the realist,
realistically it probably occurred while I was shaving. Could the
sound of running water have penetrated her wax earplugs? Possibly.
Dr. Mack's but guarantee twenty-two decibels of filter and my sink
is, shall we say, above the average in its sonic aspect. You'll marvel
once again at my restraint, at the Spartan economy of my design,
for in one of my less definite compositions, the accidental wetting
of her diaper would have triggered such baroque climax and
dénouement as to make Richard Crashaw demur. As it stands, it's
all I can do to light a cigarette calmly and touch two cautious
fingertips to my dayold frenchbread hardon. I can feel my pulse.
With an effort almost superhuman, I remove my fingers and do
absolutely nothing. I take a deep drag off my cigarette. I stare at the
wet, slightly yellow, slightly sagging diaper. It whispers to me
unspeakable promises, chants softly *she's pissed herself* over and
over again. I am lashed to the mast against its song, yet am even

more sanguine, for the only bonds which hold me are those intangible links to my future greatness. I withhold. And deny. And exhale slowly. I am held in check by a larger design, though I am driven near mad by the diaper wet before me.

You may laugh, you who are not, like Jim and I, among the soiled and sodden brotherhood, at the sight of one in thrall to the intimate inanimate, one completely absorbed by raiment and remnant of irresolute trauma. You may even deny the identification, for surely Joyce didn't stoop to the depravities implied by diapers. But you're fooling yourself, or being fooled by the shellgames of language and history, for what are *drawers* but *diapers* preincarnate, mere substitution of equidistant sets of letters? I have about as much use for a set of Edwardian underwear as Joyce would have had for a style of diaper invented in 1962 (Pampers, Proctor & Gamble). Sex, like everything else, occurs in time, and much of the trappings of the excretory fetishist are accidents of history. Joyce's style of diaper, of course, occurs on the first page of *Portrait*: "When you wet the bed first it is warm then it gets cold. His mother put on the oilsheet." Were he alive today, Joyce would be what we quaintly call a rubberist, for the cloth diapers of yore were far more nebulous garments, calling for a whole array of waterproof supplements, oilsheets, rubber pants, etc. (You still see the odd rubberist today, withered old men haunting the shores of Brighton in search of dusty magazines, probably diapered themselves now by necessity rather than choice. They are, sadly, a dying breed.) Note too that while the bulk of *Portrait* is written in the past tense, the excerpt above begins in the present habitual, bespeaking continued interest. Had we time, I could regale you with tales of my general underwear fetish, but even then, your derision probably wouldn't convert into belief. The truth will only come out, as it were, in the wash, when the century has turned and my potential finally bloomed in works of monumental achievement. You mustn't blame me if, like Joyce, I'm predictive of my future greatness; it's simply in my character.

We were speaking, a moment ago, about the accidents of history, and I think we are at last about to witness one. Her back has broken into a sweat, and this moisture portends great things. She seems now to merely hang from the handcuffs in exhaustion. We must be down to minutes at this point, and I stub out my cigarette in the sink. She is under strict orders to fight it as long as possible, otherwise it wouldn't be accidental. But the length of that possibility grows shorter and shorter. I watch a bead of sweat begin at the base of her neck, wending its way along the curve of a shoulderblade and down the groove of her back, disappearing beneath the waistband of the diaper. The diaper looks exhausted too, its once crisp, once taut surface drooping under the weight of sweat and urine. We must be down to minutes, if not seconds. My penis glistens in anticipation. The event is inevitable, but the inevitable takes some time. Then suddenly it begins.

The sound begins like the sound of someone tearing perforated cardboard, then like a string of firecrackers heard through a window, then liquefying viscous like someone squeezing paint from tubes, and a vile acrid smell from too deep in the bowels hits my nose like pepper, and the diaper expands obscenely like the cheeks of someone vomiting. And I have dropped the condom down my penis like a set of blinds, tugged the seat of the diaper aside and shoved my penis ballsdeep in her ass, before I realize the sound has stopped and the sound I hear is now the barefoot sound of shit dropping on kitchen tiles and bathroom tiles, and my crotch and legs are warm like I'm fucking mud and her shit runs down our legs in noxious brown rows. And I reach around with my dirty hand and claw her breasts, and I shove my clean hand down the front of her pisswet pisswarm diaper which is stretching and ripping and I frig her clit viciously and sink my teeth into her shoulder. And the reek is not like a row of portajohns in a week of sun but something infinitely deeper and more terrifying like operations and cemeteries and each shove forces more brown liquid out of her. And soon the diaper falls to the floor and my chest and her ass and back are covered in black and stinking filth and I can feel flecks of it hit my chin. And I know I'm about to come and redouble my fingers against her clit and her nostrils are working furiously and I can feel her body working up to a pitch and even though I shoot off first I keep shoving and clawing and tearing until I can no longer feel my penis, if it's hard or soft, inside or out but I keep shoving and biting

her neck and shoulders over and over until I feel her body start to
tense and then seize and her legs are trying to clamp as if she'd
break the spreaderbar and all I can hear now is the liquid sound of
her nostrils flaring in and out and slowly then suddenly completely
her body loses rigidity and she droops from the bolts and I can feel
her pissing down our legs and the piss spreading beneath my feet
when I suddenly hear a sound I've never heard and without
thinking I reach my shitsmeared fingers up to her mouth tear off the
tape and a long greencrimson jet of vomit flies out against the
mirror the sink and the floor and her mouth is making the sound
of screaminggasping like the sound of someone pulled out drowning
from the ocean.

— —

*Her fantasy, just fantasy: kidnap, torture, and rape. Mine: well,
you have some idea. An interesting problem for the artist to solve:
how to hold disparate ideas in tension, so the field between them
hums with magnetic strings whose pitch you can only begin to
sound. I think I succeeded admirably as she and I are concerned.
The abstract figure you saw before you, bolts and diapers, sodom and
shit, handcuffs, earplugs, and tape: a smudge of ink off which we
read unnumbered scenarios. The kidnap victim shitting herself from
fright; the brutal thief; prison guards on holiday; crucifixion, passion
and death. A blueprint for troughs and moving walls. Admire my
solution, defeating the odds at which desires seemed to stand. My
art right now consists of these fleeting and minor works; it takes
place not on paper but in temporary installations. Consider this a
progress report on the strides I've made to my own inexorable
destiny, sketch of impending masterpiece. Consider me an apprentice
in indefinite probation, during which, much like Joyce, I'm not
above dining out on the strength of future accomplishment. This is
mere rehearsal for my work in the coming age.*

ATTENTION
Beth Nugent

When my husband comes in—well, he is not really my husband, but this is what I call him, and what reason is there not to, just because it is not, strictly speaking, true?—when he comes in, he has already noticed that the dog has gone. I am at the sink with my back to him, but I can feel his eyes on me.

—I had that dog since he was a pup, he says, and when I turn around, he is gazing out at the backyard, where, until this morning, the dog was tied to a tree.

—A pup, he repeats, and shakes his head, though I remember finding the dog trotting down the edge of some road somewhere. It was where we met, more or less, the three of us, some road somewhere, and now the dog is gone.

I turn back to the sink, and I can feel his eyes back on me, vaguely suspicious.

—I'm going to go look for it, he says, and for a moment I can see the dog looking up at me, its trusting face. I do not remember letting the dog go, untying it from its tree, and so I could not have done it, but with his eyes on me, I can see the dog, its trusting face.

—O.K., he says, and he is gone. My hands are in water up to my wrists.

When he comes back, I am at the table, listening to the radio. Snow is falling all over the country, but here it is sunny and warm. He jerks his head out at the yard, then goes into the other room. After he has gone to bed, I look out the window. In the light from the streetlamp on the corner, I can see a dark furry shape, and next to it, another. All night they make noises in the yard—whining, an occasional bark or growl. I wonder what the neighbors will think. I mention this to my husband, although I am not sure if he is awake, and he opens his eyes, looks at me a long time, then closes them.

In the morning, he sits at the table and reads the newspaper. He spends most of the morning doing this every day, but I am never

sure whether or not he really reads it. Sometimes his eyes seem not
to move for minutes at a time, not even to blink. Occasionally he
will read something out loud, and every morning he reads our
horoscopes. He says that he does not remember exactly when he
was born, so he reads them all and picks the one that appeals to
him most. Usually it has something to do with making a lot of
money. He reads his first, out loud, and then mine. Mine too seems
to be more or less always the same. Pay attention to signs, it often
says, and nearly every day: expect the unexpected. It never says the
unexpected what.

Outside a dog snuffles in the yard, and my husband looks up briefly,
then back to the paper.

—Listen to this, he says. —When two people are repeatedly alone
together, some sort of emotional bond forms. He shakes his head,
and turns the page, reads for a while, then nods.

—Money, he says. I'm going to come into some.

He looks back at the paper. —Hmmm. he says, and looks up at me.
—Expect the unexpected.

Outside, the dogs are both lying on their sides. One of them has only
three legs, but where the fourth leg would join the hip it is smooth
and furry; except for a slight lumpiness, it feels almost normal, as
though the dog were born like this. The other looks fine, and aside
from the leg, they are almost identical—black chows with bright
brown eyes. Both thump their tails when my husband comes out to
stand above us.

—I should name them, he says. He stares down at them for a while.
—Chow mein, he says, then turns away and leaves.

The dog we had before was a tiny jumpy thing, always hopping
around the car like a miniature kangaroo. We never named it. We
had it only a month or so.

We ourselves have only been together a month or so. I suppose you
could say we don't really know each other all that well. When we
met—although perhaps it is not entirely accurate to say we met,
since no one introduced us—when we met, my car had broken
down by the side of some road, which was not as bad as it might
be, since I was going nowhere in particular, just driving. He stopped
along the side of the road, nearly half a mile ahead, then backed all

the way up along the shoulder until he got to me. He looked at my car, shook his head, and removed the license plates. No fines, he said. We have been together since then. Where we are now is a little house in a little town that seems made up entirely of houses. How we got here is another story, but not a very interesting one, and not one I remember terribly well, just a lot of driving and looking in the rearview mirror. Gas stations were the main attraction, and somewhere along the line I began to call him my husband.

My husband will pay for the gas, I would say to someone inside a service station, and the words had a kind of reassuring sound to them, as if I were getting back into the car with someone I had made an actual decision about, some kind of commitment to, which, in some way, I suppose I had.

He never asked me anything about myself, and so I never told him anything. Before I met him is another story, too, and also not a very interesting one. It is the kind of story you'd expect from someone like me, someone whose car breaks down when she is going nowhere in particular, just driving, and it is so familiar that sometimes I am not sure if it is actually my story, or a series of events I've seen in movies and television shows. Probably some of each. At this point I'm not sure how much it matters what is true and what is not true of the things I remember. We are here now, in a little house in a little town, and now we have two dogs. The things that came before seem to matter less and less every day, and sometimes this seems to be all I have known—really known—up to now. We are alone together repeatedly; we are forming some sort of emotional bond. We do not really talk much, but we are repeatedly alone together.

When my husband leaves to go wherever it is he goes, I sit down on the ground next to the dogs. Next door one of the neighbors comes to the window and watches for a while, then emerges, holding some sort of gardening tool. She waves it at me, then kneels on her own grass, but gradually moves closer and closer to the bushes between our two yards. She nods, then points her gardening tool at the dogs.

—Those are big dogs, she says, and I nod.

—Chows, aren't they? she says, and I nod again.

—Chow mein, I say, and she looks at me oddly. —That's their name. Chow mein.

—I hear chows can be mean, she says. —Temperamental.

—I don't know, I say. —Mostly they just lie there.

—Yes, she says, sighing, —but with all the children in the neighborhood . . .

—I guess so, I say, and she clips a few leaves from the top of a bush.

—They look like they might be diggers, she says, and we both look at the dogs.

—Diggers? I say.

—In the dirt, diggers in the dirt. Big dogs like to do that.

—The one only has three legs, I say. —I don't know how it would dig.

—Uh huh, she says. She clips another little branch from the bush, and heads back into her house. It is a house almost exactly like ours. The four-legged dog gets up and walks to the bushes, sniffing near where the neighbor stood. Later from the kitchen window, I see it digging a hole at the edge of the bushes; it keeps at it for a while, then goes back and lies down next to the other dog. My neighbor is at her window, watching.

When my husband comes home, he drags a large easy chair into the house and carries it to the middle of the living room. He brings home a piece of furniture almost every day, most of it brand new.

—From my old place, is all he says whenever he brings it in. Like this he is furnishing our house, day by day, piece by piece. We have two dining room chairs, but no table, and he has set them up in the dining room, facing each other, separated by the width of the table that would be there if there were a table. When I tell him about the neighbor and the digging, he goes to the window and looks out, then goes into the yard. He walks over to the hole the dog has dug, and kicks some dirt into it with the side of his foot, then walks around the yard, inspecting the borders closely.

When he comes inside, he sits in the easy chair he has brought in, and unfolds the paper, though it is the same paper he read this morning.

—Look at this, he says, and holds the paper up for me to see. He shows me a picture of a man sitting in a chair; a woman is standing behind him, and on the man's lap and on the chair and on the ground everywhere around him are cats, what appear to be at least a hundred cats. The man's face seems almost expressionless. If anything, I suppose it is a little mystified.

My husband turns the paper back and reads for a while.

—200 cats, he says. —200. And the house is spotless.

He looks up and glances around our house. There are little pads of dust in the corner, bits of dust drifting across the floor.

He turns a page of the paper, stares at it, then looks up at me.

—Expect the unexpected, he says. —Pay attention to signs.

Outside there is the sound of digging.

When I wake up in the morning, my husband is already gone, and so is the four-legged dog. The other one lies in the sun. When I open the back door, it barks several times at me, then lays its head back down. I wonder if the two dogs were alone together long enough or repeatedly enough to form some sort of emotional bond.

When my husband comes home, he walks from the car to the yard with his arms held out in front of him; something squirms in his hands, and then he dumps it on the ground. It is a cat, a skinny yellow thing that runs immediately under a bush. The neighbor watches from next door. I ask my husband if he couldn't find one with three legs, and he looks at me a long time, as if he is trying to remember some important fact about me, something he can say right now, but then he shakes his head and looks away, then lights a cigarette and drops the match on the ground. From under the bush, the cat's head swivels from us to the dog, back to us.

The next cat is black, with a spot behind its ear. My husband calls it Snowflake. He calls both cats Snowflake, and for several days, instead of furniture, he brings home with him a new cat, sometimes two. Some of them are wearing collars, one or two with little nametags. He calls them all Snowflake.

—Strays, my husband says, looking out at the cats prowling around the dog, who raises his head to bark at them occasionally.

He shakes his head and lights a cigarette. —People should take better care of their pets.

For several days cats seem to come and go—they do not always seem to be the same cats, but when one disappears, it seems to be replaced, so that there is more or less the same number of cats in the yard; some of them come in the house at night, through the open windows and my husband always looks up and says there's Snowflake. At some point, he seems to lose interest in them. They don't appear to bother him, it's just that he does not seem to notice them at all. A cat winds through his legs while he reads the horoscope, and you could not tell from his face or the tone of his voice that he is aware of any physical feeling. Every so often the dog begins to bark in the back yard, and after a while other dogs in the neighborhood join it. They can go on for hours, barking, and he will sit and read the paper, and when they stop it is as if nothing has happened.

One day he brings home a box, which he sets in the middle of the living room. It rustles and squeaks, and when he opens it, several small animals are scrabbling at the edges of the box—little white mice, a couple of guinea pigs, what could be a hamster. He stands and looks at them for a while, then turns the box on its side, and the animals tumble out, then scurry to different parts of the room, under what furniture we have. He nods, then smiles at me.

—These are very popular pets, he says. —They say they make good company.

A cat dozing on one of the dining room chairs lifts its head at the sound of a mouse scurrying past it into the kitchen.

After the rats, there are no more animals. For a few days nothing at all happens. My husband sits in his chair, staring at the newspaper. All around the house are little bowls of food—carrots and lettuce, cat food. During the day all you see are cats, but at night sometimes there is the rustle of something small, and a quick furious chewing. My husband stands in the middle of the room. Something's missing, he says, and leaves the house. When he comes back a few hours later, he carries in another easy chair, which he places across from the chair he sits in, and then returns to his car a few times, bringing back a lamp, a table, and two footrests, which do not match the chairs, but which he sets in front of them.

He turns on the light and sits in his chair, his feet on the footrest.

He sighs and waves his arm around the room.

—This is it, he says. —The American dream. A house. Some pets. He closes his eyes a moment. —I don't know, he says. —I guess we could use a TV. Maybe a microwave. Something.

When he brings home the television the next day, he turns both of our chairs to face it, but he does not turn it on, does not even plug it in; still, though, in the evening, we sit facing it and he reads his paper. I sit across from him.

—Listen to this, my husband says. —Baby found in dumpster. He shakes his head. —People, he says. —People ought to take better care of their kids. He stares at the television for a long time.

—They really ought to, he says. He goes back to the paper.

We are alone together, repeatedly. I close my eyes and wait for our emotional bond to form, whatever form it will eventually take. Sometimes when he touches me at night, I have to remind myself that he is my husband. And always there is the sound of animals— chewing and barking and the scrabble and click of paws as one scurries to get out of the way of another.

We have almost a full house of furniture. Finally a dining room table appears, but still we eat our food from take-out restaurants, and do not use the table. I am never hungry until he brings home something to eat, and then I am hungry for hours.

—Listen, my husband says. —Baby abused by mother. Kids abandoned over holidays. He watches a little white mouse dart across a doorway. —Baby found in dumpster, kids left in grocery store. He is not reading, but staring at the doorway, where the mouse was. —Child bludgeoned to death by mother's boyfriend. The newspaper is in his lap, and he looks at me. —Oh, he says. —Pay attention to signs. Expect the unexpected.

There is a large dumpster in the alley at the end of our street. Most days it is full of garbage, except on Tuesday, when it is empty. I poke around it a bit, and there is a rustle from under the garbage, but it turns out to be a squirrel or a rat, some quick brown animal that has been startled by my presence.

On the corner of the street is a small girl, who always plays alone in her yard. I stop on my way home to watch her. Sometimes it seems to me that men slow down as they drive past, to watch her play, and I think: there must be something I can do.
I walk by her and smile the kind of smile I think a small child would trust.
—Four, she says, when I ask her how old she is. A face appears at the window, and I wave, as if I am a neighbor strolling by, which is in fact what I am, more or less.

My husband is edgy, restless. He walks from the kitchen to his chair and then stands at the dining room table a long while. There are four chairs now, all grouped around it, and a candle sitting in the middle. The kind of place a family would sit.

My husband and I are driving, going nowhere, really, just out for a drive. It is Sunday, and this is something he says people often do, especially families: they go for Sunday drives. He seems surprised to hear that I haven't heard of this. He slows down as we pass the small girl on her little lawn. She looks at us, and after a moment, seems to recognize me, then waves. I wave back.
—Cute kid, my husband says. He lights a cigarette and flicks the match out the window. He looks in the rearview mirror as we drive away from the girl.
—They shouldn't just leave her out like that, he says.
We drive for a while, mostly around our neighborhood, and then he turns back.
—I was thinking, he says. —We could use some kids, he says.
—Maybe a couple.
—You'd have to quit smoking if we had a kid, I say, and he looks at me a long time, so long I think he might crash the car, but somehow he keeps it right on course. Then he blows smoke against the windshield and says —I think this weather is going to hold.

When I come home from my walk the next day, my husband is standing in the back yard. The black chow lies at his feet, and my husband is staring up at a tire hanging from a branch of the tree.

He reaches out and pushes it tentatively, then again, when it returns to him. When he turns and sees me, he smiles, then bends and scratches the dog where its leg would be. Hey Snowflake, he says.

My neighbor hangs her clothes up carefully; I take note of how she holds the clothespin in her mouth, then attaches it to the line. She nods at the tire hanging from the tree.
—So, she says, —are you going to add to your little family?
—Some of the cats are new, I say, and she smiles.
—I know honey, she says, —but what about children?
I wonder if my husband can hear this, from his chair inside the house.
—I don't know, I say. —The cats and dogs are a lot of work as it is.
—That one is awfully cute, she says, pointing to a little cat my husband calls Snowflake, but whose name, according to the little tag on its collar, is Muffin. My husband opens the door and looks out at us.
—Well, my neighbor says, —you'll want to be attending to him.
She turns back to her laundry. Bright sheets flap in the air about her head. We have been alone repeatedly together, she and I, but I am certain we haven't formed any sort of bond at all. I turn to my husband, standing on the back steps. He is looking out at the yard—the cats and dogs, the tire swing, me—all assembled here, like the furniture inside. His face is as foreign to me, and yet as familiar, as that of one of the mice that scurries about our house. As I walk toward him, his eyes fall on me; they do not resemble the eyes of anyone I have ever known. A dog growls at my side, and I think of all the people I might be walking toward instead of him, but as something like a smile comes across his face, I remind myself that he is my husband, and that all I can do is listen for the sounds of animals, the sounds of children, and expect the unexpected.

MULTIPLE UNIT DWELLING
Albert Mobilio

Apartment 4C: Afternoon

Somehow, I feel him as soon as he gets close. It's not like I feel him out there sending off a signal or coming in on a tracking beam. No, not as if he were getting nearer and his scent, his step, the jangle of his keys were building like a wave about to break over me. It's not something out there getting stronger with every breath. When he gets close I simply feel him. His hand cupped in my underarm, or his knuckles grazing across the bottoms of my feet. No drumbeat of approach. He's already exactly here. The air in the room shifts to accommodate him; his shadow bobs and bends across the wall. He's here and I feel him. Then I don't. Then it's over, but I know. He's at least as close as the wig shop or the bakery that does First Communion cakes, or maybe as far away as the chicken place. He's out there a few thousand inches away and swallowing them in bunches.

There's plenty of time for me to stash what needs stashing. Wash my hands and face. Some Listerine, some buttons buttoned. A blown kiss in the hallway as my neighbor smooches back, taking the stairs, johnny-atta-boy that he is, two at a time. I was so damn close when I felt him out there touching me. Almost there, with Mister Upstairs tonguing me to beat the band, when that familiar, unshaven chin rubbed twice across my forehead, making two parallel lines, one at my hairline, the other just above my eyebrows. I snapped upright, my thighs reflexively clamping around this guy's head, a contraction which spurred him on, me too for that matter. But the road traced across my head steamed like freshly poured asphalt; I pushed atta-boy away. Breathing hard through wet lips, my neighbor asks, "Was I too rough?" Not apologetic, but curious, hoping to make precise adjustments. He's really such a doll. "No, babe," I say. "But you've got to go. Pronto."

When he's gone, I check myself in the mirror—cheeks still flushed, eyes glassy. I need some more deep breaths; need to think calm thoughts, play that perfume commercial in my head, the one with long, white curtains blowing slow-motion in morning light. I make myself yawn a few times as I fluff the pillows. I toss some sections of an untouched newspaper around the bed but keep one, fold it to the crossword puzzle and begin with a pencil, just filling in anything, erasing empty boxes. My husband's fries and Coca-Cola breath dusts my shoulder. He's roaring in at me now. In the hallway, up the stairs. Inches flickering away as the tether between us pulls tight. We can stretch apart but something shivers down the tendrils in-between. We're kids talking into tin cans tied together with string; we vibrate from mouth to ear. It's not love. I mean, we've got that in the usual way but this is something else. It's like having a spy living in your own skin. I know he feels it too. Feels the office phone grow warm in his hand when I'm calling and he's on the line with someone else; hears me sniffling with a cold even though he's in a cab coming in from the airport.

A key in the door. Damn! I left the door unlocked and he'll wonder why. Got to be cool, parcel out the right measure of sleepy focus on my puzzle. Let some other day's tedium weigh in on my eyelids. His coat is being hung in the closet; a hanger clanks on the floor and I catch a whiff of the mushroomy smell of fucking. My belly twitches—a stone plunked into its smooth pool. Steady, girl. It's too late to open the window anymore. Instead, I scrub the air with the wind that's blowing those imaginary curtains. Somehow this irons out the agitation and gives my body back the heft and drag of boredom. I'm heavy enough to sink through the floor. Pour down like syrup into the place downstairs, where I'll get mopped up by my goofy neighbor there. My husband's maybe five seconds from sitting with me here on the bed, his hand returning to the heat he left on my brow only minutes ago. As he moves down the hallway his footsteps roll ahead of him and burst through the door. And then there is quiet. He's here. He's with me no more or less than he was before. I feel him again and somehow I feel myself. That is, I feel myself really here, an arrival just off the train from some suburb's suburb. As his hand combs back a few strands of hair from my downcast face, my eyes fix on a crossword clue, a six letter word for Anatomical Ring.

Apartment 4C: Late Night

Burning in through sleep, the mosquito's bite has upended an otherwise drably surreal account of my office life in which I sit at a school desk in the rain while my supervisor prowls past driving my landlord's van. In fact, when the van stops it is my landlord who gets out and comes to my desk to ruffle papers. He finds some non-work-related scribblings. At this juncture the message announcing the penetration of my skin and injection of chemical irritants must have begun arriving in my brain because the scene shifts radically to the dusty streets of a Middle Eastern village. Somewhere a child howls long, snot-choked howls of pain. I am aware that this child has hit another child with a large, flat rock and now she has been shut up behind a wall. Dust devils whirl through the streets. The town shifts to Texas, something out of *The Wild Bunch*. I approach a group of children and begin to speak but my mouth is dry, my lips are gritty. The burning sensation now pulses steadily from my neck and forehead. In the dream, I am staggering forward, my wax-dry mouth humming with unpronounceable words. The children look at me impassively, as if I were a familiar presence on these streets. My entire face and neck feel subjected to a single, enveloping needle prick. I am just beginning to wake when I hear myself ask the children, "Did I hear this on the nightly news?"

Awake, my skin sizzles with fresh attack. It's late October, yet the past few days have been summer-like. The predator must have laid low through the first frosts, like one of those Japanese soldiers that was found hiding twenty years after the war ended. I turn on the light and put on my glasses. I check my wife's face to see if the bug's feasting there. Her legs, having bicycled the sheets into thick, ropy twists, are also unmolested. I fish among newspapers and magazines beside the bed and retrieve today's paper. No good. Newsprint comes off on the wall. The paper is folded to the crossword page and I notice my wife has filled in some boxes with outsized letters. She's printed AREOLA in bold capital letters surrounded by a halo of erasure. I wonder, is this some Mediterranean island or a new crispy taste treat? Then the sounds— Are E Olah—vaguely animate my tongue and I get it. The ring around the rosy.

Vibrating at a micro-velocity, the bite on my wrist sports its own areola: a red collar around a raised mound of distended skin. It reminds me of my deadly business. An old *Smithsonian*, whose snowy cover photo—for an article about ice-climbing—won't smear the wall, offers the necessary heft when rolled. To stalk the pin-nosed monster, I squintingly examine the walls, taking warning swipes at specks on the white expanse. The huntress Diana in boxer shorts. In the overbright overhead light, the walls seem filthy. I hadn't realized just how filthy our room was. Nicks and smudges have registered our days. A chaotic overlay of fingerprints rings the light switch panel; the wall at the head of the bed is shadowed by contact with our pillows which, in turn, had absorbed our night sweats; the baseboards are speckled with scuffs; and even the ceiling bears scars of past magazine flailings—the occasional wing matted in a faint smear of blood.

City dwellers paint their apartments white to give the cramped rooms an airy, open feel; what's called the illusion of space. And it works. But now I could plainly see at what price. These walls got dirtied up by mere living. Nothing special, we don't do taxidermy or host bare-knuckle brawls. We sleep, iron clothes, and separate our change by denomination into little piles on the dresser. How could we have mucked up the place so thoroughly. Next time, a darker, more forgiving tint is in order. A beige or pearl gray. But not white. Or was it off-white. Or maybe even white white. In any event, those subtleties are gone. It looks like we've been living in a cotton bandage that's soaked up every untidy excrescence. And now, at 3 AM, my forehead dampening under the 100 watts of GE's finest, I feel unclean. We've soiled this white swab with our daily disease.

My wife sleeps on, undisturbed by either bite or the overhead roar of the light bulb. I scan her face and legs again. Bug-free, mouth slack, she breathes noisily. She never gets bitten, her sleep is never roiled by sting and swelling. Something in her blood, maybe. Or pheromones. Mosquitoes are drawn by heat and oxygen. Could it be she's a notch chillier than me; a smidgen less oxygen rich? Or am I just too appealing a meal? Once besotted with my brew, they leave her at peace and buzz off to the nearest wall to digest and contemplate the night. And that's where I usually swat them—splattering another pinprick's worth of blood into the wall's ongoing record of nightly aggravation.

Between the nightstand and the bed, in the shadow they both cast, hard by the magazine pile from which I've selected the instrument of its death, sits the mosquito in question: genus, Culex; life expectancy, nil. It's a tough angle for a server's swing so instead I deliver a rapping backhand that still yields a deliciously fat smack. Always the moment of uncertainty. Did it escape? Find a forgiving fold in which to hide? I inspect the weapon—the steep slope of Mount Rainer is scarred red—and then the wall—where a whiskery leg stands outright from the flattened wings and thorax. "He shoots, he scores," I hiss, aware dimly of flies and those wanton boys and the general absurdity of imputing personal motive to an insect. My triumphal glee is on par with that of the Supreme Creator who, after sinking a crowded ferry in Bangladesh, punches the air and cheers "Die fuckers!" Nonetheless, I do not stint myself. I have hunted. I have killed. Now I can dance the dance of the fathers around the sacred hearth. Or just crawl back to bed.

Just before dousing the light, I quick-scan the room for comrade predators. The walls glow; the nicks and knocks are like bruises on holy flesh. In catechism class, the nuns said our souls were like sparkling clean milk bottles and that our sins would show like black smudges. I flick off the switch and the bulb sucks our filthy nest back into the general smudge of night. I unknot enough of the covers from my wife's legs to accommodate my legs. Still asleep, unperturbed by the butchery, she clutches her pillow at her shoulder as if it were a sack she was carrying. Our ankles clang together as we both shift into new positions and I feel something down there at my feet, something sharp pressed into the tangle of sheets. I reach down and retrieve a creased bit of foil. Smoothed out, it is a square that's been torn open; it gives off a familiar oily, medicinal scent. But not so familiar that I've smelled it anytime recently. I stand up by the bed and toss the empty package on my pillow by her head. As my eyes roam the boxed-up dark, I believe I can see the wall's dirty marks. They seem darker than the surrounding dark—radiant scars. I reach for the lightswitch. The hunter is home, fresh meat in his mouth.

Downstairs, Apartment 3C: Afternoon & Late Night

Her door shuts and the broadcast descends. Dress shoes beat down across the floorboards, each step a whip-crack curling around my waking brain. A deeper, more seismic pounding tells me that she's on the bathroom's tile floor and it won't be long until the pipes ache and rattle as she fixes a bath. Always, for me, some calm to be found in the meditative thrumming that spreads out over my bathroom ceiling as the faucet gushes full-out into the tub. Back out over the floorboards into the bedroom for the spongy bounce when she sits on the edge of the bed. As both shoes clunk on the floor, one after the other, the simultaneity of their drop leads me to suspect that she uses her heel to loosen each shoe, hands no doubt employed with buttons elsewhere, and when both shoes hang open-mouthed from her toes she knocks them together—truly no place like home when a hot bath awaits—to send them tumbling. The muffled scuff of bare feet repeatedly criss-crossing from closet to dresser drawers dizzies me as I lie on my bed, imagining myself on a grassy slope, summer thunder rolling through low-hanging clouds. Back in the bathroom, the downpour drones in the nearly full tub and I can barely make out her entry—two gong strokes—as her feet touch bottom. From my medicine cabinet I retrieve my green onyx pipe and some hashish. I light up and listen hard for those rubbery bass notes as she shifts against the hollow body of the tub.

And I have been listening hard for almost a year now. When I moved in last fall she and her husband were friendly, loaning me a window fan, giving me the low-down on the landlord. Since I work at home—I write jacket copy for business books—I sign for their packages and a couple of times they've left keys for me to let in the super. That's how I got to know their apartment so well. Where her dresser is, her exercise bike, the big papasan chair where she watches TV. My place is directly underneath so the layouts are exactly alike—except where I have an office space, she has a little workout area. When she pedals, I hear the wheels in the airshaft; I listened for months trying unsuccessfully to locate in their insect whir the sound of her accelerated breathing. She works half-days as a personal trainer, going off at dawn to give executive types some chiding and chat while they sweat. By early afternoon she's home and, for me, that's prime-time. Her husband's not due till dinnertime so I can dog her solitary echoes as she bangs around the house.

Of course, after tummy crunching with her clients, the first thing she wants is that bath. It warms and relaxes me too. I do get edgy wondering whether she's coming home or has gone off to shop or lunch with a friend. But the frame-shuddering slap of her door—she's thoughtlessly noisy, thank god—dispels my fidgets. A few deep draws on the pipe fine tune my audio acuity—soon enough the whole apartment's an eardrum alert to her every vibration. The throaty gurgle in the drainpipe ends the bath. Then there's the sink faucet's breathy howl, like brushes on a high-hat cymbal; a good long job on the teeth, no doubt. After a few minutes more of bathroom clamor, she heads for the living room, putting on, I'd guess, the burgundy colored robe I once saw on the back of the bathroom door. A quick stop in the kitchen for, perhaps, a glass of juice, some carrot slices, and then she's curled up in the papasan chair—its bamboo base totters and squeaks when she sits or gets up. A TV announcer's baritone mumblings and the sibilant clatter of an audience sift down through the floorboards. I could probably tell if it's *The Price Is Right* or *The Newlywed Game* if I put an ear to the steam riser or climbed my stepladder to cup a glass against the ceiling. Yes, I've done that. I know it's not, well, sporting of me, but the improvement in fidelity is dramatic. Once, I heard her yelling, apparently to herself, and knocking around the kitchen. Bad news on the phone? Drunken fit? The only way to figure it out was to listen with fervor, right up close. After a long time pressed to the ceiling I fixed on the probe-like use of a broom-handle in the pantry. Yet the clincher was making out the words, "Come outta there you little sucker." Such a ballsy piece of work, she is; when I heard a decisive thwack and her half-mad victory cry I nearly toppled from my perch. She would never stand on a chair and scream, "Eek, a mouse!" I blew her a triumphant kiss and would have kissed the plaster itself, but the ceiling, I was surprised to learn, can be a very dirty place.

Some days, those that end with my vow to get out more, she calls the jock-boy law student from the top floor and invites him down.

Her phone is in the kitchen by a window and his must be too since
I can hear his phone ringing in the airshaft followed by her jangled
laugh. Today, she hangs up and unlocks her door so he can slip in
without knocking. They don't waste much time. His thick-footed
stomp is gone in minutes and the bedsprings begin their kittenish
yelp as they undress. My own bed is exactly underneath hers; my
window is open on the airshaft we share. A belt buckle smacks the
floor, pocket change showers down and one coin skips a long way
into a corner. Its wiry drumroll hovers in the air above my face.
They too seem to be waiting for what should follow. Does he
hesitate a moment, make a mental note of its location so he can
fetch it later? Faraway, out on the avenue, a tractor-trailer grinds
down through the gears to come to a squealing halt. There's some
indecipherable talk and she pops up, fairly prancing back and forth
across the room. A towel, a condom, an extra pillow? Some more
talk that's gilded around with teasing laughter. I strain for signs
she's not really pleased with all this. A slight souring in the voices,
a sudden, jagged word ricocheting off the bricks outside. Her
silence, maybe. But soon she can be heard—her fleecy croon riding
a downdraft past my window—and then comes the bed's ever so
slight scrubbing motion, a cadenced rub that polishes my forehead
even as it works into those tarnished grooves not easily reached.

Just as I begin to gleam under this scouring, it stops. Among the
sudden scatter of footfalls I can hear two distinct plunks—he's
hopping into his pants—and the cushioned closing of the door.
Scrambling back and forth she taps out an alarmed tattoo
accompanied by the bugle call of the bathroom faucet's ringing
hiss—it's all hands on deck. Finally she comes to rest in bed and
just a few minutes later I hear her husband's ragged shuffle on the
stairs outside my door. It's hours before he's usually home. Did she
know he was due early? Did I miss some bad business between her
and law-boy? Were they just in a hurry and lucky because of it? He
fumbles around the hall closet before entering their bedroom. I
scramble atop my armoire and press an ear against a glass—the best
is the tall drink type with very thin walls. I've got my favorite, a
Yogi Bear jelly glass on which Yogi dips his porkpie hat Sinatra-
style while Boo Boo looks on with admiration. But today this

acoustic high-performer yields nothing. The faint timbre of sporadic small talk hums through the glass and nothing else. After a while my neck creaks, my ear is flattened. I climb down and decide to go out and get some fresh air. A glance in my bathroom mirror shows my reddened ear encircled by the impression from the bottom rim of the glass. A rosy ring. An aural target . . .

The middle of the night and they're going at it. I don't need Yogi. The whole building can probably hear them. He draws out long tenor deep riffs of invective. She's quiet until he runs out of breath and then she's peeling out brassy staccato bursts. She stalks off to another room and he follows; he spits out something ugly, slams the door and stalks off too. She follows close behind, blaring at his back. I wish I didn't have have to hear this. But I need to. I'm tracing their steps one floor below, sucking up the lungfuls they expel. A scavenger for human tunes. And there's always so much to gather, down here or anywhere. People are messy. We always leave some of ourselves behind. The scent of stolen chocolate in a toddler's goodnight kiss, a whispered word on the telephone overheard by someone in the next booth. A torn condom package in the bedsheets. We leave scrape marks on the sunlight when we look at it; we smear the rain when we walk through it. We are a sloppy spectacle. I guess we're its audience, too. And some of us are more audience than show. We just listen. To the ringing. As someone else's body chimes against dead air.

The Chokecherry Tree
Marci Blackman

A chokecherry tree. That's what I told Mary I wanted her to put on my back. Over the years, the numbness had gotten worse. Guess I figured since I couldn't feel anything as it was, there might as well be a reason.

We were twisted among the sheets of the wrought iron bed she'd found on the sidewalk in front of her studio. It was our first real argument, occurring just minutes after the first time we combined SM play with sex.

After fisting and making me come (for the third time in a row), screaming and nearly falling to the floor, Mary pulled me back on the bed to recover, then planted subtle kisses on my nose and forehead.

"You know," she whispered, producing three heavy duty extension cords from under the bed. "Funny things happen to electrical cords in the middle of the night."

Laughing at her own joke, she used one of the cords to tie my wrists to the headboard. With the others, she knotted each of my feet to the sides of the bed frame. "That too tight?" she asked, slipping a leather hood over my head and fastening the straps.

I said no and closed my eyes.

Mary is a trust fund baby. The kind that feels guilt and embarrassment every time one of her working-class lovers discovers she has a six-digit bank account.

"It's no big deal," she was quick to explain when I asked. "My parents died in a car accident, when I was five, and left me some money. Too bad I can't use it to buy them back."

She was raised by her grandparents, the ones on her father's side. Until she turned eighteen, they were in charge of the money. Their plan was to teach her to appreciate the values in life, send her to the finest schools. A Catholic boarding school until the age of fourteen, then onto Mother Theresa's Prep Academy for Girls. In their minds, there was no question; Mary would go on to Harvard or Yale to study medicine, law, or some other reputable secure profession that would prevent her from squandering the money.

Then, after graduation, she would settle down with some nice fine upstanding young man—a fellow student, perhaps—from a good line and start a family.

Good Catholic girl that she was, Mary followed her grandparents' rules until her eighteenth birthday, when the money officially became hers, then informed them that there had been a change in the program. Her plans for herself were different, she said; she was moving out to experience life on her own. She would finish prep school, but she was not going to college.

As expected, her grandparents fought it; tried to prove— legally—that Mary couldn't be trusted with so much money. She was too young, they argued; already she'd demonstrated an inability to make sound decisions. Their son had worked hard for that money, too hard to let a girl barely of age piss it all away. But their meticulous planning—and the efficacy with which they carried out its design—backfired; the judge ruled to the contrary. There was nothing in Mary's make-up or history suggesting such a thing would happen. In fact, he asserted, her grandparents should be proud of the way Mary turned out. She was an excellent student and she knew the value of hard work. Her record and reputation at both the boarding school and Mother Teresa's stood unblemished. She had to face life's little pitfalls at some point in time. Since the original documents were all in order, there was no reason that time shouldn't be now. Mary waited until after the court's decision to tell her grandparents she was a lesbian.

From the beginning, sex between us bordered on the perverse. Although Mary was wrestling with her own demons about God and bondage when she first took my order that day in the cafe, we were two months into the relationship before we talked openly and called it what it was. We'd wake in the mornings bruised and confused from the dark places we'd traveled the night before. Then upon rising, over cigarettes and coffee, we'd talk about our individual plans for the day, not about what happened.

At first, Mary wanted to submit to me. Turn the tables, she said, fulfill my wishes, serve my needs. But I told her my needs demanded that she be dominant. I wasn't in this for retribution; I got involved with Mary for one reason only: like Uncle George, I believed I needed her to help me feel.

According to family legend, Uncle George was a slave. "A crazy one, too," my Mama used to say, with a penchant for running away and getting caught. But that wasn't what made him crazy. "Shoot!" Mama would add. "If there's a soul in captivity who hasn't been whipped for runnin' at least once, I'd like to meet him." What made folks look at Uncle George sideways, she said, was that every time he ran and got caught, the lashing he gave himself was worse than any the overseer could have imagined.

All tolled, he ran five times, through entanglements of birches, poplars, and chokecherries, looking for something called freedom. And each time, after the overseer brought him back and made an example of him, Uncle George found some way to mutilate himself even further. Whether it was ramming his head against the trunk of a tree until it burst open, or chopping off his middle and index fingers with a pick ax, he always managed to outdo the overseer. After the third time, when Uncle George swallowed an entire can of lye that ate up most of his insides, the overseer just stopped trying. And the next time Uncle George ran, since he was obviously doing a better job of it, the overseer decided to save himself some energy and let the nigger punish himself.

Uncle George didn't disappoint. As soon as he was turned loose, after being drug back on the end of a rope for the fourth time in a row, while the rest of the plantation shook their heads in disbelief, he took hold of one of the overseer's branding irons and burned his master's initials into every reachable spot on his body.

"It was like he was chastisin' himself for gettin caught," Mama would say. "Either that, or somewhere along the way, he stopped runnin' for freedom and started runnin' open-armed toward death. You know, figurin' the two were one and the same. Either way, he was still a fool. Everybody know death got its own timetable. And only a fool would try to change it."

The fifth time Uncle George ran was his last. The overseer was nearly doubled over in hysterics when he brought him back, like he couldn't wait to see what new castigation Uncle George had in store for himself. He wouldn't wait long. As soon as he cut him loose, before he could gather his wits to stop him, Uncle George reached for the overseer's rifle, stuck the barrel deep in his mouth and blew his head off.

"Now you know," Mama would end to scare me. "Damn curse has been with this family ever since. So watch yourself," she'd warn. "Ain't none of us safe."

Mama died before I could tell her that I knew the truth. Knew all about the numbness. And that my own battle with it had already started. The family was cursed alright, but Uncle George didn't start it, and he wasn't trying to die. When Uncle George placed the barrel of that rifle in the back of his throat, it was a last ditch effort to defeat the numbness.

—

She didn't know if she could do that, Mary answered. She had done it. In relationships past, she had always topped, but with me, it was different. She didn't know why, she said, letting her hair fall in her face as she folded into a ball at my kitchen table. It just was.

Mary never said why she was attracted to me. To be honest, I didn't really care. But I imagine it had something to do with her Catholic upbringing. "You know those Catholics," MacArthur used to say, "always takin' in some lost soul, tryin' to assuage that guilt."

After fastening the hood, Mary began to weave a knife around my breasts. Figure eights, in and out and in and out, coming to rest, pressing hard against my nipples. I would find out later that she drew blood. She called me names: Bitch, whore, slut, worthless. But never nigger. Never the one I wanted. She reminded me that at any moment, if she felt like it, she could slit my throat, then balanced the knife on my pubic hair and told me she knew I wanted it, wanted the knife inside.

I lay still and silent.

"You want this?" she asked, pressing the blade against my labia. "You want my knife inside you, gutter bitch!?"

"Yes," I whispered, muffled through the hood.

"What was that?" she commanded, pressing harder. "I can't hear you, bitch!"

"Yes," I said louder. "Yes, I want your knife."

But she refused to give it to me. Instead, she told me that I'd been bad. That I had mumbled. And that now I was about to find out what happens to sluts who mumble and don't behave.

She loosened my wrists and untied my feet. Then flipped me onto my stomach and reknotted my hands. She left my feet free. The cord was too tight, cutting off my circulation. I slid my wrists back and forth to loosen it, but it didn't help.

"Aw, did I tie it too tight?" Mary asked, laughing. "Am I hurting the little whore's little wrists?"

I shook my head no; the mockery in her voice told me that if I answered yes, she would tie them tighter.

"I didn't think so. Now get up on your knees."

As I crawled to my knees, she started to flog me. Soft and fast initially, then hard, slow and rhythmic. At first I thought she had doubled-up one of the extension cords, but soon realized (when she shoved its handle deep inside me), that it was a whip. A cat-o'-nine-tails, I would discover in the morning, with metal beads tied to the ends.

In the beginning, I felt nothing. Then, as the whip slowed down, each lash began to feel as though it were ripping up my skin. By the end, when the measured strokes of rawhide began to soothe, I got off on them. Wanted them. Needed them. I wondered if this was how it was with Uncle George. If, when the overseer had tired, when there were no more bare patches of skin to rip open, if Uncle George had begged him not to stop, as I was begging Mary now.

But she did stop. The urgency inside my begging must have scared her, she said later. Abruptly, she put down the whip and untied my wrists. Carefully turned me over, then removed the hood. Gently, she pressed her lips against my eyelids, brushing her cheek softly against my nose, running her tongue slowly across my lips.

"I'm sorry," she whispered over and over. "I'm sorry."

When I opened my eyes, her face glistened with sweat. She was massaging the blood back into my swollen hands. "Are you okay?" she asked.

I nodded and smiled.

"Let me take a look at your back."

She helped me sit up, then traced the fresh welts with the tips of her fingers. "Mmm, nice," she hummed. "Those'll stick around a few days." Wrapping her arms around my shoulders, she kissed the back of my neck and held me. Slowly, we started to rock. Neither of us spoke, just rocked, slow and steady.

I hadn't expected to like it. Truth is, I hadn't expected much of anything past beating back the numbness. But even that was short-lived. Already, as Mary began to drift off to sleep, the numbness started to crawl up my legs again. And lying there in the darkness, I could feel my body twitch as it cried out for more.

"I want a tree," I whispered.

"What, baby?" she answered, nuzzling her nose into the nape my neck.

"A tree. A chokecherry, like Sethe's in *Beloved*."

"Like who?"

"I want you to put a tree on my back. I'll be Sethe, and you can be Schoolteacher."

"You mean role play?"

"Yeah, only I want you to use a claw whip, a real one. No safe words, stopping only when the nerve endings are gone, dead."

"Po, that's sick."

"Is it?"

She sat up in bed. "Think about what you're saying."

"I have."

"This is crazy! A claw whip? It'll kill you."

"Maybe, maybe not. Didn't kill them. Didn't kill Sethe."

"Po, this is stupid. If this is supposed to be some kind of twisted joke, it's not funny."

"I'm not joking."

"Po, Sethe was a character in a book for Christ's sake! A disturbing book at that. And what's up with this 'them' you keep talking about?"

"Sethe was based on reality. And you know damn well who they are."

"Yeah, well, I think you're going a little too far on this one." She climbed out of bed and started pacing. "This is ridiculous. I don't even know why we're discussing it. I'm not Schoolteacher; I can't go there with you."

"Yes you can. Besides, you're a hell of a lot closer to Schoolteacher than you think."

"Fuck you! So now I'm some kind of evil overseer? I didn't do anything you didn't want me to."

"Yeah, well, now I want you to do this."

She stopped pacing and looked at me.

"I can't," she said, quietly. "I won't." Then out of nowhere, frustration maybe, she slammed her fist against the wall and stormed out of the room.

I woke in the morning wrapped in the sheets, alone, with no feeling in my wrists or back. It was raining. The city clock chimed eleven times. I rubbed my eyes and got up to go find Mary.

She had fallen asleep in the bathroom, curled up in one end of the footed tub. There was no water. An ashtray—filled with cigarette butts—sat on the ledge of the tub beside her. Her neck and shoulders were squished in the corner. Drops of rain echoed down the drainpipe that ran past the window. I made coffee and brought it to her.

"Hey," I whispered, shaking her gently before handing her the mug. "Stay like that much longer, and it'll be permanent."

"God, you sound like my grandmother," she answered, clearing her throat.

"Wanna talk?" I asked, squeezing into the tub beside her.

"How's your back?"

"Sore," I lied.

"I'm supposed be taking care of you, remember?" She took another sip of her coffee.

"Yeah, well, I slept in a warm bed last night."

"Po, you know I can't do what you're asking, at least not now."

"I know."

"And I know you think this thing you're fighting isn't about me. But it is, you know? If we go there, I'll be there with you. Then I really will be Schoolteacher." She started to cry. "I'm just not ready for that."

I set down my coffee and put my arms around her, held her. I've since forgotten the number of times the clock actually tolled that day, but our bodies stayed like that well into the night, adhered together in one end of the tub, wrapped inside the blanket of the music of the drain pipe, thinking and saying nothing.

Tree Planting Ceremony
John Yau

She doesn't know why it started happening with him, why, one Saturday night, her parents visiting a friend's in the country, certain words began wriggling and popping out of her like worms, like all of her was rising toward an indentation of damp and teeming earth, this opening from which he had moved a rock. A flat, sharp one covering her mouth. It had been a wheel he somehow managed to roll away, while they were sitting in front of the fire, drinking beer and listening to music.

It must have let the light in, what he did, and the light must have found its way to the little school table where she had been sitting and writing in a book she had been sure to show no one, not even herself. The book with a heart-shaped lock she told herself someone else is methodically filling with spiderwebs of purple ink. The book she knows by heart, each and every pink page, some of which he has now glimpsed.

An acorn. The first time she did it in front of him, she used a large polished acorn attached to a long yellow handle. He had dared her, she tells herself, but she had been smart enough to take the dare one step further than any place he had ever been, much less imagined, knowing there was no one he could tell, no one who would believe him. She, after all, had a steady job; and he didn't.

It took place in front of the crackling logs of her parents' fireplace, which always made her feel safe, his soft incessant whisper urging her on, his big flat hands beginning to slap the dusty slate floor beside her, as if she were a sweaty racer and the bleachers were full. She didn't want to tell him, didn't have to, but she was the one who was in control, and he was just a puppet mouthing the words she had taught him.

This became one of the things they did whenever he was there and her parents were not. Lying on the animal whose body has been taken away, her head near the poor swimmer's head, its mouth half open. She just simply had to lie back, unbuckle her belt, and he would practically stop breathing.

The polished brass acorn she slowly guides inside her, like a doctor of the interior. Curling her eyes up inside her skull, remembering the sharp black bristles at the other end of the handle. Then spewing worms up the chimney, faster than the night air can swallow them.

His hairless face bobbing beside her, an apple jammed onto a stick.

Some things are too small, others are too big. This is the trouble with the world, nothing fits. When do you finally get to be inside the body you inherited, rather than dreaming about another body? The real trouble with the world. Men get to be inside bodies other than their own, while women get to be inside the body they want to exchange. She possessed too much and too little of everything, and she can't shift these mounds of dirt around; she isn't, after all, a boy.

from THE AGE OF WIRE AND STRING
Ben Marcus

"Intercourse with Resuscitated Wife"

Intercourse with resuscitated wife for particular number of days, superstitious act designed to insure safe operation of household machinery. Electricity mourns the absence of the energy form (wife) within the household's walls by stalling its flow to the outlets. As such, an improvised friction needs to take the place of electricity, to goad the natural currents back to their proper levels. This is achieved with the dead wife. She must be found, revived, and then penetrated until heat fills the room, until the toaster is shooting bread onto the floor, until she is smiling beneath you with black teeth and grabbing your bottom. Then the vacuum rides by and no one is pushing it, it is on full steam. Days flip past in chunks of fake light, and the intercourse is placed in the back of the mind. But it is always there, that moving into a static-ridden corpse that once spoke familiar messages in the morning when the sun was new.

II.

I-It

The Haile Selassie Funeral Train
Guy Davenport

The Haile Selassie Funeral Train pulled out of Deauville at 1500 hours sharp, so slowly that we glided in silence past the platform on which gentlemen in Prince Alberts stood mute under their umbrella, ladies in picture hats held handkerchiefs to their mouths, and porters in blue smocks stood at attention. A brass band played Stanford in A.

We picked up speed at the gasworks and the conductor and the guards began to work their way down the car, punching tickets and looking at passports. Most of us sat with our hands folded in our laps. I thought of the cool fig trees of Addis Ababa and of the policemen with white spats painted on their bare feet, of the belled camel that had brought the sunburnt and turbaned Rimbaud across the Danakil.

We passed neat farms and pig sties, olive groves and vineyards. Once the conductor and the guards were in the next car, we began to make ourselves comfortable and to talk.

—Has slept with his eyes open for forty years! a woman behind me said to her companion, who replied that it runs in the family.

—The Jews, a fat man said to the car at large.

Years later, when I was telling James Johnson Sweeney of this solemn ride on the Haile Selassie Funeral Train, he was astonished that I had been aboard.

My God, what a train! he exclaimed. What a time! It is incredible now to remember the people who were on that train. James Joyce was there, I was there, ambassadors, professors from the Sorbonne and Oxford, at least one Chinese field marshal, and the entire staff of *La Prensa*.

James Joyce, and I had not seen him! The world in 1936 was quite different from what it is now. I knew that Apollinaire was on board. I had seen him in his crumpled lieutenant's uniform, his head wrapped in a gauze bandage, his small Croix de Guerre caught under his Sam Brown belt. He sat bolt upright, his wide hands on his knees, his chin lifted and proud.

A bearded little man in a pince-nez must have seen with what awe I was watching Apollinaire, for he got out of his seat and came and put his hand on my arm.

—Don't go near that man, he said softly in my ear, he says that he is the Kaiser.

The compassion I felt for the wounded poet seemed to be reflected in the somber little farms we passed. We saw cows goaded home from the pasture, gypsies squatting around their evening fire, soldiers marching behind a flag and a drummer with his mouth open.

Once we heard a melody played on a harmonica but we could see only the great wheel of a colliery.

Apollinaire could look so German from time to time that you could see the pickelhaube on his bandaged head, the swallow-wing moustache, the glint of disciplinary idiocy in his sweet eyes. He was Guillaume, Wilhelm. Forms deteriorate, transformation is not always growth, there is hostage light in shadows, vagrom shadow in desert noon, burgundy in the green of a vine, green in the reddest wine.

We passed a city that like Richmond had chinaberry trees in the yards of wooden houses hung with wisteria at the eaves, women with shears and baskets standing in the yards. I saw a girl with a lamp standing at a window, an old Negro shuffling to the music of a banjo, a mule wearing a straw hat.

Joyce sat at a kitchen table in the first compartment on the right, a dingy room, as you entered the fourth wagon lit counting from the locomotive and tender. His eyes enlarged by his glasses seemed to be goldfish swimming back and forth in a globe. There was a sink behind him, a bit of soap by the faucet, a window with lace half-curtains yellowed with the years. Tacked to the green tongue-and-groove wall was a Sacred Heart in mauve, rose, and gilt, a postcard photograph of a bathing beauty of the eighties, one hand on the bun of her hair, the other with fingers spread level with her dimpled knee, and a neatly clipped newspaper headline: A United Ireland and Trieste Belongs to Italy Says Mayor Curley at Fete.

He was talking about Orpheus preaching to the animals.

—The wild harp had chimed, I heard him say, and the elk had

come with regal tread, superb under the tree of his antlers, a druid look in his eye.

He described Orpheus on a red cow of the Ashanti, Eurydice beneath him underground making her way through the roots of the trees.

Apollinaire stuffed shag into a small clay pipe and lit it with an Italian match from a scarlet box bearing an oval wreathed with scrolled olive and wheat a portrait of King Umberto. He tapped his knee as he smoked. He batted his eyes. King Umberto looked like Velázquez's Rey Filipe.

My wife, Joyce says, keeps looking for Galway in Paris. We move every six weeks.

There came to Orpheus a red mouse with her brood, chewing a leaf of thoroughwax, a yawning leopard, a pair of coyotes walking on their toes.

Joyce's fingers were crowded with rings, the blob of magnified eye sloshed in its lens, he spoke of the sidhe turning alder leaves the whole of a night on the ground until they all faced downward toward China. Of creation he said we had no idea because of the fineness of the stitch. The ear of a flea, scales on the wing of a moth, peripheral nerves of the sea hare, great God! beside the anatomy of a grasshopper Chartres is a kind of mudpie and all the grand pictures in their frames in the Louvre the tracks of a hen.

Our train was going down the boulevard Montparnasse, which was in Barcelona.

—How a woman beats a batter for a cake, Joyce was saying, is how the king's horses, white and from Galway, champing in their foam and thundering against rock like the January Atlantic, maul the sward, the dust, the sty, the garden. Energy is in the race, handed down from cave to public house. Ibsen kept a mirror in his hat to comb his mane by, your Norse earl eyed his blue tooth in a glass he'd given the pelts of forty squirrels for in Byzantium, glory to Freya.

Apollinaire was showing his passport to a guard who had come by with the conductor. They whispered, head to head, the conductor and the guard. Apollinaire took his hat from the rack and put it on. It sat high on the bandage.

—*Je ne suis pas Balzac*, he said.

We passed the yellow roofs and red warehouses of Brindisium.

—*Ni Michel Larionoff*.

—Whale fish, Joyce was saying, listen from the sea, porpoises, frilly jellyfish, walruses, whelks and barnacles. Owl listens from the olive, ringdove from the apple. And to all he says: *Il n'y a que l'homme qui est immonde*.

Somewhere on the train lay the Lion of Judah, Ras Taffari, the son of Ras Makonnen. His spearmen had charged the armored cars of the Italian Corpo d'Armata Africano leaping and baring their teeth.

His leopards had a car to themselves.

When we rounded a long curve I could see that our locomotive bore the Imperial Standard of Ethiopia: a crowned lion bearing a bannered cross within a pentad of Magen Davids on three stripes green, yellow, and red. There was writing on it in Coptic.

We passed the ravaged and eroded hills of the Dalmatian coast, combed with gullies like stains on an ancient wall. There was none who looked at the desolation of these hills without thinking of the wastes of the Danakil, the red rock valleys of Edom, the black sand Marches of Beny Taamir.

From time to time we could hear from the car that bore Haile Selassie the long notes of some primitive horn and the hard clang of a bell.

Moths quivered on the dusty panes, Mamestras, Eucalypteras, Antiblemmas. And O! the gardens we could see beyond walls and fences. Outside Barcelona, as in a dream, we saw La Belle Jardinière herself, with her doves and wasps, her sure signs in full view among the flowers: her bennu tall on its blue legs, her crown of butterflies, her buckle of red jasper, her lovely hair. She was busy beside a sycamore, pulling water out in threads.

—*Rue Vavin!* Apollinaire said quite clearly, as if to the car at large. It was there that La Laurencin set out for Spain with a bird on her hat, an ear of wheat in her teeth. As her train pulled out of the Gare St. Lazare, taking her and Otto van Waetjen to the shorescapes of Boudin at Deauville, where we all boarded this train, where we were all of us near the umbrellas of Proust, the Great War began. They burnt the library at Louvain. What in the name of God could humanity be if man is an example of it?

Deftly she drew the crystal water from the sycamore, deftly. Her helper, perhaps her lord, wore a mantle of leaves and a mask that made his head that of Thoth, beaked, with fixed and painted eyes.

We were in Genoa, on tracks that belonged to trolleys. Walls as long and fortresslike as those of Peking were stuck up all over to a height with posters depicting corsets, Cinzano, Mussolini, shoe wax, the fascist ax, boys and girls marching to *Giovanezza! Giovanezza!* Trees showed their topmost branches above these long gray walls, and many of us must have tried to imagine the secluded gardens with statues and belvederes which they enclosed.

He lay with his hands folded over his sword, the Conquering Lion, somewhere on the train. Four spearmen in scarlet capes stood barefoot around him, two at his head, two at his feet. A priest in a golden hat read constantly from a book. If only one could hear the words, they described Saaba on an ivory chair, on cushions deep as a bath, a woman with a bright mind and red blood. They described Shulaman in his cedar house beyond the stone desert it takes forty years to cross. The priest's words were as bees in an orchard, as bells in a holy city. He read aloud in a melodious drone of saints, dragons, underworlds, forests with eyes in every leaf, Mariamne, Italian airplanes.

An unweeded garden, Joyce was saying, is all an inspired poet rode rickrack the river to usher to us. Her wick is all ears, the lady in the garden. There is an adder in the girl of her eye, dew on the lashes, and an apple in the mirror of the dew. Does anybody on this buggering train know the name of the engineer?

—King's Counsel Jones, cried James Johnson Sweeney.

He had pushed his way between the federales of the Guardia Civil, Ethiopian infantrymen in tunics and pith helmets, quilted sergeants of the Kwomintang.

I though of the engineer Elrod Singbell, who used to take the mile-long descending curve of Stump House Mountain in the Blue Ridge playing "Amazing Grace" on the whistle. I remembered the sharp sweet perfume of chinaberry blossoms in earliest spring.

Joyce spoke of an Orpheus in yellow dancing through bamboo,

followed by cheetahs, macaws, canaries, tigers. And an Orpheus in the canyons at the bottom of the sea leading a gelatin of hydras, fylfot starfish, six-eyed medusas, feather-boa sealilies, comb-jelly cydippidas, scarlet crabs and gleaming mackerel as old as the moon.

—Noe, Apollinaire said in a brown study.

—Mice whisker to whisker, Joyce said, white-shanked quaggas trotting *presto presto e delicatamente*, cackling pullets, grave hogs, whistling tapirs.

La Belle Jardinière. We saw her selling flowers in Madrid, corn marigolds, holy thistles, great silver knapweed, and white wild campions. In Odessa she pranced in a turn of sparrows. She was in the azaleas when we went through Atlanta, shaking fire from her wrists.

Would that be the castellum, Joyce said, where the graf put his twin sons together with a commentary on the Babylonian Talmud in a kerker dark as the ka of Osiris until a certain lady in jackboots and eyepatch found her way to them by lightning a squally night she had put the *Peahen* into the cove above Engelanker and kidnapped them tweeling as they were sweetening Yehonathan and Dawidh a sugarplum's midge from Luther into the wind and stars but not before twisting her heel by the doorpost and wetting the premises.

Shepherds! Apollinaire cried to the car, startling us. We had no shepherds at Ypres. We have no shepherds now.

We were crossing the gardens of Normandy, coming back to Deauville.

Somewhere on the train, behind us, before us, Haile Selassie lay on his bier, his open eyes looking up through the roof of his imperial car to the double star Gamma in Triangulum, twin suns, one orange, the other green.

F

Jessica Hagedorn

What you see is what you get.

Oh yeah, baby.

You gotta have rhythm, in your soul. The word SOUL. Something funky and torrid by James Brown, juxtaposed against a lush green landscape, manicured and mowed to perfection.

A jungle, jagged and forbidding, female and tropic.

Green perfume: the scent of mildew and rot. You can see your breath, like in a steam room or a Turkish bath. It is unbearably humid. Prehistoric birds are . . . squawking.

The word "bath" is subtly erotic. The marriage of "Turkish+bath" unbearably so.

A dead body lies in the midst of this lush green splendor.

Think of Antonioni's *Blow Up*. Think of a golf course. Think of me.

Always a dead body. Always a corpse. Always a surprise. But arranged beautifully; arranged to stun and shock and titillate. All things beautiful and mysterious, to the bitter end.

Death is my fetish.

And Saint Sebastian.

And God.

And get thee to a nunnery.

The word "nun" for example.

Death is ultimately at the bottom of this coy little rant (the word "coy," the word *coy* italicized). Not just any death, mind you. But a sense of foreboding, something ominous and looming in the background. Dissonant chords, the distant wail of a siren.

Sudden betrayal. *I've been made to feel like a fool.* Baby, baby. I have danced towards the edge of an abyss. On the edge of a razor blade. Ooh, baby. The word *abyss* itself. Onomatopoeia is my fetish, the word *onomatopoeia* itself. (I've always been able to spell it correctly, even as a child. Drawn to it like a magnet.)

Decaying beauty in architecture is another delight. Those faded green colonial mansions in the tropics, for example. Ravaged slowly from the inside and out by heat, rain, animals, and time itself. Faded, crumbling, peeling paint on the walls. Vegetation choking architecture: I could brood about that for days.

Rust.

Ruin has been cheapened nowadays, become a trend called "distressed."

Distressed jeans, distressed interior design. Pathetic.

Decay, like anything else of value, has to be earned.

—

I celebrate Havana slowly sinking into the sea. Manila slowly sinking into the fetid Pasig River. The boxer's broken nose, broken teeth, swollen eyes, and puffy lips. The convict's lovingly detailed tattoos.

The word *skeleton*, italicized, has possibilities.

—

My desires are inherently Catholic. The face of a fallen angel makes me hot. And mind you, angels exist in New York City. In Barcelona on the Ramblas, in Berlin in those squatter encampments, and in Manila almost anywhere. Probably in Bangkok too, though I've never been there. I'm not referring to sentimental, fat cherubs or beatific, asexual ethereal creatures. I'm naturally referring to Lucifer, fallen archangel, a major cliché, darkness as the other side of light.

—

Here's what I crave: salt, shoes made of buttery leather, and the power of certain words said aloud. Blood, for example. Fallen angel. Hunger.

—

A fallen angel, a young man with a bleeding, sinewy torso sticks his head into the garbage, foraging for food. A shirtless, barefoot young man lurching down a Greenwich Village sidewalk in a stoned stupor. He stinks: he is hungry and dirty and evil incarnate. He will die soon. His mind is gone. I fall in love with his face, the face of vice. The face of **F**: feral, feline, fucking, fallen.

If I had the balls I'd offer him a cup of java. Or a juicy burger, a milkshake and some fries. Then . . . nothing too graphic here. Nothing too obvious. I'm a good Catholic girl.

I understand taboo completely. The need for it.
Sex=death=divine=damned=heaven.
The word "taboo" is absolutely pornographic.

⁓

I like 'em young. But not too young. I like 'em when they're
poised on the brink of the abyss, of manhood—past adolescence but
not quite seasoned yet. Not ready for death but ready for the
forbidden. Tattooed biceps, form, but . . . not too pumped up. In
fact, I hate muscle boys. Much too obvious. I prefer a juicy burger
every once in a while. I usually stick to vegetables and fish, but I
can appreciate an expensive slab of meat. Well done. For someone
who likes blood (the idea of blood, anyway) I don't care for rare
meat.

I am the least visceral person I know.

I'm a bundle of infuriating contradictions.

An element of danger is always delicious.

Gardens gone to seed, black and white movies. It's no accident
I'm a film noir buff. Black film. Dark film. Ominous, ambivalent
film. A dead body, usually a woman's somewhere in the lush green
landscape or in the gloomy lobby of an elegant, empty building.

When you least expect it.

The word "desire" is music to the ears. Desire: a fallen angel who
knows how to kiss. A lithe demon who carries the memory of hell
in his little black heart: that's heaven. A taste for expensive meat
and the dank, green smell of rotting gardens.

⁓

Despair. The word "despair" excites me. The eerie cadences of
high mass, sung in Latin. Dead languages. Pretty to the ears. The
word *agony*. Close to death, but not quite yet. You keep me hangin'
on.

⁓

F for fetish. F for father. Bless me F, for I have sinned.
F for futile. F for fact, F for fiction.

⁓

Sublime. There's no end to it.

After He Bought a Dog
Robert Kelly

A house where a tongue is masculine. He lived in it.
Like a language, or a furrow.
A shoulder.
Things are quick when one another.
A house where the fireplace is full of fur. He had arranged it with
all his mothers that they were, and a river not far but the same.

It was enough and always. There is something young about
supposing, supposing and a car and a glass full of girls.

A house where empty places are clean and the full places are
borrowed and nothing blue. A wristwatch lying looped around a
fountain pen and a dog irritated by the night. Things go in circles
and there are addictions.

In a tongue where a house is masculine, the word the dog says
has to make the night upset. It was not a place to eat between the
meals. The meals were copious and no one was to admit the hunger
in between times or remember that food is not about certain times
or certain feelings. Food is about itself and happens when the
thought of it arises in the hands.

Eating is a restlessness of mind, to be sure.

Dogs preach this among their seldom. Evangels of the appetite to
move. Eating is moving and drinking is having, why some are fat
and some are drunk and ordinary people are ordinary all day long.

If you do not want to eat you must read. If you do not want to
drink you must listen.

These are the answers. Paint the shutters of the house blue then.
Paint the walls with delicate stenciling that reminds one of Indiana.

Some of what one does reminds one, some is fresh and some
forgets. What one hopes is everything, and everything is too much
to carry and too little to describe, so there it is, a wall with blue on
it and a dog.

Ycy est pourtraict le vizage dhomme he was able to read though
nothing in the painting made sense since he saw a field of wheat,
a Doge saying farewell to his barge of state, a poet in his garret

starving, a lawyer choking on a gobbet of pork. Or was it corn?

Of course the eye can know the difference but the dream was wheat. He saw a Studebaker smoking by the side of the road along some great corniche. He saw an apple exploding as the bullet passed through it. He saw an opera shuddering to its end in a small Central European opera house where a man in the front row of the second balcony just in front of him was slumped asleep or drunk or dead all through the desperate cabaletta of a one-time diva assoluta.

He saw a bishop purple as a plum. He saw a cross cast its shadow up against the lowering clouds beyond his lawn. He saw himself grovel before an unknown god whose face was that of a teenage girl and whose body was that of a vast pulsating bee-queen.

Swarms of diptera he saw whose hives were built differently, some on the base seven and the others on the base eight war with each other and common reality. He saw the colors break inside the rainbow and fall slithering down the arch and enter earth. He saw gold.

A nosebleed.

A jungle war.

Hexaploids meant to nourish us. A nurse a pratfall an accent mocked.

The candle kept remembering all night long which irritated the dog who didn't bite the cat that slept at the foot of the comforter quilt and the bed thickened towards morning with fearful sleep.

Waking in the taste of blood a VCR still spooling and the drowsy actors making up their lines.

Breakfast was a cloud. If a hammer were falling from heaven if bronze could fall nine days and nights and then on the morning of the tenth arrive on this all-enduring planet speaking an oriental language.

If not bronze a sailor would send a postcard whose wife would weep an hour. The car goes on depreciating as usual locked in the driveway while albino hamsters chitter in the neighbor's orangerie.

Suburban life really is all about what Heraclitus said, there is enough water in a muddy footprint to cleanse the world if water could make clean. There is enough fire in a casual remark to light the galaxy anew if fire still knew how to burn.

But first of all things was language, which some men took as water though women knew better and knew it by a different grain.

The badly decomposed panel still bore its images plain enough for him to read them (like any other language) but not to understand (like language too).

Stand-oil was made from walnuts and flax.

The empires of the steppes concelebrating a Christmas despite the brutal cold, a noun with nine cases besides the instrumental.

Deep as sex in all the common mind, the Pope stood at the altar in the center of the poem waiting for the Youth whose arms, already weary with the brazen lance head dripping some body's blood, lifted towards him to be blessed.

Thou art a messenger of Christ and don't forget it and all over southern Illinois the masonic temples flicked their floodlights on to bathe the gentle lawns around such absent mysteries.

The world is a singular compulsion. A pond and a heron watching it. Then a heron walking on a wall.

PROBLEM, WITH CHERRIES
for Jacques Roubaud
Robert Kelly

On the table is a white plate. On the plate are seven cherries. This is the problem and I don't know the solution. I will try to set out the influences that condition the event. An event is not a problem, any more than a nest is a bird. But the event is the straw and the spittle, fur and twigs in which the problem ripens.

Pick a number. Seven. Say: there are seven cherries on the plate.

Whose plate? What color is it? What size? Are the cherries ripe? If not, why are they there? Black cherries, pink cherries? Who made the plate? Whose tree do they come from? Who picked them? Who laid them on the plate? What pattern do they form on the plate? If there is a pattern, is it intentional? If there is a pattern, does the pattern have a name?

There are other questions. Lippe must not ask them. Lippe is looking at the cherries on the white plate, it is white, a plate wide enough for his hand to span, thumb to outstretched pinky finger, no bigger. Lippe is looking and trying to ask none of the questions he wants to ask. He wants instead, a bigger and more important he thinks want in him, to ask a question. About seven.

What is it, this number? Not this very number, but this business of a number. Or this very one, in what way are these cherries specially seven? In what way is seven particularly the case with cherries. These are more like the question Lippe wants to ask.

And this is even more like it: Is there a region, there must be a region, somewhere between seven and cherries, somewhere between cherryness and sevenness, where the two properties pass into each other. The blend. The zone of blending. Which must also be the zone of de-definition. The tide of sevenness comes toward the cherries. The cherry entity, hacceity, is at first subtly then grossly deformed, informed, reformed, by sevenness.

What then is this sevenness? What is seven such that we can say of things, there are seven of them, seven and not six, seven and not eight? Yet seven cherries on a plate are different from eight. Eight of them. Lippe knows this is some part of himself he can't call by name, but this part knows. This part does Lippe's knowing for him. And this part knows all about seven, eight, cherry, plate. Lippe sometimes thinks he's just the vessel, the irregularly shaped room where such knowing goes on.

And then he wonders: is there such knowing without chambers? Not just, in the old-fashioned sense, are there ideas existent previous to, or at least apart from, those who conceive them. But in this sense exactly, is it the nature of the container, this very irregular room, which provokes or even creates a sort of noumenal persuasion of which "seven" might be a type or an application? Do we think numbers because we are embodied as we are?

We may think (Lippe is thinking) that number is objective and built into the structure of logic, but we may think so because that is the way we must think. Ourselves possessed of discernible parts, we apprehend reality in numerable entities. Five fingers make one hand. Two hands make one man.

Lippe was confused. This isn't what he thought he meant to be thinking about when he began thinking. Is there a point when one begins thinking? That isn't the point. Lippe was confused.

What he had wanted to think about was this: what was sevenish about those cherries? What was cherryish about seven? Is there a huge plenum or field only partly filled by seven, partly by cherry, partly by each and every nameable thing? And if so, is there a zone or terrain where seven and cherry overlap, so much so that a moment comes when someone, looking up from something else (is there anything really else?) stares at the white plate and says or thinks: *there are seven cherries on the plate.*

What is seven about those cherries?

Lippe shook his head. This wasn't it exactly, and it must be exact, this ignorance of his. You must know exactly what you don't know, if ever you hope to know it. Yet (and many have said this), perhaps you know what you don't know only after, when some knowledge has come along that has, almost without your consent, dawned on you, and by filling precisely the gap in reason where your ignorance lay, revealed to you at once the truth and your need for it. As if one could know a need fully only after the need was satisfied.

And that isn't it either. Lippe held his head. Be careful, Lippe, he breathed to himself, get it right. Not: what is seven or sevenish about the cherries. No. What is sevenish about seven. That's more like it. Or: what is seven like? Or even: what is seven?

(O Lippe, Lippe, there are easier ways to walk those cobbled and all too familiar streets, noisy with the racket of cheap scholastic shoes, behind old Middle European universities, perhaps not the first-rate ones but picturesque still. They know the answer is: Seven is a counting number. Use seven in inquiries of the form: "Seven what?" Seven is not a who or how word.)

But Lippe must go his own way. He has read the mystics, learned Spanish to read the translations into that language of Ibn-al-Arabi, he knows the distinction between stages and states, knows that seven is a stage (on the way to six or eight, depending which elevator you're on), not a state, at least according to ordinary people. But what if seven were a state? Not a state of mind but a state of being, as most assuredly, every rod in his eye was telling him this, every finger on his hand repeated it, a state of being it is.

That there are only seven cherries on the plate is only the tip of the iceberg, Lippe spoke aloud, only the tip of the immense, submerged universe of seven. In sunlight it counts our cherries for us—but what does it do in the dark? What does seven do when no one is looking?

Lippe knew, knew certainly, that there is something to numbers beyond counting with them, however sophisticated the manipulation might grow. And something beyond imaginary and transfinite numbers too, irrationals, surds, something beyond all that. Or not beyond at all, maybe, maybe just this side of the number; as all that beyond is on the other side, the beyond side, so this ardent and mysterious (feels violet-colored, dark churches on Lenten evenings shot through with the red of offering lamps) otherness is on this side of number, something between the man and the numeral, something previous to all the cherries in the trichiliocosm, a seven in the heart of things. Lippe knew this, knew it with the certainty that knows that the middle finger of the left hands feels utterly different from every other finger, *semblables et frères* though they well be. This finger is not that finger. This finger has its own scope, domain, history, habits, whorls of fingerprints familiar to M. Poirot. And this finger, which elementary calculations could identify as Finger No. 3 or Finger No. 8, is by itself that very ambiguity of ordinality (such a phrase, Lippe! Are you mad? Silly? Lovesick?), proof of the otherness of numbers. Cardinal numbers, he remembered the old phrase, and hugged his ratty cardigan snugger round his neck. It was getting cold.

But he wondered, not for the first time, aren't the whims or phrases of one's mind natural, aren't we parts of nature, aren't the mind's fussy divisions and distinctions really nature's own edges and crannies and rims and basins steaming with the cooked and the raw?

Cardinal numbers. What comes in sevens? He tried to think of them. Sisters. Brides. Days of the week. Sacraments. None of those were naturally numbered, they were conventions, the number seven numbered seven somethings only the mind knew or mind (like seas) decided the limits of. Everywhere Lippe looked he found traces of that ancient Semitic patterning, seven somethings, but never seven itself. The Chinese and the Peruvians had no weeks, there are only six stars in the Seven Sisters, *Seven Brides* is just a play, the seas are one sea, endless, unbounded. Just conventions, conventions. Nothing comes in sevens.

JOMINY
(An Art History)
Shelley Jackson

That's our insignia on the cover: a waft of vapor over a mattress. It commemorates my ancestor, the Lady Jane (Jenny to me), who gave her heart to an incubus. Virgin births? She survived twelve of them, though her babies were said to be hamster-sized when they popped out of her naïve apparatus, making for easy delivery. They attained their natural heft only afterwards, though even then they were given a leg up on the easy life: rocked in air a foot above their beddings, they grew symmetrical in all directions like a pot on a wheel.

That's what my mother told me, anyway, and I believe her, even though at a glance it's another story, a sadly typical one in some respects. In this stiff and anglophile tome, commissioned out of snobbery by our California cousins, it goes down as both quaint and a tragedy. It was neither, of course, or so my mother taught me.

The paintings reproduced here bear a generic arthistorical gloss. They are minor works that have survived thanks to sentiment and the uninterrupted good fortune of the family line, whose walls they've decorated for centuries, as they decorate mine. The cousins would like to buy them from me. I will not sell, though not for the reasons they suppose. Stiff and garish as they are, the pictures tell the truth about my ancestor.

pl. 1 (Madonna and Child, egg tempera)

This painting is almost certainly the first time Lady Jane appears in the artist's oeuvre. The maternal figure is recognizable from other works as the artist's own aunt, Jenny's nursemaid. The baby might be any baby. I am sure it is Jenny by the look on its face: she bites down on the nipple with an air of great concentration.

The nursemaid had the uneasy feeling Jenny was too dogged for a girl child. Her squashed blank face looked like a soldier's. Fortunate, then, that her marriage was arranged, her future secure. The nursemaid's too: she would go along when Jenny travelled to her new home. This might be soon. Both parents were ailing, and many in the area had died. The parents of the groom-to-be (himself just six) stood to gain a fortune. It came later than they thought. Lady Jane was eight when she came to her husband's house to stay.

pl. 2 (*Young Girl in Mourning,* oil)

The future lady of the manor arrived with her nursemaid in a carriage which her intended noted from his window seat was much finer than his own. A bit too much wrist and ankle showed below the black. The dress had lain ready for some time.

The young artist had watched her all the way. He wanted to find out how you look when you have lost your parents. We know what he saw because he painted it later—much later, when he was losing his eyesight, and his paintings became stranger and maybe better. Her face is a pierced white escutcheon sunk in the black mass of the seat, from which her dress is nearly indistingui-shable. Out the window the pale blotch crotched in a long V of trees must be the house.

She stepped out of the coach, into dark passages. The servant who led her in was already small and far away. In frames great ladies suffocated under varnish.

pl. 3 (*Portrait of Lady Jane,* oil)

As she climbed the stairs toward her new bedroom the house grew more solid. It was paying attention. Am I imagining I see this here, in her first formal portrait? Each of the many glass panes in the cabinet of curios holds her image, even those that tilt the wrong way. If a room may have a face we would know at a glance, this face is turned toward Jenny. She averts hers. Archly: she knows she is being watched.

The perspective employed by the artist is worth special comment. This is his first attempt at rendering deep space, like the gallery visible through the doorway behind her. Unfortunate for his reputation yet of interest to us is his disregard for the convention that parallel lines converge toward a point on the horizon. His lines do converge at one point. It is located under the Lady Jenny's breastbone.

The furniture behind her, consequently, broadens with distance, while what approaches narrows until it resembles, more and more, an arrow pointed at her heart.

pl. 4 (*sketch*, terracotta pencil)

The young Lady Jane sat on a velvet ottoman by the window, feeling formal and alone, sipping water from a glass. She lifted the glass to the light and looked through it at the black twigs. The water began to swirl, forming a little whirlpool like a silver thimble.

Outside a cloud thinned in the center and became a ring. Other clouds lined up and leaped through, pop, pop, pop. She laughed. The bright sky lit her eyes.

The fine lines describe the swags of cord on the ottoman in finicky detail, and the shadow cast on the flagstones, but the model herself is a sort of hedge of faint strokes; you can make out a full skirt, thin torso, narrow shoulders stiffly held. The artist tried the head in two positions, first bowed, then (in firmer strokes) tilted up and aside. He left the face blank. Maybe Jenny lost patience with sitting, maybe someone called her away.

pl. 5 (*A Lady's Chamber*, pen and ink)

This exercise is superficially appealing in its wealth of detail (I make out a small pair of slippers beside the canopy bed, and on the small table a thistle-blossom, a fan, the skull of a small bird) yet these encrustations do not hide the fact that in the artist's faulty rendering the floor tilts, the walls lean. In the drawing the bedcurtains are closed. Behind them: Jenny, encased in an enormous linen nightgown. She lies still a long time waiting for her attendant to retire. Then scrunching and pleating she works the nightgown up under her arms and stretches her bare legs against the sheets. Now she can put those thin white fingers (they look so hard in the portrait, pl. 3) into the welter between her legs, the witches' cauldron.

She's afraid of men with their tufts of body hair sticking out of the decent cloth. She is afraid of the husband-to-be, who travels home from university only once in a while, who is a stranger. She is not afraid of the watcher. She has laid out messages for it (on the windowsill behind those thick curtains whose folds, so patiently modeled with minute cross-hatchings, yet so stiff, seem made of marble), patterns of pebbles and seeds, unknown fluids and juices pressed from grasses, torn writings, and scraps of clothes.

The incubus drifts above her, sniffing the small breaths, listening to sleep's quiet fit. Dreaming, the child is running slowly in place; she leaps obstacles, tucks herself into hiding places. Jominy hovers over her and copies what she does.

The girl turns her shoulder against the dark and drives her head into the pillow. Or flaps her hand dismissively. She doesn't know how to love the incubus, at first.

pl. 6 (*Reverie,* oil study)

Here Jenny is the picture of prim. Her gown cuts under her tiny breasts so tightly she bends forward to take the strain across her back. She is staring past the painter at the window. Maybe she is imagining someone there, an impossible hand on the sill, thirty feet above ground. She is stiffly fingering a twig: the painter's kitten refused to be a prop, it didn't like her cool tight grip, the mesmerized stillness of her frame.

pl. 7 (*from the artist's sketchbook,* colored pencils)

Who invented the innocence of little girls? Jenny untutored craved the flesh, without knowing anything of men outside a few uneasy suspicions centered around the pink tubing of that prince of hounds, Domino, who tended to lose his dignity when begging for table scraps. She had her own opinions, and in the way of demons, her familiar shaped itself to her imaginings, so that what Jenny touched when she touched it one day in her room resembled nothing exactly human: a ridged cone flaring over her, red and yellow, translucent as horn but made of flesh. A silver ball beads at the tip and bounces down the ribs.

Jenny catches it in her mouth; it's warm and burns like peppermint. She swallows it. The cone contracts and gently clasps the sides of her face.

pl. 8 (from the artist's sketchbook, colored pencils*)*

She wears the red fur hat all day and no one notices, no one but the painter's kitten, who taps at the pompons from on top of a bookcase.

pl. 9 (from the artist's sketchbook, colored pencils*)*

The quill running with violet ink writes funny rhymes on the sheets, and signs them *jominy.* The maid clutches the pillow to her mouth and runs out of the room. When she returns with help, the words have melted to a shimmer.

pl. 10 (A Country Manor, brown ink and wash*)*

A house in which a little girl is inventing sex is not the same house it was before. Fires run along the seams, between the stones. Iron railings softens and reform. The house lifts itself and hangs clacking its stones together like an enormous mobile. See, in the drawing, how the curdy clouds compete with it for mass. Jenny runs her hands over parapets of flesh, into pockets and purses. Jenny slides her fingers in a pouch and strokes a baby mouse, pulls a chocolate doll out of a butterfly net. The servants hear her laugh in an otherwise empty room, hear her sigh.

pl. 11 (May and December, or, Innocence and Experience, oil*)*

"Jane," said her guardian, behind the secured door of his privy study, door of oak and green leather, "have you had commerce with demons?"

"No," said Jenny, lips tiny and angelic. In this picture she is littler and blonder to suit the artist's conception, a pale cherub surrounded by dark and massive furnishings: the dull gleam of brass fittings, the stopped snarl of a bearskin rug half out of sight under the heavy table.

"No one can hear us, Jenny," said Milord, bending over her (and he is an aged cherub himself, in white curls that brush his collar), "you must trust me; there are things we can do to rid you of these pests."

"No," said Jenny. In the end they exorcised her anyway,

festooning her with herbs so she went about fragrant and rustling and the cook pinched leaves from her foliage to flavor the stew. At night they burned the herbs in her room. Behind her curtains she coughed, and smiled at things they couldn't see.

pl. 12 (A Country Lass, watercolor*)*

In the morning they let her run outside with herbs pinned to her shawl and skirt. Jominy announced himself in the form of a glint off a broken chamberpot. Ducks' clean bills in the morning sun gave her a hard satisfaction like painted toys. Low-lying mist struck damp down to the tree-roots in one unstopped slow rain.

Worms orgasm in the ditches. Jenny prods their pale ridged muscles, and it's jominy who twines round her fingertips. Long grass wraps its clinging hanks around her ankles. A dead squirrel, its skeleton displayed in its flat side, does a sideways dance on the dirt for her, little bones jigging. In this painting we look down upon her from above—the vantage point someone looking out a window in an upper story might command, the window of her guardian's study, for example. Even from this distance he could tell she was laughing.

pl. 13 (Portrait of a Clergyman, oil*)*

Her guardian sent for help. Weeks later the forest disgorged a somber young man in black, who introduced himself to the gatekeeper as the witchfinder.

The witchfinder was not imposing. He was stark scared of witchery and fonder of a cold leg of turkey in the kitchen and a jaw with the maids than of the abstruser points of heresy, which confused him so much he went mum for fear of uttering something heretical himself, which hysterical muteness and the round cap of black hair that brushed his short lashes in front gave him the uncomfortable preoccupied look of an owl about to spit up a ball of bones.

He was as a matter of fact a fond collector of owl pellets, which we can make out on the table before him, among bezoars, tumors containing hairs and teeth, and even the innocent mummy of a lizard, run over by a cart and dried to a wafer: souvenirs of the witches he had ousted. The dull rounds of his eyes moistened when he turned the dung-colored baubles over in his hands, so you might almost think him a warlock himself, until you learned he was a man of meager imagination, who adored God in church and cross and sought the devil in bones and amulets only because that was where he had been told such eminences were to be found.

pl. 14 (Night Watch, oil)

The witchfinder conscripted two priests and the nursemaid to watch over Jenny every night while she slept, to distribute snuff and herbs if the rugs hung over the windows should move, or the netting draped over the bed. He warned them to watch for the devil in any of innumerable disguises: a bit of floating hair, a crawling insect, the too-beautiful call of a bird (which should be out-clamored by banging the pans provided). He instructed them to note any especially pleasing or ambiguous fragrances. He advised them to arm their spirits against the sight of prodigies, for example: a miniscule devil might ride in through the window on a flaming votive candle, or in a little boat of orange peel stitched together with the hairs of a nanny goat, or astride a pen writing verses of soporific loveliness, or in a phaeton hitched to a team of baby mice, their blind eyeballs steering an unerring course.

In the painting the three featureless dolmens on their stools cast long shadows up the walls; it is probably a cracking in the glaze that creates those strange figures, resembling hieroglyphs, visible only here in the darkest parts of the work.

pl. 15 (Studies of Eyes & Thumbnail Sketch of the Manor, from the artist's sketchbook, pastel)

A careless onlooker will see a page of unrelated sketches, no more. A closer look finds a story in these juxtapositions. Jenny peered out at eyes, her nursemaid's eyes pale blue, with yellowish curds swimming over the whites, the priests' eyes bulging between red fat lids, their lashes pale to invisibility and straining individually to stand upright in the still air. When they close, a striped fur purse drops in her lap. In it she finds a tiny house with a catch on its side she releases with a fingernail. The house springs open and displays

all its rooms, staircases, hallways; her own room, her bed. She puts
the tip of her baby finger in the window seat where she likes to
dream.

pl. 16 (untitled [Night Watch #2], oil)

The witchfinder, hearing that Jenny had taken her pleasure under
the very eyes of her watchers and despite fumigation and psalm-
reading, entered her bedroom himself, pulled up a stool and took
hold of her ankle. The others followed suit. They held her spread-
eagled all night, watching her body for signs. The painting of this
scene, long buried in a private collection, verges on pornography.
The artist has placed himself near the ceiling (in Jominy's place?),
from which vantage point the girl is splayed on the white sheets, her
head thrust so far back in the downy pillows it all but disappears,
except for a sliver of check wet by a white highlight. She is a pink
X on the ends of which dark figures cling, making a sort of heavily
burdened swastika. (The symbol had not yet acquired the meaning
it has for us, of course.)

Despite the restraining hands Jenny's body lifts itself toward the
ceiling. The witchfinder's dedication was growing firmer by the
minute, and he regretted only that company kept him from taking
other, more drastic measures. His grip on her ankle was tight
verging on cruel, but as he watched her stomach rise and fall he
knew the demon had already covered her with his suede wings,
kindled her with an invisible flint. A pearly shine winked just once
between Jenny's legs, a fleck of zinc white that might only be visible
to someone up there, on the ceiling.

*pl. 17 (Anatomical Studies, page from the artist's
sketchbook, pastels)*

In the previous (pl. 16) the faces are too stiffly rendered to show
emotion. The attitudes of the four might be better expressed by
parts that don't show up in the painting: for example, their thighs.
First the nursemaid's, soft and broad, built up out of sketchy strokes
of lavender, peach and chartreuse, with somber blossomings of burst
blood vessels in true red. The lavish highlights show she's sweating
in the Venusian cloud of steam and other emanations that belled her

skirts, byproducts of her excitement and the pork and beans of luncheon. The two priests are duplicates; their plump thighs (in full front and three-quarter view) keep a firm clasp on the baby carrots, whose stirrings are not strong enough to counter the inertia of the flesh. The witchfinder's thighs are a faggot of sticks parcelled in hide and tense as fencing, holding their distance from the cold, surprised erection, which hangs there like a tool in the hand of someone who has forgotten what it's for.

pls. 18, 19, 20 (from the artist's sketchbook, watercolor)

Jenny strokes a flap buried in hair until it stiffens and slowly flares open, revealing the trembling pages of a book.

A little bird on a stalk of flesh shakes out its feathers and lifts its wings when she brushes the stalk with her fingertips.

A sponge drips blue syrup into a shallow pool. When she blows on the pool, cascades of bubbles the size of salmon roe spill over the lip and across the bed. When they burst on her arms and legs they dry into dots of blue sugar, and she licks them up.

pls. 21, 22, 23 (Studies of Rustic Types, from the artist's sketchbook, pen and ink)

The servants begin to hang around the witchfinder's door. They corner him with their own stories:

The head housekeeper found in her heap of sweepings a little grey man, light as a husk, curled up in a spiral like the casting of a snail.

The vintner sampling an aged red saw an oily scum on the surface, which, swirled, became the profile of a young man, clear as a cameo glass.

The housemaid spread her legs while emptying a bucket of dirty water and felt a business underneath, and later she discovered the miracle: her stockings without having been removed had been tied between her legs in a tiny knot, which she would be happy to show off to anyone who asked, but especially the inquisitor.

pl. 24 (Medical Examination, brown ink and wash)

The child was innocent of carnal relations in the ordinary human sense, the witchfinder announced. He had made sure of this himself.

The girl's vagina would admit nothing larger than a pen nib. Far from being a good sign, this was virtual proof she had a demonic lover, since no innocent maid knew such pleasure in her own flesh as the Lady Jane enjoyed. In this picture the Lady Jane is wearing clothes more befitting a peasant girl, no doubt to divert the attention of scandal-mongers from the family. Note as a matter of medical curiosity the large basin of steaming water, the giant forceps and scalpels; not called for by this examination, these are no doubt added for atmosphere, like a stuffed alligator on the wall of an alchemist.

pls. 25, 26, 27 (Studies of Rustic Types, from the artist's sketchbook, pen and ink)

Jenny, locked in her room, was let out only for dinner. The cook whispered to Jenny, passing her a bun on the sly, "Is it like desire buttered over every brick and table-leg, instead of sitting cool in its pot?"

The gardener pelted her window with sods and called up, "Is it like every vegetable in its patch resembles you? Is it like being seed instead of an elm tree, sifting everywhere and itching to sprout?"

The old lord alone in his room muttered, "Is it like sweat breaking out on a dry page, collecting in letters that smell something like the ink of a virgin who was measured with a quill, that spell something like a recipe for eternal youth?"

pl. 28 (The False Clerics, oil)

The priests recited in unison the substances thought to drive away demons: "rue, St. John's wort, verbena, germander, Palma Christi, Centaury, diamonds, coral, jet and jasper, the skin of the head of a wolf or an ass, a woman's menstrual fluid," but this last item choked them with images of red superfluity, buckets and buckets of red milk, smothery breasts squashing the earth from a reddened sky, red cows trotting ominously home to be milked, and in a horror they whispered Jominy's name as if it might be some kind of antidote. The hellish "visions" awkwardly afloat in the smoke of the censer are derivative of Hieronymus Bosch.

pl. 29 (The Messengers, oil study*)*

This piece is an awkward pastiche of Greco-Roman references and Renaissance chiaroscuro. It is not surprising the work for which this was a study has never surfaced. The witchfinder is on his knees in the stone niche where a suit of armor once stood. Naked, the candlelight shining off their sweating scalps, the priests come running down the hall. They seize him by his arms, panting. "The scriptures are correct," they exclaim, "except in this—": that God was a woman—hence rain of blood—earthquake in Lisbon— seasons of plagues and marvels—all these being signs of God's menses—that the earth is God's egg—that with each menses another planet is spit from Her fallopian tubing and lodged in the rich pulp of the ether, joining the billions already there. That God like any woman is foul tempered ere the moon is full!

The witchfinder is exercised by this obscenity, and finding himself engorged shakes off their hands and hurries downstairs. His manhood has lately slithered out of his grip. This time it does not desert him. He finds the servants eager to assist him and gives the first bottom a bumptious ride, and when he closes his eyes and spends sees a planet all mucky with clots of menstrual blood and clear skeins of vaginal fluid, wreathed in fishy mists of fart and pubic sweat. The globe wobbled provocatively in a dark matter that seemed to convulse regularly, as with a heartbeat.

pl. 30 (Tending His Row, watercolor*)*

From this point on the witchfinder knew that the witch, or her airy spirit, was polluting his judgement, instilling fancies that blurred his vision of Purgatory: a dry knoll that practically filled his narrow skull, where the guilty worked off their sins in the dust of constant traffic. He liked to keep his sights on that hill. This was his private heresy, to believe he could preempt judgement, that earth itself was only the rather broad base and foothills of that purgatorial hill, where onc might (with sufficient humility) work off part of one's sentence in advance, calculating the demerits for every sin, the man-hours for every demerit, and setting to. The sprite upset his arithmetic, just as the damp clouds of unreason that hid in the folds of her curtains rusted his compass-needle right down to the pin in the center. He hurried outside to pour ants down his collar and stuff his trousers with rose branches until the gardener ran him off with a pitchfork.

pl. 31 (The Invalid, colored pencil*)*

The witchfinder, his pants jutting strangely, knocked on the door of the master of the household. "She is bewitching the whole house," he insisted. More drastic measures had to be taken.

They tied her wrists to her ankles and left her bound and naked on her bed for two days, then when her nursemaid protested that she'd sicken in the cold, they built up the fire until the sweat poured off and she begged cup after cup of water. The witchfinder held a spoon in the fire and laid it against her left thigh, where a sizzle convinced him the spirit was beginning to fear him.

pl. 32 (from the artist's sketchbook [water-damaged], charcoal*)*

The witchfinder found that all it took to achieve a knobby, noble stiffness was to take the skin of the wench's neck between his teeth, jam his bristled chin against her vertebrae, and imagine her head the sexual planet-egg, provocatively swathed in clouds. The effect was heightened if he wrapped the maid's head in a towel.

pl. 33 (The Blessing. Or, While She Sleeps, silverpoint*)*

They put her to bed in wire underwear, yet the witchfinder saw a smile pass over her lips while she slept.

pl. 34 (The Groaning Board, oil*)*

Jenny was whipped until the blood came up in cross-hatchings on her small body. She took herself to be a painting when she saw the deep carmine of the strokes. In this she took little solace. When she was allowed to sit at her window and saw a small pig running loose in the garden she sent her agony into it, as jominy told her to do, bundling it together like a great red hairball and thrusting it across space into the little body. At dinner she wept for the pork roast, which was deeply cross-hatched by the fat-soaked strings that bound it, and wreathed with parsley.

pl. 35 (Their Old Father, charcoal)

The witchfinder required the servants to carry him on their backs; he perched on their planetary buttocks and tweaked their ears to guide them, steaming the backs of their necks with his foul breath.

pl. 36 (Peasant Unrest Calmed by Mighty Right, oil)

When they burned her labia with an iron, a squirrel fell flaming from a tree and set fire to a field of hay, and all the fences burned, so that all night crying chickens ran from one shrub to another under Jenny's window, and the servants spent the night in the woods calling the pigs. The next morning they arrayed themselves outside the witchfinder's door in silent protest. In due time he emerged with his decision: since the finest netting could not strain the demon out of the air, whether because he made himself small enough to creep through a chink, or large and vaporous enough to breathe right through, that smoke didn't choke or hexes pox him, that from close study delirium derived, and that the entire household was practically possessed, the witchfinder concluded they had no choicc but to pack her off to the asylum. And so on a day too misty for rain but too rainy for mist, when it would be easy to mistake acorns for *eggs,* and hatch hummingbirds from an oak, or eggs for acorns, and plant a feathered tree. They set out, it was the wrong day for kicking out a demon, but they knew less than little about such matters, and

pl. 37 (Young Girl in White or, Spring Outing, oil)
Jenny did not tell them, but sat in the carriage as mild as an avocado. With jominy up her sprigged sleeve.

pl. 38 (Woodland Glade or, Aphrodite, oil)

They arrived at the somber asylum gates in good time, perhaps a little sooner than they anticipated, but then the roads were clear and it had not rained for three weeks. Their time of arrival and the names of the priests, the nursemaid, the two servants and the driver who accompanied her are recorded by Jenny's lawyer, who took their testimony. Their accounts are similar: they describe the dim hall and the narrow office, the smiling doctor and towering attendants, the cries they heard when the door opened to admit her, their pity and relief as the door closed behind her. But her name does not appear in the records of the asylum. Admittedly these were haphazard at best. The office of the asylum also differs in important details from that described in testimony: it faces south, not east; it is lushly carpeted, not paved in stone. The lawyer's journal has the Lady Jane on the stoop of his office in the city scant hours later. Did Jenny escape the asylum somehow? My mother doubted it; the mad and haunted were locked up and closely watched.

My mother claims that if the servants had known what to look for they would have seen the doorframe tremble when Jenny set her hand on it. They would have heard the cries swell when she raised her head and subside when she lowered it, and seen the doctor watching his patient's hands, like a soloist keeping an eye on the conductor. She told me Jominy only knew what love looked like by what he saw in dreams. He shaped his body after fantasies, opinions, rumors, fleeting thoughts. Love that day was a grey narrow building with an iron gate. Jominy had plucked it out of their minds, and set it up beside the road to receive them.

Behind the last door, where imagination failed, Jominy gave her the one thing you can't expect: freedom. Rustle of leaves, caw of a startled crow. She stood in a forest clearing in a spot of advantageous light. In her white dress she is so bright as to suggest overexposure, which makes the painting appear startlingly photographic, hence stopped, momentary, present. Note the simplified forms of the trees, conceived as columns. The carriage is nowhere in sight.

She followed a stream back to the road and hitched a ride on a farmer's cart headed for the city. The agreement her parents had signed with her guardian had a proviso. Her parent's house, lands and legacy reverted to her if on firm grounds she decided not to marry. When she returned to her guardian's estate she took her lawyer with her.

pl. 39 (Studies after Breughel, red chalk*)*

This page looks at first glance like a mish-mash of sketches after nature (radishes and eggs) and drolly prurient doodles. I think it conceals a story.

Note the hurley-burley of quick curved strokes. The household was already in confusion. Many of the servants had left. Those who stayed, many of them half-finished sketches, raved of disembodied hands that plucked and poked. (The flotilla of "anatomical studies" of hands, many in accusatory poses, substantiates their claims.) The master of the house was reading aloud in his study and would not unlock his door. They found the inquisitor with his pants down and his groin mud-caked, in the custody of the gardener (a stocky rural character straight out of Breughel) who had dragged him out of the vegetable patch. He was pulling up the radishes and inserting himself in the holes they left; he had convinced himself that he was the apocalyptic sperm-bearer who would finally fertilize God's great Egg, and found a race of heavenly giants, among them the husband God needed to tame her wild ways. The little priests' heresy had persuaded him—every mishap of history came from the premenstrual madness of a virago god—here depicted as a monumental nude, with stylized rays of light emanating from her groin.

pl. 40 (Court Scene, charcoal pencil)

The witchfinder went to the asylum whose office faced south. Jenny, coached by her lawyer, was pronounced sane if excessively imaginative, and fit to press her case in court, before a gallery of rough ovoids. Jenny's intended husband, his face a scrawl, released her with a speed suggesting relief, and she returned to her parent's estate, to live "alone" the rest of her life, and create a roaring scandal by giving birth to a whole bevy of bastards. The nursemaid fled and took her nephew with her; it is doubtful he ever saw the Lady Jenny again, though he painted her for the rest of his life.

This, however, is a sketch my mother made of me when I was a girl. I have been told I look like Jenny .

Who told me? Discretion still advises silence on some matters.

BODY
Brian Evenson

I. Body

I have been privately removed to St. Sebastian's Correctional Facility and Haven for the Wayward, where they are fitting me for a new mind, and body too. Most of my distress, they believe, results from my having a wayward body and no knowledge of how to manage it. As mine is a body which does not sit easily in the world, they have chosen to begin again from scratch.

The body, says Brother Johanssen, *is not simple flesh staunching blood and slung over bones, but a way of slipping and spilling through the world.* While others slip like water through the world, the world is always bottling me up. The only way I can come unbottled is to crack the world apart. *One cannot refashion flesh and blood*, Brother Johanssen tells me, *but one can refashion the paths that flesh and blood take through the world.*

In a way you can remake the flesh and blood too, whispers Skarmus, *or unmake it, as you know, dear boy.* It is late one midnight, and I lie bound to the slab. I have no answer to this. His fingers are pushing through my hair. In the dark, I imagine I hear his grim smile in his voice. *That you hear what others see*, Brother Johanssen tells me, *is but further index of your waywardness.*

It is true, as Skarmus says, that I have acquired a certain skill at unmaking flesh and blood, dividing it and sectioning it into new creatures and forms as a means of transforming the distress of my wayward body into pleasure. Put into the brothers' terms, the only commerce I can stomach is with the dead. In a little time, I know to work away my distress by transforming the object of my affection into a stripped-and-lopped-off dark lump of flies. They do not know all of this, though they surely suspect. For the little they do know, I am conscripted in Saint Sebastian's, subject to all things as I prepare to take up another, purer body.

—

Four buildings, four stations, four doors. Before I may enter any station, I am required to salute the doorframe of the remaining three. First lintel, then post, then lintel again, addressed in such fashion first with my right mitt, then with my left, then my body must spin sharply and stride to the next door.

Skarmus has been assigned as my private demon, tasked by the brothers to insure I meet all proscription regarding motion, that I salute doorframes in proper order and fashion, that I locomote as they would have me do. I am to be impeded and interrupted by him. All is an effort and the brothers' belief is that my mind in the face of that effort must opt for the construction of another body.

There must, for reasons never explained to me, be an interval of five seconds between each gesture, no more, no less. I must regulate seconds as Skarmus challenges me with hands and voice. When my movements are irregular, the intervals inexact, I am forced to begin again. If I fail a second time, Skarmus is allowed to tighten the flap over my mouth until I can barely respire and slowly lose consciousness.

I do not know if Skarmus whispers his own opinions by night or if his words are part of the brothers' larger plan for me. I attempt not to respond to his whispers or actions, attempt as far as possible to ignore Skarmus and lead him off guard. I have twice, despite the padded restraints engaging my hands and feet, despite the system wiring my jaw closed, beaten Skarmus senseless. Indeed, I would have beaten him dead and attempted, despite my restraints, commerce with the remainder, had not the brothers rapidly intervened.

Four stations: the Living, the Instruction, the Restriction, the Resurrection. I have entered all stations save the Resurrection. There, Brother Johanssen believes, I am not yet prepared to go.

The Living: I am strapped flat around chest, wrists, ankles, throat. The mask is undone and set aside, the lights extinguished. I am allowed to sleep if I can so manage with Skarmus mumbling over me.

At some point, lights flash on. A tube is forced between the wires encasing my mouth and I am fed.

Brother Johanssen arrives, the jaw screws are loosened, I am allowed a moment of untrammeled expression.

"How are you, brother?" Brother Johanssen asks. "Are you uncovering a new body within your skin?"

"I have a new body," I tell him. "I am utterly changed. I have given up evil and am becoming pure."

He shakes his head, smiling thinly. "You believe me so gullible?" he asks. He makes a gesture and the jaw screws are tightened down, the mask re-initiated.

You must learn to deceive him, whispers Skarmus. *You must master better the art of the lie.*

Then we are up and outside and walking. The weights and baffles and mitts, always varied slightly from one day to the next. The restrictions, Skarmus' constant tug and thrust as I walk. My body remains aching and sore, unsure on its feet.

Skarmus is beside me, a half pace behind. Brother Johanssen is somewhere behind, out of sight, the other brothers as well. I am at the center of a world whose sole purpose is to circle about me.

The Instruction: I am made to listen to Brother Johanssen, Skarmus still whispering in my ear. *That which is wayward must be angled forward, the body surrendered for another*, Brother Johanssen preaches. I have, I am told, been wandering all the years of my life in the darkness of my imperfect body. Only the brothers can bring me into light.

You cannot be brought into the so-called light, whispers Skarmus. *You shall never survive it. For you there is no so-called light but only so-called darkness.*

I fail to understand the role of Skarmus. He seems intent on undoing all that Brother Johanssen attempts. Together, it is as if they tear me apart.

The beauty of the world, Brother Johanssen is saying, *is objective, impersonal. For a body such as that which you still persist in wearing, an affront. Affreux. You must acquire a body which will live with beauty rather than against it.*

There is only against, states Skarmus, later.

The Restriction: when I am inattentive, when I resist, when I follow Skarmus' advice rather than that of the good brother, when I fail to fulfill my tasks and motions. The mask is tightened almost to suffocation, the flaps zipped down to block my ears, eyes, nose, the hands chained and dragged up above the head. The back of the rubber suit is loosened, parted, a range of sensations scattered over it or into it by devices I cannot perceive. At some point sweat begins to crease my back, or perhaps welts and blood.

The process all revolves around not knowing. I cannot say if it is pain or pleasure I feel, the line between the two so easily traversable in the artificial distance from my own flesh. The dull thud coming distanced through my blocked ears, the flash of sensation flung across the skull at first and then barely perceptible, the damp smell within the leather mask.

"How are you, brother?" Brother Johanssen asks. "Have you found your new body?"

"I have a new body now, dear brother," I say. I strain against the straps. "I am a changed man."

He shakes his finger back and forth over me slowly. "I see you take me for a fool," he says.

A brief flash through the stations, a day in the space of a moment, my mind at some distance from my body and the light goes off. I feel fingers in my hair. *You cannot believe any of this*, Skarmus says. *You must not allow them to take away what you are.*

Lintel, post, lintel with right. Lintel, post, lintel with left. The muffled blows the mitt offers with each strike.

A slow turn, the foot coming up. Stumbling to the next door, Skarmus clinging to one of my legs.

"You are not prepared for the Resurrection," says Brother Johanssen, leaning benevolently over me.

You'll never be ready, Skarmus whispers.

The chains tighten. I feel my back stripped bare. In the darkness inside my mask, I see streaks of light.

I open my mouth to speak. They are already screwing my jaw down.

A remembered ruin of bodies and myself panting among them, yet with no complete memory of having taken them apart.

I am different from anyone else in the world.

He is smiling, waiting for me to speak. I close my eyes. He pries them open, waits, waits. Finally lets them go, tightens the jaw screws until my teeth ache and grate.

Skarmus falls slightly ahead of me and for a moment I feel myself and my body clearly my own again. He stumbles and I have my mitts on either side of his head and am holding his head still as I strike through it with my own masked head, as I lift him up to bring the side of his skull down against my muffled knee. Were I not so restrained and softened by padding he would be dead. As it is, it is a sort of awkward game.

I try to snap his head to one side and break his neck but the mitts give slightly and the neck groans but refuses to snap. There is a flurry of bodies and Skarmus is dragged away and other hands are holding me down, pulling the mask off, holding my own head down. I see the brief glint of the long needle, feel it pricked into my skull, just above the rim of my eye.

"An inch more," says Brother Johanssen. "A simple rotation of the wrist, brother, and you shall have little relation to any body at all. Is that what you choose?"

I move my eyes no, feel the pressure of the needle.

"Are you telling me that all our time has been wasted?" He looks at me long, without expression, the needle an everpresent pressure, a red blot now drawing itself into my vision. "It is too late for a full cure," says Brother Johanssen. "Your body is too stubbornly the way it is. We can only redirect it slightly."

Brother Johanssen gestures and I feel the needle slick back out, see it fluxed and dripping blood, moving away. There lies Skarmus, his jaw blistered black and blue. He is silent for once.

"The Resurrection then," says Brother Johanssen as blood curls over my eye. "We have done all we can do. May God forgive us all."

II. Shoe

In the polished ceiling of the Living, in the few moments I have free of the mask, I see the flesh above my eye gone dark and turgid, swelling like a third eye. Below it the original eye wavers and falls dim. In a few awakenings its vision is altogether gone, the enormous fist of death beginning to open in its place.

They sedate me and scrape the eye from the socket and drain the ichor from it and scald the socket clean. Skarmus speaks muffled, morphined, his jaw wrapped, his voice mumbled.

I was right, he means to say. *I was right all along.*

His gestures of impediment have subsided, seem half-hearted at best. I am allowed to touch each doorframe largely unimpeded, move in my wires and chains into the Resurrection at last.

It is a simple station, a single room, a low light in the center of it. Brother Johanssen is already there, waiting, at attention, his simple garments exchanged for brighter brocaded robes.

I am made to sit. I am strapped in place and into a head-brace locked so I am forced to regard him.

"These are the initial terms of the Resurrection," he says:

Top Lift

Eyelet

Aglet

Grommet

Vamp

He holds it up, cupped in his hand. He displays it in the light.

"Do you see the curve here?" asks Brother Johanssen a few sessions later, tracing along the side. "Employ your imagination. What does it conjure up?

They are trying to change you, whispers Skarmus.

"On a woman's body, brother. What does it recall?"

He brings it close, traces the curves, holds it close to my face, describes the minor shadings and traces. When I close my eyes, Brother Johanssen commands Skarmus to hold them open, both of them, the missing and the whole. He is touching the shoe, caressing it, speaking still too in a way that makes the shoe steam and glimmer, glister in the odd light as if threatening to become something else.

Quarter, he says.

Cuff.

Counter.

Heel.

When I wake he is there, leaning over me, my jaw already screwed open. "Do you accept the fruits of your new faith?" he asks.

"What?" I say.

"What?" he says. He stands and begins to weave away. "What?" he repeats, "What?"

Throat, someone says behind me.

Tongue, someone says.

He dims the central light, disappears himself somewhere behind me. A square of light as big as myself appears, flashes onto the wall before me.

You are in it, says Skarmus. *Too late to step back now.*

The square of light goes dark, is exchanged for the image of the forepart of a woman's shoe, the dip between the first and second toe captured in the low cleft of the vamp. It flashes away and is replaced by pallid white flesh, the dip of a dress, the slow curve and fall of the woman's body.

There may be a resemblance, says Skarmus. *Yet it is entirely superficial.*

The images are flashed back and forth, one replacing the other soon with such speed it becomes difficult to know where one image stops, the other begins.

Breast, someone says.

Cleave.

Box.

I hear the clatter behind me, the square of light pulsing and then a shoe fading up and angling in and transforming into a woman. Then the shoe again and a different place, followed by a section of the woman. The clatter, swirling motes of dust bright in the beam of light.

It is her breast, its breast, her feet, its foot, her neck and shoulder, its neck and shoulder, cleave, cleave, thigh, thigh, box, box, counter, counter, welt, welt, looping to begin all over again.

Skarmus is speaking filth into my ear.

The film is sped double time, looped over and over. In my good eye I am seeing the parsed shoe, in my missing eye the parsed woman. At some point there stops being a difference.

Sole.

I feel his hands through my hair. I test my bonds, find them tight.

Every shoe was once a woman, he says. *A shoe is a woman in a new body. There is, for your purpose, no distinction.*

Welt, he whispers. *Box.*

When I open my eye there is a flash of gold, pendulant, turning back and forth above me. I try to lift my head but cannot lift it. I do not feel the pressure of the jaw screw, yet my jaw will not move.

There is the steady sweep of Brother Johanssen's voice, speaking slowly and calmly and with authority, his body invisible except, above the flush of gold, a pale and disembodied hand. Skarmus is nowhere to be seen or heard.

Brother Johanssen's cadence changes, his words coming slower, matching the rhythm of the swinging gold. "One," he intones. "Two. Thr—"

I have lately been experiencing some uncertainty as to who I am and where and when. I am becoming strange to myself, caught somehow outside my own skin.

I hear a noise like the snap of a bone.

⁓

I am in the Resurrection, not knowing how I have come to be here. The padding and restrictions have been removed from my arms and instead I hold in my hands the subject of all my time in the Resurrection.

I stand still, holding it, observing it. I begin to stroke softly, my heart beating harder, until I feel my arms overwhelmed by other hands and the object is falling out of my hands, and I am crying out into the closed surface of a mask.

The mouth flap is tightened, and I feel the breath slowly leaving me. The baffles are fitted over my hands. Brother Johanssen moves until I can see him through the eyelets of the mask. He is smiling. He has picked the subject up, holds it suspended from a single finger, swaying, near my face.

"Dear brother," he says, leaning forward as my air gives out. "Welcome to the fold."

⁓

They hold me down and in place and strip all the apparati from me piece by piece until I am bare and shivering and in a heap on the ground, lost without the sweat and smell of baffles and rubber and leather and wire. They carry me by the arms and legs, toss me. There is the moment of collision with the floor, a sensation more naked and complete than anything I have felt in some time.

As I am getting up, stumbling in my body, I hear the sound of the door snapping to.

I can barely walk, the ground wavering under my feet.

I am, I know, in the Resurrection. In the cast light, centered, a woman of red leather, sleek and low cut, satined inside, without eyelets, aglets, grommets, perhaps twelve inches from heel to toe box. She is lovely, her shank perfectly curved, needle heeled, her vamp v-shaped and elongated.

I am moving forward. I reach and pick her up in my hand, touch her against my long encased skin.

After that I cannot explain what happens. There is a rush of dizziness and when I awake she is destroyed, strips of leather and thin wood and metal is scattered about, the heel broken off and free. There is, as always in the first moment, tremendous regret and shame, fading quickly.

I turn to see Brother Johanssen and Skarmus together, complicitous in the doorway. I lift my shoulders, try to think of something to say. Then all the brothers are upon me in a rush, ladening me down, binding me again.

Each day I am stripped to my skin, left alone with her. I may, Brother Johanssen tells me, remain with her as long as I do not destroy her.

I do what I can to resist. I make conversation. I resist, for a time, touching her. When I do touch her it is merely slightly, turning her, attempting to perceive, briefly, a new aspect. I let things build slowly, but in the end am always lying spent, strips and fragments of her scattered about me.

Yet each day she is there again, the same, velvet on the outside, silken innards. I can destroy her, but she keeps returning. It is, after all, the Resurrection.

That's right, says Skarmus. *Keep destroying it.*

It? I wonder.

The film gets stuck. I watch the image darken, bloom black and dissolve into light. I am not the only one who destroys.

There is some confusion in me about who I am, what I desire.

I keep destroying her. I am not changed, my body just as wayward as ever. Yet they are happier with me. I understand none of it.

—

Then I am stripped and thrown in again. Yet this time there is no woman, only an odd and curious creature, the same size as myself, much like myself, a man only not a man. It grimaces, brushes back its hair. It is all familiar somehow.

"This is your body's test," says Brother Johanssen. "Do not fail us."

I do not know what is expected of me. I approach slowly. It makes no move, seems at ease, relaxed. It begins to mumble words that I can't quite string together.

Breast, throat, quarter. I can see the woman hidden in it, luminous, the leather and satin hidden just beneath hair and teeth and skin.

Though her skin I brush her vamp, finger the damp welt. They cannot conceal her from me in such a carapace. In a minute, I know, I will have shucked the carapace and she will be strips of leather, her box torn apart and open, her throat undone, all of her gone.

THE FEET OF JOHN YAU
Gordon Lish

The thing of it with me is, speaking to you personally, the thing of it with me as an individual as far as speaking about my own personal philosophy as far as my own philosophy of life goes, it's like, you know, it's like okay, it's like there's feet which you like to look at and then there's this other type of feet which, you know, which forget it, oh my God, forget it, forget it, it's already making me sick just for me to sit here and think about it, those type of feet, the other type of feet, which face it, face it, it's like okay, okay, it's like everything everything everything else which they are all of them always sitting there constantly never quitting from carrying on about—the works, the works!—in their books, in their books!—in this book, in this book!—it's all of it, it's just to all of it get you not to stop and think to yourself okay, okay, what is the type of possible feet which we are dealing with as far as this particular individual goes?

So you see what it is?

It's all a smokescreen, a smokescreen, a smokescreen!

It's all of it like a red herring—everything the mob of them are always standing around making all of these constant constant big deals about, it is all of it just to get you to quit paying attention to them as far as the type of feet which they have the personal tragedy to have.

Like take the feet of John Yau.

Do you see what I mean?

Okay, I cannot sit here and personally swear to you that I Gordon Lish have ever actually had a decent chance to inspect the feet of John Yau.

But I am willing to bet you anything you want that here is a person who went ahead and made up their mind to be the editor of this book just so there would not be all of these other human beings always coming over to him and thinking to themselves yes or no, pro or con, what the fuck is the story here as far as the feet of John Yau?

Please, do you honestly think Gordon Lish does not know what's going on?

I promise you, Gordon Lish knows what's going on.

You scoff.

Don't think I don't hear you scoff!

You think Gordon Lish does not hear scoffing when it's going on?

Fine, fine, scoff if you dare. Your feet, your feet, it would probably make me vomit if I had to see them or even just even for two seconds had to think about them. Hey, if I had feet like you have, you know what? I would run go see a doctor. I would run go to the ends of the earth to find myself a genius with a miracle treatment if I had the type of feet which you have the horrible fortune to have. Believe me, there is always help for everybody, even the worst person. The way to start is go look the truth square in the eye.

This is what is wrong with John Yau.

This is what is wrong with this book.

There is no looking the truth square in the eye, which is why you should get down on your hands and knees and thank God Gordon Lish is the one human being who is not knuckling down to public pressure and selling out.

(And one more thing, asshole—fetish, you looking for a fetish, what's the fetish, where's the fetish, is it feet which is the fetish or is it instead, uh, isn't it instead, uh, not feet but even plainer to anybody with any brains in their head than even the nose on the face of you or of God or of Yau?)

DAY OF SORROW, DAY OF DARKNESS
Dennis Barone

Just why we enjoy October captures the densest wit. He had begun too roughly with the foot. The weight and the strength of the Doc Martin knock-offs protected both feet from his obscene gestures. The profession the editor selects will not normally exceed the black edges of well-formed souls. She should conform to shifts in their classes or study subjects such as transportation, housing, and parks and recreation. These shifts necessarily reflect changes in styles, though not in shoes. Still she wears those thick-soled and heavy clunkers. The point, they say, is painfully clear.

The European thespian in a side-splitting story will make sparks fly. On this date, at that time his eyes have trouble focusing on the hunchback and instead feign a sleepiness that allows his downward glance or glare to the soft folds of redolent slippers, pussycat slippers all a-furred and bewhiskered, comfy and cushy. This he fears may be his undoing, an extraordinary story of a ten-year-old boy who suffers from a rare genetic disorder. Perhaps. Ah, there. There a toe wiggles and is then transformed into the orb of romance. Their mouths open in astonishment.

Even so, the importance of understanding culture cannot be overlooked, his mom warns him and so he pursues Claire and Linda whose toe shoes he regards as just another machine grinding at his soul. So, perhaps his mom was right? Or his editor? The director maybe? This issue poses tough questions for him, but, nonetheless, he takes full responsibility for making all final decisions about what to pursue after all. It is sentences such as this that flush out his character. Everywhere he looks he sees four feet, four red silk-covered feet flat against a floor or the ground or up on point. So what's the difference? he wonders. Claire? Linda? The secrecy demanded by military research, he decides, is deplorable. It is exactly eight o'clock. Eight o'clock in the a.m. Just how good is he at keeping secrets?

The mission is, as a consequence, being transformed. It affects all. Clogs, whose manufacture is now controlled by computer chips, are especially strong. Consider a heart-pounding trip into the thrill zone and how the click-clang-klonk of one's clogs can accentuate it. Consider a cloned dancer under the direction of a hilarious subscriber who wreaks havoc on a captivating drama about a regular guy and how this can all seem finer, more eloquent and elevated if all wear clogs and the sounds get looped later. Anyway, an elite group of terrorists seize control of the set, of the state. Right? They always do, he thinks. So why not have a little fun in the meantime? he wonders. Why not lose your heart and come to your senses in clogs now while you can. Right? Now is the moment, now, he repeats as he walks down the street, to take what pleasures the gods allow and then, just then he hears it: click-clank-klonk. He is in the Vogel Market in Antwerp and loving it. It is his holiday and everything has been reduced, especially the clogs.

To some degree the answer to all these questions is yes. He has become accustomed to the transfer of globally exchanged information. It is possible to develop his character by situating it in a particular time and place, by contextualizing it, but, dear reader, that alone will not explain it. An unbroken continuum binds figure to philosophy. In other fields stable jeans by no means should bring all this running from a certain angle to the money of a wealthy granting agency. (See, for example, its mixture of different people.) There may be no more difficult problem than remembering. This shocking historical tale of deceit and sexuality; this sweeping, epic tale; this bizarre comedy of high voltage; this magnificent fantasy adventure; this comical spin on a classic story—that's for sure; this gripping drama of good and evil, love and passion; this game; this particular night; this favorite; this sling back sandal; this weapon capable of wiping out his heart.

While I was preparing this discourse, I noticed that we had already lost more than eighty percent of the series. Intellectual work requires an ungodly amount of time and all during this time I had one shoe on; one, off. Well, half-off anyway. Half-off and dangling from one nylon-encased foot that I moved around and around in a circular motion as a way to pass the time while I composed this discourse. During this time—my highly trained mind is more than capable of several thoughts held simultaneously in mind, a simultaneity that I cannot communicate to others in either prose or speech—I had four thoughts: 1) the unspoken, the unwritten; 2) the discourse itself; 3) amazement and wonder that the sandal would not, did not fall; 4) that this whole time I was being watched, a trial by ice of sorts for all such unseen eyes are cold, cold as the desert of Itabira. I do not mean that politics has nothing to do with morality, and I quickly realized the situation was both a political and a moral one. In the distance I could hear football teams practicing, grunting. It was, after all, late August. The ground was dry with the autumn approaching and their cleats made strange sounds as they turned left and then turned right, as they pushed on straight ahead into those blocking dummies.

We are witnessing a remarkable moment that demands reflection. We know that there is a "he" who does not watch the film, but stares at the feet and we know that there is a "she" who is so very astute that she can hear the strange sounds that young boys' cleats make in the distance. Can "he" and "she" be brought together? People of my generation went to college to answer this very question. The large abstractions common to such questions have alarming and I think very revealing consequences, but such treatises are put together by people who are not perfect, adequate, or graceful and so forgive me if the end is austere and lacking in that nostalgia people feel for sensational entertainment, fierce and disturbing. They were brought together—"he" and "she"—brought together by you-know-who. In a terrifying story with plenty of exciting twists and turns? In a compelling character-driven drama? In an auto accident at the age of thirty-nine? Alas, no. Oh, day of sorrow! Day of darkness! Day of no tomorrow! When at last they met by the fountain of the Plaza, at the top of the Eiffel Tower, rafting down the Colorado, on an island off Greece where all the buildings are white, in Seattle he wore Asics and she wore Birkenstocks.[1]

—

Postscript

"A rapturous love story."
— Gene Shalit, *Today Show*

"Powerful! A real special piece of work."
    — Gene Siskel, *Siskel & Ebert*
"The special effects are beautifully effective."
    — Kenneth Turan, *Los Angeles Examiner*

Note

[1]Would their child, had they had one, have worn Candies? Perhaps Converse basketball "Attack" sneakers? And if so, would the child as a young adult have played in the CBA and struggled to get into the NBA? From what we know of the mother and father—though they had no child, though they did not get together—can we tell how they felt about this child and his arduous yet always courageous struggle? In an attempt to shed light on these matters a special commission of several of the academy's brightest minds has been formed. We anxiously await the results of their deliberations. Meanwhile, we may consider the critically acclaimed film that has the basketball-playing lad doing *almost* anything to insure victory for his team in a full-court, fast-paced comedy that has scored a swish with critics even though he has little ability to believe in himself and puts all his confidence—his hopes, his dreams—in his shoes which in the end get stolen, lost, replaced, discontinued, too smelly to wear any longer, endorsed by another player whom he doesn't even like because he won't play fair. This is the one. A delight. Magnificent! Gorgeous.

THE PORNOGRAPHERS
Cybele Knowles

Picture of utopia, or perhaps just a case of mistaken identity. Respectfully submitted for your consideration, a place which is now, a time which is a town like yours and mine. An otherwise ordinary society transformed completely by a puzzling anomaly—the custom by which people write out each other's deepest sexual fantasies, transcribing the pornography generally scribbled down in private hearts. It's a transfer of goods and services, one balcony seat in a moviehouse full of dust for a ring inscribed with the motto of a secret, favorite shame, an adaptable form of socioeconomic exchange, pornography in this kingdom surpassed and now replaces those previous and partial satisfactions only still known in memorializations of the querulous old—heartfelt customer service, the ministrations of their wives and darkies, the decorum of traveling attire. But consider from your distant place in the time-space continuum the present alternatives, a range of possibilities that begins with the quarterly receipt of optimistic erotica from your broker and ends with the logistics of taping a snuff for the love of your life, the one who left your ass. The benefits of widespread production and consumption of pornography are practically limitless, but we cite just a few examples, first and foremost the fact that literacy is generally on the rise, and specifically that most people finally begin to understand the proper uses of the comma, the ignorance of which is a sad inadequacy in our own reality. We also observe a markedly improved ratio in the incidence of fucking to coitus, and the Harvard-trained economists call our attention to an explosion in the markets for fresh towels and Kleenex Man-Size— industries both in need of a good, healthy boost.

Ideally, pornography as they know it is a contract of mutual benefit knowingly entered, but in that world as in ours there's pornography stolen and pornography unbidden. Pornography we might call "found pornography," such as that in the handwriting in the one you love, the one who'll never know you love him. Pornography, for the division chief who adores a woman best when she's wearing a very large sanitary pad, coming over the Kimberly-Clark information line. He hangs on the rep's every word when she says, with all the vigor of someone reading from the company literature, "At times a body needs a *thick* pad!" Pornography is happening at the shore, where a man with the face of a sad vulture watches girls of five and six playing in the waves. In a small notebook he writes a little story, never to be delivered, which he still hopes is suitable to the kindergartners' taste and experience. It concerns the bulky load of sand that collects in the cotton crotch of one's bathing suit after a few hours in the surf. Even in that place, pornography struggles with its last bastion, the domestic life, where there are still so many excuses and deferments—headaches, no paper in the apartment, so many of my fantasies that we haven't gotten around to yet. But should you find your coordinates warping around you and suspect that you have crossed over to *there,* consider yourself lucky, and accost the people around you to make sure. Flay them in ordinary conversation, and you'll find first not the bone of their inhibition, but the Wild West of what turns them on. Cameo, in fact, of the parallel me in that trapezoid universe, not the one waiting for prince charming, but the one writing pornography—for my mother, a bodice-ripper; for my father, a tract of genteel sadism; for my sister, a kind of millennial divination.

from SHOW ME THE GOOD PARTS
Kenneth Goldsmith

Cunnilingus & Fellatio

An employee takes a picture of one of the company's officers in an informal moment. In order to get a telling shot, he makes a little noise, and the subject raises his head from between the thighs of the married woman he is making love to. He first lays a strap across the back of the lovely girl then spread-eagles her across a Purina box and buries his head between her thighs in contrition. His examination is very thorough, and she undresses completely, even though she only has a sore finger. He is a cunnilinguist, to her disgust, but after some time and some literary investigation, she comes around to her predilection. They are steady lovers, and he bugs her about her past, with special emphasis on oral sex. She admits to having done it, and does it for him. They go all the way. Their loss of virginity is both upsetting and exhilarating. One of them expresses her outrage to an uncle, who gives her sympathy in a sexual form that enthralls her. She unselfishly wants her sister to experience this ecstasy, so when the uncle comes padding around in the dark to her bed, she switches places with her sister.

Exhibitionism

Two Quaker children, a girl 16 and a boy 13, are in a barn. "If thee show me, me will show thee." So she shows he and he shows she. His bragging and boasting about his prowess as a lover leads to a night of voluptuousness followed by three whores who gyrate and flaunt their charms in the face of the Good-Time-Charlies.

Consciously or unconsciously she is always showing a part of her anatomy. One evening her provocative display excites the refined young man and he charges into her bed and into her waiting arms. She dances. She sheds her veils and reveals her tantalizing breasts. She dances. Her body has filled out, making her even more desirable in bed. She makes Salome seem like a clod.

Her penchant for form-fitting sweaters inspires the admiration of a lot of men and the enmity of a lot of women in the small town. A 16-year-old boldly declares his love. He sneaks into her room one night and, despite her feeble rationalizations, talks his way right into her bed.

She is a triple threat: she is a sexual queen at home, on the stage she is a stripper par excellence, and in the cinema she stars in obscene movies. Tireless praise of her anatomy follows. Impressed by the dimensions of her bust, he buys a dozen brassieres as an offering. She excites him by doing a private striptease for him. He tells her that she need not remove all her clothing, because he can fill in the missing parts from imagination.

His hobby is photography. He takes Peeping Tom shots of nudes. When he's not working in his darkroom, he's out raping women. In this scene, he conducts a normal bit of business with a girl he has persuaded to model in a bathing suit for him. He is sexually conditioning her for the first time when, unbeknownst to her, he will rig up cameras and ultraviolet light, and take dirty pictures of her and him in action. His ambition is to outdo a set of Japanese pornographic photos he has. She undresses to the waist to show him something she has to offer and exposes a firm breast while driving. His distraction causes a collision and doom.

Part of her routine is to involve a guy, usually a repressed, embarrassed type. She errs in judgment and is vigorously handled. Her mask of geniality falls, and she tells the men they are "sons of bitches."

Another guy, who is "educating" his girl, takes her to a strip show. She is fascinated by the artistic peeling. When they get home, she gives a few society women a private and more daring performance. The women get in the spirit, shed their garments, and play a game called "living statues." She reflects on her early breast development and her pendulous mammalia and while serious talk is exchanged, she dopes a strip routine until conversation becomes too difficult. She takes off her clothing so that each will know what they have to fight with. It is a draw, except that one is more sunburned. The goal of every bra manufacturer is to have the honor of her splendid bosom modeling it.

Fearing impotence she goes through some elaborate machinations to make herself a demonic lover. She takes hormones, vitamins, and nude photos of herself in lewd positions. She goes so far as to interest another woman in her husband so that her passion can be whipped by jealousy. Her efforts succeeds and she dies of his sexual exertions.

Soon she is pressured into a private leg-comparing contest that broadens to include thighs and navels. All ends happily in a blaze of floodlights as the photographer's true love sheds dainties before the camera. She allows the photographer to tie her to a table and snap a simulated horror picture of her with some red stuff on her breast.

One of the girls tells of her first steps down the "primrose path." She was conned into posing for some suggestive photos and then blackmailed into modeling hotter ones. The bastardly photographer takes her virginity after completing his picture essay.

Frigidity

When she was eight years old, she heard her mother tell someone that in the 26 years of her married life her husband had never seen her naked body. This statement warps her life. She tries the policy on her husband, whose response to this coyness is to rip her clothes from her body during their honeymoon. The expensive honeymoon is impaired because she sleeps at the edge of the bed. The husband, after struggling for his rights, gets his reward in the form of a hollow and loveless marriage.

Very little sexual excitement can be gotten out of a woman the young man is having an affair with. He manages to work her up before the act, but her motor always runs out during it. She wants to reassure herself that she is not frigid and that she will give her husband-to-be good value. He tries to arouse his frigid wife. He fondles her, but all he gets for his efforts is a kiss.

They play analyst with each other and startling revelations emerge. With both their ardors dampened, he tries nevertheless to fiddle around with her in bed and arouse her. The frigid woman is defrosted; with a correct mixture of gentleness and firmness, he helps her overcomes a psychological block against sex that was plaguing her.

She goes to a therapist for counsel and asks, "Could a woman *want* to do things like that . . . it all seems so disgusting somehow." She is shown a sexy dance and taught that her thoughts were wrong, that a woman could be *too* good. Armed with this new enlightenment, she drops her pale reserve and dons an "insidiously intoxicating" perfume designed to arouse the pure brute savage.

Homosexuality

He is a homosexual who seduces altar boys. Shook up by his traumatic experiences, and fearing himself to be "queer," he does all kinds of crazy stunts to prove his manhood. He has intercourse with an old prostitute just to see if she has VD.

He has been performing admirably with women but is suddenly swept by a strange yen while sleeping spoon fashion with a male friend. The big romance between them comes off but slipped in during the bacchanals and revels are two homosexual bits. He is washed by the boys and becomes excited. Some of the children are over-fondled.

He and a lesbian, in an effort to go "straight," try a heterosexual arrangement, but fail. A monstrous freak show of homosexuals, lesbians, perverts, masochists, and sadists begins. (The author warns the readers that the following is a homosexual part of the narrative; and if the reader is uninterested, he should skip the section. Ha!) Looking through a one-way mirror, the man can see the owner inspect and select members of his stable and hand them out to clients. He views men who have to be draped in chains and cursed, others who masturbate, and one who kisses his own reflection in a mirror.

The boy's eerie adventures continue as he looks for love with male strangers in parks and toilets. He finds one deviant who whips and then caresses him. He wants to stimulate him in less orthodox ways and tells him that he is the first woman he has ever had. He then speaks of his early sexual acts with men.

Doomed by his homosexual conflicts, he watches the two lovers and thrills at the thought of playing the girl's part. He views himself in a mirror and imagines himself a woman. He shaves the hair off his chest. The young man knows he's "that way," and lets his sex life lie dormant. To the strains of "Liebestod," he enters an older man's arms.

He views his naked body in a mirror and is annoyed by the large protuberance, which he feels spoils the symmetry of his body. He is cruelly tormented by some boys in a gym. They kid him about the largeness of his organ and then their play becomes rougher and they attempt rape. He falls in love with the brawny fellow who saves him from being raped and describes to him what he does with girls in the hay. The account gets them both excited. He is a docile and willing fly. His homosexual mentor is a charming spider.

A traumatic episode in his youth, in which he watched an older boy have sex with a stupid girl, seems to be a contributory factor in his personality development, for he grows up to be a handsome homosexual. He persuades a young beautiful boy to drive home with him. It builds in intensity to an almost unbearable account of homosexual perversion. (Youth, it seems, is the most important commodity among homosexuals. After a certain age you must pay for love. There is a popular song entitled "There'll Be Some Changes Made." One of the lines of the lyric has been parodied and bitterly sung as "Nobody wants you when you're old and gay.")

He reveals to his analyst that he had a homosexual affair with an actor, now dead. He corrupted the actor by telling him that being straight was square and that a bisexual policy would open many more doors for him, a delicate soul who goes mincing through the twilight world of Paris and New York.

The two boys are swimming and wrestling. Homosexual feelings flare up and they make love. For one boy, it is an experiment and a romp; for the other, it becomes a way of life and the memory of this first love dominates him. The twilight boy keeps his secret hidden. Given a little freedom from their usual strict supervision, they have themselves a wild orgy in the shower room.

Sea Tang & Nino
Jeff Clark

You left for the ends of your sphere . . . We found together our spheres are immense anemones, the centers tender flesh, the perimeter those spikes, but you had the will to collapse yourself to Essence and move through them as if through parking lot lamps.

⁓

Beside her pool in autumn, Nino nursed little cousin. I had walked across town to fetch her F Britannica.

Knock-knock-Nino?

Out here!

The left strap down the arm, cousin detached from her breast to see me.

Hello Bunnyboy.

Hi Nino.

Cousin no longer drank, the chaos of three Disneylands stood still, Nino leaned against the conch-pink cushion of the lounge chair, legs out to naked feet. She smiled up with a hand across her brow to kill the Cahuilla Fireball behind me. Cousin still stared up here. A gorgeous Malmedy Mound atop the breathing cage. A droplet fell off her dark circle.

Does that taste strange, Nino?

You reverse corpse!

She pushed herself up with her bottom, and gathered it. Politely I bent and tasted—Lozenges of Ancient Colostrum! and throttling impressions of flesh. Cousin was laid out on a towel beside the chaise, and my face pulled down again and held. The chair in a while reclined and something was placed between baby and pool. Blue nails pealed away the veiling cotton. Agreement with our eyes that neither was criminal. We pulled off her suit bottoms and as I nursed again some anonymous Benoit wizarded my nephew joy into primeval South Tante. Overwhelming interior noise, each liter and portion of spirit deserted its place and shifted to the shaft. She had two hands with blue fingernails. One finger, which?, wet itself and stroked upon my button. Presently the hole was opened, and

Nino
Bunnyboy   fffffff   you love me
I

She kissed my mouth. Two o'clock. Ineffable sphincter meccas
were made rulers of my torch—the locus left the head and grew
janglier. Flame crept down toward the base and invaded a new
zone high inside. Our mouths sucked. Vapors must have escaped my
face for she pulled me out of her and kneed my feet back to the
cement, pulled my bottom and across her belly, set it on her breasts,
lifted her head from the chaise, and assented, assented, assented . . .
A flock of atomic herons was let go and disappeared.

Then we swam! In godly water corrupted by shifting shades of
a dead palm I submerged and saw the forelegs of a horse
trampolining red-bronze spheres. My lips' coronation in chlorinated
hazy beige. My tongue's coronation in the small Drain of Angels.
My first witness of how a tit changes. Nino was a ballerina and had
eaten raw falcon: in space now with her animism and her mouth of
English novels. Her thighs that everlastingly inspire quarries of
Serpentine in Tactile Rooms.

You oughtn't talk like that.

Who are you?

Hilma Gazebo.

Where?

Above the West. You oughtn't talk like that! Pure things don't
require decoration—

I'm trying—

Your mouth is like aluminum foil! If, in your life, you worship
only love and silence . . . why do you speak like an antique
motorcycle? Why do you speak at all?

Are you—

I see the straw that goes into the skull.

— —

Cream Lincoln Continental out on a jetty. The other ones left it to
go down the beach, Nino asleep against me, clutching a coat to her
belly. Ocean Man was to drive us to The Palomino. Nino breathed
her black bangs up. A red-orange blouse of forgotten print, and the
other ones were quite away down the sand now. My pink paulownia
in its own high July was punching further up quickly. Gently, with

breaks, I stole the coat from her arm and bit it a moment and, still supporting her drowse, unpanted my lit business, tightened my arm around her to drop the coat over its sparkling . . . but her drowse was wrecked, she awoke and saw what was there and instantly took the coat away and united us.

On her floor of pillows I began to pray and my cock erected. The blessings I asked for my loves became a clenching and releasing of ass on the silk cases. The head lifted itself from the surface of the torso. The entire piece pumped with the heart and wanted to sidewind to the bellybutton. It was either finish prayer or ejaculate before Ocean Man came back. I rolled over and drove it against chance mounds, into accidental shafts.

Legless Throne of your pink infantry! You loved that room—
Your green Chinese pillow.
Its memory elates your king and pawns.
The scent of your hair and halos of your mouth that suffocated my court. Corpses, but so fresh!
At that birthday, you remember?, we let the maddened slab bump my bottom in phony reaching . . .

To return in the front from petty terror and see it pressed to the seat. "Put your cock through my splendid hair." The interior of that big car was a den. I know someone has kept our dust there. She lifted the armrest and then her dress and, like a Countess, annihilated her nephew.

Riding in Hosie's car, we pretended we were his merry children, and frolicked; we slapped one another and were uxorious of the passing scenery. "Oh! Look!" Then we calmed when he barked from the wheel. I drilled your face with my eyes and silly grin until, at last, you comprehended and made the sign with it of, What?, and looked down to my roughening cob aimed at Hosie's chirking leather. "Oh! Enlargement of a Spanish toy spaniel!"
What are you two talking about? he whined.
That little spaniel over there!
Wouldn't it be wonderful to squeeze such a gorgeous dog?

Memory is a prop for the fatuous. But her telepathy, the spirits in her bottom, its constant revivals in my mind, the flashing and vanishing legs and bang that effortlessly load the hand—and sleeping so peacefully she was magnificent to see, to sit with! Her pillows were expressly for my flesh! as were her rubbing oils and her speed and parasol. Strange, though, that the body is not expressly and always for another flesh, rather for itself, for its own days and dreaming, and for orange shafts of afternoon, for silken hillocks. Once, as she rinsed off sea, I set yellow verses upon her green pillow of Chinese motif, redolent of sea tang and neck, and tugged my pants down for some liberty. Was it madness to love blood? It was sanity . . . petite tan anaconda of a virgin Prince. Juvenile Nutella! She loved a young man and anyway her ticket had already been bought by gods. I have the Chinese case, redolent now of lesser places.

THE HONK OF THE M'JOOB
Rikki Ducornet

The author of the following entry is indebted to Sultan Hen Egg Tekke's detailed inquiry into the origins of Old Ubar's most mysterious artifact: the Honk of the M'Joob.

1. Construction

An articulated frame of Flap is said to be the bones of the Honk and its blood. The sustaining walls are made of wood treated with herbane juice and jequirity beans: density is essential. In the early stages of construction, a splinter could prove fatal to the carpenter.

Once the walls and bottom are secured to the skeleton with a saddle of struts, the interstices—which by law cannot be caulked—are inspected for seepage: the Honk is set to float, perhaps indefinitely, in the dung of Dowager Queens diluted in horseradish dressing. The prolonged soaking neutralizes the poisons and causes the wood to swell; the best Honk are soaked for six years. Such is the cabinetmaker's skill they always float. Approaching the tub at this time in order to scrutinize the Honk is effectively discouraged. Although such rules seem strange today, even the elderly are denied special privileges. Fatalities, nonetheless, are not infrequent.

2. The Primal Voyage

Popular tradition would have us believe that the M'zab of the M'joob is populated by the descendants of Old Crock who, heeding the prophecy of a harpy, took to the sea in a Honk. Guided by a Hungarian map, he and his family floated for twelve years helping themselves to the occasional egg that fell into their Honk from the sky. In tedious conversations they wistfully recalled the secondary helpings of obligatory Blast served in better days. It seemed to them that the appallingly intimate circumstances could be gladly overlooked if only a large Whoop, fully roasted, along with the required relishes, materialized as prophesized; it never did.

During their ordeal, they invented the consonantal alphabet, the notion of the poles and the theory of Archimedes which states that all bodies plunged into the sea suffer a vertical paradox that, like sexual desire, starts at the bottom and rises to the top. The valve of this paradox is equal to the density of the ocean thus displaced; the planets and moons in their orbits function within the celestial ether in much the same way. In other words: *gravity always rises.* A comet hitting the earth would cause the sea to rise up from its bed and remain suspended for as many minutes as it would take to navigate the star's circumference—an impossibility.

3. The M'Zab of the M'Joob

When, after twelve years, Old Crock heard a loud knock and dared lift the lid of his Honk, he was relieved to feel a fresh breeze tugging his beard toward an island so fertile its meat moths could be seen from afar. As soon as the Honk hit land, Old Crock proceeded to dig a shallow pit and fill it with kindling in order to roast Yowl. This culinary habit explains why the fingers of the peoples of the M'zab of the M'joob are always brightly stained with scales, just as those of the saffron pickers of Spain are always yellow.

4. Yowl

Yowl forms the staple diet in the M'zsab, and this culinary rigor, neatly observed, sheds light upon current cosmological concerns, as well as decorative motifs so common on crests and clams. Close ocular inspection of Old Crock's codpiece reveals the meat moth's jugal furrow.

5. Honk and Yowl

The Ancestral Honk on view in the Treasury is over two thousand years old. It is no bigger than a cracker tin—clearly too small to have served the First Family as described. Its diminutive size is explained in this way: Having need of a vessel no longer, Old Crock now required a tight casket to keep his Yowl. Attentive to this new necessity, the gods, once obliging, reduced the Honk's size. Today its dimensions are thought to be perfect, and throughout the M'jab the system of measures and weights depends upon the venerable artifact.

The Honk is the Mjoob's one miracle. The people have no notion of clerical intervention, no gospels, no sacred edifices. It is the Honk that fulfills the numinous functions which so burden others with dogmatic contradictions. A perfect model of order in chaos, a constant reminder of fortitude, the Honk is always kept to the right of the Tock in the hut beside the hearth, filled to the brim with Yowl. If a Coot's handshake is not sticky with Yowl, he might as well croak.

Pure food, emblematic of pure thought and eventual beatitude, these bodies serve a function not unlike that of the Holy Wafer in France.

MANDRAKE
Rikki Ducornet

Attributed to the Crimson Library, the *Tale of the Patriarch*
reveals the erotic origins of the Tlonic *mandraked* and *to mandrake*.
According to Manda, *to mandrake* is to seduce, glamorize and
inspire sexual exuberance.

The Tale of the Patriarch

1.

When the Patriarch went out to harvest wheat, he found instead
a thicket of mandrakes all singing with the voices of sirens. At his
approach they began to whisper together:

"See the mortal man! See how his sex rises to greet us with a
blessing and a promise of rain."

Their voices rose and fell like a field of wheat in the wind of
summer and were so sweet the Patriarch fell to his knees and
ejaculated into their leaves.

2.

Later the Patriarch returned to his wives. And although their breasts
and buttocks tumbled across his eyes and they nibbled his balls with their
little teeth, the Patriarch could not forget the voices of the mandrakes, nor
how his seed glistened on their eager leaves like dew. When he tore
himself from his wives' embraces, his hands were sticky, as when he
harvested myrrh. His palms bled a little, pierced by unexpected thorns.

3.

The mandrakes heard the Patriarch's feet before they saw him.
"Come live with us!" they sang with earthy voices. As he lay down
among them, his sex thrashed like a branch in a violent storm.
"Keep dreaming among us!"

The Patriarch laughed to see his body catch fire. The Patriarch
could not stop laughing.

4.

That night the wheat field, unharvested, blazed red under the
moon. Naked and filled with longing, the Patriarch's wives walked

to the field alone together. Standing tall and golden the wheat tempted them.

"Embrace me!" it whispered. "Take me between your teeth, against your tongue."

"Let us do what the wheat asks of us," one wife said to the other. "Sister, unbind my hair."

It was a harvest unlike any other.

TUSK

by Steve Aylett

After a pert little heist one day Easy Fortezza felt unaccountably reluctant to remove his mask. It was the amiably layered face of an elephant. He wasn't even meant to participate in such heists, let alone become transmogrified into a tusken behemoth during the procedure. Because he was a favorite nephew of Eddie Thermidor the gang boss, everyone indulged him. But when after a whole week he was still wearing the bonce, some of the house hoods had a sit-down about it. "So he's got a attitude problem," shrugged Larry Crocus, cracking his knuckles.

"Attitude," grunted Moray.

"Maybe it's a phase," said Sam "Sam" Bleaker.

"Phase," grunted Moray.

"You guys'll be the death o' me," laughed Barry Nosedive.

"Death," grunted Moray.

"I mean it's not like he's done any harm," Nosedive continued. "Maybe he's evolving under the pressure."

"He poses the threat of a good example," hissed Shiv, examining his knife.

"Sure. We'll get a reputation."

"Death," grunted Moray.

"We can't waste Fortezza," stated Nosedive. "He's good—irreplaceable."

"He appears to have been effortlessly replaced by an elephant," muttered Mr. Flak without inflection. He was a man who did not have to raise his voice as he cared little whether anyone heard him—and no one ever did.

"This droopy mammal," hissed Shiv, "cow-eyed and inscrutable, will kill us all."

"The boss don't even know Easy goes out on them installation pieces," added Bleaker. "He finds out about this the lot of us'll be found on an empty lot with our future round our ankles."

"And our ears stuffed with mini veggies," hissed Shiv.

"Let me talk to the boy," muttered Mr. Flak. "He trusts me."

No one heard the older guy.

"Death," grunted Moray.

Mr. Flak visited Easy's apartment for a friendly chat on the matter of the boys' decision to send him to the ivory yard. As he waited for Easy to show, the boys planted a bomb on each corner of the building in a deliberate deviation from mob hit method. Only one went off, obliterating Mr. Flak and the apartment, and the feds suppressed knowledge of the others thinking it was another covert job gone sloppy. Thermidor clocked the mob style but concluded it was a rival gang—maybe Betty getting above her strata. Considering Easy and Mr. Flak were both dead of dispersion, he declared gang war.

Easy meanwhile went on the skitter deep underground in Beerlight City, too tired and tangled to retaliate. Had he offended, or been offended against? At what point had he diverged into this dumb fugitive routine? He knew that among those who suspected his survival he was banished. He wept tears thick as glue.

But he finally found he wasn't alone regarding the masks. There was even a support group for crooks in just his situation. One night he was listening to one of his brother sufferers address the group. "My name's Josh," the brother was saying. "And I've been wearing Newt Gingrich's face for . . . three years now. Unlike many of you, I can never feel pride. But I'm resolved to live with the abuse, the scorn, the hatred—and live life as best I can. That's all I have to say." There was applause as Josh sat down. Easy later heard that a plastic surgeon had altered the mask to Boris Karloff by shortening the forehead.

But that evening as Josh sat down, Easy beheld a pale horse sitting to his right—she was the sleekest creature he'd ever seen. After the meeting she approached him. "You don't need this any more than I do, tusker."

"So why you here?"

"Ill will hunting. I'm Lady Miss V. Short for Voltaire—I run the Fist of Irony under Valentine Street. The meek are welcome to the earth, Easy." The pony girl led him across town and down a stairwell to a basement entrance. She pointed out a light meter over the door to measure PVC gleam intensity and took him in.

The Fist of Irony illuminated all the ghostly bones of the heart.

Rather than just biting the bullet, these people strapped on a feedbag. Among the laser-sprayed crowd were Chewy Endeavor, a skeleton glossed with wetlook leather, Annie Drawback, who'd disconnected her headskin to make it a draw-off woman hood, Ted Gloot, a man trapped in a cop's body, and hundreds more who, sick of being stared at in drab America, had resolved to legitimize the stares. Someone had grown a beard consisting entirely of facial muscle. Others had directly stained their skulls with a likeness of their own face so as to retain personality in the grave. A black guy had had himself tattooed all over with the U.S. flag so that police assault might result in prosecution. Couples into acting out alien abductions found common cause with the enema crowd. Ariel Hi-Blow was such an invert he stuck himself to the ceiling and put a mirror on the floor. "Molecular solvent," he laughed, and Easy looked up, startled. "I can see up your pants."

FMJ the gunhead wore a bullet suit and had had Lady Miss construct a giant Charter Arms .44 Special to his precise specifications.

"Tonight's the night," he said.

"Go girl," yelled Ariel from the ceiling.

The Caere Twins were in the corner with a guy in a void coat—one pushed an arm in up to the elbow and brought it out dripping with ectoplasm. The man extruded an etheric valve and slathered them in blown ghost—the entire corner bulbed into a pullulating chrysalis, sickly with spinelight. Peering at the indistinct forms which wrestled within the calyx, Easy was hustled on past a series of doors. "Tug-of-War Room—don't go in there. Hillary Room—private party. Firing range—need a license. And here's my chamber." Lady led him into a stable. "America kisses with its mouth closed, Easy. Want to try something?" She placed a bit between her teeth, separating her jaws, and buckled the strap behind her head.

"We can't do this, Lady," stammered Easy. "It's unnatural—we're different species."

Lady shrugged off her clothes and knelt over, gleaming white. Easy felt like an airbag was being deployed in his skull. An explosion sounded over the building as FMJ reached for the sky.

Two whole years passed. Easy became part-owner of the club. Moving in a different world, he kept clear of the mob. For a crook to become attached to his disguise was an offense without duplicity. It was rejection—growth, even. Like others at the Fist, he'd given up trying to deny the worth of worship. Holdup masks never went out of fashion—one afternoon Larry Crocus, Moray, Shiv, Bleaker and Barry Nosedive were due to perform a heist behind the faces of a regular menagerie. They were inside the vault when Shiv, who had selected the face of a walrus, raised a gun at the others.

"Cut it out, Shiv," they laughed nervously. With a rubbery flourish, he drew off the walrus mask to reveal that of an elephant.

"Fortezza!" gasped Larry Crocus.

"That's right," said Easy. "Don't let anyone persuade you character takes orders."

Nosedive pushed forward, the ears of his dog mask flapping. "Hey we gave you the cod eye!"

"I have different information."

Crocus, who wore the face of a pig, gestured to Easy with his snubgun. "Where's the face we shut."

"This is who I am." He drew a bead on Crocus. "And these beans want planting."

"Four guns to one, Dumbo," honked Moray from behind a cat face.

At that moment, Sam "Sam" Bleaker tore off his horse mask to reveal that of a horse.

"Who the hell are you?" shouted Crocus as the pale horse aimed her gun. "What you do with Bleaker and Shiv?"

"You bore me," said Lady.

"Tied up in a closet at the gang fort," said Easy. "They didn't come along on the bomb run, after all."

"So it's about the old man. We don't got any gripe with you Easy but I'll put you on a keyboard if I have to."

"I don't bluff empty armor, guys. Lemme ask you, is crime what happens when you miss the target, or hit it? I put glue in your masks."

The three mobsters dropped their guns and began scrabbling at their heads as Easy and Lady Miss backed out of the vault. It was Ariel Hi-Blow's molecular glue. A scream tore out as a face came away with a fake.

An elephant never forgets.

VOTIVE: CHALICE
from *Beauty Is Convulsive*
Carole Maso

3, 7 and 9 are your magic numbers. Are your lucky numbers. You put them in a glittery box. You add a pink ribbon, a drawing, a lock of hair. You are no fool. The end is nearing. You draw a right foot, a right foot. Right foot.

You return now to the women. In the calm violence of your being. You draw a right foot. As you drag yourself across the page to this final place of desire.

Your tears are nails. You hold them in your mouth. That saltiness, Calvary. The women praying their dark rosary—the tone of the cross, 10 our fathers, 10 hail marys, the drag and hum of the cross.

Cackling clutching rattle your fetus in a bottle. Formaldehyde. You are no fool. Singing Mexican drinking songs. Your country of broken blood and roses. Your hands arranging flowers in the dark. You finger your pendants, charms.

Forcing the ludicrous death head between your breasts—a sugar skull.

Laughing madly fingering dancing last things, imagine fingering, you draw with speed. Slap paint.

Free. The V of *Viva, Vida*—a dipping up and down. Slap paint.

In the upper register a frieze of androgynous profiles shedding tears.

From the operating theater looking up you hear voices and you are dying again in the garden, whispering, and you are dying in their formal garden of posthumous appraisals and praise and disdain. Those plaster pedestals. *Leave me be.*

A pair of red legs severed from their body—and between them a pair of lips.

Hair on fire hair on fire tiny shrunken Frida heads. Tongues are lapping, lapping in the last grotesque. Total eclipse on fire. A dancing pair of lips. Insisting insinuating, separating now you see—

In one 1951 *Still Life* (now lost) the flagpole's pointed tip emerges inside the halved fruit's soft dark interior.

And I am still caught in it, in you again, and writing the Frida études and singing little patriotic songs demented songs let's hear one, in the bleak hilarity of the end. Lips lowered. Magenta. Wayward songs and love. Making a muffled song up.

away
a hand
an eye
everything we usually need a mouth a wing
hair on fire
look over there
It's like floating
Your hands arranging
Pulque—a kind of ambrosia . . .
Sing me into the end she begs.
Black rose of blood
flowering in the eye.
Crow feathers glittering in the corners of the room.
   Where does your life go? You put it in a box. Marked 3, 7, 9.
   Where does your life go? Fingering a necklace of hummingbirds
and crows and thorns
   dark corridor.
   down the dark corridor.
   to the crematorium.
   The visible wing of the misshapen angel.
   I am the disintegration, you scrawl, you scratch, paw, dark
corridor. Are you leaving then?
   No.
   Touch me with your disembodied hand. It will be like floating,
living some.
   How bad do you want it?
   —other side.
   carrying a wooden box.
   other side tonight.
   Men in black ascend double staircases carrying a wooden box but
you are watching the solar eclipse.

Not yet.

But you are singing off-color songs in front of a falling curtain of velvet and blood. In the furious theater of you.

Men ascend looking, looking for you.

But you are out painting solitude.

drawing a right foot.

drawing

hair on fire. Hair on fire. Shaking your fetus in a bottle.

Frida adored children

The tone of the box 10 our fathers

the hum of the box. More our fathers

They are ascending double staircases with roses and weeping.

But we are in another corner of the dark garden altogether

force-feeding each other flowers.

What links us to each other is a tendril, a fragile line of paint, a word.

It's like floating. Sort of. Hair on fire. Body. Ashes. Hair on fire. Smirking

Goodbye on fire

Fetus in a bottle.

Viva la vida she writes in blood red with only one week left to live. *Viva la vida.* Amputated leg and life on fire. The grave we dig all night.

The grave we dig all night now.

Dress of fire halo, tendril.

Toward the end of June when her health improves she asks,

What are you going to give me now as a prize since I'm getting better. I'd like a doll best.

The strange dancing legs.

I would like a doll most.

She covers her wooden leg with boots made of red leather with Chinese gold and bells embroidered. One more time she dances. But only once. Heartbroken. Hair on fire. How badly tonight.

Life. Begging for it by then. Remembering she smiles.

Dwindles.

A perfect day: make love, take a bath, make love again.

And sucking drugs and roses. *If you could feel what I feel now.*

And she carves a rose. The drone of the box and the cross and the word. *love, love.*

Knife through the succulent melon. Knife through. All the weeping fruit. She whispers, bites my ear but gently blurs, seduction, love, *no blood*, she whispers, biting as-*Shh-Shh-or they'll hear.*

Men ascend with dirges but.

With glory be to the Father and to the Son but.

Men ascend with testimonies, reviews, dirges but you refuse. With double recriminations but you refuse. Carrying their wooden box but.

And we are dying in their formal Gardens of recriminations and petty jealousies and mean spirited judgments. Falling off the ludicrous pedestal. Breaking into arms and legs. Dance away. Resilient one. Trying to keep up. A three-legged race.

Men ascend with passions, compliments but—

The names painted in pink on her bedroom door now are:

Maria Felix

Teresa Proenza

Elena Vasquez Gomez

Marchila Armida

Irene Bohus

Maria Felix you cry!

Men ascend

As you step over the love-lorn woman cup of poison fallen dead at your blue door, cupped your hands reveal a little bird, a box, a 3 7 9

Your very blue door, then door of earth, you wave the fetus cackle babble drugged: abyss

the pigeon made mistakes
it made mistakes.

Instead of going North it went South
It thought the wheat was water
It made mistakes.

We look into the abyss. See birds and see a little deer and see your father closing the aperture now.

hourglass
pyramid a deer with 9 arrows
because I suffer, die.
Confined to an apparatus
her toes now blackening
   Te vas?
   No.

Hair on fire. Hair on fire. Halo.
In Aztec mythology and iconography the image of the deer stands
for the right foot.
Viva la vida she scrawls on my breasts. And I am trying to
extricate myself—in anticipation of the end.
Coward, you hiss.
Viva la vida.
Her ruined leg
Hair on fire fetus in a bottle chalice garden fur and lipped and
fruit yes there yes there yes good no yes O.K. more paint no scrape
it—no O.K. that hurts like that. O.K. and there and there—to reveal
9 arrows—upside down, now up, now down, hold there, look. oh
look—love

I am the disintegration.
The amputation.

Color of poison
Everything upside down.
Me? Sun
and moon
feet
and Frida
te vas?
No.

It's so hard.
Slapping paint.
Live your life. *Viva la vida* she writes.
Holding a melon on the eve of her death. Free.

Trying to let go of—
3　7　9
tenacity and wildness
of the day
of the night

And they force-feed you tubers and the end.
Men ascend double staircases with dirges but.
With Glory be to the Father and to the Son but.
You are driving in a Lincoln Continental convertible with Doctor
Polo a little free. Your jangling. Charms. Drinking a double tequila.
Men ascend with the wooden box looking for your body but.
She winks. *Viva la vida.* Free. Free of.

Life on fire.

Recalling your small twin votives: vision, devotion

Diego

Long corridor to the crematorium.

In the incineration she sits upright
In the furnace, forced by the heat. Her hair on fire like a halo.
Love. I am the disintegration. She smirks goodbye. She laughs and
waves on fire.

The *alegría* girl with glee.

The chalice of your life. Everything you held and hold.
Devour, hovering, glowering
burning chalice
red legs—red dancing lips.

Free
Free of.

Free.

Against the blue door you pose a moment longer. You wink and

then walk. And you walk one-footed down the hall, poor paw, poor
paw and you say *live* once more, and you say *love*

And you pick up a brush.

THE SON, HE MUST NOT KNOW
from *Southernmost*

Michael Brodsky

So much bloody effort required to procure the toy, the toy that is a man's, a father's, rightful due. All day, a day of calm, of springlike pronouncements, though of a pomp foreign to spring itself, yet towards evening a steady dark prison-bar drizzly downpour, and at the very moment when, having dragged home, to homey ground, the gadget vital to their operation, I had still to go out and borrow my toys from the storehouse.

Through the rain I carried my toys, after the toymaker tried, having never laid eyes on me before, to make pleasurable conversation and to show that as long as I paid my way there would be no pronouncements over a sick man's taste.

Smuggled into the home-front once I was sure the son was in bed, cuddling up with his bear, the toys, kept in their shell, were consigned to the closet until I was absolutely ready to proceed, that is, done with ablutions and with at last no reason on earth to be called away from the degradation site, labeled DS on the grid of my afflictions. And so, seating myself, I gave way to what the toys had to offer in the way of a slant on that self. It was hard this time, I must confess, to remain synchronized with the way of the toys, either because they were moving far too fast or not at all and so I had to fill, disappointed, their void with my own movement.

The son, he must not know the excesses, that is, the essence, of the father for in his father's house there are many closets. And so, the son, he must not know. After a night of riots he, the father, had to dispose of its-night's-toy as adroitly as he knew how. He tiptoed into the bedroom where wife and mother was breathing too lightly and placed it high up on the closet's highest shelf. There it lay, until daybreak, for after a night of riot—the malice aforethought of the toys having once again clogged every crevice of his own invention—the father found it harder than usual to sleep, as was his custom, till noon, being constantly interrupted by morbid anticipation of the rites of return. For what is borrowed must be returned and the toy was a borrowed toy. Of course, the father could have bought a toy, many toys, but on some level he must have preferred the borrowing even if, precisely because, it involved a borrowing visit and a returning visit (whereas an outright buying would have involved but a buying visit).

He tossed and turned, his dreams illuminated by a spasmed sketch of what they, in the toy store, must think of him, a grown man, head of household, returning what he was bound by law to return. The toys had been ejected from the gadget needed to operate them at home, to make them go. The toys were in the closet. But even if safely above the son's reach did this mean some toy was not still and at the same time inside the gadget, purring. Acts normally mutually exclusive were no longer so now that it was a question of fathers and sons, or rather, of fathers being found out, caught in the act, by sons, suspicious since a long time of something yet still not sure of that for which they were searching.

So he kept getting up to verify, not the continued presence of the toys on the highest shelf in the house, for that placement did not exclude their—the toys'—continued presence purring in the gadget slot reserved, in the living room, for any given toy. So he kept getting up to verify the nonpresence of the toy in the gadget's roomy, furry slot. But done verifying it was as if he had never verified or done far far less than verify. It was as if he had sabotaged all possibility of verification at some point unspecifiable in the very near future, of daybreak in the city. But such uneasiness did manage to momentarily quell the uneasy spasms familiarly preparatory to returning the toys and meeting their maker, now his maker.

The day dawned grim and bluish. A vacation day for him, no work, only drizzle, only the curve of self-generated tasks to appal the vacancy defined by no tasks imposed from without. He took the toys down from the shelf and when the apartment was empty at last marched with them out into the soccer field towards the subway station. He sat down on a bench in the soccer field, there where his son had so often played and he had refused without even the slightest hint of a reason for his aversion to come and watch. He sat himself down and removed the toys from their hide, to make sure he had them all, for there were several. He counted them over and over and over, fighting against distraction by their lurid surfaces. And then he put them back in their hide and their hides back in the bag nondescript as any other bag, only more so, more so. And he continued his walk across the soccer field, and along the river smelling of sulfurous waste. A solitary tug, secretly, expertly green though blue and white to the unpracticed eye—He, the father, wished that some one could keep him on the soccer field by the river as long as possible, making the starkest novelty out of its penury of props, its wintry staffage. He, the father, wished that some thing would weld him forever to the contour of the field and to the river beyond and to the sulfurous hide of that river beyond.

But the presence of all the toys in all their hides and all those hides in their bag did not prove that the toys were not still at home, in the gadget's slotty slit, just waiting to be discovered by the son on his return from school, satchel slung over his shoulder, mouth a-work with bubble gum, a normal lad, with no need, with every right not, to be afflicted by the sins of the father's toys. There was no warranty that the toys, every single one of them, were not still at home, in the place most conspicuous for a son's recovery.

How he dreaded the moment of the toys' return to its maker, moment of contact with the smug little faces of the makers, at war among themselves yet never averse to parasitizing some plausibly common enemy shot down, compliments of this ghastly addiction, in their midst. How he loathed their conspiratorial glances over the counter, over his head but not, contrary to what they believed, over his head. For they assumed one so preoccupied with so many toys must be a bit pudgy thereabouts, either to be desiring so many in the first place or from the self-abuse consequential to mismanagement of those so many. Maybe it wasn't even the number of toys. But he had to guard against assuming that others shared his belief in the number of borrowed toys somehow mitigating the scandalousness of the activity they enjoined. The toy activity.

How he, the father, dreaded return of the toys, the waiting for them to verify that all the toys were in fact intact, as pure of defect as when they had been rented a day ago or several years ago, during puberty's perilous midnight. But now, he saw it now, under the soccer field's leafless catalpas, his only guarantee that all the toys had been returned, were, that is, no longer on the highest shelf in the house or in the toilet or in the gadget's innermost furry slot of a slit—the only guarantee would stem from a protracted attendance on their—the makers'—perpetration of a merciless scrutiny on the body of the toys. So the act that he had most dreaded and often did not wait to undergo completely (imagining as he fled that he heard those makers' sneering imprecations on his sloppy elusiveness)—the very act he most loathed . . . was the act he now most craved to reassure himself that he had managed successfully to withhold, far from his schoolboy son, all the evidence, all the brandishable evidence, of his affliction. So this must be the purpose of the toy life—to create these shifts in perspective, i.e., meanings—preferably on a soccer field denuded of all bloom and at best impaled on a few catalpa stumps. Only through the toy act could a single event— encounter—come to have an opposite valence at last. Now he was looking forward to the encounter he had dreaded most among all those constitutive of the act of toying. Now he was looking forward to his meeting with the makers, the smug little makers, or rather, "looking forward to" had a new meaning, a capsized meaning. Now he was hoping, the father was, to prolong the very event that he had most dreaded and that had accounted for so much sleeplessness. An encounter with his makers was the crucial confirmatory finish to a night of riot, merest hallucination outside the context of such a finish. If he had bought those toys instead of renting them then there would have been no encounter to be looking forward to and so he might have ended up channeling the frenzy now consecrated to mastering horrified anticipation of their makerly contempt— elsewhere, far far far from whatever it was that made the act of toying an authentic act. He might, living the toy life without benefit of the straitjacket of return, have ended up a toy himself, bandied about on the trading floor.

And so bravo I say, he said, bravo! bravo! for the makers eyeing him smugly, eyeing smugly my overnight gluttony. He thought once again of leaving the toys in a hurry, without awaiting the truculent nod, reluctantly conferred, that all was as it should be. But then there would be no craved guarantee from without, definitive because obtained under conditions of excruciating shame. But hadn't he opened up the nondescript sack on the soccer field to verify that indeed all toys, beneath the catalpas, were present. But verification could not negate—couldn't he get that through his thick fatherly skull—some other moment in the process. For the reality of the toys was a process and his sullen stabs at verification could only injure that process. All stages coexisted. There was no such thing as contradiction. The toys were in his hands on the soccer field, there where the tugs only appeared to be bluish grey, yet still at home, not even on the highest shelf but inside the furry slit of the gadget, secreted in the most attention-getting way, hidden in a way that was more overt, more of a message, than throwing them, unzipped, across the kitchen table. For no verification, no such prophylaxis was as powerful as the image of that horror: the son's promised end of coming straight upon them, the toys, and failing to himself digest these leavings of his father's trespass. That was a film more gripping than any definitive verification had the power to impair. That was more powerful than verification/nonverification. The horror pursuant to the son's discovery and consequent revulsion subsisted, then, in a plane that was vastly inaccessible to the comfort of data derived from measly stratagems of verification.

I circled around the site several times, making sure nobody I knew was within eyeshot, and soon the whole street was deserted as if alert to the crucialness of the spectacle. But at the moment of entering the toy boutique I was still not clear whether in fact some of the toys were not still at home and in a position supremely compromising to the delicate boyhood of my son, and so I was torn between running home to verify, that is, re-verify, and allowing the maker to spread out each item for inspection, a common enough procedure, but one for whose entirety I never allowed myself to remain, being so overwrought as I was with fearing despair for the visible grimaces of his contempt for my predilections, whereas, in fact—I could see it now!—strictly speaking—I could see it now!— inspecting he was never in the least interested in the light each toy might cast, in its present linkage to my bulk, on this or that paraphilia of the moment, but rather, but only, in determining whether they—all my toys together—were still shipshape enough to rent to some other.

So here is where telling rescues the obvious, one stumbles on the unforeseen and what is the unforeseen but articulation of the obvious, the all-too-obvious, the too obvious to be rescued, that is, articulated, and therefore transformed into something new and fragile. He, the toymaker-cum-store manager, alone with his tools on a windy night in the middle of the day, was suddenly and already a pivot point, a pillow shot, resonating towards the next customer, his eyes greedy with anticipation of just the oleaginous defect to displease that worthy, whereas I was still slumbering (misreading his gaze) in the present casting a retroactive ray of reprobation on the night's riot spread out before him and in which he had not the slightest interest, veering as he was futurewards.

Between the two of us—the two of us incarnated in the gaze I lent him—embodied past, present, and future, thereby transmogrifying a simple stolid encounter stuck in a single time zone. I waited for him to compute the sum of toys and assure me with an indifferent grunt all was in order, and therefore no need for fear, at home on the sofa, the bed, the highest shelf, in the toilet, of their continued presence. He grunted but no grunt satisfied. Perhaps he was being strangely negligent and miscomputing. How get a definitive response. He was waiting for me to leave, no further reason to stay. If only I could manage to substitute some anguish irrelevant to all this so as to distract myself from its overwhelming resonance in a world otherwise anguishless. But no anguish was forthcoming, no other anguish materializing to create a sense of far too many anguishes to permit focus on a single one.

So nothing to do but trudge out into the inscrutable cold, under the horizon blood-red as a mallow's subtropical heart, except where pierced for all time by skyscraper accessories: belts, fins, scrimshaw. Nothing for it but to button up and leave and assume that nothing had been left behind at home for the son to uncover, even if that image, of his coming home to my vices, was so mesmerizingly veridic as to vitiate every conceivable reassurance of its impossibility. How annihilate it, that sonny image, or somehow make friends with it, how.

The son must not know yet the son must know. I want the son to know. About the toys. Father-son-toys. Why not be more explicit? Why not call things by their right names? But to call the toy by its right name is to impoverish it, to extract the beautiful aura conferred, through no fault of its own, by *toy*, that is a wrong name and at the same time a more generous, general name. No thrashing free of this menstruum of wrongness and greater generosity. Father-son-toy. The soccer field swamped with tugs and catalpas. It must be called a toy but not just for purposes of concealment. For purposes of aggrandizement, not of myself, the father, but of the experience with which I have been burdened, saddled, through every fault of my own, and to prove myself, father, noncommensurate with the fit of a certain straitjacket—father.

The toy debauch, the toy affliction, the toy affair, demonstrates among other things that the act most loathed—encounter with a clerk of the court—is the act most devoutly wished because the only road albeit through shame to authentic warranty. The toy episode, the toy affair, demonstrates that the toymaker's scowl, because it inflicts a painy shame and shameful pain, does not lie, installs me in a world beyond the need for verification where contradictions no longer rampantly subsist untamed by the law of mutual exclusion. The scowl ensconces at last in a world of either/or. Either the toys were returned or they remain on the highest shelf in the soccer field's smallest closet. When my son came home the toys were definitively gone. He never suspected the enormity of my debt to toys, to their maker and taker. He never suspects that it is only through this marginal event that I am able for the first time to tell the father/son disease as I live it, as it was meant to be told. And by naming wrongly and in general—father, son, toy—marginality salvages itself from the slagheap of the too-specific and becomes everybody's autobiography, that is, cure. Only through toys, oh my son, and the father-son-toy triad, oh my son, do I worm notochord into that robust territory (of father-son business ventures: foreign direct investment in good health and good housekeeping) too long estranged from a claimstaking prerogative as rightful as anybody else's; my own.

THE SUBSTANCE
Dennis Barone

All these occupations would not have had any concrete audience had they not been well-rehearsed in logical sources and moral reasons. The others are to direct a slow stroll down the edge of an individual's conversation. His spoon to his mouth; his eyes to the fading moon: this kind of harmony tackles the initial precautions taken to protect his own projections on the stage. Fantasies, that is, face-to-face interactions, appear to be in line with the real crime of this confidence man. Betrayed, famous music at three o'clock also entered the program before us.

Next, there is the old, persistent question of deception, the highlighted that becomes the convenient label for standard parts. Quick now, one illustration of this may be the smile on an actor's face in profile. There are grounds for believing practice makes perfect. There are grounds for believing that the desire to perform suggested the individual's significance to others, to me, to the most skilled and patient—to Beatrice. Upon careful observation a particular performance with the full round of routines had to some extent an expressive interaction with these fish and potatoes men. This loyalty from which a tattered man always chases a sparrow can be made to give the impression of the ideal doctor. Consider aspects of a "complete recall." Consider the laborers who must rely on the good breeding of their audience. Everything, then, seems to have to do with impressions.

This slip of the tongue, in spite of our willingness to continue with the production, is not meant to image the hair-dye or make-up of the least sophisticated. It is the reason we began to act, after all. It is the reason why Beatrice had whiskers all throughout the first act. These were hard times and a fifteen-year-old boy who drives a car or drinks in a tavern is undesirable in the best of times. Beatrice would lay down the law, such as it was, or else she would lay down the body itself, magnificent! The American law became intolerable, a blue line down the page. Who did it? we wondered, but we were never to be consoled. Right now somewhere else at this precise moment someone is doing something else. While the people in the fields move, the people in the rooms are immovable. Just ask Beatrice. Just ask the audience. It is raining and that is all that has brought them inside this evening.

How far is it possible to go with the performance if it is a sacred thing? The false one that fabricators assembled for us the poorest of the poor watched from rooftops and hence perpetuated their lowly position. We relied on Beatrice for the truth as well as for grand performances. The individual is like that, something that must be enacted and portrayed, a professional. No more, please, of your "let it ride." Participants, we have taken to the stage all of your most valued impressions. She won't be flattered that quickly and still more must follow. I went home and put on the new jeans, but already they felt a little bit too tired and worn, a bit too close to the skin.

If the members of Beatrice's troupe were to disengage from her, then Robert's cue word would just have to be "propel." We were that firm about it. We were actors and actors perform. But who had written the scene, the dominant one that only Beatrice could play? We ought not to assume it, but she can ill afford to wear a fixed smile throughout this tragic scene! She can ill afford to doze off a bit! She better stay alert and stop pretending to read that old book of hers! We will adapt ourselves to the well-dressed gentleman, otherwise.

Robert, though, speaks too much about bedrooms in lower-class houses, of kitchens and bathrooms and all that is done to the human body. His methods are too real. They become openings to the back regions of business buildings, to the private Bacchanalian reveries of an executive. We speak to one another and emphasize the nature of the conflict, the pitch of the denouement. We speak to one another so as not to think of him as the sole force operating here. We remain teammates ready to kick the ball back to Beatrice whenever and wherever we are asked to do so. Play on. We are the performers who put on the show.

A final point must be made about backstage revolutions. This will involve two types of secrets. They might be called the political and the criminal. Agents of the underground not only find their condition, their faculties, their conduct exactly as if it were hardly their share of the business, but all the office stratagems, intrigues, unspoken feelings and bluffs share a community of fate with the failures of the stage. It just had to happen.

It is to be noted that the dignity of the oral tradition had no place in the new theater. Robert saw to that. In a very limited manner Nelson aligned a party of progressives with Beatrice and her company. I think this is true. Together we put on a show that delighted every audience. But backstage activity often takes the form of a council of war and once again, despite our "allies," we were defeated. It seemed that very soon we would even run out of paper on which to propose a performance or impress a potential producer.

In the course of my last conversation with Beatrice she broke down. She could no longer even appreciate my infinite tribute to her—for Nelson, after certain unspeakable grimaces and gesticulations, had turned against her, too. It appeared that Robert had won and that the theater as we had known it terminated before a furtive public. Harry Mulisch tried to speak of this in his novel *The Last Call*, but doodling or going away to imaginary places— perhaps because that reality of which he spoke so eloquently was just too troubling—ruined the architecture of his prose, made it all too diffuse.

I have considered one subject, for one reason and one alone: my undying love for Beatrice. Might I expect her to unbend just a little sometime soon? I would like the therapeutic gratification of her non-verbal activity, of her smile. In any case, many of us are willing to tell our secrets to the same specialist if it will do us any good in meeting our unquenched desires. Whatever it is that generates human desires, few remove the mask behind which they hide their marijuana smoking, their telephone voice, their appeals to the other to be shown themselves. This, you see, is the substance of the theater as we have understood it when under Beatrice's benevolent hand. In short, I advise all to rehearse the routine, to enter ethic organizations, to play dumb on dates, to forget about the theater given that dramaturgical rules rule us both on stage and off. They are the only rules that all of us share. They are the richest ingredients of air. Breathe deep, all furies of the night.

Snow White and Her Seven Dicks
A Fairy Tale of Tails

Janice Eidus

The walking, talking, detached dicks of seven Rock Stars, past and present, are lined up outside my hotel suite, which is huge and magnificent. My four-poster bed is king-sized. My windows reveal a view of the city at night, stunning, aglow. A chandelier on the ceiling glitters.

Room service is in and out, bringing me the best champagne, the most flavorsome caviar, the sweetest chocolates bursting with the juice of cherries.

The reason I'm here, in this luxurious hotel overlooking the park, is because I, Snow White, the Beautiful and Famous Best-Selling Novelist, am touring the country on a multi-city book tour, and today is a special day. Today is the day my most recent novel, *Hot Spot*, is Number One on the Best Seller list. Until today, I've been number three, and number two, but never Number One.

The reason that the dicks of seven Rock Stars are lined up outside my hotel door today is simple: they're my reward for being Number One.

Years ago, long before I ever dreamed of becoming a Beautiful and Famous Best-Selling Novelist, I was the one waiting in line outside the Rock Stars' hotel rooms, along with hundreds of other nubile, horny, desperate female groupies. While we waited in line all those long hours, we spoke only of our unrequited, passionate love for this or that Rock Star, of how we yearned, desperately, to be the sole object of the Rock Star's desire.

When we were lucky enough to be one of those chosen to enter the Rock Star's room, we obeyed commands: lie still, spread your legs, blow me, bite me, ram me, suck me, eat me, bend over, do it with my manager, my roadie, my brother, my wall-eyed, illiterate childhood best friend. We performed for them in threesomes, and foursomes, with men and women. We danced naked, we hung from the ceiling, we cleaned up their puke, we cooked up their heroin for them.

Or, well, the *others* obeyed these commands. I never got further
than a few French kisses, a quick hand on my breast, a peek under
my ruffled panties. I, Snow White, had gotten a reputation as The
Virginal Groupie. It started when I was twelve, standing in my very
first line outside a hotel door. I'd confided in the others that I was
still cherry, and word got around to the Rock Stars and that was that.
I became an object of curiosity. Not that there weren't lots of other
prepubescents hanging out, sometimes jailbait even younger than I,
and the Rock Stars didn't hesitate to give those girls all the dick they
had. But those girls had all "done it" before. About me, they'd say,
"Uh oh, it's Snow White, The Virginal Groupie," and they'd bounce
me on their laps, affectionately tweaking my nipples and patting my
butt, before they called in the next girl standing outside the room,
usually an 18-year-old, six-foot-tall aspiring model from Wichita.
    The Rock Stars always insisted I remain to watch. This excited
them even more, having The Virginal Groupie as their audience. I
sat quietly on the sidelines, desperately wishing that I could be the
one tied to the bed, that I could be the one being hit over the head
with a bottle, having hot wax poured all over me, spreading my legs
for the Rock Stars' dicks.

⁓

All we groupies ever really wanted from the Rock Stars was four
things, which didn't seem too much to ask. We wanted them to
perceive us as individuals, not as nameless, faceless sets of tits and
asses jumping at their commands. And we wanted them to reveal
intimate, true things to us that they'd never before revealed to a
living soul, the things they didn't dare tell *Interview* or *Rolling
Stone*. We wanted expensive, gaudy presents. And, finally, we
wanted those Rock Stars to fall madly in love with us, so that after
our one night together, they'd be changed men, yearning, pining,
and lusting for us. We wanted them to return to their homes in
Malibu and St. Tropez and to write the greatest songs of their
careers for us. We wanted them to marry us, and never to sleep with
anyone else as long as they lived.
    But we never got those things. Whenever the Rock Stars fell in
love, it was with assorted socialites, actresses, and models with
names like Tisa, Tara, and Tiara. It was never with me, Snow White.

⁓

But that was then. This is now, and there are seven Rock Stars' dicks lined up outside my hotel room door. I'm The Virginal Groupie no longer. I'm the Beautiful and Famous Best-Selling Novelist with the Number One Book, and I gave up on Rock Stars years ago. I grew tired of yearning for the unattainable, for men who thought only with their dicks. I wanted to be the one in control. I wanted power. So I re-invented myself. I got myself a literary agent, and began writing steamy, sexy books. I've been around the block plenty of times since then, and, believe me, I'm never the one left in the lurch, yearning, pining, and lusting.

Still, in honor of my days as The Virginal Groupie, I've tied my hair into two girlish pigtails with pink ribbons. Apart from these two ribbons, though, I'm unadorned, stark naked, ready to greet the seven Rock Stars' dicks in my birthday suit, the way they so often used to greet me. Because I'm a Beautiful and Famous Best-Selling Novelist, I can afford to work out with a personal trainer and to eat the best and healthiest foods. My breasts and thighs are perfect. My body is bathed in an earthy, musky scent. My eyes are bedroom, come-hither eyes; my lips are lush and pink.

"Well," I say loud enough for the seven dicks to hear me, from my prone position on the king-sized, four-poster bed, "which of you shall be first?"

I hear cries of "Me!" "Me!" "No, Me!" outside my door. I wrap my tongue around a chocolate. I take a sip of bubbling champagne. Giddily, I call out, "Let's start with an Oldie-But-A-Goodie, one of the older dicks. No," I amend that, "two oldies! Salvatore! Curtis Lee! Come in here!"

And in they come: the dick of Salvatore, the pompadoured, Brooklyn born rocker from the fifties, lead singer of Salvatore and The Six Stars, heartthrob of city girls everywhere, side by side with the dick of Curtis Lee Grant, the raw country boy from the Deep South. These are their youthful dicks of course, from when they were at the heights of their singing careers, before Salvatore grew fat and Curtis Lee grew too skinny, bald and alcoholic. Salvatore's dick walks just like a Brooklyn boy: tough and swaggering. Curtis Lee's dick swings raunchily from side to side, mimicking the way his whole body moved back when he opened for Elvis, playing those Southern honky-tonks, long before either of them got rich and famous and inspired teenage girls everywhere to swoon and sweat.

They climb up—six inches each, at least, maybe seven—onto the foot of my bed and stand erect, alert, gazing at me with awe, reverence, and lust.

"Yo, Snow White, I love your books," Salvatore's dick says gruffly to me, in his thick Brooklyn accent. "They changed my life."

"Honey, your beautiful, sexy novels about the trials and tribulations of contemporary women and men make me bawl like a baby," drawls Curtis Lee's dick.

They each hold out copies of *Hot Spot* for me to sign. "Maybe later," I say coolly. I lie there, legs apart, naked, stroking myself, playing with the pink ribbons in my pigtails.

The next thing I know, Salvatore's dick has scampered up between my breasts and is rubbing me hard, and Curtis Lee's dick is down below, burrowing inside me, a little locomotive of lust. Salvatore's dick bites my nipple, gently, then harder. Curtis Lee's dick expertly plays with my G-spot. I'm enjoying myself, but I've also got other things on my mind, more important things. Like, how to dress for my next TV interview, and how to spend all the royalties I'm earning. Just the way they used to have more important things on their minds back then, when, even as the other girls were obediently biting and sucking, and I was obediently watching, they were on the phone with their managers, setting up tour dates and arguing over the cover design of their next album.

"Okay, boys," I say, yawning, "that's enough. Sing for me." Right on cue, Salvatore's dick, perched on my left breast, breaks into a heartfelt rendition of his biggest hit, "Coney Island Cutie." Curtis Lee's dick, standing up tall and proud at the foot of the large bed, huskily croons, "Mint Julep Eyes."

"Not too bad, boys," I say, yawning again, "now tell me a secret."

"I'm not really a poor boy from Brooklyn," Salvatore's dick admits, shamefacedly, still perched on my breast, "I was a rich kid from Scarsdale."

"And I didn't grow up in the cotton fields," Curtis Lee's dick mumbles. "My dad's a Harvard grad."

Meanwhile, I hear shouts outside from the other dicks who want their turn. I send Curtis Lee's and Salvatore's dicks on their way without signing their books, or even saying thank you. I remember exactly how it's done.

~~

"Okay," I say loudly, "Rick and Slick, next!" And in they march, the little dicks of Rick and Slick. These dicks, too, are youthful, from the seventies, heyday of the cult-inspiring heavy metal group Mother Load, before Rick's face got pudgy and bloated, before Slick began looking like an aging hooker with a bad wig. From my days as The Virginal Groupie, I vividly remember Rick's fondness for whips and chains, and how he liked to be the one in control, spanking the girls. To show who's boss this time, I tie the two dicks to the doorknob. I'm all-powerful here, I call the shots, Gulliver in the land of the Lilliputians.

A long, thin whip, coiled in the closet, is waiting for me. Without any hesitation, I give Rick's dick a light smack here, and Slick's dick a light smack there, and then I smack them both just a tad harder. Between grimaces of pain, they harmonize on "Hey Girl, Get Goin', Fast," Mother Load's interminably long rival to Led Zeppelin's "Stairway To Heaven," while I keep smacking. When I can't bear to hear the chorus one more time, I untie them and put down the whip. "Pretty good, but watch those high notes. And now, a confession from each of you," I demand.

"Sometimes I can't get it up," says Rick's dick, sadly, rubbing his wounds.

"I can never get it up," says Slick's dick, looking at me with great big puppy-dog eyes, and holding out a copy of *Hot Spot* for me to sign, which I ignore, of course.

~~

Next, I opt for Bobby London and Sig Rooster. In sashays the skinny, pouty dick of the freckle-faced Bobby—whose career, like The Beatles and The Rolling Stones, began in the dark, smoke-filled clubs of Liverpool—and the manly, chocolate-colored dick of Sig, the Afro-haired, flower-and-bead-wearing San Franciscan guitarist, whose signature was the peace sign he made with his gorgeous, agile fingers at the close of every concert, melting the hearts of sweet young things everywhere.

I turn over onto my stomach. Together, Bobby and Sig enter me from behind as I bark commands: faster, slower, gentler, rougher, there, not there, there! We do this until I hear them panting with exhaustion. "Boys," I murmur, "it's showtime."

Bobby's dick goes first. He sits lightly on my butt and delivers a soulful rendition of "Lovely Ladies," the soft ballad that remained number one for over a year.

Then Sig's dick whips out a guitar from somewhere. He stands on my shoulder with military bearing, and with his little teeth plays a riveting "Star Spangled Banner," to express his fierce allegiance to me. His version may not be quite as good as Jimi's, but it's still pretty damned good, indeed.

"What have you got to say for yourselves, boys?" I ask, after Sig's dick takes a timid little bow.

Bobby says, pouting once more, "These thick, luscious lips aren't all mine. I use collagen."

Sig slumps his shoulders. "I was really a hawk, not a dove. All that peace and love stuff was bogus, just a way to get girls."

"Oh well," I yawn, ignoring their pleas for me to sign their copies of *Hot Spot*, "see ya sometime, boys." And off they go.

In struts the seventh and final dick of the day, all by himself, the black-haired, big-shouldered, beer-bellied Gavin Later, the self-proclaimed "White Trash Bad Boy of Rock 'n' Roll," known for his misogynistic tirades, drunken brawls, and no-show concerts. His startlingly teeny-tiny dick boasts a fetching tattoo of me—Snow White, the Beautiful and Famous Best-Selling Novelist—right on its tip. I lie on my back, knees up. He enters me fiercely, then pulls out all the way, then comes back harder, just the way I like it. Since his dick is to be my last of the day, my final reward, I let myself go. My orgasm is the stuff that wet dreams are made of: I heave, I gasp, I writhe, I moan, driving him all the more wild. We come in unison, also the way I like it. Still, I yawn very loudly afterwards, because that's the way the game is played. "Sing for me, boy," I say, through my yawn.

Obediently, he sits on my pillow, swinging his legs, shouting the words to "Bad, Badder, Baddest Bitch," the song that catapulted him to instant fame.

"Stop. It's Revelation Time," I command, interrupting him mid-song. He runs around my bed, jumping back and forth, a zig-zaggy,

manic path. "I identify more with the sensitive female characters in
your novels than with the insensitive male characters," he says,
landing on my pillow. "And I like to wear women's underwear," he
adds, swinging from one of the bed's four posts. I don't sign his
copy of *Hot Spot,* either.

When it's all over, I send the seven dicks away, despite their tears
and protestations. I call for room service and more bellhops arrive
with more champagne, more caviar, more cherry-filled chocolates.

I modestly pull the covers up to my chin as I sip and eat, while
another group of bellhops brings in the gifts the dicks have left for
me outside my door: a diamond ring; a bracelet made of emeralds;
a deed for a brand new house in Bel Air. I'm unimpressed. As the
Beautiful and Famous Best-Selling Novelist with the Number One
book, I can buy these things for myself.

The notes attached to the gifts profess the Rock Stars' dicks'
undying love for me. I toss both the gifts and the notes aside. I stand
up, untying my pigtails and discarding the pink ribbons. I comb out
my hair into sophisticated waves, and I put on my clothes, the kind
of clothes a Beautiful and Famous Best-Selling Novelist like myself
wears: a silk black slip of a dress, a tailored jacket, high-heeled shoes.

As I dress, I smile to myself, imagining the seven little dicks
strumming their guitars, singing their songs, yearning, pining, and
lusting for me, weeping, wailing, and shriveling up. I imagine them
reattached to their owners, sitting at night with copies of my books
in their laps, rereading my words, remembering, forever, our one
night together. I imagine them growing depressed, canceling tours,
spending the rest of their lives on the verge of suicide. I imagine
them getting arrested and being hauled off to jail for trying to climb
over my back fence, even though I've taken out a restraining order
against each of them.

I've had those Rock Stars' dicks once. I don't need them again.
They were groupies, not to be taken seriously, just today's reward
for being Number One. I'm Snow White, the Beautiful and Famous
Best-Selling Novelist. I can have any dick I want. And besides, I'm
going to be very, very busy, writing my next novel, the one destined
to sell more than all my other books combined, the one I shall title
Snow White and Her Seven Dicks: A Fairy Tale of Revenge.

BAKER BETTERLAUGH TODAY
A. G. Rizzoli

Being a chapter for a story with Betterlaugh hero, both in embryo and of undecided title.

"Well, no engagements for tomorrow," Victor Betterlaugh sighed regretfully as he studied his diary of dates, "but for Friday there's Miss Adeline Deloars to manipulate; well, that's comforting." Already retreated to his rooms, he retired thinking pleasantly of Adeline, wondering what he should do to make the day remembered. He fell asleep with the happy thought of approaching—and having—Zenith Manlimaid accompany him. "What's the idea of conscripting me?" Zenith protested as Victor urged acceptance.

"Look here, Zannie, this brand new five dollar bill is yours the moment you acknowledge receipt saying 'received of—five dollars for service rendered in accompanying—Betterlaugh to Miss Deloars, Friday, one o'clock.' "

The sight of the bill blinded Zenith to all thoughts of declination. That settled, the two men were at ease until Victor called with his car for his companion.

"Yes, Zannie, she's a perfect lady in every way, barely twenty-one, and no man to my knowledge has paid court to her," Victor volunteered as Zenith sought details.

"Probably not well-off and probably old-fashioned."

"Most unfortunate, none the less, quite true," Victor agreed. He became surprised to hear a familiar lusty voice hallooing him. Looking over Zenith's shoulders he saw Toilman Brightpit gesturing to stop.

"Hey, Vick, what are the chances to take in the cool, comfortable countryside this afternoon?"

"Nothing doing," Victor laughed, "but if you crave feminine company then hop in."

"Golly, how sensible you can talk at times, Vick," Brightpit flattered lustily.

Driving slowly roundabout in South Bend District, Victor finally parked his car in front of 821 Spotten Sandal Street, his companions evincing disappointment upon beholding the two-story, rustic-covered, rather common-looking house—though of better appearance than the neighboring—which they were soon to enter.

"How's this for keeping engagements? One o'clock sharp, and Addie, I'm simply dying to don that apron of mine the moment I reach your cosy kitchen. By the way, look what I picked up," Betterlaugh essayed familiarly as Adeline met him at the door. Surveying his companions, she took their introductions calmly, wondering how she could be sociable without neglecting Victor.

"Golly, what's in the offering?" Brightpit asked lustily as he saw Victor doffing his deep sea-blue slip-on sweater, preparatory to harness himself.

"This may be an afternoon of relaxation for you, Tub," Victor ventured, addressing Brightpit, "but to me it means hours of laborious work."

"And a chocolate cake it's going to be," Adeline exclaimed musically, surveying Victor and his two companions discreetly.

"Make yourselves comfortable, ladies and gentlemen, while to the kitchen I retreat," Victor suggested, leaving quietly. Familiar with the premises through force of habit, Victor moved about with enthusiasm, passed through the dining room, reached the kitchen, and then from a cubby within the pantry obtained his starchy white cook's apron and cap, the cubby containing among other things his file of recipes, spices, and utensils most generally used. Disdaining to neglect Victor for her new-made acquaintances, Adeline, too, preferred the kitchen, hinted that Victor's companions follow suit, else make themselves comfortable in the living or dining room. Brightpit readily assured her that he was amply capable of looking after himself, eagerly appreciative of the comfort of others at the same time, "but I'm not so sure about our man-of-the-hour pal, so untalkative and morose at times his very presence seems to take all the joy out of life."

"Never mind me," Manlimaid protested. "I'm charmed to meet Miss Deloars and shall endeavor to offer as little interference as possible. Silence is golden, it's said."

Presently all four were in the somewhat-compact kitchen, Victor stepping lightly about to tackle his task; Brightpit talking, arguing, asking, pacing restlessly about simultaneously; Manlimaid standing in the doorway to the dining room; and their hostess looking rather puzzled upon beholding the composite group of singular bachelors, eyeing occasionally Victor sympathetically, Brightpit cautiously, and Manlimaid wonderingly.

"All set and roarin' to go," Victor cried merrily as he had sorted needed utensils and prepared in their order needed ingredients, now sifting eagerly the flour.

"What! The dough or whatever you call it isn't ready yet?" Brightpit demanded lustily as he looked into the kitchen for the fifth time. "Had I known it, I could have had the best bakery in town deliver the most delicious cake imaginable. That gives me an idea. Show me your telephone so we can in the meantime chew on fruit-footed sweetmeats." He addressed Adeline, but seeing the telephone in the hall, stepped thereto, disregarding her attempt to offer objection. Manlimaid marveled at the way Victor mastered his fascinating task while Adeline, whenever the opportunity afforded, offered aid.

"In a minute, this wholesome batter will be ready for the oven," Victor hinted cheerfully. "Golly, I must hurry and have it in by two-thirty."

Meanwhile Brightpit communicated with his favorite candy shop, ordered a generous box to be delivered immediately, the saleslady assuring him delivery could be effected in fifteen minutes or thereabouts. Slowly accustoming himself to the environment, Brightpit learned in time through direct questioning that made Manlimaid blush and stare protestingly, taking his questioning too impudently, that Adeline's mother, semi-invalid, was in bed upstairs, that her father was a mechanic rather neglectful of the family, and that a brother likewise employed comprised the household.

"Into the oven of heat went the three pans of batter," Victor exclaimed, preparatory to gathering together utensils no longer needed.

"Most likely our best yet," his hostess flattered sympathetically. "Isn't that tall, handsome gentleman lively, rather restless though at times?" she reminded in a low voice. "And what can be ailing your other companion—so untalkative and unresponsive that I dare not talk to him directly?"

"Probably what to do with that five dollar bill in his pocket is blinding Zannie to all thoughts socially," Victor hinted casually, friendly.

"Come here, one and all!" Brightpit called lustily as the delivery boy left a bulky package. "This box of dainty sweetmeats at your disposal. If we had to wait until Vick's cake's done, we would be starving. Here, sister, take a handful."

"Count me out," Victor protested. "Tasting such sweetmeats would ruin my appetite for the homemade cake soon to grace yonder platter."

Helping himself out to five or so pieces, Brightpit passed the box on to Adeline; she in turn presented it to Manlimaid, who after some hesitation finally helped himself. Adeline, delighted at the goodness before her, too, finally picked herself a piece.

"Boys, she's all set for the filling, frosting followed," Victor shouted from—bringing his two companions once more into—the kitchen.

"But look at the watch—already three o'clock," Brightpit retorted, adding contemptuously, "We'll need a case of lemonade to down that stack of dough. That gives me an idea—and a quart of ice cream on the side." Again he telephoned his order with the request that the delivery be made immediately. "Brace up, Zannie, show some pep, and hang around and we'll yet see Adeline's dress wet all around," he instructed, when they were alone in the parlor. "What! Her mother in bed? Nothing like investigating to feel certain." Stepping kitchenward, he found Victor busily occupied in—what appeared to him—blending sugar and chocolate, Adeline watching attentively. "Stop! That's hot," he yelled, catching Adeline by her right forearm as she attempted to remove a saucepan. Sensing Brightpit's strong hold, to the point of nearly making her lose balance, she marveled at his strength and aggressiveness, and—now urged to let him see her mother—Adeline wondered if she might not yet be victimized, perhaps brutally attacked. With Victor agreeing to follow—and seeing Manlimaid trailing along—the quartet went upstairs, beholding presently in bed a rather plump middle-aged woman nervously—annoyed of face. Other than suggesting that the candies be brought upstairs, Brightpit behaved gentlemanly, in fact, no sooner introduced than sought leave. The doorbell ringing reminded him of the delivery due momentarily. Prophesying correctly, a case of assorted bottled water and a goodly supply of ice cream were soon available, Victor excusing himself to put on the finishing touches to his layer cake; the other three were persuaded to make merry in the adjoining dining room, Brightpit persuading Adeline to keep drinking lemonade, consuming three glasses before she felt herself full. That she took to the ice cream freely, too, encouraged Brightpit to feel aggressive. "She will be wet all around yet," he cautioned Zenith during a moment when they were alone. "Come on, sister! Do away with the ice cream before it boils itself away."

"Really, I can't down another spoonful," adding laughingly, "look at my belly—oh, how thoughtless I'm at times, I mean my stomach—full to the rupturing point. There isn't an inch of space left for Victor's delicious cake."

"Ah ha, better there isn't. We had better let Betterlaugh taste it first—to see if it's digestible."

"Wait till you see whipped cream topping this sweet-love chocolate frosting—won't it make your mouth water," Victor snapped back from the kitchen.

Finding herself more comfortable seated than stepping about, Adeline felt eventually she must seek relief, but hearing Brightpit calling lustily, her thoughts were directed elsewhere.

"Hey, Vick! Look what I found. Isn't she hot?" He made his way from the parlor to the kitchen via the dining room carrying to Adeline's embarrassment a small portable frame photo of a young lady barely draped. "And I thought your sweetie was pure-minded."

"Pipe down, Tub. Look lightly upon her faults and laud her virtues. Isn't the sight of this delicious cake watering your mouth?"

"Not by a long shot; neither is this photo. Hey, Zanny, look here. Just a dime a glance. Isn't she hot?" Brightpit thrust the photo into Manlimaid's sphere of vision.

"Enough to make stored-up steam-hot liquid love flow at random," Zenith commented rather humiliatedly.

The excitement over, no harm resulting, and seeing Brightpit returning the photo to where it was, Adeline felt her fullness urging relief, but feeling delightfully, excitedly withheld herself, though seeing only Manlimaid observable, she pressed into the region rather conspicuously in the way little girls do to overcome discomfort. Unable to avoid her movements, Manlimaid felt extremely uneasy with erectible pressure, sensing allied wetness imminent.

"Who shall be first to taste this tasty chocolate cake?" Victor shouted merrily, proudly displaying his culinary product, and placing the platter upon the dining table, looked surprised to see the group scattered, Manlimaid unduly burning of face.

"Ladies first!" Zenith laughingly answered, glad to be so readily responsive for once.

"Out of the pan into the fire jumped Vick's doughy bolognas," Brightpit retorted snappily.

"Satisfy your own appetite first, gentlemen, while I run upstairs for a moment," Adeline ventured, finding the moment opportunely to seek relief.

"Quite a clever girl: quiet, home-loving, and sympathetic," Zenith commented, breaking the silence hovering over them. "Still, I'd rather leave for the open than remain another minute."

"Brace up, Zan!" Brightpit retorted lustily. "Snatch a hug or two now and then, else grab her by waist."

"And help us bring back that boyish feeling," Victor intercepted. "Let's make weatherworn gargoyles stand up and take notice."

"What! Four-thirty already, and I should be in the office by four o'clock!" Brightpit exclaimed, studying his watch closely.

Their hostess returning and feeling delightfully relieved, having touched up her cheeks in the meantime, she felt enwrapped in joy, romancing a personality irresistibly fascinating. With Brightpit quieting down, poring over whether or not he should leave or continue to be the life of the party, allowed Adeline opportunity to laud Victor's comely creamy cake, the frosting showing creamy whirls decidedly appetizing.

"Hey, fellers! Let's decide one way or the other. Which shall it be? Save the cake or allow each person present a goodly quadrant piece?" Victor suggested merrily.

"With all the candy I chewed away, a slice one quarter inch thick is all I'll be able to bear. Get this clear, Vick. It's not that I distrust you, but I feel that I should be officebound right away."

"All right, I'll eat it all myself. Here goes a goodly quarter piece. Look at its fine texture. Look at its thick fillings and creamy frosting—not a drop of skimmed milk nor an iota of axle grease in it—nothing but fresh butter and cream and sugar and chocolate. Oh, boy, how my mouth's watering. Yes, Addie, our best yet," he admitted after insinuating the first mouthful, and a chunky piece it was. Adeline, after serving her guests steaming black coffee with cream on the side, sliced herself a modest piece. Manlimaid, hesitating, finally took a piece. And Brightpit, slicing the thinnest piece possible, ate it from his hand.

"Fine stuff, Vick! Fit for a king, that's that. Thanks all around; I must be going." In a moment he was off. Manlimaid, finding himself uncomfortable with desire, likewise left presently, leaving Victor and Adeline enjoying the cake they baked, and not yet half-consumed.

"Sure, Addie, another bite won't do us any harm," Victor hinted, helping himself to a modest piece.

Already after five, his hostess stepping excitedly about to prepare dinner, Victor found the interval a moment for much needed relaxation, and as was his practice, bade Adeline goodbye as the clock indicated six o'clock.

1934

from THE SEX SPHERE
Rudy Rucker

Lafcadio Caron hated the physical universe. As a Platonic idealist, he deeply resented any claims that the crass world of matter might have on immortality. So he devised a theory according to which any bit of matter eventually decays into light, and a second theory according to which light eventually gets tired and trickles into folds of spacetime; and a third theory according to which space and time will die of disuse once all mass and energy are gone. "Here today, gone in 1,040 years," he would say, twisting his features in desperate, irrelevant laughter. The man had problems.

But, yes, he was a genius. He spent much of his time slouched in a leather armchair in the University of Rome's physics library. Graduate students and foreign research fellows would cluster around him as he lolled there, long skinny legs stretched out. The legs were like grasshopper legs; and like a grasshopper, Lafcadio would rub his legs together as he talked, chirping and buzzing about Ultimate Reality.

His constant companion was a roly-poly Hungarian woman named Zsuzsi Szabo ... an exotic name which translates prosaically to Susan Taylor. She had short blond hair, high tartar cheekbones, huge pillowlike breasts, and a washerwoman's arms. The State had originally sent Zsuzsi to Rome to learn the latest developments in nuclear-reactor design. But instead she had attended Lafcadio's lectures, fallen in love and defected ... heedless of her Budapest family's fate.

Zsuzsi was a wizard at experimental design, and Lafcadio took her into his full confidence. They made a striking team: Fat Lady and Thin Man, Sancho Panza and Don Quixote, Earth and Fire. The graduate students speculated avidly about the pair's sex-life. It was, indeed, intense.

"You are my wild exotic particle," Lafcadio might say, mounting her. "Let me split you into quarks, my darling."

"Cling close, svheet one," she would respond, ardently reversing position. "I am absorber for your titanic energies."

Biologically, the union was barren. But Lafcadio impregnated Zsuzsi with the design for a beautiful second-generation proton-decay experiment. It was this experiment that led to the Mont Blanc laboratory's capture of a speck of degenerate hypermatter. Hearing the news, the proud couple named the particle Babsi (Hungarian for "little bean), and hurried to see it.

Aosta, Italy, February 8

Wet snow is falling. The sky is gray and it looks like there will never be a sun again. From some random crag we watch the slow crawl of lights up the valley . . . cars and trucks laboring through spaghetti-turns to the Mont Blanc tunnel. There in the distance is the tunnel's mouth, a small upside-down U, sad and surprised.

Moving closer, we see the concrete customs shed and tollbooths. Closer. A Fiat stops, the driver shows a pass. The car is colorless with dirt, the driver white with cold. Lafcadio.

Zsuzsi, for her part, is pink with breakfast, loud with pleasure. "Zo, finally vhe have a little Babsi."

"This would seem to be the case. If Signor Hu is to be believed." Lafcadio holds up a cautious bony finger.

They pull into the tunnel. *10Km*, reads the sign overhead, indicating the distance to the French end of the tunnel. The Mont Blanc tunnel is filled with an eternal roar, a Hephaestean clangor. Huge trucks labor past, shaking Lafcadio's tiny car. The light is yellow and smeary. Everything is covered with wet grit. The air itself seems to grow thick. *9 Km.*

Zsuzsi glances at the car's ceiling. "I hate it in here. All zat mountain over us. Kilometers and kilometers."

Lafcadio laughs his strangled laugh. "All slowly decaying, Zsuzsi. Slowly returning to the one." *8 Km.*

"I whish vhe vhere already zere," frets Zsuzsi. "I don't trust that Chimmy Hu to keep za Babsi stable. He doesn't really understand your zeory."

Lafcadio snorts briefly. "Doesn't believe, is more like it. No one but you, dear Zsuzsi, has really believed in my vacuumless vacuum, my cube of Absolute Nothingness. But only in such an incubator can Babsi live." *7 Km.*

"How much did Hu zay she vheighs?"

"Variable. Up to a full three grams," Lafcadio crows. "Can you believe that? Apparently she comes from a cascade of the most energetic proton-decays yet observed. And your mono-field caught her, Zsuzsi, swept her into the vacuumless vacuum. We'll celebrate with a trip to Venice, you and I." *6 Km.*

"Svheet dollink! But zlow down. Vhe're here."

They turn into a sort of underground parking garage. It's a hard turn to make, and the canvas-shrouded truck running behind Lafcadio's Fiat comes dangerously close to ramming them.

They're out of the car as soon as it stops, hurrying across the cold, damp garage to a door in the far wall. Lafcadio has a key. White light streams out, making a brief bright trapezoid on the garage's rough concrete floor.

Inside it's bright and warm. An old guard waves them on. They trot down the hall. At the end is a large room with a lot of machinery. A smiling Chinese man in tan corduroys and dark blue sweater greets them.

"Lafcadio," he calls happily. "Zsuzsi! It is stable."

"Zats vhonderful, Jimmy." Zsuzsi tosses her overcoat onto a chair. "Let's zee." She wears a tight red sweater, wide skirt and high boots. Pushing Jimmy Hu to one side, she leans possessively over her machine. Lafcadio crowds up behind her, watching over her shoulder.

The machine looks something like a video-game, with dead-black screen set high in a console. Pipes and cables writhe out of it like tropical lianas, brightly colored root-vines feeding on the satellite machines: vacuum pump, ion drive, gas chromatograph, differential analyzer, macroprocessor, monopole accelerator, quantum fluxer, quark scanner, relativity condenser, gravitomagnet, strong/weak force junction, supercooled bloog tank, hyperonic veebletweeter, two-tier furglesnatcher, black boxes, boxes, boxes, boxes. Lights blink, needles wag, speakers hum here deep under the mountain, far from the eye of God.

Behind it all is something that looks like a huge Beuys sculpture, a four-meter stack of iron plates interleaved with gray felt pads. Tubes and wires snake out of the felt, feeding the machines.

"Babsi," croons Zsuzsi, staring into the screen. Looking in with her, we see a pulsing point of light . . . neither far nor close, just there.

"It is werbling on a four-millisecond cycle," whispers Jimmy Hu. "Shall we cut into the resonance drive?"

"Don't ask me," chuckles Lafcadio. "All I know is that I'm right. A particle is the hypersection of a four-space construct,"

Zsuzsi grunts wetly and lets her hands drop down to a row of knobs. Close shot of her fingers diddling the dials. Her nails are short and bitten, lacquered pink.

Laboring whine of machinery being pushed to its breaking point, "You see," exclaims Lafcadio. "It is still growing! There is no practical upper limit to the size of a particle,"

Wunh-wunh-wunh-wunh-wunh-wunh-wunh: an alarm-hooter. Zsuzsi and Lafcadio are staring in at the golfball-size Babsi, but Jimmy Hu is worried now. He backs away from them, glancing up at the hooter, then back at the console.

"Don't try to manipulate it," he warns. Not at this energy density."

"Nonsense!" cries Lafcadio. "Listen to me, Zsuzsi! We must knot Babsi into our space for metastability. Use Hinton double-rotation."

Her sensitive, stubby fingers dance across the dials. The object behind, or in front of, the screen begins to spin. Another flick of the dials. Babsi flattens a little and dimples in at the poles. The sound of the hooter is faint and musical, synched to Babsi's growing buzz. Jimmy Hu's voice is shouting something, but the sound warps into a gabble.

"Z-axis," hisses Lafcadio. "Donut."

Zsuzsi is playing the console like this year's high-scorer. Babsi's polar dimples dig in and meet. The mottled manner flows in one pole and out the other. It's a torus now, a spinning vortex ring.

But then . . . as we stare at the Babsi the . . . spinning stops and . . . goes over to the room.

Babsi, Lafcadio, and Zsuzsi: the three are motionless, while all around them the blurred room races. Engine, impresario and operator: poised at the center of the merry-go-round gone mad.

"Tie the knot," urges Lafcadio. He is gaunt, gray, and wild-eyed. "Use XZ surgery and W-axis hyperflip."

You have the feeling the Babsi particle wants to escape, for the flowy little torus jerks back from Zsuzsi's touch of ruby laser light. She throws a switch and a glowing blue net of field-mesh holds Babsi fast. The surgical red ray cuts in.

The distant hooter is a dull, repeated scream, *aenh-aenh-aenh-aenh-aenh*. Look at Zsuzsi's fingers, slick with sweat.

Now the Babsi folds in on itself and two circles link. The shifting outline of a Klein bottle is there, a meaty bag whose red neck stretches out and punches in to eat its own bottom: a tortured hairless bird with its head stuck in its navel and out its ass. The world-snake. Klein-bottle Babsi-bean slides in and through itself, tracing impossible curves. Slowly it settles down, smoothing out and shrinking a bit.

The room has stopped spinning. Zsuzsi throws a relay, and the machines idle down.

Lafcadio laughs and hugs her. "Ready to take our baby to Venice?" As Zsuzsi watches, he draws out a tiny gold key and twists it in a little lock next to the console screen. There is a hiss of air and the screen swings down like an oven door. Lafcadio reaches in.

The space in there is funny. As Lafcadio thrusts his arm in the *front*, we see his hand angle in from the *side*. Undismayed, he seizes the little bean and takes it out.

Close shot of Lafcadio's palm. Resting on it is a spherelet. It glows slightly. There are lightly shaded lines on it, as on a peeled orange-pip.

"*Babsi*," croons Zsuzsi, motherly bosom aheave. "*Edes kicsikem*." Sweet little one. She prods it with a trembling finger. It shrinks away, avoiding her touch.

When the little sphere shrinks, the surrounding space distorts . . . It's like seeing Lafcadio's palm through a wrong-way lens. But then the Babsi bounces back, bigger than before. It tries to shrink away, and again bounces back. The space-knot is holding.

"Come zee, Jimmy," calls Zsuzsi. "Vhe really trapped a hyperobject."

Jimmy Hu edges back in the room, loosely laughing, shaking his head.

PPPPFFFFFFWWWAAAAAAPP!

A huge ball of tissue is flowing over Zsuzsi . . . eating her! Suddenly only one hand is still showing. Blood drips off the fingers as they clench, unclench, go lax. Bones crunch.

Lafcadio has been flung back against a bank of machines. His face is rigid with horror. Tubes and cables snap, gas is whistling out in foggy plumes, sparks are jagging, and now a sheet of flame sweeps across the room.

Lafcadio falls to his knees, gone all to pieces, moaning, eyes rolling, tongue lolling. The blood-flecked superparticle edges toward him. Jimmy Hu grabs Lafcadio's foot and pulls him away. The giant Babsi bulges forward, hesitates, then SLAMS down to point-size as fast as it can. The floor beneath it bulges up with space pressure . . . but the hyperblob can't get free.

Lafcadio's clawed fingers rake the floor as Jimmy drags him out of the room. The door slams. The little bean lies on the concrete, angrily buzzing in a puddle of blood.

I woke up with a start. I knew who I was. Alwin Bitter, kidnapped by terrorists. My back was killing me, and my hurt finger throbbed. I looked at my watch. Quarter of ten. Lafcadio still sat on the sofa, guarding me with the robot and the machine gun on his lap. He hadn't noticed yet that I was awake, and I studied him through slitted eyes.

His dry black hair stuck out from his head in asymmetrical tufts and auras. There was a festering scab-crust along the outer curve of his left ear. His skin was a sallow yellow, blued along the jawline by sixteen-o'clock shadow. His mouth was a thin twisting line, never quite at ease, never quite amused. It was as if he were constantly holding back both screams and laughter. He kept his eyes squeezed almost shut, possibly in an effort to valve down the boom and bustle of consensus reality.

He wore a plain black suit, shiny with wear, and a stained white shirt with no necktie. The suit pockets bulged with worthless objects. Now as I watched he fished out a sheet of paper with some sort of geometric diagram and studied it intently, turning it from side to side like a monkey would. His hands were off the machine gun . . . but this did me no good, as the chain fastening me to the wall was so short. Yawning loudly, I sat up.

Lafcadio put away his diagram, and then smiled to me in a friendly sort of way.

"*Stavvi Minos orribilimente, e ringhia: essamina le colpe ne l'intrata; guidica e manda ch'avvinghia.*" Apparently he spoke no English . . . strange for a physicist, but not impossible, especially in Italy.

"I'm sorry." I threw out my hands. "I can't understand you at all. I only understand about twenty words of Italian. *Non capisce.*"

But that didn't stop him. He wanted to talk. He had something on his mind. *Luna,*" he said, molding an ass-shape in the air. "*Baciare e entrare.*" He made the traditional hand-gesture for coitus, the erect right index finger bustling about in the loop of left thumb and forefinger. Apparently he was asking if I liked sex.

"Sure. *Molto bello.* Me and my wife every night." I pumped the air with both fists, as if lifting myself up and down in bed.

Lafcadio went to the door of our stone room and peered out. Was he going to set me free? Tell me a secret? Assault me sexually?

"*Ecco,*" he said, laying his gun down on the sofa and stepping close to me. He fumbled for something in his pants pocket and then brought it out. A tiny bean or seed it looked like, lying in the center of his dirty palm.

Looking lovingly at the little lump, Lafcadio began . . . blowing kisses at it. Pursing his lips and making coaxing noises.

"*Smeep smeep. Smeep smeep smeep.*"

The little sphere seemed to twitch, to grow a bit.

"*Smeep smeep*" went Lafcadio, pausing to grin and nod encouragingly at me. I was supposed to help.

"Smeep," I went, dry lips puckered. "Smeep smeep smeep."

"*Smeep smeepy.*"

"Smeepity smeep smeep."

The little ball grew, its surface flowing. In a way, I felt like I was being hypnotized, or having a hallucination. But yet the . . . *presence* growing and taking shape in crazy Lafcadio's cupped palms seemed real enough. Another order of reality, I thought, when suddenly . . .

There was a crash of footsteps, an explosion of gunfire, and Lafcadio pitched toward me, his chest gushing blood. With what must have been his last act of volition, he passed the magic sphere

to me. It shrank to the size of an orange-pip. I pocketed it as I
stepped back from the intruders.

Going through my pockets I found the little spherelet which
Lafcadio had given me. Had that really happened today? Was this
the missing sample? The tiny ball glowed mysteriously in the pitch-
dark room.

"Smeep," I went, pursing my lips. "Smeep smeep." The ball grew
slightly larger. There were faint patterns on it, like half-seen
continents on a clouded planet. I felt a stirring of excitement in my
loins. The thing gave off an incredible aura of sexuality.
Pheromones—the airborne organic molecules that people give off
when they're sexually excited. Invisible little PLEASE FUCK
ME's. Leaning over the sphere was like putting my face between
my wife Sybil's legs. Without really knowing why, I licked my lips
and began smothering the tiny sphere with kisses. I was just so
lonely. The sphere grew and became warm to the touch, bigger and
bigger. What was going on?

With an effort I drew my face away from the magic sphere and
looked it over. The side facing me had a cleft down it, like a
peach . . . like a woman's beautiful ass. My hands dropped away in
astonishment. The mildly glowing sphere hung there weightlessly.
Now she was turning, showing herself off.

The perfect buttocks rotated out of sight, and I was facing the
lovely naveled round of a pregnant woman's belly. I reached out to
caress—her, running my hand down through her wiry pubic hair to
fondle the pouty labia. The sphere hummed gently and floated
closer. On top were the mounds of two stiff-nippled breasts.
Between the breasts nestled a perfect, full-lipped mouth.

My hands were wooden and trembling with excitement, with
rechanneled hysteria. I fumbled my pants open and drew the sex
sphere down onto my distended penis. This was madness, but I
couldn't stop.

My cock slid in easily. The sphere's mouth smiled loosely up at
me, showing white teeth and a pink tongue. I leaned over, trying to
kiss her, but she was just out of reach. Obligingly, she grew a bit
larger and plastered her sweet smelling wet lips against mine,
shoving her tongue into my mouth.

I came.

In the sudden silence I could hear one of my captors shifting in bed next door. Was this really happening? I stared down at the object in my lap. A skin-colored sphere the size of a giant beach ball, with breasts on top and a mouth between the breasts. At the bottom were my generous buttocks, a crinkly anus and a vaginal passage containing my rapidly limpening penis. Was this safe?

The sphere giggled, shrugged me out, and rotated one hundred and eighty degree about the horizontal. The intoxicating scent of her south pole filled my nostrils. Pheromones locked into receptor sites. Her soft lips and sandy tongue were at work on my genitals. I sighed with pleasure and sank my face into her deeply rounded cleft.

The harder I licked, the bigger she grew . . . past beach ball size, past the size of the library's big Earth globe, past all reasonable dimensions. My arms could no longer reach all the way around her. The huge mouth held my testicles as well as my penis, and her luscious vagina covered my entire face.

I came again.

Once more the sphere rotated, and I noticed a twinkling brown eye set in her side, just below the crease at the base of her breast. Next to her eye was the delicate shell of an ear.

"Who are you?" I breathed. "Where do you come from?"

The fat breast nudged me and I tongued the chewy nipple.

"Who are you?" I repeated. "Talk to me."

The smiling mouth came swinging around to plant some sticky kisses on my face. The mouth was almost a foot long now. The teeth looked very big and strong.

"Please shrink a little," I begged. "You make me nervous like this."

Obligingly she dwindled down to a more manageable size . . . maybe a meter in diameter. I happened to be holding her breasts as she shrank, and it was a strange sensation . . . not as if she were a balloon losing air, but rather as if she were sliding out from under me. Yet when she was through shrinking, her breasts were still in my hands.

"Thank you," I said, planting another kiss on her mouth. "Please talk to me."

She pressed her legs together and rocked sweetly one-two, one-two from left to right. Shaking no. Then blew a last kiss at me and shrank slidingly down to orange-pip size.

I smeeped fruitlessly awhile, then put the bright spherelet back in my pants pocket. I decided to call the sex sphere Babs. The two orgasms had left me tired and relaxed. I stretched out on the couch and fell asleep.

There were stairs up to the street, deserted. Trying to look every which way at once, Sybil skittered across a bright intersection and darted into the shadows of some modern apartment buildings.

Another roar rose from the castle. The whole sky up there was red. A block away, two drunks hurried past. American soldiers. A bottle smashed on the cobblestones. Sybil stayed in the shadows, thinking hard.

Not far from here there was a little-used trail up to the castle's L-shaped grounds. If she used this trail she would come out at the opposite end of the L from the castle, far from the crowd, and with a good view of what they were up to.

The drunks' clumsy footsteps and hoarse voices faded away. Senses strained to the limit, Sybil moved forward. *I'm ready to kill,* she repeated to herself. *I'm going to kill Alwin and Babs.* She held a weapon ready in each hand.

In some of the buildings children were crying. But the streets were totally deserted. Everyone was up at the castle: all the men and all the sex spheres. Sybil found the path and hurried up.

There was a lurid red glow over the castle park. Someone had set most of the trees on fire. As Sybil climbed higher she could see more and more of the bizarre celebration.

In the background were the jagged castle ruins, hollow and dead. Set there in the crowded park was a single huge sex sphere . . . a giant ass with a gaping hell-mouth cunt. The crackling trees and many flares bathed the scene in jumpjump eldritch light. A few late-arriving sex spheres shot past and merged into the mass of the one great Babs. The air tingled with pheromones.

Men with horrible twisted faces pressed up to the giant sex sphere like sperm seething around an egg. One by one, they were worming their way into the vaginal rent: damaged souls entering the gate of hell, children following the Pied Piper under the mountain. All naked and distant, they looked rudimentary, like forked parsnips. In their sexual frenzy, some coupled together. Others hunched twitchingly against the sex sphere's sagging breasts, or rubbed their faces against the sphere's broad, glistening anus.

The livid mob spread out from the sphere's crack like a pool of standing urine. Body by body, the pool grew smaller, as one man after another reached his heart's desire, reached that stinking wet hot dark embrace. An odd little figure darted around the edges of the manpool, herding them forward. The figure was short and yellow, and seemed to have a wheel instead of feet. Occasionally, he would pause in his feverish activity to stare attentively towards the top of the sphere. A single man squatted near the sex sphere's summit, just beneath her huge, pleased mouth. Sweating and grinning, he shouted down instructions. He was the procurer, the Devil, the Pied Piper: Sybil's husband, Alwin Bitter, me.

＞＜

I could feel the bullets coming, sense them with my field. The first burst would have hit me in the head if I hadn't jumped clear.

I landed on a fat man wedged in between Babs's labia. Sybil was still firing her Uzi. I could see the tracer-bullets *thipp*ing past.

"*Pass doch auf, sie doofe Narr,*" hollered Fatman: "Look yes out, sir goofy fool." Skull-faced Thinman, just ahead, pulled Fatman fully in.

Men seethed around me. Ugly men with warts and wens, limps and humps, scars and age-spots, blind white eyes. I was lost in the crowd, and crazy Sybil was firing at random. Sudden blood-flowers bloomed in th-th-th-th-there on Babs's hide. Men screamed like women. I stayed low and worked my way around to the shelter of the sphere's other side.

Wheel Willie, I called with my mind, *come help me!*

Tilted over at a high-speed angle, the little rascal came buzzing around the great curve of flesh. After my *Schnookeloch* knob-job we scored him some hash, and he was in good spirits.

"Everything's right on, Alwin! Babs'll haul this whole bunch off to Hilbert Space in a few minutes. Is it really trippy there? Are we going too?"

"Not yet. I still have much to do. When I return to Hilbert Space it will be in glory. The reason I called you is . . ."

Suddenly the smooth wall of the sphere above us split open. A tightly collimated beam of pale-purple light punched through. I recognized it as a particle-beam. Sybil was shooting a particle-beam laser at Babs!

The beam had eaten a hole right through the sphere, but no important centers had been cut. Babs rose hugely off the ground, looking this way and that for her attacker. All but a few dozen of the men were lodged in her womb, and she moved heavily. Thirty meters away stood Sybil, a tiny courageous figure with a weapon in each hand.

"That's my wife," I told Wheelie Willie. "We have to save her."

The sphere's great mouth opened to show cruel teeth. "Vhell, vhell," she boomed. "Little Sybil Burton Bitter." A plump, struggling figure slid out of Babs's stuffed twat and dropped maggotlike to earth.

Black-painted and tense, Sybil stood her ground. Another beam of purple light flicked forth. Babs dodged it and zoomed fifty meters straight up. Her bulk seemed to cover half the sky. For a second the angry firelit monster hovered, and then she dove.

With our minds tuned together, Wheelie Willie and I had formed a plan: a desperate suicidal rescue. As Babs dropped, he and I surged forward. I flew like Superman, my arms stretched out. He followed right behind, his wheel a screaming blur. Directly above us, the sex sphere's mouth was swooping down.

I snatched Sybil and sped away. Babs's piggy eyes were too far around her curve to see. Noble W.W. poised himself right on ground zero. He made there by his one oblation of himself once offered a full, perfect and sufficient sacrifice and satisfaction for my sins. He gave himself as substitute, fooling Babs's gross mouth.

In a flash I'd landed Sybil in the shelter of the _Gesprengter Turm_, the Sprung Tower, Babs thought she'd eaten Sybil, but she was looking for me with her eyes and her hypersenses as well. I used my mental powers to disguise our vibes: we would scan as a bush and a rabbit. Babs searched vainly for another minute, then settled down to spread for the remaining men. Perhaps she thought I'd gone off to grieve.

"Let me _go_," said Sybil, waving her Uzi.

"Put that down."

The Sprung Tower was "sprung" or blown in two, by the troops of Louis XIV, some three hundred years ago. Half of it still stands, and half of it lies on the ground in one huge piece. Originally it was used as a fortress, with several floors and lots of gun-slits. What remains of the top floor is good and solid. Sybil and I were up there, peeking down at Babs through one of the tower's loopholes.

"I've sworn to kill you, Alwin."

"Be reasonable, Sybil. I haven't done anything to you."

"You killed all the women in Heidelberg. Turned them into sex spheres."

"Babs did that."

"You didn't stop her."

"I know it *looks* bad. But Babs is trying to bring freedom and immortality to everyone. You should see it in Hilbert Space, Sybil."

"Help me kill her. Or else."

Sybil poked me with her Uzi. That was once too often. With a twitch of my will, I melted the gun-barrel. Sybil dropped the hot weapon with her exclamation point of pain.

"There's only way I know to stop Babs," I said. "And it's not the particle-beam laser. You have to realize that she's infinite-dimensional. Nothing we can do to her in this space can amount to more than a pinprick. But there is maybe a way."

"Save us, Alwin. It's your duty."

"Why should I do anything for you? You tried to shoot me about five minutes ago."

"Think of the babies, Alwin. The poor children. Having the world disappear is fine for you . . . you're bored with it. But they're just beginning. Shouldn't they have their chance too?"

"Well . . ."

"All the children in Heidelberg are alone. Locked up and crying. Is that fair?"

"You don't realize what a sacrifice you're asking me to make," I complained. "Wheelie Willie already died for you, isn't that enough?"

"What are you talking about?"

"Wheelie Willie, the little man I used to draw at Rutgers. He was alive. I found him in the Nekar and just now he let Babs eat him so she's think you were taken care of."

"That . . . impossible, Alwin. You must be going crazy."

I paused to recall exactly when Wheelie Willie had appeared. I had been chatting with Huba. Just before that I'd been about to doze off; no, I'd been thinking about Hilbert Space. *Moving* in it. What must have really happened was that I'd shifted the nature of reality. Probably the shift that made Wheelie Willie real had been the same as the shift that had turned all the Heidelberg women into sex spheres.

Enjoyable. It had been an enjoyable afternoon with Wheelie Willie, partying in the old town. Huba had turned back up, not really too pissed-off about his wife, and we'd gone barhopping. The funniest moment had come when we'd passed some really loud and plastic-looking American tourists. "*Deine landsmänner,*" Huba had said, nudging me. "Your fellow-countrymen." Around sunset, all the spheres had flown up to the castle, as if roosting there for the night. We men followed them up and found that they'd merged. One humungous ass, and everyone wanted in. Crazy? Sure. But I hadn't questioned it 'til Sybil came blazing her way in.

Duty. Should. Fair. Wife words. But maybe she was right. There was no rush, really, to destroy reality. In the Zen sense, there's nothing to destroy anyway.

A gleam of light from a gun-slit lit up Sybil's face. Wide mouth, deep eyes. A strong face, a good face. She smiled. I kissed her.

"All right. I'll do it."

There are many possible realities, infinitely many. Yet most of them are not . . . alive. Most of them are like possible books that no one ever actually wrote. A group-mind, like humanity's, lights up one given world. What makes this world different from some ghostly alternate universe is that *we actually live here.*

In my trip to Hilbert Space I'd learned how to take hold of human reality and move it about. The first thing I'd done was to fix it so that I had superpowers. And then I'd begun shaking things, trying to get our group-mind free, free like Babs. But now I was going to have to undo everything I'd done. More than that, I was going to have to move our group-mind across the dimensions to

some other universe where Babs might not find us. Dodging her
was not going to be easy.

"How will you do it?" Sybil leaned against me, familiar, intense.

"In a minute Babs will disappear. She'll take all those perverts
up to Hilbert Space. While she's gone we'll run away."

"To Frankfurt?"

I laughed shortly. "To a different layer of reality. I'll move the
human race's group-mind to a different place and hope that Babs
can't find us."

We peeped out of our stone loophole. The last man was in Babs
now. Her sides swelled out like a hamster's cheeks. Then she
shrank . . . smoothly sliding off into hyperspace.

"This is it," I told Sybil. "Say your prayers."

I let my consciousness flow out. First to Sybil. Her complex self:
part bad-girl, part old maid. Past her, to the children in Heidelberg.
Then up and down the Nekar. Fleeting images, snatches of German.
Europe now, hold it all, Asia, Africa, Australia, the Americas. The
mystical body of Christ, of Brahma, Buddha, you, me too.

Suddenly I'm thinking of a children's book, *Make Way for
Ducklings*, Father Duck looking for a place to land. God, the
sunset's bright. Hurry up, the sphere is coming. Down there is a
safe spot, a mote in golden light. Hurry. Circle down . . .

We live in Virginia now. I'm sitting at a typewriter. There's a
magnolia outside my window. The kids are in school and Sybil's in
another room, working on a painting. I think I'll go ask her if she
remembers how we got here. One thing: if you see the sex sphere,
I don't want to hear about it.

III.

Us-Them

DEAR MOTHER
Harry Mathews

This is where I once saw a deaf girl playing in a field. Because
I did not know how to approach her without startling her, or how
I would explain my presence, I hid. I felt so disgusting, I might as
well have raped the child, a grown man on his belly in a field
watching a deaf girl play. My suit was stained by the grass and I
was an hour late for dinner. I was forced to discard my suit for lack
of a reasonable explanation to my wife, a hundred dollar suit! We're
not rich people, not at all. So there I was, left to my wool suit in the
heat of summer, soaked through by noon each day. I was an
embarrassment to the entire firm: it is not good for the morale of the
fellow worker to flaunt one's poverty. After several weeks of
crippling tension, my superior finally called me into his office.
Rather than humiliate myself by telling him the truth, I told him I
would wear whatever damned suit I pleased, a suit of armor if I
fancied. It was the first time I had challenged his authority. And it
was the last. I was dismissed. Given my pay. On the way home I
thought, I'll tell her the truth, yes, why not! Tell her the simple
truth, she'll love me for it. What a touching story. Well, I didn't. I
don't know what happened, a loss of courage, I suppose. I told her
a mistake I had made had cost the company several thousand
dollars, and that not only was I dismissed, I would also somehow
have to find the money to repay them the sum of my error. She
wept, she beat me, she accused me of everything from malice to
impotency. I helped her pack and drove her to the bus station. It
was too late to explain. She would never believe me now. How cold
the house was without her. How silent. Each plate I dropped was
like tearing the flesh from a living animal. When all were shattered,
I knelt in a corner and tried to imagine what I would say to her, the
girl in the field. What did it matter what I said, since she wouldn't
hear me? I could say anything I liked.

Next day after eating lunch out of a plastic container I went back
to the field. I'd found my stained suit on the floor of the closet
where I'd dumped it. The added rumpling and dirt made it look

even worse. I put it on anyway—I'd been wearing it at the beginning of this misadventure, and I wanted to be wearing it at the end. I do not know if this was a mistake or not. The little girl was playing not far from where I'd seen her the first time. I stood at some distance inside the edge of the field and spoke to her in a voice neither loud nor soft. I said that my wife's lawyer had called earlier to say that she was filing for divorce, but that I would never blame her, the little girl, for that. I told her that she was beautiful, that in a way I loved her, that even though I was utterly unhappy I would remember the scene of her in the field without bitterness. I had more to say, but the girl had stood up and turned to me as though she had heard me, which it soon transpired she had. She was not so little, either, but rather tall and, as she approached me, plainly of a more nubile constitution than I had conceived from afar. She pointed toward me and in a confident voice cried, "That's him!" to persons that were out of my sight for the good reason that they were standing behind me, three men and two women in serious garb, whom I took to be officials of some sort. I then sank into such a torment that I suffered a kind of seizure, from whose effects I have taken several months to recover. It turned out that I could not have fallen into better hands, for those five strangers were medical people, and they have tended me, I assure you, with extraordinary care. My indisposition nevertheless has kept me from writing to you sooner, and that is why now, before recounting the most recent events, dear Mother, I hasten to send you the melancholy intelligence of what has recently happened to me.

Early on the evening of the eleventh day of the present month I was at a neighboring house in this village. Several people of both sexes were assembled in one of the apartments, and three or four others, with myself, were in another. At last came in a little elderly gentleman, pale, thin, with a solemn countenance, hooked nose, and hollow eyes. It was not long before we were summoned to attend in the apartment where he and the rest of the company were gathered. We went in and took our seats; the little elderly gentleman with the hooked nose prayed, and we all stood up. When he had finished, most of us sat down. The gentleman with the hooked nose then muttered certain cabalistic expressions which I was much too frightened to remember, but I recollect that at the conclusion I was given to understand that I was married to a young lady of the name of Juniper Simmons, whom I perceived standing by my side, and I hope in the course of a few months to have the pleasure of introducing to you as your daughter-in-law, which is a matter of some interest to the poor girl, who has neither father nor mother in the world.

I looked only for goodness of heart, an ingenuous and affectionate disposition, a good understanding, etc., and the character of my wife is too frank and single-hearted to suffer me to fear that I may be disappointed. I do myself wrong; I did not look for these nor any other qualities, but they trapped me before I was aware, and now I am married in spite of myself.

Thus the current of destiny carries us along. None but a madman would swim against the stream, and none but a fool would exert himself to swim with it. The best way is to float quietly with the tide.

ABSENT
Beth Nugent

There are parts of my father's body I cannot bear to touch. The slackness at his throat. The throbbing there. Sometimes the cave behind his knees when we bend his legs, the delicate tendons along the sides. But mostly the hands. The hands are what give me the most trouble. Something about the webbing between the fingers The knobs of knuckles. They are like something moving, something constantly moving.

They remind me of crawfish, the way they twitch, crawfish scrabbling about on rocks. I tell my brother this, and he just looks at me, then shakes his head. He has problems of his own, he says, problems I know nothing about. He looks away from me out the window; on the little pond in the park across the street there are two swans, circling. They are always here when we visit. They mate for life, my brother tells me.

Later when we are home again, together, he looks up from his work, and stares at me a longtime.

—Crayfish, he says, not crawfish. He stares out at the table in front of him, the stacks of notebooks and papers and pulls one toward him, opens it, flips to a blank page.

—Crayfish, he says, as he writes, then looks up at me, Crayfish. They're not the same thing. He looks back down the page, then closes the notebook. He shakes his head.

—Sometimes, he says, sometimes. I don't know where you get your information. He looks at me a long time.—It makes me worry, he says, and don't you think I already have enough to worry about, with my work. He spreads his arms out, gesturing across the table. He shakes his head.—Crawfish, he says. These are the kind of conversations we have. We have been having them for our whole lives, it seems, and I no longer bother to agree or disagree, because usually that entails more of the same, and there is already enough of the same.

But back to my father's hands. No. To my brother's work. He is writing a book, he says. A book on the nature of suffering. Among, he always adds, other things. There are other books, too. Memoirs. Medical dictionaries. A book on taxidermy. His book on suffering, though, is what he refers to as his major work. So far he has gotten only as far as a title and a table of contents. The title is *Facts*, and the there are three chapters: Love. God. The Body. These are the main causes of suffering, he says, and the absence of them is what will end suffering. And who, he sometimes asks of no one in particular, who should understand suffering better than he? He has been writing this book as long as I can remember. There is not a time I remember when he was not writing this book, but then my memory is fragile and does not serve me well. This is what my brother says: Your memory, he says, does not serve you well, and though everything about how he says it is annoying, I can hardly disagree.

But back to my father's hands. Sometimes I close my eyes and pretend they are someone else's hands. My mother's. The hands of a stranger. My own hands touching my own hands. My father wakes every now and then, or at least opens his eyes, and looks at me.

—You, he says, with no inflection and who can say what he means. We see him once a week, my brother and I, since we have brought him here.

When we come here, my brother waits for me to sit with my father and watches the swans. Did I tell you, he says, that they mate for life. He says nothing should mate unless it mates for life. He is impatient to return to his work.

—This is not, my brother says, a home, not technically speaking and I suppose he is right, if you consider that, technically speaking, a home is a place where people live together, not a place where they are put when their children are waiting for them to die. It is, rather, my brother says, a place for people like our father, who are what he delicately refers to as "absent." He used to live with us, but it became tiring—this was my brother's word—tiring—to have him around all the time, although he was almost never awake, and required very little from us, and if there was a place like this, a place for people like him, and if he had a pension to cover it, then why not take advantage of it? Men like my father drift by. Absent men, my brother says, men don't know what is real, any of them. Reality is like a movie to them. Our father, he says, does not know what is real, and that is what became tiring about having him around, even though he was always asleep, just being in the same house with someone who didn't know what was real was a strain. It was interfering with his work. His work. I have never seen him write in his book on suffering. He stares out at the papers as though he is looking at maps written in foreign languages. He is collecting his thoughts, he says. There is so much to try to understand. This is what I do not understand, he tells me sometimes—that work like this takes time, thought.

Sometimes when he is working, and I am sitting on the couch reading magazines, I can see that he is watching me. Or thinking of watching me.

This is how we live. This is how we have always lived except that our father used to live here with us. Without him, there is some kind of absence, though it would be hard to put a finger on it exactly. My brother is changing, or has changed. He said our father was watching him all the time, and he had to get him out of here. That and the reality problem. The important thing, he says, is to know what's real, and the only way to know what's real is to pay attention to the facts. Sometimes he says the "facts of the matter," or the "facts of the case," but in any event, he keeps a list of these as well. The world, he says, is facts, nothing else, and to pay attention to them is the secret. And facts, he says, are everywhere. You just have to know where to find them, where to look. Of course the kind of facts he's talking about are things like Mice give you headaches, which is something he said he overheard in line at the grocery store. He wrote it down as soon as he got home. Of course I know that facts like these are wrong, but sometimes when I watch him write something down, I wish I had something so certain to think about. Lately he has begun to read them to me.

When we return home, the children who live next door to us stop playing and look up, stare at us as we enter our house. My brother stares back at them, until one of them, the smallest, sticks out his tongue. My brother shakes his head. Children are monsters, he says, and when we get inside, he pulls out his book of facts.

—Children, he says as he writes, are monsters. They are not even human beings. They do not understand facts. He closes his book and looks at me. His face seems to be changing somehow, growing paler or thinner or somehow just less like itself. He looks at me a long time.

It is, of course, only a matter of time before I leave him.

THE SPRAY
Jonathan Lethem

The apartment was burgled and the police came. Four of them
and a dog. The three youngest were like boys. They wore buzzing
squawking radios on their belts. The oldest was in charge and the
young ones did what he told them. The dog sat. They asked what
was taken and we said we weren't sure—the television and the fax
machine, at least. One of them was writing, taking down what we
said. He had a tic, an eye that kept blinking. "What else?" the oldest
policeman said. We didn't know what else. That's when they
brought it out, a small unmarked canister, and began spraying it
around the house. First they put a mask over the mouth and nose
of the dog. None of them wore a mask. They didn't offer us any
protection. Just the dog. "Stand back," they said. They sprayed in
a circle towards the edges of the room. We stood clustered with the
policemen. "What's that?" we said. "Spray," said the oldest
policeman. "Makes lost things visible."

The spray settled like a small rain through the house and
afterwards glowing in various spots were the things the burglar had
taken. It was a salmon-colored glow. On the table was a salmon-
colored image of a box, a jewelry box that Addie's mother had given
us. There was a salmon-colored glowing television and fax machine
in place of the missing ones. On the shelves the spray showed a
walkman and a camera and a pair of cufflinks, salmon-colored and
luminous. In the bedroom was Addie's vibrator, glowing like a fuel
rod. We all walked around the apartment, looking for things. The
eye-tic policeman wrote down the names of the items that appeared.
Addie called the vibrator a massager. The dog in the mask, eyes
watering. I couldn't smell the spray. "How long does it last?" we
said.

"About a day," said the policeman who'd done the spraying, not
the oldest. "You know you c-can't use this stuff anymore, even
though you c-can see it," he said. "It's gone."

"Try and touch it," said the oldest policeman. He pointed at the
glowing jewelry box.

We did and it wasn't there. Our hands passed through the visible missing objects.

They asked us about our neighbors. We told them we trusted everyone in the building. They looked at the fire escape. The dog sneezed. They took some pictures. The burglars had come through the window. Addie put a book on the bedside table on top of the glowing vibrator. It showed through, like it was projected onto the book. We asked if they wanted to dust for fingerprints. The older policeman shook his head. "They wore gloves," he said. "How do you know?" we said. "Rubber gloves leave residue, powder," he said. That's what makes the dog sneeze." "Oh." They took more pictures. "Did you want something to drink?" The older one said no. One of the younger policeman said, "I'm allergic, just like the d-dog," and the other policemen laughed. Addie had a drink, a martini. The policemen shook our hands and then they went away. We'd been given a case number. The box and the cufflinks and the rest still glowed. Then Addie saw that the policemen had left the spray.

She took the canister and said, "There was something wrong with those policemen."

"Do you mean how young they seemed?"

"No, I think they always look young. You just don't notice on the street. Outdoors you see the uniforms, but in the house you can see how they're just barely old enough to vote."

"What are you going to do with that?" I said.

She handled it. "Nothing. Didn't you think there was something strange about those policeman, though?"

"Do you mean the one with the lisp?"

"He didn't have a lisp, he had a twitchy eye."

"Well, there was one with an eye thing, but the one who stuttered—is that what you mean by strange?" Addie kept turning the canister over in her hands. "Why don't you let me take that," I said.

"It's okay," she said. "I guess I don't know what I mean. Just something about them. Maybe there were too many of them. Do you think they develop the pictures themselves, Aaron? Do you have a darkroom in the police station?"

I said, "Probably." She said, "Do you think the missing things show up in the photographs—the things the spray reveals?"

"Let's just keep it and see if they come back."

"I wish you would put it on the table, then."

"Let's find a place to hide it."

"They're probably doing some kind of inventory right now, at the police station. They'll probably be back for it any minute.

"So if we hide it—"

"If we hide it we look guiltier than if you just put it on the table."

"We didn't steal anything. Our house was broken into. They left it here."

"I wish you would put it on the table."

"I wonder if the police do their inventory by spraying around the police station to see what's missing?"

"So if we have their spray—"

"They'll never know what happened!" She shrieked with laughter. I laughed too. I moved next to her on the couch and we rolled and laughed like monkeys in a zoo. Still laughing, I put my hand on the spray canister. "Gimme," I said.

"Let go." Her laughter faded as she pulled at the can. The ends of several hairs were stuck to her tongue. I pulled on the can. And she pulled. We both pulled harder.

"Gimme," I said. I let go of the can and tickled her. "Gimme gimme gimme."

She grimaced and twisted away from me. "Not funny," she said.

"The police don't have their SPRAY!" I said, and kept tickling her.

"Not funny not funny." Slapping my hands away, she stood up.

"Okay. you're right, it's not funny. Put it on the table."

"Let's return it like you said."

"I'm too tired. Let's just hide it. We can return it tomorrow."

"Okay, I'll hide it. Cover your eyes."

"Not hide-and-seek. We have to agree on a place. A locked place."

"What's the big deal? Let's just leave it on the table." She put it on the table, beside the salmon-colored glowing box. "Maybe somebody will break in and take it. Maybe the police will break in."

"You're a little mixed up, I'd say." I moved closer to the table.

"I'm just tired." She pretended to yawn. "What a day."

"I don't miss the stuff that was taken," I said.

"You don't?"

"I hate television and faxes. I hate this little jewelry box."

"See if you're still saying that tomorrow, when you can't see them anymore."

"I only care about you, you, you." I grabbed the canister of spray. She grabbed it too. "Let go," she said.

"You're all I love, you're all that matters to me," I said.

We wrestled for the can again. We fell onto the couch together.

"Let's just put it down on the table," said Addie. "Okay." "Let go." "You first." "No, at the same time." We put it on the table.

"Are you thinking what I'm thinking," she said.

"I don't know, probably."

"What are you thinking."

"What you're thinking."

"I'm not thinking anything."

"Then I'm not either."

"Liar."

"It probably doesn't work that way," I said. "The police wouldn't have a thing like that. It isn't the same thing."

"Don't."

"You said it wouldn't work."

"Just don't. It's toxic. You saw them cover the dog's mouth."

"They didn't cover themselves. Anyway, I asked them about that when you were in the other room. They said it was so you wouldn't see the stuff the dog ate that fell out of its mouth. Because the dog is a very sloppy eater. So the spray would show what it had been eating recently, around the mouth. It's disgusting, they said."

"Now you're the liar."

"Let's just see."

I jumped up. "If you spray me I'll spray you," I shouted. The spray hit me as I moved across the room. The wet mist fell behind me, like a parachute collapsing in the spot where I'd been, but enough got on me. An image of Lucinda formed, glowing and salmon-colored.

Lucinda was naked. Her hair was short, like when we were together. Her head lay on my shoulder, her arms were around my neck, and her body was across my front. My shirt and jacket. Her breasts were mashed against me, but I couldn't feel them. Her knee was across my legs. I jumped backwards but she came with me, radiant and insubstantial. I turned my head to see her face. Her expression was peaceful, but her little salmon-colored eyelids were half-open.

"Ha!" said Addie. "I told you it would work."

"GIVE ME THAT!" I lunged for the spray. Addie ducked. I grabbed her arm and pulled her with me onto the couch. Me and Addie and Lucinda were all there together, Lucinda placidly naked. As Addie and I wrestled for the spray we plunged through Lucinda's glowing body, her luminous arms and legs.

I got my hands on the spray canister. We both had our hands on it. Four hands covering the one can. Then it went off. One of us pressed the nozzle, I don't know who. It wasn't Lucinda, anyway.

As the spray settled over us Charles became visible, poised over Addie. He was naked, like Lucinda. His glowing shoulders and legs and ass were covered with glowing salmon hair, like the halo around a light bulb. His mouth was open. His face was blurred, like he was a picture someone had taken while he was moving his face, saying something.

"There you go," I said. "You got what you wanted." "I didn't want anything," said Addie.

We put the spray on the table.

"How long did the police say it would last?" I said. I tried not to look at Lucinda. She was right beside my head.

"About twenty-four hours. What time is it?"

"It's late. I'm tired. The police didn't say twenty-four hours. About a day, they said."

"That's twenty-four hours."

"Probably they meant it's gone the next day."

"I don't think so."

I looked at the television. I looked at the cufflinks. I looked at Charles' ass. "Probably the sunlight makes it wear off," I said.

"Maybe."

"Probably you can't see it in the dark, in complete darkness. Let's go to bed."

We went into the bedroom. All four of us. I took off my shoes and socks. "Probably it's just attached to the clothes. If I take off my clothes and leave them in the other room—"

"Try it."

I took off my pants and jacket. Lucinda was attached to me, not the clothes. Her bare salmon knee was across my bare legs. I started to take off my shirt. Addie looked at me. Lucinda's face was on my bare shoulder.

"Put your clothes back on," said Addie.

I put them back on. Addie left her clothes on. We lay on top of the covers in our clothes. Lucinda and Charles were on top of us. I didn't know where to put my hands. I wondered how Addie felt about Charles' blurred face, his open mouth. I was glad Lucinda wasn't blurred. "Turn off the light," I said. "We won't be able to see them in the dark."

Addie turned off the light. The room was dark. Charles and Lucinda glowed salmon above us. Glowing in the blackness with the vibrator on the side table and the luminous dial of my watch.

"Just close your eyes," I said to Addie.

"You close yours first," she said.

POISON IVY
Eileen Myles

It's just called alcoholism, it runs in my family. We have a genetic disposition towards it and depression, I believe. The first night I went down the train tracks with my friends and Colt .45 to knock back a few. You could feel the world pushing against its own size, that night. Expanding. Yet booze was a baby drink. Drinking was cute. Arm around my friend Lorraine and we were five, revolving around the telephone pole, huge thing, at the corner of both our streets, Swan Place and Swan Street, singing our baby hearts out, "Show me the way to go home, heek, over land and sea and foam, you will always hear me singing our song . . ." then some adult would walk by and laugh. I hear in the Middle Ages they only had booze on holidays, the whole town would get drunk, say for spring or the harvest and everyone would fuck each other in the hay, and then all the booze was gone and they'd go back to work. I mean I know the kings continued to get drunk, to make history, but the peasants had these episodes, gigantic, and just that. Who would want to hear about a king?

In Arlington the whole town was drunk. It was the only dry town in the state of Massachusetts, it was like South Boston in the suburbs, so it was one nice thing a drunk could do for his family, buy a house in Arlington. I walk down the train tracks all my life. Burnt gravel, the future. The pond. It seems strange in retrospect, it seems like a stage. The long mound of the empty tracks. The direction to Cambridge, Boston, and out. Dear Mom, I'm gone. Steal horses in Medford, Triple A stables, Texas to get hats. We drew this map. Ate our sandwiches on the tracks. Covered in jungle in either side, bushes. I was with Patty Delay and Ruthy. The Delays did it large, introduced me to the world of plant poison. I mean, they were covered in ringworms, bites and sores, one of them, Gracie, had false teeth at fourteen from coasting, no one ever had their eyes poked out, close, and of course they got poison ivy, poison sumac and poison oak. We didn't in my family. We just didn't have it, we were inimitably unlike the Delays. Our dolls were intact, we had no dogs. We read. We went to the library. Our meals were quiet, no one would come wrestling out the screen door and four others to restrain him, or worse to call the cops. We sat there eating, kind of happy, kind of sad. You could not make our skin blister and itch. No one in my family had gotten poison ivy. Yet.

Look I said to the Delays, and eight lips sneered, socks with my sneakers, snob, Eileen Myles lifting a greasy branch of the stuff. And I will prove it to you. I won't get it. Rubbing leaves on my arms, laughing, I scrubbed some on my cheeks and eyes. They were all watching. I was not like them, it was impossible, the Delays would see. It was absolutely one of the worst cases of poison ivy anyone ever saw, short of hospitalization. Deep in the bowl of that summer, I was lolling in the fumes of yellow soap, thick pink calamine lotion, I was guiltily engaged in fevered scratching, the near-orgasmic itch, my eyes were caked, almost sealed, blind, while big summer fans were aimed my pitiful way, I was a giraffe. All afternoon kids were coming by with old comic books I could barely read so they could see how bad (ha-ha) show-off Myles was.

I was human, I decided. I knew my weakness, like Kryptonite and I could do it again. I was not a bad kid. I always pushed it, but not so far. I had a deal with God. If I failed to do homework, in the absent-minded way I wouldn't get caught. If I skipped it on purpose, watching teevee, I'd get nailed. God protected my spaciness and innocence. We had an understanding that things would essentially go my way if I was generally good, God was fair, God cut me a margin of error. I was safe. And bad kids got caught. I could never afford to get caught. It was sad in my house, now, with my father being dead, and my mother now so totally alone, again, after her enormously sad childhood. Also I must admit there was some lingering mystery around my father's death and sometimes I wondered if she killed him, and maybe she would kill me too. I was afraid of her.

To keep things cool I made utterly sure I was never so bad a nun had to see my mother. I didn't do much. Laugh and pass notes. And once in a while I drummed. The wood of our desks was about an inch thick. They were hollow, stuffed with old papers and half pencils, gum wrappers, school smell, and if you slapped the joints of your fingers just below the tips on the band of golden wood that surrounded the inkwell you got this low thudding that felt like your whole body got released in that place, it was like drawing, but no pictures, just this oooooooo strumming nervousness, a sweet sound. The desk played tight like close to the rim of my bongos which no one ever heard. I had this record by Jack Costanza, Mr. Bongo, and he had a straw hat and a bowtie and a vest and behind him was a long-haired woman with castanets, her head flung back, really beautiful, she was dancing to Jack, and so were the kids in the room when I played. It was a joke, I knew I was being a jerk, but it sounded so good in the empty room, and I was doing my beatnik imitation, eyes closed, and the nun turned around from the board and said, Who is that boy who is banging his thumbs on the desk. I stopped. The room grew silent now. Who is that boy. The bowl of the room was so loud. The traffic on Medford Street hummed, the trees were shaking with their teeny green buds practically smiling in the breeze. If everything stopped and I was silent, the nun would give up. Kids were turning around. Who is that boy. The room was silent. It's Jack, I prayed. It's not me, it's Jack. I was sweating now. Sister wouldn't stop. She bellowed. I will keep the whole class after school if that boy will not stand up right now and have the manliness to admit.

I stood up. Everyone hollered and screamed. The boys went Myles. Kids were dying. The girls giggled and blushed. Janet Lukas and Suzie were imitating me, silently playing their drums on their desk. I felt so ugly. Tell your mother I want to see her at the convent tomorrow evening. The worst. My mother loves nuns. She wanted to be one. What shall we do about Eileen. The nun and my mother sitting on velvet furniture. I started to try and make a deal, which I always do. I got as close as I could, I whispered. Let me do a punish task, I was practically bowing to her in front of the class, lifting my paws, pulling her dress. I will be perfect, I whined. No young lady, and she spat lady out like what a joke and the class got it and sneered . . . Catholic school was choreographed abuse. I've seen, I've heard your kind of perfect. I need to talk to Mrs. Myles, and we'll decide what perfect is for you. I slunk back to my desk. I must do something. My head was bowed. 1962. I had a permanent.

I banged on the Delays front door. Dickie came to greet me, he was tall and handsome. He was scratching his belly. It was a special confident guy gesture. Dickie was in high school. He had dark red hair. Short. All the girls had crushes on him. He looks like Dr. Kildare, which I couldn't see. He wore grey athletic teeshirts that hung loosely from his thin strong frame and Dickie held the door with one hand and scratched his lightly furred belly, with the belly button kind of protruding and you could see the top of his BVDs. For a boy I didn't think was so cute, I memorized every fucking thing. He turned his head yelling loudly into the house. Ruthy. He turned to me quietly and said, she'll be out in a minute. He had something to eat in his hand and he lowered his head and took a bite. He looked at me for a second then he vanished into the dark of the house. I waited a moment. I yelled, Ruthy.

I need some poison ivy. I can't go to school tomorrow. You're shitting me. Yes. Ruthy threw her leg over the railing, and then we went over the fence. It was before supper. For years we came home at the six o'clock train. Myles you are nuts she said as I rubbed the shiny leaves on my legs and my arms. It was a suspiciously even-handed attack. And it kept me out of school. Good thing you didn't get it on your face my mother sniffed.

THE CHINESE BOY WHO LIVED UP TO HIS NAME

John Yau

I'm closing in on forty-five, and the odds are that I'm not going to be remembered for anything I've done. Thank god, I'm married, and my wife and I have two kids. I'd like to say they're normal and healthy, but I'm not sure they are. At least not yet. Anyway, I can't tell if the kids take after me or my wife, Harriet. Maybe they're the perfect distillation of the two of us, the mud we made. That's the thing. We're just ordinary people who dropped two ordinary children onto this dirty old planet. Well, maybe we're not ordinary, just dull. We're part of a growing group that possesses no hidden potential of any kind, no aptitude for anything, and it seems likely they don't either. We're blots, dust balls tumbling towards the future, until it stands outside and knocks on the door.

The kids call her Harry. Usually on Sunday when Harriet is trying to usher us all off to Mass. It's the only imaginative thing they've ever said in their entire lives. Call my wife, Harry. Boy was I happy when they started doing that, showed they had some spunk lodged, however tiny, in their shapeless little bodies. Can't make me harry it up any faster, they like to announce in loud exasperated voices, high pitched, just short of puberty. I suppose that's why I'm calling you.

I don't need to see your face. What's the point? I read the ad. Just as long as you're really Chinese and bear more than a passing resemblance to your picture. Maybe it doesn't matter if you're Chinese or not, just as long as you say you're Chinese. Right now, that's enough for me. You see, I have this thing about the Chinese. I don't know if it's a good thing or a bad thing. It's just a thing I have. Part allergy, part addiction.

I got married late, but you don't need an abacus to have already figured that out. Aren't the Chinese good with numbers? You're like a taxi meter, aren't you? I bet you're good with numbers. I bet you remember how many phone calls you get each night and what each of us says to you and how many times we say it. I bet you've heard it all. Well, little honey, you're in for surprise this time, because you haven't heard my story before, and I'm paying you to tell it, paying you good American dollars. Isn't that the American dream in a nutshell? Getting paid dollars without getting your hands or sheets dirty?

Did you know I played the tuba in high school? No, how could you know that? You may be Chinese, but that doesn't mean you're clairvoyant. You know why? Because fat kids with freckles, red hair, and pale skin have to play the tuba in my high school. We're the only ones that look right with a bright snake's flawless body circling a dumpy red and green sack. That's why we had to wear a uniform and a hat; we had to be covered up. We had to protect you, yes you. Because there are no fat albino Chinese, their bodies all squishy like warm lard.

One morning I got on the school bus. It was two weeks before Thanksgiving, the big game was coming up. Our team had a shot at the state championship. Everybody was humming with excitement, a bunch of air conditioners needing new parts. Dripping, they were so excited. And what did I do? I forgot my instrument. Yes, that's what I called it when I ran down the black rubber aisle, and told the driver that I needed to get off right away, that I needed my instrument, a whole busload of kids screeching at me, as I'm yelling about my instrument. Lurching down the aisle of a moving bus, like a drunk looking for a doorknob in a dark room. It's funny now, but it wasn't funny then. Nothing was funny then. Not even a bus load full of parrots beating the windows with their beaks and laughing.

I didn't forget my instrument this time. In fact, that's why I'm calling. I can't forget about my instrument, I can't even try to forget about it. It does the lurching these days, and I follow after it, like a dog who knows he'll never be fed.

You see, when I was nine my parents, those little bags of soggy potato chips, got the bright idea that I should go to summer camp. Probably so they could spend more time playing bingo at the church.

You know what the place was called? Camp All-Saints. A church camp. Ten boys to an A-frame made out of white fiberglass. Smelly green cots. Gray wooden floor. Mosquitoes as big as donuts and a brown pond paved with leaves and black mud. Counselors with tattoos they did late at night in some schoolyard full of broken glass. These guys were from the part of the city my parents assiduously avoided.

The cabins were named after saints. I slept in Saint Augustine's Cabin. You know who he is? Well, he lived a life of sin until he had a vision. With me, it's the other way around. I had a vision and ever since then I've been trying to live a life of sin, and to tell the truth I'm not doing a very good job either. That's why I'm ordinary, and why I'm sick of being ordinary. So I called you, because it's your job to lead me to bliss. Should I go on?

My parents thought going to summer camp would be good for me. Being in the outdoors. Learning to swim, play baseball, going on cookouts, taking hikes in the woods. Raise my dexterity in arts and crafts. That was the biggest joke. Arts and crafts. Ever trying to make key chain holders out of plastic coated wire. The square knot. The diamond knot. Ten worms for fingers. And my parents inform me that I should be a good boy and bring them home a pair of key chains, a red one for dad and a blue one for mom.

Six horrible weeks later I brought home a plaster bust of Abe Lincoln that I painted green with red eyes. Told my parents it was a streetlight for civil rights. I'm glad they didn't ask me what I meant because I didn't know. Not then, at least, but I was already on the right track. I just didn't know that then.

Most of the kids that went to Camp All Saints didn't ride on a schoolbus, like me. They walked or took a subway, came from the part of the city few of us ever visit, much less stop in. It's the first time some of them ever been in the woods or gone swimming. And you know what, they liked it. They liked swimming. They even learned how. This is what got me, kids who had no swimming pool anywhere near them learned how to swim.

I should have been sent to a fat camp, but my parents didn't seem to know I was fat. That I didn't run, I lurched. That I had no table manners, didn't know any dirty jokes, hadn't seen a naked woman in a magazine, that I was a dismal failure and I was only nine. You know what it means to be a failure at nine? No, how could you? You're Chinese.

There was this Chinese boy at camp, a con artist who could talk a snake out of his spots. He knew everyone thought that Chinese kids never misbehaved and he took full advantage of this myth, not that I blame him. His name was Victor. I hated him then; and I hate him now. Meanwhile, everyone thought he was a nice boy, just a little wild, but I knew better. I knew he was a creepy little deviant. Nice, the very word makes me sick. He could swim and play baseball, which isn't right. Chinese boys aren't supposed to know how to play baseball or swim, but scrawny Victor did.

Victor was twelve; it was his third year at Camp All Saints and my first. He was an altar boy in his church, I was the fat boy who wore thick glasses and ugly blue sneakers, licked the knife after he stuck it in the peanut butter pail. Victor had a friend, Jack, who was also an altar boy. They went to the same church and were some pair. Jack was going to a New England private school named after some Mayflower family, so he was worse than Victor because he had already spent the entire school year practicing little tricks he could play on younger students, enlarging his repertoire. But it was Victor that got under my skin. It wasn't right that he could play baseball and I couldn't.

They always made fun of me and they never once got caught. One night, while I was asleep, Victor and Jack decided they should masturbate, and they made me the target. They had been talking about Mary, some girl who went to their church and wore tight dresses because nothing would fit her. They had seen her lacy bra, the freckles on her breasts, and they were imagining what the rest of her looked like, what they would do to her after she drank some sherry they stole from the priest.

In the middle of all this, which I was listening to and which they must have known I was doing, Jack decided he and Victor should have a race, see who could ejaculate first and get it on my head, my red hair. If you need to know, that's what fat boys have to put up with every day in America. There was nothing I could do, so I lay under my blanket, kept pretending to be asleep, and listened to them chattering away like monkeys, laughing, and pumping themselves faster and faster. A bunch of shotguns aimed at me. And they probably don't even remember doing it.

I know you people are unholy. That's why there's so many of you. Because you're unholy about it, because you can't restrain yourselves, because you got nothing better to do.

You want to know why I'm calling you. I'll tell you why I'm calling you. I'm calling you because Victor lived up to his name and won. Because if it wasn't for him, I wouldn't be here panting in your ear. That's why I'm calling you. I'm calling you because of Victor. And if you're married or have a boyfriend, maybe you'll think about what I said when you see him after work, when you get off the phone and go back to your life, as if I never called, never paid you good money to listen to what I had to say.

Swallow
Inspired by Edgar Allen Poe's *Berenice*
Laurie Weeks

The TeeVee was on, I was watching *Dark Shadows*. Quentin hissed to Angelique, who was sitting beside him on a stone bench in the *Dark Shadows* park, If you don't do such and such a thing for me, your whole body will look like this by midnight tonight. Gasping in horror Angelique raised her hand into the frame. The flesh had disappeared from her wrist and fingers, which is to say they were bones. Music swelled, as did, I was confused to note, a sensation of heat between my legs, and later that night, tossing in a semi-hallucinatory state of longing and dread, I waited for Angelique's exfoliated hand to rise from underneath my bed. A chill light from the institutional windows next door irradiated my sheets, and my little sister slept peacefully in the bunk bed below.

I lay in my grave. At first I'd thought myself to be in bed, with my brother sleeping above me. Blood poured from my gums across my tongue, as if my gums were crumbling into soil. The groundwater of my body poured across my tongue. When I tried to lift my head I hit the coffin's lid. Hardly able to breathe, I gurgled my brother's name.

Mostly I don't have any memories except the first one: falling in love. This person, my sister, vanished almost immediately it seemed, before my very eyes, in fact it was the onset of her disappearance, sadly, that first truly drew her to my attention, and I lay in an erotic haze day after day with my book, dreaming of the seductive mirage released by her flesh as it evaporated from her bones, of her beautiful teeth unveiling themselves from beneath the thinning tissue of her lips.

Though spawned from the same strange loins, my brother and I had different temperaments. In the beginning, I'm not sure he ever loved me like I loved him. Until I was 11 or so I'd thought him the weirdest of boys, though I adored him. He'd never come outside to play when I asked him, he just stayed in the den reading books—

but there came a day when the slenderness of his hips and thighs, his long tangled hair, his gloom, made him seem almost girlish, like a rock star, and I developed a passionate tenderness for him.

⌐⌐

We lived in a house at the end of a cul-de-sac overshadowed by a hospital for diseases of the nervous system, and through the window you could see the hospital and its patients wandering the grounds. Beyond that was a vast riverfront landscape of factories and chemical vats. At a certain point this room in which I enjoyed watching *Dark Shadows* had started to feel like a quarantine chamber. With our romance we exposed ourselves to a strain of pathology that was almost unendurable, it came up through the vents inside our cage or bedroom it was hot, we had sheets not curtains across the windows. By the time we'd passed the incubation stage in our strange carpeted atmosphere, by the time we'd grown up, so to speak, we were like extraterrestrials, our perceptions were ESP due to the fact that language no longer had any relation to what our bodies experienced from one moment to the next.

⌐⌐

The more in love I felt with my brother the more he ignored me and I wandered through the house like an alien. Confused by the way my body would confuse itself with his, I'd slip in and out of my own outlines just trying to make it to the bathroom, to examine my body. I couldn't figure out if my features were ugly or cute; was I short or tall, fat or thin? On what basis did people make such decisions?

⌐⌐

Sometimes it comes back to me, how we learned to ride bikes together after my sister's sixth birthday, how the whisper of tires as she rode felt to me like the sound of a pathologist's depression as he makes his report, the report that even now sits on top of the television under stacks of *TeeVee Guide*. I was never free of my suspicion that biopsies were in the forks, lurking behind everything, especially shows on TeeVee, I had no words for it then, my sense of dread, to which she was cheerfully oblivious as she pedaled away her balance and proficiency so superior to mine. I wobbled along behind her. The street itself the spiky line of fever on a grid. The bike tires going around and around like the motor in a cat scan. There are soft tissue tumors and tumors of the bone.

~ ~

My front teeth had grown in crooked and chipped because my brother had accidentally knocked me off my bike when I was seven. Boys used to say to me, "Hey, Buckteeth," at school, but then I learned to say jokingly when they opened their mouths, "I know, I know, I look like a beaver." Actually, I'd never noticed my teeth until someone informed me how ugly they were, and when I checked in the mirror after school I saw it was true. I thought if I said it first boys would laugh and realize I was a good sport who shared their perceptions, but instead they'd get a strange expression on their face and, for the most part, fall silent. After my braces were off and the dentist had filed away the broken edges, the comments ceased altogether.

I was nervous, however, about my breasts. My tiny nipples had grown swollen and pointy, and a hard lump of tissue developed beneath each one. They ached all the time. My undershirts rubbed harshly against them and I felt embarrassed at the way they poked through the cloth during calisthenics. At night I lay sleepless in my bed, panicked at the thought that the new tissue beneath my nipples was a cancer. I didn't want to go to sleep because I was afraid I would die. Sometimes, after lying awake night after night for months, my terror would become so unmanageable that I'd stammer in shamed whispers to my brother that I felt scared, though I didn't say of what. In the beginning, he'd tell me to shut up and let him sleep. Still, it was his calm presence in the bed above that let me rest at all—it just seemed like I couldn't come to any harm with my brother in the room.

~ ~

Until she got sick I hardly noticed her—she was just an overly healthy child whose animation alarmed and irritated my senses, though my aggravation only seemed to fuel her clamoring for my attention, which, given that it didn't exist, was easy to withhold. Her presence interfered with, diminished, the pleasure I took in my books, in television, in photographs—these things were my world, all else seemed hallucination. To me my sister was a dream, it seems weird now to think that in her almost pornographic health she was as distant as a dream, though I must say this dream had the annoying properties of a persistent insect. She agitated my nerves, I perspired unpleasantly. Why did I never stroke her hair, or pet her, I wonder—she who was just a sweet kid with a stutter—until the flesh had begun to wither from her bones?

The more books he read the more carbonic became the gleam in his eyes. He ate little, as though stories themselves provided a chemical nourishment which instead of adding freight converted his frame into metal. I myself was hungry all the time, and this made me feel somehow gross, out of control, like I was an entity both soft and putrid, contaminated with rank and craven desires. A gravely sick person demanding constant attention, beset by insatiable cravings, was me, I felt, in every situation, whether simply walking to the store for candy or stealing up to the top bunk to watch my brother's face while he slept. Though I knew this was my defect, it felt like love. I felt humiliated in my need, I wanted to be hard and independent. I wanted what my brother had, to me he seemed delicious, like a crystal clear piece of candy your body turns into energy, productive and pure. Thinking about him made me get the same eerie, romantic sensations I felt when an ambulance siren sounded deep in the night, or I'd see radio towers transmitting red messages in the distance. My brother would be off somewhere and I'd sit at the nighttime window, bathed in radiation from TeeVee, unbearable longing for his presence mixed up in my head with the alien, erotic beauty of industrial machines aglow and pulsing beside the river. I loved my brother, if I could eat my brother I'd be clean.

Once she fucked me in the water, looking serious, more serious than I was taking it at the time, it just seemed like something to do. We were standing up in the shallows of the river, at the swimming park, sort of enjoying the fact there were people all around, except she was so serious about it, being extremely young you see she had all these romantic notions about me, the first person she had sex with, etc., and that got mixed up in her head, I suppose, with the movies we'd spent our life together watching on TeeVee, so every moment with me during this time was an epiphany to her. I tried to smile at her while we fucked to wipe the serious look from her face, and when that didn't work I dragged her from the water, which terrified me at any rate, and continued fucking her hard on the ground in some rushes by the water's edge. I remember my panic when she opened her mouth. Like I was pushing myself into dirt soft enough to collapse, suck me under, swallow me up.

— —

I used to talk a lot but with the onset of my illness I found myself remaining silent more and more. I was still ravenous, though food itself had grown repellent. I had begun to get words mixed up with food; if it came inside my mouth, a thing seemed to have the ability to change me in unpredictable ways, so that biting, for instance, into toast, delivered the sensation of sinking my teeth into a prosthetic device. At the same time, I had for some reason become convinced not that my brother could read my mind, but that he knew what I was thinking the way your own skin does, the way your flesh responds to fluctuations in the muscle underneath. This was the effect on me of his stare, which itself was a new and unnerving experience. Suddenly some days I would look up to see him gazing at me intently—ME! who by now I practically considered invisible, even to myself—producing in my chest a dizzying and instantly addictive rush of pleasure. Conversation seemed unnecessary; besides, I often said things I neither intended nor felt, as if words congregated in my mouth, foreign particles, to swarm forth and engulf me in a sticky murk from which others recoiled. I remembered my brother's near-repulsion when I would ask him to come out and play.

— —

Overnight my sister grew secretive and wasted and I looked up from my book to see her clothed in a low-grade fever contagious in its allure. Her hips were boyish in their black jeans and her hair matted in a tangle around her neck. The skinnier she became the more insistent was her presence in my mind. I thought of her all the time and found myself perpetually aroused. I imagined her having sex with the beautiful Angelique, Angelique older, experienced, seductive, and cruel, my ailing little sister so vulnerable and small, still just a child . . . each sinking her teeth into the other's neck, delicate feline cries of ecstasy and pain echoing through the chamber as I watched. It was as if my sister's illness gave her passage into the filmic world that was my reality, my transport. It was as if the malady was a special radioactive dye injected into her bloodstream to illuminate her heretofore invisible body, allowing it at last to register on the screen of my heart. I wanted to put my sister in a velvet-lined box, keep her beside my bed.

My brother left the house for a while and I lay down in a warm hollow left by his body on the couch. I glanced around the room. Like most people, I had tried to decorate the walls in my own inimitable style. There was a cool picture I'd bought at a thrift store, to prove my independence from him, he who hated to shop. He also loathed the picture, which was a house with yellow clouds behind it and flower petals like floating corpuscles that someone had painted in the 30s on a hit of acid. They didn't have acid in the 30s, sneered my brother, but still I really liked the painting's whimsy, it made me feel giddy and relaxed. Also on the wall was a photo taken by me, shot from an angle flush with the ground. The figure was a tiny paper doll onto which I'd pasted a xerox of my face. The doll was propped up in some backyard dirt and being stalked by a housecat made monstrous in the print's low perspective.

I started taking pictures because my brother did, aiming his camera out the window at patients wandering slowly like ghosts or dying movie heroines across the hospital grounds. At such times his breath came quickly and he would wave me away. When he wasn't looking I learned to use his camera. I wanted to be an artist in my own right: I speculated, in the days before my illness that perhaps when he saw my sensibility was no different from his he would return my affection. These days I myself take pictures of girls from books and put them into my photos, where the blood slides across their bodies, a dress.

A commercial came on TeeVee and I collapsed across the couch. Your beloved shadow fell on me at this point, fell on me, I might say, with something like abandon, and I found myself consumed. I found myself immured if you will in the walls of a house the address of which I could hardly remember, let alone its place in architectural history, who the designer was, etc.—details whose importance ordinarily held me in thrall. From the couch I watched the weak autumn sun stain our walls, as though the wallpaper itself were expressing a thin fetid fluid from infection. The wallpaper was a grassy pattern selected by my mother, who channeled all her libidinal energies into projects of interior decoration involving the selection of compatible earth tones. I wandered through the house waiting for my sister to call my name the way you wait breathlessly for a physician to make his diagnosis, to stroke his finger instructionally across the outline on the X-ray of your naughty internal organs. I tried to read but couldn't concentrate, so insistent and mesmerizing had become the image of your teeth superimposed across the text.

When I got sick he starting shooting pictures of me, his camera sucking images from my face and mouth like kisses, or like people obsessively drawing smoke into their lungs. It seemed the thinner I became the more my brother liked me; something was wrong with me and of this he obviously approved, producing in me almost involuntarily a sense of pride. Before, I had felt perpetually sick and ashamed, though physically healthy: now I was truly ill and nearly euphoric. I felt stoned on some chemical manufactured by my own starving tissues. I felt that now my disease spoke for me, that it reflected the seriousness, the depth, that my flesh and childish prattle used to hide. I was really into poetry, also music.

Almost every day, my brother, who had great taste, would bring home a new CD. He'd put it on and I'd pose for him, opening my mouth for the lens as though receiving nourishment, or medication. Occasionally, embarrassing seizures of unexplained horror swept through my torso; my body would shudder into a frigid sweat and seem to be suffocating with me inside it. Smoking Marlboros, I'd feel my lungs soften, bits of them begin to drift toward my feet; I'd get dizzy. During these spells, my brother watched me and took pictures, tape-recording my descriptions of vertigo and panic, with the new CD playing in the background like a soundtrack. Usually it took a while for me to come down but the clicking of the shutter was for some reason soothing, its steady whirr affirming my presence in the world until I could breathe again like a normal person. When the session ended I took pictures of myself in my darkened bedroom, trying to figure what exactly it was about me that my brother suddenly loved.

— —

I abandoned my books for the darkroom. Every afternoon she bled into focus beneath my touch, her teeth in particular rising from the paper like a phantasm that would consume me. I wanted to lick the teeth, they were irresistible. My attraction disturbed me, but I couldn't help it. Under my hands the mouth that anchored my sister's teeth disappeared and they swam by themselves in the iridescent flow of chemicals; the gradual evaporation of her flesh revealed to me the correspondence of her teeth to the ideas I so loved—fixed, eternal, clean, more real than the surface attractions of so-called reality . . . there were times I found it difficult to breathe, so intense was my excitement at the image of her teeth drifting across their field of RC paper like those withering patients materializing on the hospital grounds.

— —

My gums bled into his palms which he cupped. I wanted to pour the blood back into his body, which was mine. He reacted like my blood was a battery acid decomposing the flesh of his hands. Undoubtedly this metaphor comes to me because of the thing with Angelique. He flinched. I'm sorry, I whispered through the blood. Keep quiet, he replied, and while I gazed back at him, an infant, his finger entered my mouth. It was as if his fingertip produced its own secretions of coagulant and morphine, for gradually the bleeding stopped and I felt myself relax as he moved his finger tenderly back and forth across my upper then my lower gums, stroking my teeth, my gums, my teeth again, lingering on each tooth with a soothing tiny circular motion while his other hand held my forehead. I closed my eyes. Gently he waggled my front tooth back and forth to test its mooring in the crumbling tissue. I was ashamed of my sore and hideous gums but thankful for the teeth that resisted decomposition and for the moment at least were clean. My brother rested his finger on my tongue and tickled it a bit while I looked at him until, impassively, he withdrew himself from between my lips. I wanted to spit my teeth into his palm, a gift. Get away from me, he said. I looked back when I left the room and saw him wiping my blood against his jeans.

THIS IS NICE OF YOU
Gary Lutz

I was a man dropping already well through my forties, filthy with myself, siccing my heart less and less on the locals, when, taking a turn at the toilets one close-buttoned afternoon, I met two brothers—they said they were brothers—who swore they had a sister, a schoolteacher, an officer of instruction at the county college, a whirlwind midlife turmoil of everything already put to ruin, who had gone off from a new marriage in an old car, an upkept and ennobling sedan, but who had returned now to the apartment and was living there alone with the little runoff there was from the marriage—some outcurved appliances, apparently, and low-posted furniture promoting its own mystery but becoming figurable in certain concentrations of TV light—and, above all, a telephone (on a pedestal, they insisted), the handpiece of which she gripped in lieu of exercise, or in fury, and I thus let out my little reliable cry that I was in fact a student of the telephone, that it was a debasing apparatus in the main, with its meager economy of bells and tones, and the intimacy of the mouthpiece that sent your breath, tiny aftervapors of it, back toward your lips, so that regardless of the party accepting the outgoing products of your voice, you were, at most, in a further rivaling exchange with yourself alone, and this is what must have brought the two of them around, the men who professed brotherhood with the woman, because they offered me her phone number, put it at my disposal on a piece of paper one of them had already committed it to, a tearing from a menu, and the looks the men were now giving me had deletions in them, already, of my exact beanpole size and shape, so off I went to a pay phone, the nearest canopied one I could find, and put the call through. The woman answered after the second ring and said she needed a lift right that very moment into the little racial city close by.

She was idling in the doorway of the building when I pulled up in front, and I helped her into the car and got in myself. I had always had a way of not having to look at people that nonetheless brought them to me in full, and so I am still certain of the susceptive and impressible complexion, the shimmer on the mouth, a lipstick of low brilliance, a difficulty around the eyes, the hair short and prickly, skin gristly and bagged up over the elbow bone, conflict even in how her arms stayed at her sides—in sum, a spinal loveliness for me in the nuisance dress she wore; an off-blonde quantity with shadowed, thumbworn hollows that put me out of whatever I might have known of women before.

I set the two of us into the narrow traffic and remember telling her, by way of explaining the little burden which I had shifted, by now, from the shelf of the dashboard and onto my lap, that when you lived in filth, as I then did, a daily newspaper came to count for a lot, though instead of the thick-supplemented local paper I bought a trimmer one from a backlying town—not, of course, for any affluences of native data it carried, but as an article of houseware: a rough immaculacy in four lank sections, a set of fresh hygienic surfaces to come between the table, say, and whatever I had going for me at the table, if the table was where I was going forward—because what else so cheap comes so clean and far-spreading?

The woman told me that her own trouble with paper was that through a modest hole, no larger than a quarter, that had been drilled a foot or so above the floor (the standard height, she had reasoned, of legitimate electrical outlets), and by means of which her faculty office had at last gained communication with the roomier but unoccupied office next door, she more and more often shot a single sheet of paper, plain copier paper she had rolled just barely into a tube, so that after landing on the floor of the neighboring office the paper would preserve little if any of the curl, and there would be nothing written or typed on it, of course, and it was always a blank sheet that had been aging on her desk for some time and had already been moved around, or advanced, from station to station on the desktop, coming into further creaselets and crimps and rucks and other infirmities—paper, in short, still too clear, too bare and unfraught, to be thrown responsibly and forgettably away, and yet too seasoned and beset with irritations of the surface (a molelike blemish, say, or what looked like a tiny hair, an eyelash, sunk into it, or frecklings, or notational pressings of a fingernail), too wrought, in sum, for the paper to be appointed to any secure curricular purpose. Her office, she claimed, was in fact full of such paper, much-handled and singularized sheets of it by the loose, functionless hundred.

I had to get across to the woman that I myself no longer had an office, or any other place to divide me reliably from everybody else, and that for much of the daylight I thus appeared to be among people because I kept putting myself where people came together into even closer-fitting assortments, the viewing areas and showrooms and rotundas and such: I took in the rigged, lean-to look of the women, the tongues coming and going in what the men kept thinking of to say—whole families of low knees for me to bark my shins against during the crowded and involving way out. At home afterward, in the one room where my life was packed down, I would keep my nose stuck in the safehold of the phone book, where the names of people suffered reduction to mere episodes of the alphabet and underwent humbling declensions down every column (Lail, Lain, Laine, Lainerd), and the names of streets, of the towns and townships, got docked in crude, heedless abbreviations (the vowels almost always the first to get poked out), and I would run my eyes over the telephone numbers themselves, each sequence of digits another fallible run of the infinite. I thus corrected my feelings for people and assembled myself emotionally into whatever else I had at hand—the obligating arms of the clothes hangers, usually, or the keen-angled understructure, the guardian legginess, of the ironing board.

The woman said that in her case, though, it was more a matter of making slow circuits of the classroom where she had to put across the Emporial Sciences, retail theory and methods, to heat-giving and suggestive young women, some of them world cruelties already. There was the cooing of empty stomachs in the hour just before lunch, and the braying and fizzle of loaded stomachs in the low hours of the afternoon. She would recite her notes in a voice barely loyal to any one octave, a tiny alluvium of slaver hardening at the corners of her mouth on the days she gave the glassy lozenges a slow, warming suck, and she would take lowering notice of how whatever she said succumbed at once to freak spellings and prank paraphrase in the big dividered notebooks; and because in mid-afternoon light the world looked as thorough, as filled in, as it was ever going to get, a better way to set about ruining her eyes was to review how hair had established itself on the arms of the young women, because almost every arm had brought across itself a welcome and diversifying shadow. On one girl it would be a fine, driftless haze afloat above the white of the arm, never seeming to touch down on the skin itself. (An atmosphere, at most, of chestnut brown.) On another, it was as if copper wire, the narrowmost lengthlets of it, had been stuck into the fleshy batter of the thick, freckled forearms. On a third: a field of it—wheat-colored, thin-spun. On a fourth: a differencing, darkish updrift that shaded off as it approached the inner bend of the elbow, re-emerging at the base of the upper arm as whiskery fringe. On others it was a brassy or rust-colored frizz, or it was coarse as cornsilk, or it looked fussed on, as if the arm had been slowly stroked with charcoal.

But here the woman broke off, or I may well have made an interruption of my own—I think I must have asked if she was hungry, and she said if I was, and so on one of the lesser streets I parked the car and led her down into a belowstairs eating house I still remembered. Sandwiches were presently lowered in front of us. I watched her remove the festooned toothpick from hers and then play her fingers over the toasted planes before she took a fond first bite.

"This is nice of you," she said.

I must have looked at her in the way I then had of getting people to speak so they would not seem to be dwelling any longer on my features, because if on the well-set face the mouth and eyes are said to seem frozen in elegant orbit about the tip of the nose, then mine was a face that beholders, regarders, could not help trying to round off with greater success, to goad the particulars of it back into the arcs they had wandered away from—the mouth, for instance, having been pursed and pinched suchwise that it seemed resident more on one side of the face than the other—and there were further signs of original strife to be busied with (slapdash eyebrows unbunched, it appeared, from reserves of hair elsewhere on my person; a showing of adult acne, a shrivelly little relevance of it, confined to the declivity of my nose); and so to be polite, the woman thus sank her gaze into her sandwich, and told me, in a voice lowered accordingly, that, one late-childhood summer, she had devoted herself to collecting postage stamps: it was a tongue-involving sideline to early-arriving puberty, and she liked having to lick the pale, gummed hinges instead of the sticky backs of the stamps themselves before entering everything into the hosting album; and once, during some foul weather between her and a brother (the older, thrown-over one who had already made a habit of fooling the underside or his arm across the top of hers and calling her "pussified"), she reached for the shoe box in which she had let duplicate stamps accumulate— Spanish ones, mostly, of a feebled orange—and sent the box slooshing through the lower air so that the stamps showered onto the brother's bare legs with a full delicate harm all her own.

The woman was now touching up the surface of her iced tea with tiny activities, initiatives, of the longspun spoon. I myself was good at getting my touch onto things, though in a way that seemed to mix up the motive atoms inside them, but I was satisfied that for the moment my sandwich, the unbitten-at half of it, was still displayable and fit and local to my plate.

The woman went on to say that, as a child, she had been bundled off, many an afternoon, to the slope-ceilinged quarters of a bachelor uncle who, when speaking of anybody not immediately present, could not bring himself to use the person's name but instead would say "an acquaintance of mine in . . ." and then mention the name of some lapsed homeland, or little-loved rural orchestra, or backset building about to come down; and it was never a riddle, this device of his (not once could the girl have been expected to identify any of the subjects), and no matter how often and aloud he insisted that particularizing persons any further— bringing even a first name down upon any one of them—would have been indecent, he claimed, much like doing things to people while they slept, the girl accepted all of the uncle's prim and extravagant evasion for what he surely must have intended it to be: a neat, protective trick to space the world out a little further in her favor, to scatter the population so that wherever her hand might at last come down, it would have to be on herself alone.

And here I could sense that the woman wanted it from my mouth, an account of as much as I myself might have ever managed of attachment, so I told her I had once owned a house (a rising, really, of much-fingered, handwrought architecture that amounted to a little family of rooms above garages: a boxlike building with a rattly thorax of downspouts and drainpipes and an unfolded but full-toned fire escape), and I had had for a time a boarder, a student, a high-colored, loose-packed representative of declining girlhood, hung with necklaces and barettes, a girl of precise but shifting leanings and inclinations; and the afternoon she had come round to ask after the room, I stood in the entranceway, handshaken and asweat, and from what would later be my memory of the girl I made off with, first, how every pore of her nose seemed to be sheltering within itself a tiny dark seedlet, a grain of something immediately and enormously valuable. And a lipless mouth (just a slit, practically), the teeth inside looking wet, watered—it was my life's chore, at that instant, to keep from sending the back of my thumb blotterlike across the line of them (I was later to learn she drank everything cold and through the narrowest of straws). And her hair: it was tea-colored hair she had, long and reachful, an unstopped downcome of it. Tall for a girl, but she managed to stay out of much of her height and put herself across as somebody backward, or behind.

I must have told the girl, as best I could, that I of course had a wife, a full-faced imperishable partner, though for the moment she was gone otherwhere in the marriage, and here the woman, my present companion, my tablemate, whose feet were now parked, in parallel, on the grade of my upper leg, interrupted to say that her husband, too, had been such a liar, and what could I bring up by way of reply other than that a lie is a truth struck through with other, further truth, or that a lie is the present multiplied by the past, or that a lie is an outcry of borrowed hope? The woman gave me an allowed look of disgust, her eyes lowered but still popular with me, and on I went with what had now become the girl of my story.

For there had been a great, gainful carpet in the room I put the girl into, a matty expanse of coarse, grabby piles, an engrossing affair that took things into itself and held them tight, hoarded them, and I of course insisted that the girl not bother herself with its upkeep, that I enjoyed weekly access to a prestigious upstanding vacuum cleaner; but as soon as the girl was out of the house each morning, I would withdraw from my room, where time was unportionable, and loose myself into the ticktock impertinence of the girl's room and get down on my knees, and, going after the carpet first with my fingers, then with a forceps, and finally by unspooling lengths of clear package-sealing tape and pressing them against the tufts in neat rectangles to catch what I had missed, I brought vast tracts of the carpet to depletion, recovering not simply the girlinesses, the girleries, one would expect (buttons, straight pins, downed jewelry), but flirtier personalia in the form, say, of a stray confetti brought into the world when a page had been wrung without caution from a spiral-bound notebook, or some pleated paper shells of the chocolates she required, or one of the budget antihistamines she took to get her naps going, or a trash-bag tie whose plastic-coated sheathing was ragged enough to show the kinked line of the wire within (this I would wind around my finger), or a cough drop enwrapped like a bonbon (I would undo the wings of the wrapper and have to decide whether to suck the drop all down or begin chewing it midway)—I became the following, the public, that these things, these off-fallings, had come to have; but mostly there was hair, afloat above the uppermost pushings of the fabric of the carpet an almost continuous haziness of loose hairs of all lengths and sources, and I would have to set them out on a fresh sheet of paper and assort them according to the regions of the body they had taken their separation from, and in no time I had nestlike filiations of broken filaments and smaller involvements of the hairs that made me think of hooks, of barbs, and each pile required a separate envelope, to be filed in a separate shoe box for every sector of the body until, I hoped, the boxes themselves would no longer be enough and I would have raised something semblable, brought up something equal in volume to the comprehensive girl herself.

And her wastebasket! For every bit of rubbish, every dreariment she tossed into the thing, I would, in secret, deposit a reciprocal discard of my own, matching a spotty confidential tissue of hers with a lurid throwaway after my own heart—the cardboard substructions of a fresh parcel of underwear, maybe, or tearings from pantyhose I now and again pressed against a span of my forearm to work onto it the complications of female shading I otherwise made do, choosily, without.

I thus built the two of us up together in her trash! One afternoon—it was another of those vital, unsampled days on which the world humors us each a little differently to keep us nicely on our last legs—I discovered in the wastebasket an inch-deep textbook of hers, a paperback with a celery-colored cover that had come partly unglued, and this dilapidation I paired off, naturally, with a name-your-baby guide to whose pages, during my recurrent turnings of them, in bed or at table, I had contributed dried preserves of my person, a chemical splendor entirely mine. This coupling sent a sudden spigoty thrill from me that forced an unbuckling and an unzipping and a cleanup with a handkerchief I then ventured responsively into the wastebasket as well.

In the bathroom afterward, I found a suds-clouded puddle on the unlevel floor of the tub, a little undrained remainder, rimmed with offscum, of the girl's prolonged early-morning soak, and this was as much as I needed to get on my hands; I pressed them flat against the wet porcelain, then flapped them around in the air, and that was when I noticed it—in the amphitheater of the toilet bowl, an orange-yellow tint, or value, to the waters.

When the girl came home that evening, I told her, of course, that I had discovered fresh, unforeseen trouble within the tank of the toilet (a misalignment of the trip lever, a waywardness of the float ball, a misarticulation of the lift wires, kinks and defects, really, throughout the entire system) and that in fine it was an apparatus now operable only by means of advanced and strenuous equilibrial manipulations that it would be unseemly, inhospitable, of me to presume to burden her with—so that from here on out, following any leak or evacuation she need merely lower the lid and then, before quitting the room, ring the handbell that had been placed on the sink; I would see to everything else.

But the bell never rang, not even once, and from my window the next morning I watched the girl carry from the house a little plastic bag distended balloonishly, much like those bags you will remember having seen in the hands of children bearing homeward their solitary carnival-prize goldfish. In fact, I never ran across the likes of the girl again. The man who came to collect her things—not the father, apparently, but an advocate, an upholder—I found to be dull-eared and lax in his speech, and the better part of his face seemed to have already begun making tiny, rotational departures from whatever it was that the eyes, themselves impressively mobile, were just that moment having to take in. (Was there a lamp in the house that was not that night slopping its wattage over everything?) I guess I was waiting for the man to take a laggard, last-minute interest in me, and by now I was pushing everything into the doubled first-person—it was, I said, "*Our* night shot," and I began including the two of us in whatever it might be doing out, the expected sprinkles and such—but he was no friendship buff, and he paid no heed to my telling him that the only dress of hers I'd ever fidgeted myself even partway into had been the simplest of them all, a large-buttoned pertinence of deliberate blue, and then only on the principle that one naturally fits whatever one has into whatever somebody else had first, or how else would the world keep getting any taller with people? The man just went about the removal of the girl's things and did not have to be reminded too noticeably, I guess, how every dick hangs by a thread.

The woman, though, had by this time brought about some becoming slowings of her arm—it was an arm inclinable to langorous diagonals and magicianly swoops through the air above the tabletop—but it no longer was involving itself with her plate, so I suggested we shove off, I made payment for the food, and on our way to the car, and then in the car as I took to following her pointings, the directional tilts of her head, she said that you naturally kept putting more and more of yourself into another person, at first wondering how much she can take, how much of you is accumulable and how much she can hold, and you're letting things out, unpiecing yourself, and you've soon got things set up in her, a structure, a ghost skeleton hovering above her own, and room is being made for even more of you, and if you bring this off with enough people, even two or three people at the most, what you've got is at first a comfort, because you can pass yourself along and move a little more widely through the world and leave it to these others to man your grievances, your disappointments; and what brought this to mind, the woman said, was a term of financial hardship she had contrived for herself a few years back, an unpaid leave of absence from scrupling letter grades onto quiz papers (propped-up As, and lopsided, unascending Bs made to look, rather, like rear ends, all As and Bs, no Cs or anything lower, the difference between an A and a B having less to do with the accuracy of whatever facts might have been convened, or impounded, in the space the woman had provided for an answer than with anything rememberable about the way the enrollee had conformed her body to the confining perpendiculars of her chair and the navel-level writing surface that projected from it, or the way there might one day have been an unignorable blush on the instep of a once-moseying foot, disburdened of its shoe, that had got itself trapped in the grillwork of that cagelike involvement, intended for books, that was welded to, or otherwise schemed into, the underworks of the chair)—this had been a duration, in short, of controlled difficulty when the misexpenditure of even a twenty-dollar bill had set her thrilling, gloating, over everything she would miss out on, and one afternoon she had made an engagement for a haircut, a trim, and very early in the session the haircutter, a woman ill-defined in the face but otherwise full of conspicuities of emotion, set down the prevailing scissors and pressed the flat of a lukewarm hand against the woman's cheek, held it there for a good minute and longer, while the other hand eventually found its way into a drawer, a shallow treasury of slender specialty scissors, one pair of which the cutter withdrew and began routing deductively through the woman's hair, the other hand staying put on the cheek, longer and longer, and the woman went home and for weeks afterward the bathtub was now a more likely destination than any of the upright furniture, and it got easier to fill the tub with further clarifying volumes than to clear space on the difficult heights of the sofa, and she was hardly claiming to have become a cleaner person in result— she in fact would often discover, voyaging about her body, a browned fractionary detail of a larger crepe of toilet tissue that must have got itself stuck in some assy crevice and was impossible to get plucked out of the revolving suds—she was saying only that she spent more and more of her time thus immersed, ill off in water, and the haircutter had surely had a hand in it, the woman was doing some of the cutter's life now, coming into some of its wrong, because you sometimes have to look to somebody else's life to get dimensions set back even part of the way around your own, and it should not have to be any less your own life when it comes from somebody else, and you could surely fudge a society out of any one available person and get this person doubling for the many, so that in the little run of things perpetuable from one person to the next, every loose moment stood to become a complete, active finality.

But by now this was a new day, with only an hour or so off it already, and the place the woman had had me bring us to, the man's place, with the promise that the man was elsewhere—this was on a little slip of a street, a stewy efficiency apartment the color had long ago gone out of; and when, once in bed, still clothed, I found among the sheets and blankets a spoiling pair of the man's underpants, one of the leg openings of which was bunched and narrowed into an avid, sloppy mouth, I held myself accountable for redisposing the fabric until I got a befitting featurelessness back onto it; but all the while, I am sure I had to make myself go over again in my mind that if the body is the porter of as many organs of affection as there might one day turn out to be, then the idea was to let the thing carry you to where you would never otherwise have reason to arrive, because I listened for the unmelodious downslide of the woman's zipper, and then the woman made me put myself out of my own clothes, the attritional corduroys and bloused-out overshirt, and got herself up at last onto the subject not of the man whose apartment it was (because his story was scarcely the story of how the boy who decides he is half a girl no sooner starts to worry about where the other half might be than he gets careless with where he rests his eyes, or what he gives even the flimsiest of fingerholds to, and anything, even a crumbly triangle of pie offered on a saucer instead of on a pie plate proper, comes in easy, ready, wronging answer), but of her husband, and how, no more than a couple of months into the marriage, he had begun snugging away in his undershorts a little source of chance, reliable frictions to nudge him forward through the workday—anything company-keeping that could be counted on not to slide out of the elasticky leg holes: a half-dollar packet of chocolate tittles, maybe, that was barely noticeable in the baggy surround of the widecut trousers so popular at the time.

For by now the woman had at last brought what is usually called the other mouth to within only inches of my lips, though it is not a mouth, obviously, yet I let myself go along with the goodwill behind the comparison, the way I will remain loyal to anything deliberately and faithfully misunderstood, and I fussed my tongue against the vital trifles hung inside of her, as much of the curtailed finery as I could find, and gave the whole insimplicity of it a slow-circling examinational lick, until I was taking a sudden tepid downwash on the tongue.

It was a familiar latrine indribble that must have tasted, no doubt, like trouble just starting out.

THE MONITOR
James Poniewozik

Madonna we can do. Madonna we do regular. Her too. Her, you have to give me a week or so. Well, she's a difficult phenotype. No, phe-no-type. A difficult body. Well, I did say that. Eight hundred. This is a quality service. You think you can find it elsewhere, be my guest. No problem. O.K., so you talk to your friend, think about what you want, and you give me a call. Oh, we can handle it. Can you? Mm-mhm. Bbye! Come on in, you're, just a second, Mr. Sachs and Mr. Olson? Zoe, take these gentlemen's coats?

It's O.K., I think I can just put it over on the.

The coat, Marty, you're embarrassing me. Give the lady your coat.

You'll get it back in one piece. Cross, my, heart.

My young friend's a little shy.

Just it's a little chilly, all right, all right.

Here, for you, miss. You'll excuse him. Only carries a roll of hundreds.

So I see. Drink?

Scotch rocks. Two scotch rocks. Go, have a seat. Marty. It's *lea-*thuh. Thank you, dear. Gah, that feels good. Sorry, you prefer yours neat?

They don't look like pros.

Speak up, Marty, they know what they are.

It's just, ahm, it's just, you know, it doesn't look like a. The building even. You wouldn't think you'd find one down here is my point. So near the office.

What, you think I'm going to drive you down Times Square? You and me and Joey from Great Neck cruising some walking petri dish? Cheap stuff, Marty, garish. Think it's coincidence you find that near the theater district? Caters to the same sensibility. What you got there is the *Cats* of the skin trade. Greasepaint and discount tickets, am I right, Mariel?

MID-night, not a sound from the PAVE-ment, has the moon lost her MEM-ree . . .

Whereas your gentleman of taste, he goes as it were off-Broadway.

CAN'T forget, WON'T regret, what I did, wait, CAN'T regret, WON'T forget, what I did . . . fahhh . . . anyway. You were waiting for?

Sit over here, Mar. Josh Sachs, I made the appointment? My boy here's getting married.

Married, you don't say? He's too young! You must be so excited, sweetie, where's it happening?

Ahm.

The blessed event.

Oh, we're, it's next Saturday up in Rhode Island.

Up in Rhode Island, he says, let me translate, Mariel. Up in Newport, specifically at the J. David Gobel summer estate, he means in full. Oh, yes. Our happy little Marty is marrying himself two symphony orchestras, a few buildings at N.Y.U., and half an art museum. Plus assorted communications and entertainment concerns.

What a perfect time of year. I go up every year for the folk festival. Wait, don't move. I've got something for you, for the groom. There we go. You take it, it's my gift.

A rock?

It's hematite. For potency. Traditional. So for the honeymoon?

Asia. Bali, Thailand, China.

Well don't you *try* coming back here without bringing me a souvenir. So. For the bridegroom here you requested the—

Stumm. It's still a surprise.

Right. So it's seventeen five oh up front.

'S on me. We took up a collection. *Charity case.*

Fuck you, Josh.

I'll decide who fucks who around here, son!

I'll need to give you the rundown, since this is Mr. Olson's first time here.

He knows the shtick.

Anyway. Substances O.K., but no selling; no property damage, no personal inquiries, no physicality, no photography or cameras, we'll videotape for one-fifty per, Polaroids for twenty-five. Unprotected you can work out with the young lady in advance, but we discourage and we stress *in advance*. All backgrounding and necessary prior information strictly your responsibility, not liable for omissions on your part. Now. Anyone carrying?

Hah! Sorry, that tickled.

He's clean, Mar. Mine you gotta find, though. You're cold. Freezing. Lit-tle warmer. Lit-tle warmer. Cool, oh you're warmer, you're hot, *oh*, hose me *down* you're hot, you're burning, yeah, damn! you're good, sure you were never a cop?

Jesus, Josh, that's yours?

You surprised? And here I didn't know what to pick up for your wedding present. Still time to put it on the registry. You want to be ready for Colin Ferguson when he comes to check your ticket.

Your friend here thinks he's Clint Eastwood, Marty. I knew where it was the whole time. Bang, bang.

Bullshit.

Bull*shit*. And so does Colin Ferguson, cutie. Now I'm going to put this away safe for you and see how everything is upstairs.

We could have just gone to a regular.

What, don't worry about the spiel, it's just procedure. See Mariel, you scared the boy! Strictly Disneyland here, Marty. Enjoy the ride, keep your hands inside the car only if you act up they get serious. It's just some guys, they come here with an agenda.

So you're doing Monica.

So I'm doing Monica. Quiet little Monica. Sweet little Monica. Doesn't know how good she's getting it.

My mom had a lamp like this one in the living room.

That so? I'd like to *meet* your mom someday.

Oh, *fuck* you.

Yes sir, Mr. Gobel.

It's not like I haven't been to a place like this before.

College?

It was a friend of mine, he read Kerouac and Henry Miller and stuff, if you're familiar. The idea was all these artists and writers went to whores and got laid all the time on top of it. That girls, you know, they could sense something about you. Which for me anyway worked. We went to one in Roxbury.

Where let me guess they sent you to a fleshy professional old enough to be your mother, but patient and experienced. Did she lovingly relieve you of your cherry, Marty? Did she draw you sweetly into her big mammy bosom—

Gave me a handful of Kleenex and checked her watch. Had to meet her quota or whatever. Had a freaking egg timer.

Why they call it piece work.

She was skinny actually. But old, yeah. Rodge and Howard say they'll meet us up at Sidecars later?

And Rollins, they ever unchain him. He's heavy into the AuroraPharm thing. Between you and me, I think he's sinking. Between you and me, call the Coast Guard and alert the next of kin.

Tappan coming?

Pfft.

What do you think is the deal with Tappan?

Ay Eye Dee Ess. Undoubtedly.

No way.

You want to know how I know? Washes his hands. Constantly. Mornings when he comes in, after a meeting, before lunch, after lunch. Few times in between. Infection, you see. Subway poles and so forth. Fortunate to be a young man in your position, Marty. The Lord deciding to remove so much of your competition and all.

Mm. I've got an uncle who says that. The God part.

Maybe God wants us all to be lesbians.

Mr. Sachs? We're ready in 5B. If you'll go with Desiree.

I'll see you shortly, Marty. Longly as the case may be.

Wait a minute, the black chick? Excuse me, but that doesn't— Josh, she doesn't look a damn thing like Monica.

She's an escort. Escorts you up to the.

To the actual?

To the actual. So I'll see you down here? O.K., so enjoy. Tell them to get you another drink. Mariel, my boy wants a drink.

Scotch rocks?

Sure.

Scootch over, sweetie, and you can tell us all about the big plans. I love weddings.

—◠—

It's unlocked. I'll leave you now, you can go on in or if you need a couple minutes to get into character, that's fine, too. Bbye.

Ah. Hello?

Sit down, Olson. At my desk. I'll be with you in a minute.

Anywhere? Do you need me to—

Now then. There you are. I said sit down, this is going to take a while. Don't slouch, Olson, you look like a goddamn teenager.

Wait a minute, you're—

I have a lunch meeting with Daniels and Patel, so maybe we could quickly go over the briefs if you're prepared? The briefs, oh for Christ's sake, no, don't tell me, you didn't, hsssssss, O.K. It's just as well, look I'll be honest with you, that isn't entirely why I called you in here. It's.

Excuse me.

It's about your performance, Olson. It's about, to be precise, what you're bringing into this office. I mean besides a certain dumb-jock charm and a profitable marriage, if you can think of something? Maybe you could tell me, because frankly I'm not seeing it here. Frankly none of us are.

Excuse me, but isn't there supposed to be a goddamn bed in here?

Ah. So about your, ah, performance review.

I'm a little mixed up here, I think.

I think we should start over. It's O.K., honey, you're nervous. You don't do this every day. Remember this is improv, you can say whatever you like, we'll take it from there. Everything's taken care of, you get what you want in the end. So I'll go back in the bathroom and we'll start it again. And, ah, you might want to help yourself to a little treat there? From the bowl, by the door? As in we like to keep things safe here, kiss kiss?

I, yeah. I'm sorry. You know you do look just like her.

I hope not! Kidding, it's my job. So lights, camera?

Yeah, lights.

Sit down, Olson. At my desk. I'll be with you in a minute. Now then—don't slouch, Olson. You look like a goddamned teenager.

Sorry.

I've got a lunch meeting with Randall and Patel, so I thought we could go over the materials, if you'll? Olson?

Uh, I don't actually have them on me.

Oh for Christ's, hsssss, no don't bother getting them, Olson, that's not actually why I've called you in here. It's about your performance here. In so many words, it's about what you're bringing to this firm. Because frankly we're not seeing it, Olson? Olson, what the hell are you doing?

I'm sorry, Jesus! I thought it was the cue to take, shouldn't I be taking my clothes off? I mean otherwise you could let a guy know when.

O.K., let's, just a second. The idea as I was told is you're supposed to be in the aggressor role.

In the?

In the aggress, oh wait a sec. I'm guessing you weren't prepared here. By any chance this was a surprise?

Ah, birthday present.

We see that happen. A more complicated role-play, it's really better if the person knows.

Knows?

The idea is that it's a role reversal, like, you're the boss? This Helen Chambers, I'm guessing she's some kind of boss, some kind of supervisor of yours? Or whatever they call it there?

She's both of ours, mine and Josh Sachs, he brought me here? He's been telling me about this place for months. I guess you've seen him before.

A few times. Not in that way.

No, I guess it's the same girl. He's with her now. Every time he comes in, he fucks Monica, girl at the office.

Receptionist?

Legal assistant. Incredibly smart, Dartmouth. Twenty-two years old and she's already married—pretty, but the thing is, early on, she let Josh know in no uncertain terms, you know. He's showed me a picture, picture of the Monica here, I mean damn, you guys here— it's really a great likeness.

Doesn't it creep you out, I mean, aren't you and Monica?

Huh?

In the scenario, the prep materials, you've been having a thing with Monica? I guess he just wrote that in. One point I'm supposed to grab your balls and ask does Monica ever do this for you?

No, we really—Marcia. He probably wrote Marcia. Or he meant

to write Marcia and it was you know a what do you call it. She, Marcia, well, she's actually my fiancée.

Don't worry. I wasn't expecting a ring. So maybe you want to try again?

Maybe I shouldn't.

This is what you call a highly subjective situation. You do what feels right. You want to change the game, too, we can change it. We can even do a regular. Or nothing.

Thanks. What I said before about you looking like her, like Chambers, I was talking the hair and makeup, not, you know, the body.

I know.

How does it compare here, working here? I mean not like I know whether you've done a lot, but.

Monetarily, the money is excellent. Physically, there's far less work. Do you know everyone asks me that? Like they're going to open a franchise. But really. I mean it's skilled. Skilled pays. While you can do it, skilled pays.

So you've got something going outside, I mean, you could be an actress or something?

Or something.

No personal, right? That's O.K. I—I've got this wedding coming up, you know? And, like, well, you're supposed to feel this way before a wedding, right? It's kind of a big deal. They're hiring a chamber orchestra. They're hiring a, like a juggler. I don't know why I'm saying all this.

I think maybe you should relax. Maybe you should have your personal review.

I think, yeah.

So you picked yourself out a? No don't worry, I'll get it. Pick your color?

Gr, ah, blue.

Yellow. Catch. Blue makes it look diseased. Don't you think? So you can stand . . .

. . . over by the.

Sit down, Olson, I'll be with you in a minute. At my desk. So if you'll, I said sit, Olson, this is going to take a while.

I think I'd rather stand.

I don't have time for this. Sit, stand, did you bring in the Simmons and Patel file? I've got a lunch meeting, get off the desk, Olson.

You don't want me off the desk. You've been watching me ever since I started here.

I, I don't know what you're talking about.

The, like that time, in the new-business conference last week? And you made that comment, that dumb-jock comment? Except maybe you need a little dumb jock. You're always, you're always going around, you know, so tense. Maybe you need a little relaxer?

Olson, I—

Mr. Olson.

⁓

Jesus.

You done, sweetie?

Mhn.

That usually does the job.

That was really weird. Oof, sorry.

If you'll just roll, a little, there. Yeah. So listen if you want to unwind a little, I've got a while yet. Smoke? No, it's on the house, it's good, really.

No, I should probably just. It's going to be a long night.

You mind if I?

O.K., I'll, just a hit. Pff. It's a nice desk, somebody have to move it in?

It's a set, the room. Like we have another one with a sink, so it can be a kitchen or maybe a doctor's office, depending? Pff. We've got a dentist's chair. And of course for a consideration we'll go on location, that makes some things easier. The rest are normal rooms, which a bed's a bed, whether you're with Sharon Stone or, like, your sister-in-law. But you tell them it's a *hotel* room, that's the key, then it's exotic. Then plus makeup, plus costume. It's never exact, look close here, see the eye pencil? Up close you can see that. But, I'm doing my job, then up close you got your mind on other things. Generally you give people a few key details and they'll create the illusion themselves.

Pff. Sorry, I guess I killed it.

One dead soldier. I'm not supposed to do this, but take a card. Tuesdays and Thursdays, at Fumer. My stage name's Amy New York.

So I can use your bathroom, before I?

⸺

Hail to the conquering hero, we were about to send a search party.

Sex machine! Glad you could make it!

Fuck you take off on me for, Josh? Hey Rodge, Howard, hey, Zee.

Hey, M. Sex machine, know what I mean?

You're a working man, you can afford a cab. We wanted to get things ready. And you know I didn't want to disturb your whatever, afterglow. Order yourself a drink, you know you have to call ahead two weeks for a private room here?

Helen Chambers, Josh? You're one sick fuck.

Nothing but the best. But seriously, I mean, they treat you right there, am I right? Cadillac ride, no?

Yeah, I had a good time.

M, seriously, Helen Chambers? Josh told us. M, man, I've never had a personal hero, but you're it.

I mean it's not like it was the actual.

Sit down, M, we were worried you'd miss the main event.

Don't tell me, you guys got a stripper.

Not in so many words.

You might want to watch the monitor, Marty.

The idea as I was told is you're supposed to be in the aggressor role.

In the?

In the aggress, oh wait a sec.

Oh, fucking, Josh, they *taped* it? But they can't, but I never said!

Your typical whorehouse isn't greatly concerned with the fine points of constitutionality. Surprising as that may be.

Rodge, I think we saw the, maybe you could fast-forward through some of this? Just through the—yeah! Ba-da-boom ba-da-bing! Marty, next time give us a signal! Hey, watch this—

I'm out of here.

Come on, sit, Marty, it's a joke, I'm up next. You know, you show me yours et cetera. Rodge, don't be an asshole, just let it play. Quit screwing with it.

Gah!

Does Monica ever do that for you?

Jesus.

Mm, I didn't think so.

Jesus.

Jesus!

Jesus Mary Joseph!

Turn it off, Josh.

You might want to try and pick up a little tan there in Bali, Marty, they've got those what do you call those all-around beaches.

Screw you, Howard. Josh, please.

You done, sweetie?

Mhn.

That usually does the job.

In a sec, in a sec, Marty. We've just got the denouement here. Be a sport, you went to a boys' school.

You're giving me the tape.

Anything's negotiable. But I mean we wouldn't want this to end up as landfill somewhere. We've got to consider its audience. You've got Marcia on the one hand and Chambers on the other, I'm thinking maybe we could arrange some sort of screening. Kidding, Marty, so what's taking you so long up there, you grab a shower?

Everything spic and span?

Everything, yeah, you found my tie, thanks.

So you need to go meet your friends now? Good luck on the big day, good luck with, ah, Monica.

Marcia. Hey, you know, the—what I said about the Monica thing, it wasn't exactly true. From the office? It was just one time, we were working late, we had a drink. She—I mean, she felt bad about it. After. But Josh doesn't know, as far as I know.

Maybe he's a little jealous.

Maybe he's, you know, in bed. I guess you're all not supposed to talk about that, either?

Ouch!

Hey, Josh, I'm—

Forget about it, Marty.

And et cetera, et cetera, we're past the good part here, I think, the star rises, puts on his jacket, good day, madam, pleasure to do you—

—come back and see me again some time—

—and he exits. And curtain.

Monica, M? Shit, Monica? Forget what I said about hero. You are my personal god.

Im going to be dead tomorrow. I'm going to be so dead.

Worse, you'll live. It's O.K., we'll find you a cab in a sec, Ahmed'll take you home, you'll wake up in your own filth ready to take on the world. Have some fresh-squeezed and a couple aspirin, you have a juicer, Marty? You really ought to get into juices.

I'm, I'm going to actually yak now.

Just hold—O.K., around the side, by the dumpster, if you, Christ! Aim for the wall then. Attaboy.

Cak.

Let it all out, the rain'll take care of it, don't worry.

Cak.

Here you go. Wipe.

Thanks.

Toss it. Emily buys me a half dozen of them a week, it's some personal project of hers or something.

Josh. I fucking hate scotch.

You love it, baby, you just don't know it yet. That's a punch line, I'll tell you the joke someday you're older.

I'm supposed to go to fucking *brunch*. Taxi! Shit.

So. You cut me down in front of a whore, Marty. That's priceless.

What I was saying on the tape, that was just me talking shit. About Monica? You know that?

You can't even lie sober, Marty, don't try it now. What, you think you bruised my feelings? You must think I'm one pathetic fuck. Like you need to be shielding me from the truth? Pff. Shielding me.

Josh, come on, you know I never.

Drop it. You've got nothing to be sorry for. Tell you the truth I'm glad to hear it, actually.

So you're not mad?

Mad, get over here, am I mad? What you said, it restores my faith in humanity. That nobody's above it. The sheer fuckability of people, Marty. Takes your breath away.

Maybe we should move down the block.

"Celia, Celia, Celia shits."

Who?

Come on, we'll try around Duane Street. But listen. You wouldn't mind, would you, if I were say to share this bit of information with Monica? It might add to my already considerable powers of charm and persuasion.

Give me a break.

I'm asking. If it were implied, I mean, that certain information might ultimately spread further, if you were to back me up, O.K., you're in no condition, we'll talk later.

I don't get it, Josh. She's not even that, I mean, what do you care about her?

You of all people on your wedding eve. Maybe it's love, Marty, don't laugh. Taxi!

Hey, you're good.

The best. This one's yours.

You, you've got your, gotta get a train.

I can be late. Emily—she's ceded me certain prerogatives in our relationship.

So you going to give me the tape?

Oh, the, oh good, so you remember. Pretty good clarity of mind, or was this all your I'm-not-so-think-as-you-drunk-I-am act?

Excuse me, you're getting in, sir?

A minute, a minute. Go ahead, start the meter. You're going to the Upper East Side.

Meter she runs too slow if I'm parked.

Christ, here take it, half an hour's worth, listen to the radio. Marty, I think I need to hang on to the tape. I'm inclined to think you're going to do something foolish.

Fucking, Josh, I want to go home already.

Fine, fine, you got it. Here, hold the umbrella.

Thanks.

One thing, though. That's not your tape. It's mine.

I don't want your tape.

Course you do. Keeps me honest. Our present sexual climate that tape puts me on Court TV with my jacket over my face, Monica retires on five million of the firm's money. You watched it, you know it's not blank. You've got the tape, means I'm not planning anything funny here. Means we're new best friends. Trust me for once. Some point you're ready to trade back, you let me know.

Trade me now.

Marty, I'm just not going to do that. You want to call me an asshole today, that's fine, come on, get in. Someday soon you're gonna be in that office. She's gonna be dicking you around about new accounts this and billable hours that and you're going to eat her shit and ask for seconds. On the outside. But on the inside you're going to think, I did you. Because you know you've got her, right here. Confidence, Marty. You wait. Then you tell me I'm an asshole.

You're an asshole, Josh.

Certifiable. 'Joy your brunch.

75th between Madison and Lex. How do I know you won't make a copy?

Friends forever, get some rest. Go on, sahib. Drive.

CRUSH
Wang Ping

What exactly caused the ache was never clear. But it all started with "The Little Mermaid" story I told to my sister and our upstairs neighbors—the Dong sister and brother—on the night of the last and bloodiest faction war on the island.

It wasn't supposed to happen like that, I mean the war that killed hundreds of young people in the fourth year of the Cultural Revolution. After endless fierce battles, the two largest factions between the workers and Red Guards had finally sat down to negotiate for a possible fusion into a common revolutionary committee under Mao's instruction: We want refined battles, not military ones. During those fifteen months, things slowly got back to normal. Markets and shops reopened. Some factories turned on machines. Students returned to schools for half a day to study Mao's books. But in the end, Mao's earlier teaching that revolution is not an invitation to dinner parties but thunderstorms probably took the upper hand. Overnight, the middle school building used for the headquarters was covered by the Red Guards' pledge "Fight for Our Great Leader Chairman Mao to Our Last Drop of Blood" and other war slogans. Before people had time to store food and seal windows with paper strips, the war broke out.

I woke up in the midst of heavy explosions and piercing noises at the back window. At first I thought Chairman Mao must have issued another great teaching and the whole country was celebrating with firecrackers and parades. I was looking for my clothes when Father rushed in and pulled us off the bed. "Stay low and keep quiet," he whispered sternly as he dismantled our bed in the dark and laid the mattress on the floor. Several bullets flew in our direction. Windows shattered upstairs. We all lay down on our stomachs without being told so. Before we got our breath back, someone was knocking on the door. "Stay where you are," Father said and crawled out. Soon he returned with three people who sat down immediately against the wall. Father unrolled a bamboo mattress on the cement floor, threw a blanket on it and said, "Just make do for tonight. Tomorrow I'll make it more comfortable for you."

Slowly I recognized our upstairs neighbors, the Dong sister and brothers. I saw the girl and her younger brother every day, though we rarely talked to each other. The older brother was a stranger, since he lived and worked as an apprentice in Shanghai Radio Factory. He came to visit his parents once a year. My sister poked at me and whispered in her breathless excitement as if a pancake had just dropped into her mouth from the sky. "Look, it's Dong Sheng, the oldest brother. Isn't he handsome like a prince!" In the dim moonlight, I stared openly at the sixteen-year-old young man, who was said to be the best-looking person in this compound. Living in the big city and working there in the best factory only enhanced this image. I couldn't see much except for his gleaming pale cheekbones and his long neck. Unlike his siblings who stretched out on the mattress, he leaned against the wall, his thin body trembling as the cannons exploded in the distance. He wasn't used to brutal fights, having grown up in the safety and luxury of Shanghai. "Pretty bad out there, eh?" my sister said as loud as she dared, her trembling voice saturated with excitement. To have the "prince" sleep in the same room with her! How her friends would envy her! Dong Sheng sat motionless as if glued to the wall. His sister answered, "Terrible, terrible. All the windows broken into pieces. My brother almost hit by a bullet, just two inches away from his ear. I'm not lying. I can show you the hole in the wall."

"Wow, that is really scary," my sister said. I almost kicked at her for being so phony. We were used to having bullets flying past our ears, above our heads, having our windows pierced and shattered. A bullet hole in the wall? We'd seen thousands of them. The Dong sister and brothers felt the exaggerated sympathy in her voice. For a while no one spoke. My sister grew more and more restless. She was desperate to make a deep impression on the legendary prince. If she missed the chance, she might never get another one. The Dong family kept to themselves, especially when Dong Sheng was around. She had tried hard to break into the family, and became friendly with the mother, but from Dong Sheng, she could only get a hello and a quick nod before his weekly stay was up and he was

back to Shanghai again. I knew she was dying to turn on the light
to show off her sparkling eyes and rosy cheeks, to perform her five
consecutive backward somersaults, and stand on her hands for
fifteen minutes.

The gunshots stopped suddenly. My sister broke the eerie silence
and said, "It's too scary. Let's sing a song." Not only did she have
the sweetest voice, but she knew all the songs, revolutionary or dirty
ones that circled in the underground. Often we started singing
together, and ended up listening to her solo performance. She knew
her power.

"Don't be ridiculous," Grandma intervened. "You can look for
death all you want, but your brother and I are not ready to die yet."

"We have to do something. I can't sleep. I can't stand this
silence," she said. "Grandma, why don't you tell us a story."

"Nah, you've heard them a hundred times. They're silly, those
stories about stupid sons-in-laws and horny old men. Not suitable
for you anymore." She stole a glance at Dong Sheng. Even she was
in awe.

My sister nudged close to me. "Big sister, please tell us a story."

I was moved speechless by her generosity. First, she barely called
me sister, especially in public. Secondly, she was giving me the
chance to show my talent, the only thing I could do better than she.
She could chat and sing for hours with such grace, yet as soon as
she started a story, she stuttered. I touched her arm to acknowledge
my gratitude, searching madly in my brain for something to impress
our rare guest.

"What about 'The Merry Widow's Fan'? The woman's private
part was cut off by her husband's mistress, and the husband
retaliated by cutting off the mistress' nose. Isn't that wild enough?"
my sister suggested. Before I could remind her that it was a dirty
book, that we were supposed to keep it secret, she babbled on. "Or
the stories from the Bible you found in the garbage. That virgin girl
who gave birth to Jesus, who can walk on the surface of the water
and raise the dead."

I was panicked. My sister had just revealed our top secret books
to people we didn't really know. I was about to give her an elbow
when Dong Sheng said, "Isn't it all superstition? I thought we'd

cleaned it up long time ago. Well, things are different on an island."

His soft voice carried an authority that sent my sister into silence. The bullets and cannons started exploding again outside. People were charging across the football field in the back of our building towards the middle school headquarters. Something hot rose from my stomach to my head, the same burning sensation that went down my chest when I drank boiling water or swallowed a piece of scorching bean curd. I sat up. "I have a story called 'The Little Mermaid.' It's about a beautiful human fish who gives up all she has in order to win love from a prince."

Without waiting for an approval, I started describing the beautiful sea palace, the six princesses loved dearly by their father and grandma, their impatient waiting to reach fifteen when they could swim to the surface of the water to look at the other world—the world of humans who walk on their legs. I described in great detail the exquisite beauty of the youngest mermaid, her longing for the world on land, her rescue of her beloved prince, and how she traded her voice for a pair of legs. I talked on amid the shower of bullets, the explosion of grenades and the screaming of wounded people a few hundred yards away from us, but no one seemed to care. Even Dong Sheng stopped trembling at the explosions. I'd always been a good storyteller. But this time, I was possessed. Words rolled out of my mouth effortlessly. My small, bony body seemed to have merged with the story. My feet felt the sharp pain of walking on knives with each step the Little Mermaid made, and my heart contracted with anguish as she danced with her bleeding feet at the wedding of the prince and the royal maiden, knowing that when the dawn broke, she would turn into a speck of foam among the ocean waves. The fierce battle in our backyard seemed to have faded into a far distance; only my voice bounced from one face to another. Now the Little Mermaid sat alone on the deck, watching the skyline in the east turn pink. Her five sisters emerged above the water, their hair all gone, traded for the knife with which the Little Mermaid could save herself by killing the prince. Behind them was their grandma, her hair all gray from sorrow. I was pausing to create suspense, to stop my voice from choking, when my grandma broke the silence.

"I say she's a silly girl, that little mermaid. Why the hell did she want to leave her father's palace to become some dumb man's slave? Let's not mention the way she had her body cut in half, her tongue cut out, her feet bleeding with each step. Worse than footbinding. And I'm not even going to say how she neglected her duty to her family, and the sorrow she caused."

"It's called love, Grandma," my sister came to my defense.

"Pooh, love. Can it feed you or keep you warm? I've lived sixty-five years without it, and I'm doing just fine. No severed limbs or tongues, no broken heart, like that silly fish girl."

"Oh, you'll never know what it is to fall in love, Grandma. You're too old, anyway. You never had a chance to meet a prince in your life."

"Prince or no prince," she snapped, "what good does he do for you if you can't speak up for yourself, or if he only treats you like a dumb child and slave?"

There was a painful silence inside and outside the house. The attackers seemed to have broken into the Red Guards' headquarters. Finally, Dong Sheng asked, "Did she kill him?"

His question startled me. I shook my head. "I don't know the end of the story. It was an old book, with many pages missing." I didn't know why I lied. The book, which I had stolen from my classmate after I read part of the story over her shoulder, was hidden right beneath me, inside the hole I ripped through the mattress.

Either because books with missing pages were common, or the audience's concentration was shattered by Grandma's interruption, they all seemed to have accepted my explanation. Only Dong Sheng seemed to have some questions for me, but checked himself. Soon I drifted into a dream, floating with waves until I reached the shore. I lay upon the sand, my body, starting from my feet, was melting into white foams. The prince came to kneel over me, finally realized what was going on, but it was too late. He had already married the other maiden. His tears dropped like pearls on my dissolving face.

I opened my eyes and saw Dong Sheng kneeling next to the bed, his face a few inches from mine, his breath hot and sweet, his clear eyes wide open, yet he did not seem to notice I had awakened. He lingered over my face for a few more minutes, then he bent his head closer. My heart thumped in my throat. Was he going to kiss me? He climbed on top of me, his body stiff and heavy like a rock, yet his finger traced my nose and lips with great gentleness. I dared not make a sound; my sister, grandma and brother were sleeping next to me on the same mattress, and on the other side Dong's sister and brother. I trembled under his weight, gasping for air. He remained stiff and motionless for such a long time that I began to panic. Oh God, he might have died on me. Suddenly he got up and went back to his own place.

I stayed wide awake in bewilderment until the dawn broke and it was time to get up for the morning chores. The only explanation for what happened last night was that Dong Sheng was in a trance or sleepwalking. But why me? Because I was the storyteller? He stroked my lips exactly the way the prince fondled the Little Mermaid while calling her "my dumb child." Was he acting like a prince in his dream? He must have known how people in this compound admired him. Was he taking me for the Little Mermaid? I had no beauty or a sweet voice to match up with her except that my mother and grandma also called me "dumb," with the double meanings for being stupid and silent. Why didn't he choose my sister who resembled her in every way except she talked too much? Should I feel lucky or take it as a bad omen to be chosen? After all, she was abandoned in the end and was about to lose her body and soul forever. I walked in and out of the apartment in a trance, doing my morning routine of letting out chickens, lighting the coal stove, making breakfast. When I returned from the market with food, the Dong family was gone. They would not return tonight, my sister said. The workers, armed with the weapons provided by the Navy, had seized the Red Guards' headquarters last night. Yes, many people died. Mostly students. But the battle was over, finally. All morning, the loudspeaker had been broadcasting the announcement that the workers had officially taken over the school as the ruling class, that all students and teachers must return to school in the fall to receive re-education from the working class. I listened to her chatting, wondering if she had any inkling of what had happened last night between Dong Sheng and me. Then I heard her say that Dong Sheng was leaving for Shanghai in two days. His father got him the ticket the first thing in the morning. Too bad, eh? After last night's intimacy, she was confident of getting a connection with him. And, she said triumphantly, his mother had invited her to play chess with her son, who was said to be an excellent player. "I'll let him win no matter what," she cooed. My sister was the chess champion of the compound.

Grandma came over with a rooster. "Chicken Yang is here," she said. "I want you to run out and get the rooster fixed. Hurry up. There's already a big line. He hasn't showed up for two weeks." I took the rooster and walked away with an aching heart. What my sister had just told me made more sense than what had taken place last night. How should I explain everything then? I knew I wasn't dreaming or hallucinating. I could still feel his weight, still smell his salty breath, and my lips still tickled from his cool fingers. The only possible answer was that Dong Sheng had mistaken me for my sister in his sleepwalk.

The rooster made a desperate struggle to get free. He flapped his wings, raising his head in vain. Realizing I had been holding him upside-down by his legs which Grandma had tied together with a straw rope, I turned him over and held him under my arm. I had brought him up from a bloody chick pecking his way out of an egg shell into a brown feathered, fourteen-month-old rooster. After he jumped the first hen, which was about half a year ago, he was put in a separate coop and fed with special food. Once a week, Father drew blood from under his wing with a needle and injected it into Mother's buttocks. Everyone believed that the blood from a young rooster was the best tonic. Ever since the Red Guards paraded Mother on a truck throughout the town, she had been acting weird. Her moods alternated between extreme happiness and manic depression. Her need to pinch and whip us became more frequent and unpredictable. The blood transfusion didn't change her much except for giving her more strength to hit us, but the rooster, with his blood being sucked out periodically, was a wreck. His feathers became dull and tangled. His pale crown sagged like an old breast. Father had abandoned him a week ago, and started drawing blood from Big White, our stud rooster, until the two spring roosters were ready to give blood. Once the wasted brown rooster was fixed, he

would grow plump and tender, and in two or three weeks, he would
be a delicious meal. I looked at him with sadness. His life was so
short and joyless. Did he have a soul? If he did, where would it go
when Mother ate his meat? If not, would he earn one after this long
period of sacrifice, like the Little Mermaid?

The line moved. I stepped outside and saw Chicken Yang cutting
into a rooster with his knife. Before me, everyone had one or two
haggard roosters upside down in their hands. The chicken blood
transfusion was this year's trend. And they all seemed to know the
secret that a fixed rooster tasted better. Chicken Yang took
something white out of the chicken and popped it into his mouth.
He pulled a few feathers from the screaming creature, stuffed them
into the wound, untied the rope, and returned the rooster to its
owner, who handed him a bag of chicken feathers. Yang poured it
all into his gigantic sack which was already half filled. Unlike all
other peddlers who sold noodles, bean curd or sharpened knives,
Chicken Yang never took cash for his merchandise—his malt candy
or castration service. For fixing one rooster, he took a bag of
feathers. He also accepted glass bottles, toothpaste tubes, cigarette
wrappers, books, and scrap iron. Whenever his drum rattled into
the yard and his singing "Chicken feathers, goose down" boomed in
the compound, kids would run out and chase him, singing, "Chicken
feathers, goose down, and Chicken Yang's pubic hair." Although we
tormented him like this, we couldn't wait to bring him our collected
feathers and traded them for his malt candy, something strictly
forbidden by our parents. They said his candy was made from his
saliva, that he sometimes put herbs in it to lure children away for
some dirty business. Yet they always welcomed his arrival,
especially now with so many wasted roosters to be fixed. While he
worked on roosters, we often stared at his round, hairless scalp that
was covered with greasy beads of sweat, his nose and lips red and
meaty. Adults said he lost his hair from eating too many rooster
testicles. Imagine all the male hormones accumulated in his body
that had no outlet, living alone in a remote village. But the more
our parents talked, the faster we ran to him. His quacking laugh,
his round trembling stomach and oily face, and what he did to
roosters, all terrified and fascinated us at the same time. And how

his malt candy made our mouths water as he lifted the greasy cloth off the tray, chopped pieces of his golden treasure with a chisel and lay them gently in our little palms. The sticky sweet candy stuck to our teeth, giving us horrible cavities and toothaches, but we didn't care.

"Hi, little girl, you want me to fix your rooster or not?" Chicken Yang's quacking startled me. I looked around. I was the last customer under the weeping willow where he set his stand. People behind me must have gone home for lunch or gone ahead of me while I was in a daze. I handed him the chicken. He tied its legs to a long chopstick, plucked some feathers under the wing until its pale skin was exposed. He poked at the smooth spot, then stabbed a thin knife into it. The rooster uttered a hoarse screech, but was unable to move. Slowly he withdrew the knife, turned it around and stuck the other end which was shaped like a spoon into the cut. With a few stirs, he spooned out something white that resembled a pigeon egg. Not a drop of blood. Either he was extremely skillful or the rooster had completely dried up. Chicken Yang examined the egg with a grunt and popped it into his mouth. I stared with disgust. Had he swallowed all the stuff he had taken out of the roosters?

"What are you eating?" I heard myself asking.

"Oh, rooster egg, little girl. A very good thing for men. Makes them big and strong, like me." He flexed the muscles on his arms and pounded his chest. "Good eggs are rare to find these days. The roosters people bring me are useless, like this one." He kicked at my brown rooster on the ground. "Hey, little girl, when are you going to bring your Big White? I'll give you a whole tray of my candy."

I shook my head and handed him a bag of black feathers. It was from the black hen which Mother had killed to make broth a week ago after she stopped laying eggs. Since her disappearance from the coop, Big White had lost interest in food and sex. Of the eight hens, the black one was his favorite consort. Whenever he caught a worm or found a grain of rice, he would call her over and danced around her like a dirty old man. Chicken Yang took out a handful of the shiny feathers and nodded his head in satisfaction. When he poured them into his sack, I asked, "What do girls eat to make them big and strong, hen eggs?"

He burst out laughing. "No, no, no, little girl. Hen eggs won't do the trick. It's other stuff." He looked me up and down. "How old are you, little girl?"

"Fifteen." I said, adding another year to my Chinese age, which had already increased my real age by a year and a half.

"No good, no good." He shook his head as he rubbed his chin, scrutinizing me with his meaty eyes. "Hey, little girl, why don't you come with me. Chicken Yang knows how to make you big." He suddenly bent over and cupped my flat chest with his giant hand. The heat from his palm scorched my clothing and skin. "You haven't seen your ghost yet, have you?" He looked at me with such pity in his eyes that I froze in his grip. He loosened his hand and said, "Go home, little girl. Eat lots of chickens and eggs. Grow some meat on your bones first. Next time, bring Big White and Uncle Yang will teach you some trick." He chiseled a piece of candy from his tray and slipped it into my hand.

Everyone was in bed when I got home. My lunch, a bowl of rice with some stringy vegetable stems and brown sauce, stood humbly next to a pile of dirty dishes. Grandma spoke from our bedroom. "Did Chicken Yang eat up your soul or what? I thought you'd never come back. Finish your lunch and clean up. Your mother wants you to wash the windows today. Why don't you start with the kitchen?"

I ate, washed the dishes, and cleaned the kitchen window. My family was not yet up. So I sat down on the windowsill and opened my braids. My hair hung all the way to my thighs. Whenever Mother saw me brush it, she would curse loudly. Now that she was asleep, I could take my time. How foolish of me to believe that Dong Sheng liked me, I told myself, leaning over the window to make sure no hair would fall on the floor. Even Chicken Yang didn't want me because I was still not a woman. When would I ever grow up? When would I see my ghost like my sister? She was younger, yet her blood flowed half a year ago. When she first saw the red, she came to me in tears, thinking she was dying of some mysterious disease. We sewed layers of cloth to her underwear to block the blood, until one day mother saw the thickly padded shorts and threw a rubber panty at her. Soon my sympathy turned into jealousy as I watched her waddling to show off what was going on between her legs, her whispering to her friends about her monthly visit by the "old ghost." I tried everything I could, jumping up and down, carrying heavy things, placing toilet paper in my underwear, but I remained as dry as an old hag. On my fourteenth birthday, I cracked a hole on an egg I found in the chicken coop and was about to suck it when my sister waddled over. From the way she walked, she must be haunted by her ghost again. She threatened to tell on me unless I gave her the egg. I trashed it on the ground and yelled, "It's my birthday, damn it. I'm already fourteen, fourteen, do you hear?" She gave me the same pitying look Chicken Yang did and pulled out her rubber panty. "Would you like to borrow it?" she offered. "Two of my friends wore it for only a week and the red just poured out like crazy. Very effective."

I looked down at my belly. It was even flatter than my chest. The only places that stuck out on my body were my joints and my big nose. My sister's breasts bulged just like the Little Mermaid's. So did the curve along her waist. I looked down at the Big White in the coop and rubbed the candy which I had wrapped with the cigarette paper. Should I go with Chicken Yang?

"You have the most beautiful hair on earth, my little mermaid."

I turned to the direction of the voice but dared not look. It was Dong Sheng, but how could it be true? It was impossible to be in the same dream twice. The voice came again. "Please tell me what happened to her? Did she kill the prince or did she let herself perish forever? Please tell me so I can sleep tonight."

I opened my eyes. How pale he looked! As if he had been tossed around in a storm all night and just been rescued to the shore. Perhaps what happened last night wasn't a dream or sleep-walk. But why me? I looked into his dark velvet eyes and said, "My sister said you were playing chess with her this afternoon."

He waved his hand. "Oh, I beat her in fifteen minutes. Too easy. Well, what happened to the Little Mermaid?"

I shook my head. Too easy. Was the Little Mermaid also too easy? Was it why she lost her prince?

"Come on," he pleaded. "I know you have the whole story. What can I do to make you tell?"

I almost said, "I want you to love me. I want you to make me a woman."

Dong Sheng's mother shouted from upstairs to summon her son to the chess game. He stamped his feet and stood up with a sigh. "I'll come back, you stubborn mermaid. I hope you won't make me wait too long. I'm leaving day after tomorrow. By the way, your hair looks like fire in the sunlight."

I sat on the windowsill for a long time until grandma came into the kitchen and yelled at me to get down and start making supper. I washed and chopped vegetables, watched them being sautéed in the wok, my heart sizzling in a happiness I had never experienced in my life. He likes me, and he will come back for me and for the story, I chanted silently to myself. If I have to die now, I'd have nothing to regret.

Dong Sheng never came back even though his ship was delayed for a week by the typhoon. I was glad he didn't. That afternoon while I was chopping vegetables in a daze, I forgot to wrap my head with a towel. At dinner, Mother found hair in every dish I made. She threw down her chopsticks, grabbed a pair of scissors and cut my braids. My sister took pity on me and tried to trim my short hair into some kind of shape. It didn't work. My hair stood up on my scalp like an angry porcupine. Grandma said it looked as if it had been bitten by a mad bitch. She also kept telling me *le ji sheng bei*—extreme happiness brings tragedy. I wondered if she was eavesdropping on us that afternoon.

We encountered each other again, however, on the morning he left. I was delivering Big White to our neighbor Mr. Liu, who wanted the rooster to mate with his hens. Though Big White hadn't recovered from the death of the black hen and the weekly blood transfusion, Mother agreed to his request. She had been eyeing charming and powerful Mr. Liu for a long time.

The Dong family were walking ahead of me, each carrying a parcel or a basket filled with dried sea food. My sister walked next to Dong Sheng, chatting like a magpie. She had spent every minute of her spare time upstairs for the past week. When she returned for dinner, she talked on and on about her prince, her eyes sparkling like stars. I walked behind them, praying that no one would look back and see my tangled, dog-bitten hair. Suddenly, the rooster, which had been lying quietly against my chest, jumped out of my arms and charged at Mrs. Dong, pecking at her hand with his powerful beaks, his wings wide open. He was trying to rescue the black hen that Mrs. Dong was holding upside down in her hand.

She ran in circles screaming for help, yet refused to let go of the hen. Dong Sheng turned at the sound of the turmoil and pounced upon the rooster in his heavy navy boots. Big White staggered a few steps before he fell. I picked him up, put my hand on his snow white chest, now streaked with blood. He was still breathing. I looked up. Our eyes met. He quickly turned his head. I wasn't sure if he had recognized me. My sister watched the scene with her mouth wide open. She knew how important the rooster was to our family, especially to me. If the culprit had been someone else instead of Dong Sheng, she would have screamed her lungs out and thrown herself upon him. Love had tamed her.

To my surprise, Mother only gave me a few knocks on my head with her knuckles and told me to keep an eye on the rooster. If he got better, she'd have Chicken Yang fix him. If not, she'd kill him early next morning. He'd be good at least for a pot of soup. That night I stayed up at the coop watching Big White breathe on my lap. He'd never get better again. What for? To make a better meal? I took out my handkerchief and made a knot around his neck. "Forgive me, Big White," I said and pulled. He stopped breathing without a struggle. He understood why I did this. He would be inedible by the time I reported his death the next morning. Mother would punish me, but Big White had been my best friend since he hatched before my eyes two years ago, and this was the least I could do for him—to keep his body whole.

I buried Big White and put his feathers in a new cloth bag, together with Anderson's fairy tales and my schoolbooks. I was ready to go away with Chicken Yang, let him take me wherever he wanted. But three weeks passed by. His peddler drum never rattled again into our compound. My sister announced one day at lunch that Chicken Yang had died. Someone said he was shot by a stray bullet; some said he did something bad to a village girl and was stoned to death by the angry villagers. "Too bad," she said, "no more malt candy."

PAGES FROM *Cold Point*
Paul Bowles

Our civilization is doomed to a short life: its component parts are too heterogeneous. I personally am content to see everything in the process of decay. The bigger the bombs the quicker it will be done. Life is visually too hideous for one to make the attempt to preserve it. Let it go. Perhaps some day another form of life will come along. Either way, it is of no consequence. At the same time, I am still a part of life, and I am bound by this to protect myself to whatever extent I am able. And so I am here. Here in the Islands vegetation still has the upper hand, and man has to fight even to make his presence seen at all. It is beautiful here, the trade winds blow all year, and I suspect that bombs are extremely unlikely to be wasted on this unfrequented side of the Island, if indeed on any part of it.

I was loath to give up the house after Hope's death. But it was the obvious move to make. My university career always having been an utter farce (since I believe no reason inducing a man to "teach" can possibly be a valid one), I was elated by the idea of resigning, and as soon as her affairs had been settled and the money properly invested, I lost no time in doing so.

I think that week was the first time since childhood that I had managed to recapture the feeling of there being a content in existence. I went from one pleasant house to the next, making my adieux to the English quacks, the Philosophy fakirs and so on—even to those colleagues with whom I was merely on speaking terms. I watched the envy in their faces when I announced my departure by Pan American on Saturday morning; and the greatest pleasure I felt in all this was in being able to answer, "Nothing," when I was asked, as invariably I was, what I intended to do.

When I was a boy people used to refer to Charles as "Big Brother C.," although he is only a scant year older than I. To me he is merely "Fat Brother C.," a successful lawyer. His thick, red face and hands, his backslapping joviality, and his fathomless hypocritical prudery, these are the qualities which make him truly repulsive to me. There is also the fact that he once looked not unlike the way

Racky does now. And after all, he still is my big brother, and disapproves openly of everything I do. The loathing I feel for him is so strong that for years I have not been able to swallow a morsel of food or a drop of liquid in his presence without making a prodigious effort. No one knows this but me—certainly not Charles, who would be the last I should tell about it. He came upon the late train two nights before I left. He got to the point—as soon as he was settled with a highball.

"So you're off for the wilds," he said, sitting forward in his chair like a salesman.

"If you can call it the wilds," I replied. "Certainly it's not wild like Mitichi. [He has a lodge in northern Quebec.] I consider it really civilized."

He drank and smacked his lips together stiffly, bringing the glass down hard on his knee.

"And Racky. You're taking him along?"

"Of course."

"Out of school. Away. So he'll see nobody but you. You think that's good."

I looked at him. "I do," I said.

"By God, if I could stop you legally, I would!" he cried, jumping up and putting his glass on the mantel. I was trembling inwardly with excitement, but I merely sat and watched him. He went on. "You're not fit to have custody of the kid!" he shouted. He shot a stern glance at me over his spectacles.

"You think not?" I said gently.

Again he looked at me sharply "D'ye think I've forgotten?"

I was understandably eager to get him out of the house as soon as I could. As I piled and sorted letters and magazines on the desk, I said: "Is that all you came to tell me? I have a good deal to do tomorrow and I must get some sleep. I probably shan't see you at breakfast. Agnes'll see that you eat in time to make the early train."

All he said was: "God! Wake up. Get wise to yourself! You're not fooling anybody, you know."

That kind of talk is typical of Charles. His mind is slow and obtuse; he constantly imagines that everyone he meets is playing some private game of deception with him. He is so utterly incapable of following the functioning of even a moderately evolved intellect that he finds the will to secretiveness and duplicity everywhere.

"I haven't time to listen to that sort of nonsense," I said, preparing to leave the room.

But he shouted, "You don't want to listen! No! Of course not! You just want to do what you want to do. You just want to go on off down there and live as you've a mind to, and to hell with the consequences!" At this point I heard Racky coming downstairs. C. obviously heard nothing and he raved on. "But just remember I've got your number all right, and if there's any trouble with the boy I'll know who's to blame."

I hurried across the room and opened the door so he could see that Racky was there in the hallway. That stopped his tirade. It was hard to know whether Racky had heard any of it or not. Although he is not a quiet young person, he is the soul of discretion, and it is almost never possible to know any more about what goes on inside his head than he intends one to know.

I was annoyed that C. should have been bellowing at me in my own house. To be sure, he is the only one from whom I would accept such behavior, but then, no father likes to have his son see him take criticism meekly. Racky simply stood there in his bathrobe, his angelic face quite devoid of expression, saying: "Tell Uncle Charley good night for me, will you? I forgot."

I said I would and quickly shut the door. When I thought Racky was back upstairs in his room, I bade Charles good night. I have never been able to get out of his presence fast enough. The effect he has on me dates from an early period in our lives, from days I dislike to recall.

Racky is a wonderful boy. After we arrived, when we found it impossible to secure a proper house near any town where we might have the company of English boys and girls his own age, he showed no sign of chagrin, although he must have been disappointed. Instead, as we went out of the renting office into the glare of the street, he grinned and said: "Well, I guess we'll have to get bikes, that's all."

The few available houses near what Charles would have called "civilization" turned out to be so ugly and so impossibly confining in atmosphere that we decided immediately on Cold Point, even though it was across the island and quite isolated on its seaside cliff. It was beyond a doubt one of the most desirable properties on the island, and Racky was as enthusiastic about its splendors as I.

"You'll get tired of being alone out there, just with me," I said to him as we walked back to the hotel.

"Aw, I'll get along all right. When do we look for the bikes?"

At his insistence we bought two the next morning. I was sure I should not make much use of mine, but I reflected that an extra bicycle might be convenient to have around the house. It turned out that the servants all had their own bicycles, without which they would not have been able to get to and from the village of Orange Walk, eight miles down the shore. So for a while I was forced to get astride mine each morning before breakfast and pedal madly alongside Racky for a half hour. We would ride through the cool early air, under the towering silk-cotton trees near the house, and out to the great curve in the shoreline where the waving palms bend landward in the stiff breeze that always blows there. Then we would make a wide turn and race back to the house, loudly discussing the degrees of our desires for the various items of breakfast we knew were awaiting us there on the terrace. Back home we would eat in the wind, looking out over the Caribbean, and talk about the news in yesterday's local paper, brought to us by Isaiah each morning from Orange Walk. Then Racky would disappear for the whole morning on his bicycle, riding furiously along the road in one direction or the other until he had discovered an unfamiliar strip of sand along the shore that he could consider a new beach. At lunch he would describe it in detail to me, along with a recounting of all the physical hazards involved in hiding the bicycle in among the trees, so that natives passing along the road on foot would not spot it, or in climbing down unscalable cliffs that turned out to be much higher than they had appeared at first sight, or in measuring the depth of the water preparatory to diving from the rocks, or ill-judging the efficacy of the reef in barring sharks and barracuda. There is never any element of braggadocio in Racky's relating of his exploit—only the joyous excitement he derives from telling how he satisfies his inexhaustible curiosity. And his mind shows its alertness in all directions at once. I do not mean to say that I expect him to be an "intellectual." That is no affair of mine, nor do I have any particular interest in whether he turns out to be a thinking man or not. I know he will always have a certain boldness of manner and a great purity of spirit in judging values. The former will prevent his becoming what I call a "victim": he never will be brutalized by realities. And his unerring sense of balance in ethical considerations will shield him from the paralyzing effects of present-day materialism.

For a boy of sixteen Racky has an extraordinary innocence of vision. I do not say this as a doting father, although God knows I can never even think of the boy without that familiar overwhelming sensation of delight and gratitude for being vouchsafed the privilege of sharing my life with him. What he takes so completely as a matter of course, our daily life here together, is a source of never-ending wonder to me; and I reflect upon it a good part of each day, just sitting here being conscious of my great good fortune in having him all to myself, beyond the reach of prying eyes and malicious tongues. (I suppose I am really thinking of C. when I write that.) And I believe that a part of the charm of sharing Racky's life with him consists precisely in his taking it all so utterly for granted. I have never asked him whether he likes being here—it is so patent that he does, very much. I think if he were to turn to me one day and tell me how happy he is here, that somehow, perhaps the spell might be broken. Yet if he were to be thoughtless and inconsiderate, or even unkind to me, I feel that I should be able only to love him the more for it.

I have reread that last sentence. What does it mean? And why should I even imagine it could mean anything more than it says?

Still, much as I may try, I can never believe in the gratuitous, isolated fact. What I must mean is that I feel that Racky already has been in some way inconsiderate. But in what way? Surely I cannot resent his bicycle treks; I cannot expect him to want to stay and sit talking with me all day. And I never worry about his being in danger; I know he is more capable than most adults of taking care of himself, and that he is no more likely than any native to come to harm crawling over the cliffs or swimming in the bays. At the same time there is no doubt in my mind that something about our existence annoys me. I must resent some detail in the pattern, whatever that pattern may be. Perhaps it is just his youth, and I am envious of his lithe body, the smooth skin, the animal energy and grace.

For a long time this morning I sat looking out to sea, trying to solve that small puzzle. Two white herons came and perched on a dead stump east of the garden. They stayed a long time there without stirring. I would turn my head away and accustom my eyes to the bright sea-horizon, then I would look suddenly at them to see if they had shifted position, but they would always be in the same attitude. I tried to imagine the black stump without them—a purely vegetable landscape—but it was impossible. All the while I was slowly forcing myself to accept a ridiculous explanation of my annoyance with Racky. It had made itself manifest to me only yesterday, when instead of appearing for lunch, he sent a young colored boy from Orange Walk to say that he would be lunching in the village. I could not help noticing that the boy was riding Racky's bicycle. I had been waiting lunch a good half hour for him, and I had Gloria serve immediately as the boy rode off, back to the village. I was curious to know in what sort of place and with whom Racky could be eating, since Orange Walk, as far as I know, is inhabited exclusively by Negroes, and I was sure Gloria would be able to shed some light on the matter, but I could scarcely ask her. However, as she brought me the dessert, I said: "Who was that boy that brought the message from Mister Racky?"

She shrugged her shoulders. "A young lad of Orange Walk. He's named Wilmot."

When Racky returned at dusk, flushed from his exertion (for he never rides casually), I watched him closely. His behavior struck my already suspicious eye as being one of false heartiness and a rather forced good humor. He went to his room early and read for quite a while before turning off his light. I took a long walk in the almost day-bright moonlight, listening to the songs of the night insects in the trees, and I sat for a while in the dark on the stone railing of the bridge across Black River. (It is really only a brook that rushes down over the rocks from the mountain a few miles inland, to the beach near the house.) In the night it always sounds louder and more important than it does in daytime. The music of the water over the stones relaxed my nerves, although why I had need of such a thing I find it difficult to understand, unless I was really upset by Racky's not coming home for lunch. But if that were true it would be absurd, and moreover, dangerous—just the sort of thing the parent of an adolescent has to be aware of and fight against, unless he is indifferent to the prospect of losing the trust and affection of his offspring permanently. Racky must stay out whenever he likes, with whom he likes, and for as long as he likes, and I must not think twice about it, much less mention it to him, or in any way give the impression of prying. Lack of confidence on the part of a parent is the one unforgivable sin.

Although we still take our morning dip together on arising, it has been three weeks since we have been for the early spin. One morning I found that Racky had jumped onto his bicycle in his wet trunks while I was still swimming, and gone by himself, and since then there has been an unspoken agreement between us that such is to be the procedure; he will go alone. Perhaps I held him back; he likes to ride so fast.

Young Peter, the smiling gardener from Saint Ives Cove, is Racky's special friend. It is amusing to see them together among the bushes, crouched over an ant-hill or rushing about trying to catch a lizard, almost of an age the two, yet so disparate—Racky with his tan skin looking almost white to the glistening black of the other. Today I know I shall be alone for lunch, since it is Peter's day off. On such days they usually go together on their bicycles into Saint Ives Cove, where Peter keeps a small rowboat. They fish along the coast there, but they have never returned with anything so far.

Meanwhile I am here alone, sitting on the rocks in the sun, from time to time climbing down to cool myself in the water, always conscious of the house behind me under the high palms, like a large glass boat filled with orchids and lilies. The servants are clean and quiet, and the work seems to be accomplished automatically. The good, black servants are another blessing of the islands; the British, born here in this paradise, have no conception of how fortunate they are. In fact, they do nothing but complain. One must have lived in the United States to appreciate the wonder of this place. Still, even here ideas are changing each day. Soon the people will decide that they want their land to be part of today's monstrous world, and once that happens, it will be all over. As soon as you have that desire, you are infected with a deadly virus, and you begin to show the symptoms of the disease. You live in terms of time and money, and you think in terms of society and progress. Then all that is left for you is to kill the other people who think the same way, along with a good many of those who do not, since that is the final manifestation of the malady. Here for the moment at any rate, one has the feeling of staticity—existence ceases to be like those last few seconds in the hour-glass when what is left of the sand suddenly begins to rush through to the bottom all at once. For the moment, it seems suspended. And if it seems, it is. Each wave at my feet, each bird-call in the forest at my back, does *not* carry me one step nearer the final disaster. The disaster is certain, but it will suddenly have happened, that is all. Until then, time stays still.

I am upset by a letter in this morning's mail: The Royal Bank of Canada requests that I call in person at its central office to sign the deposit slips and other papers for a sum that was cabled from the bank in Boston. Since the central office is on the other side of the island, fifty miles away, I shall have to spend the night over there and return the following day. There is no point in taking Racky along. The sight of "civilization" might awaken a longing for it in him; one never knows. I am sure it would have in me when I was his age. And if that should once start, he would merely be unhappy, since there is nothing for him but to stay here with me, at least for the next two years, when I hope to renew the lease, or, if things in New York pick up, buy the place. I am sending word by Isaiah when he goes home into Orange Walk this evening, to have the McCoigh car call for me at seven-thirty tomorrow morning. It is an enormous old open Packard, and Isaiah can save the ride out to work here by piling his bicycle into the back and riding with McCoigh.

The trip across the island was beautiful, and would have been highly enjoyable if my imagination had not played a strange trick at the very outset. We stopped in Orange Walk for gasoline, and while that was being seen to, I got out and went to the corner store for some cigarettes. Since it was not yet eight o'clock, the store was still closed, and I hurried up the side street to the other little shop which I thought might be open. It was, and I bought my cigarettes. On the way back to the corner I noticed a large black woman leaning with her arms on the gate in front of her tiny house, staring into the street. As I passed her, she looked straight into my face and said something with the strange accent of the island. It was said in what seemed an unfriendly tone, and ostensibly was directed at me, but I had no notion of what it was. I got back into the car and the driver started it.

The sound of the words had stayed in my head, however, as a bright shape outlined by darkness is likely to stay in the mind's eye, in such a way that when one shuts one's eyes one can see the exact contour of the shape. The car was already roaring up the hill toward the overland road when I suddenly reheard the very words And they were: "Keep your boy at home, mahn." I sat perfectly rigid for a moment as the open countryside rushed past. Why should I think she had said that? Immediately I decided I was giving an arbitrary sense to a phrase I could not have understood even if I had been paying strict attention. And then I wondered why my subconscious should have chosen that sense, since now that I whispered the words over to myself they failed to connect with any anxiety to which my mind might have been disposed. Actually I have never given a thought to Racky's wanderings about Orange Walk. I can find no such preoccupation no matter how I put the question to myself. Then, could she really have said those words? All the way through the mountains I pondered the question, even though it was obviously a waste of energy. And soon I could no longer hear the sound of her voice in my memory: I had played the record over too many times, and worn it out.

Here in the hotel a gala dance is in progress. The abominable orchestra, comprising two saxophones and one sour violin, is playing directly under my window in the garden, and the serious-looking couples slide about on the waxed concrete floor of the terrace, in the light of strings of paper lanterns. I suppose it is meant to look Japanese.

At the moment I wonder what Racky is doing there in the house
with only Peter and Ernest the watchman to keep him company.
The house, which I am accustomed to think of as smiling and
benevolent in its airiness, could just as well be in the most sinister
and remote regions of the globe, now that I am here. Sitting here
with the absurd orchestra bleating downstairs, I picture it to myself,
and it strikes me as terribly vulnerable in its isolation. In my mind's
eye I see the moonlit point with its tall palms waving restlessly in
the wind, its dark cliffs licked by the waves below. Suddenly,
although I struggle against the sensation, I am inexpressibly glad to
be away from the house, helpless there, far on its point of land, in
the silence of the night. Then I remember that the night is seldom
silent. There is the loud sea at the base of the rocks, the droning of
the thousands of insects, the occasional cries of the night birds—all
the familiar noises that make sleep so sound. And Racky is there
surrounded by them as usual, not even hearing them. But I feel
profoundly guilty for having left him, unutterably tender and sad at
the thought of him, lying there alone in the house with the two
Negroes the only human beings within miles. If I keep thinking
about Cold Point I shall be more and more nervous.

I not going to bed yet. They are all screaming with laughter
down there, the idiots: I could never sleep anyway. The bar is still
open. Fortunately it is on the street side of the hotel. For I need a
few drinks. Much later, but I feel no better; I may be a little drunk.
The dance is over and it is quiet in the garden, but the room is too
hot.

As I was falling asleep last night, all dressed, and with the
overhead light shining sordidly in my face, I heard the black
woman's voice again, more clearly even than I did in the car
yesterday. For some reason this morning there is no doubt in my
mind that the words I heard are the words she said. I accept that
and go on from there. Suppose she did tell me to keep Racky home.
It could only mean that she, or someone else in Orange Walk, has
had a childish altercation with him; although I must say it is hard
to conceive of Racky's entering into any sort of argument or feud
with those people. To set my mind at rest (for I do seem to be taking
the whole thing with great seriousness), I am going to stop in the

village this afternoon before going home, and try to see the woman.
I am extremely curious to know what she could have meant.

I had not been conscious until this evening when I came back to
Cold Point how powerful they are, all those physical elements that
go to make up its atmosphere: the sea and wind-sounds that isolate
the house from the road, the brilliancy of the water, sky and surf,
the bright colors and strong odors of the flowers, the feeling of space
both outside and within the house. One naturally accepts these
things when one is living here. This afternoon when I returned I
was conscious of them all over again, of their existence and their
strength. All of them together are like a powerful drug; coming back
made me feel as though I had been detoxificated and were returning
to the scene of my former indulgences. Now at eleven it is as if I
had never been absent an hour. Everything is the same as always,
even to the dry palm branch that scrapes against the window screen
by my night table. And indeed, it is only thirty-six hours since I was
here; but I always expect my absence from a place to bring about
irremediable changes.

Strangely enough, now that I think of it, I feel that something
has changed since I left yesterday morning, and that is the general
attitude of the servants—their collective aura, so to speak. I
noticed that difference immediately upon arriving back, but was
unable to define it. Now I see it clearly. The network of common
understanding which slowly spreads itself through a well-run
household has been destroyed. Each person is by himself now. No
unfriendliness, however, that I can see. They all behave with the
utmost courtesy, excepting possibly Peter, who struck me as
looking unaccustomedly glum when I encountered him in the
kitchen after dinner. I meant to ask Racky if he had noticed it, but
I forgot and he went to bed early.

In Orange Walk I made a brief stop on the pretext to McCoigh
that I wanted to see the seamstress in the side street. I walked up
and back in front of the house where I had seen the woman, but
there was no sign of anyone.

As for my absence, Racky seems to have been perfectly content,
having spent most of the day swimming off the rocks below the
terrace. The insect sounds are at their height now. The breeze is

cooler than usual, and I shall take advantage of these favorable conditions to get a good night's rest.

Today has been one of the most difficult days of my life. I arose early, we had breakfast at the regular time, and Racky went off in the direction of Saint Ives Cove. I lay in the sun on the terrace for a while, listening to the noises of the household's regime. Peter was all over the property, collecting dead leaves and fallen blossoms in a huge basket and carrying them off to the compost heap. He appeared to be in an even fouler humor than last night. When he came near to me at one point on his way to another part of the garden I called to him. He set the basket down and stood looking at me; then he walked across the grass toward me slowly— reluctantly, it seemed to me.

"Peter, is everything all right with you?"

"Yes, sir."

"No trouble at home?"

"Oh, no, sir."

"Good."

"Yes sir."

He went back to his work. But his face belied his words. Not only did he seem to he in a decidedly unpleasant temper; out here in the sunlight he looked positively ill. However, it was not my concern, if he refused to admit it.

When the heavy heat finally still reached the unbearable point for me, I got out of my chair and went down the side of the cliff along the series of steps cut there into the rock. A level platform is below, and a diving board, for the water is deep. At each side, the rocks spread out and the waves break over them, but by the platform the wall of rock is vertical and the water merely hits against it below the springboard. The place is a tiny amphitheater, quite cut off in sound and sight from the house. There too I like to lie in the sun; when I climb out of the water I often remove my trunks and lie stark naked on the springboard. I regularly make fun of Racky because he is embarrassed to do the same. Occasionally he will do it, but never without being coaxed. I was spread out there without a stitch on, being lulled by the slapping of the water, when an unfamiliar voice very close to me said: "Mister Norton?"

I jumped with nervousness, nearly fell off the springboard, and sat up, reaching at the same time, but in vain, for my trunks, which were lying on the rock practically at the feet of a middle-aged mulatto gentleman. He was in a white duck suit, and wore a high collar with a black tie, and it seemed to me that he was eyeing me with a certain degree of horror.

My next reaction was one of anger at being trespassed upon in this way. I rose and got the trunks, donning them calmly and saying nothing more meaningful than: "I didn't hear you come down the steps."

"Shall we go up?" said my caller. As he led the way, I had a definite premonition that he was here on an unpleasant errand. On the terrace we sat down, and he offered me an American cigarette which I did not accept.

"This is a delightful spot," he said, glancing out to sea and then at the end of his cigarette, which was only partially aglow. He puffed at it.

I said, "yes," waiting for him to go on; presently he did.

"I am from the constabulary of this parish. The police, you see." And seeing my face, "This is a friendly call. But still it must be taken as a warning, Mr. Norton. It is very serious. If anyone else comes to you about this it will mean trouble for you, heavy trouble. That's why I want to see you privately this way and warn you personally. You see."

I could not believe I was hearing his words. At length I said faintly: "But what about?"

"This is not an official call. You must not be upset. I have taken it upon myself to speak to you because I want to save you deep trouble."

"But I *am* upset!" I cried, finding my voice at last. "How can I help being upset when I don't know what you're talking about?"

He moved his chair closer to mine, and spoke in a very low voice.

"I have waited until the young man was away from the house so we could talk in private. You see, it is about him."

Somehow that did not surprise me. I nodded.

"I will tell you very briefly. The people here are simple country folk. They make trouble easily. Right now they are all talking about the young man you have living here with you. He is your son, I hear." His inflection here was skeptical.

"Certainly he's my son."

His expression did not change, but his voice grew indignant. "Whoever he is, that is a bad young man."

"What do you mean?" I cried, but he cut in hotly: "He may be your son; he may not be. I don't care who he is. That is not my affair. But he is bad through and through. We don't have such things going on here, sir. The people in Orange Walk and Saint Ives Cove are very cross now. You don't know what these folk do when they are aroused."

I thought it my turn to interrupt. "Please tell why you say my son is bad. What has he done?" Perhaps the earnestness in my voice reached him, for his face assumed a gentler aspect. He leaned still closer to me and almost whispered.

"He has no shame. He does what he pleases with all the young boys, and the men too, and gives them a shilling so they won't tell about it. But they talk. Of course they talk. Every man for twenty miles up and down the coast knows about it. And the women too, they know about it." There was a silence.

I had felt myself preparing to get to my feet for the last few seconds because I wanted to go into my room and be alone, to get away from that scandalized stage whisper. I think I mumbled "Good morning" or "Thank you," as I turned away, and began walking toward the house. But he was still beside me, still whispering like an eager conspirator into my ear: "Keep him home, Mister Norton. Or send him away to school, if he is your son. But make him stay out of these towns. For his own sake."

I shook hands with him and went to lie on my bed. From there I heard his car door slam, heard him drive off. I was painfully trying to formulate an opening sentence to use in speaking to Racky about this, feeling that the opening sentence would define my stand. The attempt was merely a sort of therapeutic action, to avoid thinking about the thing itself. Every attitude seemed impossible. There was no way to broach the subject. I suddenly realized that I should never be able to speak to him directly about it. With the advent of this news he had become another person—an adult, mysterious and formidable. To be sure, it did occur to me that the mulatto's story might not be true, but automatically I rejected the doubt. It was as if I wanted to believe it, almost as if I had already known it, and he had merely confirmed it.

Racky returned at midday, panting and grinning. The inevitable comb appeared and was used on the sweaty, unruly locks. Sitting down to lunch, he exclaimed: "Gosh! Did I find a swell beach this morning! But what a job to get to it!" I tried to look unconcerned as I met his gaze; it was as if our positions had been reversed, and I were hoping to stem his rebuke. He prattled on about thorns and vines and his machete. Throughout the meal I kept telling myself: "Now is the moment. You must say something." But all I said was: "More salad. Or do you want dessert now?" So the lunch passed and nothing happened. After I had finished my coffee I went into my bedroom and looked at myself in the large mirror. I saw my eyes trying to give their reflected brothers a little courage. As I stood there I heard a commotion in the other wing of the house: voices, bumpings, the sound of a scuffle. Above the noise came Gloria's sharp voice, imperious and excited: "No, mahn! Don't strike him!" And louder: "Peter, mahn, no!"

I went quickly toward the kitchen, where the trouble seemed to be, but on the way I was run into by Racky, who staggered into the hallway with his hands in front of his face.

"What is it, Racky?" I cried.

He pushed past me into the living room without moving his hands away from his face; I turned and followed him. From there he went into his own room, leaving the door open behind him. I heard him in his bathroom running the water. I was undecided what to do. Suddenly Peter appeared in the hall doorway, his hat in his hand. When he raised his head, I was surprised to see that his cheek was bleeding. In his eyes was a strange, confused expression of transient fear and deep hostility. He looked down again.

"May I please talk with you, sir?"

"What was all the racket? What's been happening?"

"May I talk with you outside, sir?" He said it doggedly, still not looking up.

In view of the circumstances, I humored him. We walked slowly up the cinder road to the main highway, across the bridge, and through the forest while he told me his story. I said nothing.

At the end he said: "I never wanted to, sir, even the first time, but after the first time I was afraid, and Mister Racky was after me every day."

I stood still, and finally said: "If only you had only told this the first time it happened, it would have been much better for everyone."

He turned his hat in his hands, studying it intently. "Yes, sir. But I didn't know what everyone was saying about him in Orange Walk until today. You know I always go to the beach at Saint Ives Cove with Mister Racky on my free days. If I had known what they were all saying I wouldn't have been afraid, sir. And I wanted to keep on working here. I needed the money." Then he repeated what he had already said three times. "Mister Racky said you'd see about it that I was put in the jail. I'm a year older than Mister Racky, sir."

"I know, I know," I said impatiently; and deciding that severity was what Peter expected of me at this point I added: "You had better get your things together and go home. You can't work here any longer, you know."

The hostility in his face assumed terrifying proportions as he said: "If you killed me I would not work anymore at Cold Point, sir."

I turned and walked briskly back to the house, leaving him standing there in the road. It seems he returned at dusk, a little while ago, and got his belongings.

In his room Racky was reading. He had stuck some adhesive tape on his chin and over his cheekbone.

"I've dismissed Peter," I announced. "He hit you, didn't he?"

He glanced up. His left eye was swollen, but not yet black.

"He sure did. But I landed him one, too. And I guess I deserved it anyway."

I rested against the table. "Why?" I asked nonchalantly.

"Oh, I had something on him from a long time back that he was afraid I'd tell you."

"And just now you threatened to tell me?"

"Oh, no! He said he was going to quit the job here, and I kidded him about being yellow."

"Why did he want to quit? I thought he liked the job."

"Well, he did, I guess, but he didn't like me." Racky's candid gaze betrayed a shade of pique. I still leaned against the table.

I persisted. "But I thought you two got on fine together. You seemed to."

"Nah. He was just scared of losing his job. I had something on him. He was a good guy, though; I liked him all right." He paused. "Has he gone yet?" A strange quaver crept into his voice as he said the last words, and I understood that for the first time Racky's heretofore impeccable histrionics were not quite equal to the occasion. He was very much upset at losing Peter.

"Yes, he's gone," I said shortly. "He's not coming back, either." And as Racky, hearing the unaccustomed inflection in my voice, looked up at me suddenly with faint astonishment in his young eyes, I realized that this was the moment to press on, to say: "What did you have on him?" But as if he had arrived at the same spot in my mind a fraction of a second earlier, he proceeded to snatch away my advantage by jumping up, bursting into loud song, and pulling off all his clothes simultaneously. As he stood before me naked, singing at the top of his lungs, and stepped into his swimming trunks, I was conscious that again I should be incapable of saying to him what I must say.

He was in and out of the house all afternoon: some of the time he read in his room, and most of the time he was down on the diving board. It is strange behavior for him; if I could only know what is in his mind. As evening approached, my problem took on a purely obsessive character. I walked to and fro in my room, always pausing at one end to look out the window over the sea, and at the other end to glance at my face in the mirror. As if that could help me! Then I took a drink. And another. I thought I might be able to do it at dinner, when I felt fortified by the whisky. But no. Soon he will have gone to bed. It is not that I expect to confront him with any accusations. That I know I never can do. But I must find a way to keep him from his wanderings, and I must offer a reason to give him, so that he will never suspect that I know.

We fear for the future of our offspring. It is ludicrous, but only a little more palpably so than anything else in life. A length of time has passed; more days which I am content to have now, even if they are now over. They are over. I think that this period was what I had always been waiting for life to offer, the recompense I had unconsciously but firmly expected, in return for having been held so closely in the grip of existence all these years.

That evening seems long ago only because I have recalled its details so many times that they have taken on the color of legend. Actually my problem already had been solved for me then, but I did not know it. Because I could not perceive the pattern, I foolishly imagined that I must cudgel my brains to find the right words with which to approach Racky. But it was he who came to me. That same evening, as I was about to go out for a solitary stroll which I thought might help me hit upon a formula, he appeared at my door.

"Going for a walk?" he asked, seeing the stick in my hand.

The prospect of making an exit immediately after speaking with him made things seem simpler. "Yes," I said, "But I'd like to have a word with you first."

"Sure. What about?" I did not look at him because I did not want to see the watchful light I was sure was playing in his eyes at this moment. As I spoke I tapped my stick along the designs made by the tiles in the floor. "Racky, would you like to go back to school?"

"Are you kidding? You know I hate school."

I glanced at him. "No, I'm not kidding. Don't look so horrified. You'd probably enjoy being with a bunch of fellows your own age." (That was not one of the arguments I had meant to use.)

"I might like to be with guys my own age, but I don't want to have to be in school to do it. I've had school enough."

I went to the door and said lamely: "I thought I'd get your reactions."

He laughed. "No, thanks."

"That doesn't mean you're not going," I said over my shoulder as I went out.

On my walk I pounded the highway's asphalt with my stick, stood on the bridge having dramatic visions which involved such eventualies as our moving back to the States, Racky's having a bad spill and being paralyzed for months, and even the possibility of my letting events take their course, which would doubtless mean my having to visit him now and then in government prison with gifts of food, if it meant nothing more tragic and violent. "But none of these things will happen," I said to myself, and I knew I was wasting precious time; he must not return to Orange Walk tomorrow.

I went back toward the point at a snail's pace. There was no moon and very little breeze. As I approached the house, trying to tread lightly on the cinders so as not to awaken the watchful Ernest and have to explain to him that it was only I, I saw that there were no lights in Racky's room. The house was dark save for the dim lamp on my night table. Instead of going in, I skirted the entire building, colliding with bushes and getting my face sticky with spider webs, and went to sit a while on the terrace where there seemed to be a breath of air. The sound of the sea was far out on the reef, where the breakers sighed. Here, there were only slight watery chugs and gurgles now and then. It was unusually low tide. I smoked three cigarettes mechanically, having ceased even to think, and then, my mouth tasting bitter from the smoke, I went inside.

My room was airless. I flung my clothes onto a chair and looked at the night table to see if the carafe of water was there. Then my mouth opened. There on the far side of the bed, dark against the whiteness of the lower sheet, lay Racky asleep on his side, and naked.

I stood looking at him for a long, time, probably holding my breath, for I remember feeling a little dizzy at one point. I was whispering to myself, as my eyes followed the curve of his arm, shoulder, back, thigh, leg: "A child. A child." Destiny, when one perceives it clearly from very near, has no qualities at all. The recognition of it and the consciousness of the vision's clarity leave no room on the mind's horizon. Finally I turned off the light and softly lay down. The night was absolutely black.

He lay perfectly quiet until dawn. I shall never know whether or not he was really asleep all that time. Of course he couldn't have been, and yet he lay so still. Warm and firm, but still as death. The darkness and silence were heavy around us. As the birds began to sing, I sank into a soft, enveloping slumber; when I awoke in the sunlight later, he was gone.

I found him down by the water, cavorting on the springboard; for the first time he had discarded his trunks without my suggesting it. All day we stayed together around the terrace and on the rocks, talking, swimming, reading, and just lying flat in the hot sun. Nor did he return to his room when night came. Instead, after the servants were asleep, we brought three bottles of champagne in and set the pail on the night table.

Thus it came about that I was able to touch on the delicate subject that still preoccupied me, and profiting by the new understanding between us, I made my request in the easiest, most natural fashion.

"Racky, would you do me a tremendous favor if I asked you?"

He lay on his back, his hands beneath his head. It seemed to me his regard was circumspect, wanting in candor.

"I guess so," he said. "What is it?"

"Will you stay around the house for a few days—a week, say? Just to please me? We can take some rides together, as far as you like. Would you do that for me?"

"Sure thing," he said, smiling.

I was temporizing, but I was desperate.

Perhaps a week later (it is only when one is not fully happy that one is meticulous about time, so that it may have been more or less) we were having breakfast. Isaiah stood by, in the shade, waiting to pour us more coffee.

"I noticed you had a letter from Uncle Charley the other day," said Racky. "Don't you think we ought to invite him down?"

My heart began to beat with great force.

"Here? He'd hate it here," I said casually. "besides, there's no room. Where would he sleep?" Even as I heard myself saying the words, I knew they were the wrong ones, that I was not really participating in the conversation. Again I felt the fascination of complete helplessness that comes when one is suddenly a conscious on-looker at the shaping of one's fate.

"In my room," said Racky. "It's empty."

I could see more of the pattern at that moment than I had ever suspected existed. "Nonsense," I said. "This is not the place for Uncle Charley."

Racky appeared to be hitting on an excellent idea. "Maybe if I wrote and invited him," he suggested, motioning to Isaiah for more coffee.

"Nonsense," I said again, watching still more of the pattern reveal itself, like a photographic print becoming constantly clearer in a tray of developing solution.

Isaiah filled Racky's cup and returned to the shade. Racky drank slowly, pretending to be savoring the coffee.

"Well, it won't do any harm to try. He'd appreciate the invitation," he said speculatively.

For some reason, at this juncture I knew what to say, and as I said it, I knew what I was going to do.

"I thought we might fly over to Havana for a few days next week."

He looked guardedly interested, and then he broke out into a wide grin. "Swell," he cried. "Why wait until next week?"

The next morning the servants called good-bye to us as we drove up the cinder road in the McCoigh car. We took off from the airport at six that evening. Racky was in high spirits; he kept the stewardess engaged in conversation all the way to Camagüey.

He was also delighted with Havana. Sitting in the bar at the Nacional, we continued to discuss the possibility of having C. pay us a visit at the island. It was not without difficulty that I eventually managed to persuade Racky that writing him was inadvisable.

We decided to look for an apartment right there in Vedado for Racky. He did not seem to want to come back here to Cold Point. We also decided that living in Havana he would need a larger income than I. I am already having the greater part of Hope's estate transferred to his name in the form of a trust fund which I shall administer until he is of age. It was his mother's money, after all.

We bought a new convertible, and he drove me out to Rancho Boyeros in it when I took my plane. A Cuban named Claudio with very white teeth whom Racky had met in the pool that morning sat between us.

We were waiting in front of the landing field. An official finally unhooked the chain to let the passengers through. "If you get fed up, come to Havana," said Racky, pinching my arm.

The two of them stood together behind the rope, waving to me, their shirts flapping in the wind as the plane started to move.

The wind blows by my head; between each wave there are thousands of tiny licking and chopping sounds as the water hurries out of the crevices and holes; and a part-floating, part-submerged feeling of being in the water haunts my mind even as the hot sun burns my face. I sit here and I read, and I wait for the pleasant feeling of repletion that follows a good meal, to turn slowly, as the hours pass along, into the even more delightful, slightly stirring sensation deep within, which accompanies the awakening of appetite.

I am perfectly happy here in reality, because I still believe that nothing very drastic is likely to befall this part of the island in the near future.

MS Ferncape
(New York-Casablanca)
1947

UPPSALA
Stacey Levine

We come from a bad family and we are disgraced.

"What time do we get there?" asks brother.

"Stop cluttering your mind with those kinds of thoughts," answers Mother. It is brother's nineteenth birthday, and we are driving off to the cabin.

We think she is terrible.

The true source of our family remains unknown though it effectively has prevented speech and compassion for the speechless.

Destination our vacation home in Uppsala.

The mountains luminously shore up the family cabin and our cheeks burn red; in our tiny battered car, we make bare progress along the road with its columnar, trembling snow.

Amidst the piercing whiteness of which exist all our wishes that combine to produce a friction of desperate severity.

Where is the family we know?

Here, only here.

My brother speaks his own language, he always did, sitting behind a TV tray, or silently loading an ebony water pistol with saliva toward the purpose of expressing both his inborn glee and the necessity for being inarticulate around Mother. Father resembles a hassock.

Suddenly, of an evening, an angry, upset scream from within the cabin. It is Mother, who saw a flea, and fleas are a sign of dirt. Soon after, another unbearable scream. She has forgotten to bring along a loaf of bread. Such occurrences are irreparable to her; she cannot contain her fear though thankfully the snow has already fallen, the dry loam that quietens all sound and sharpens our sight.

Brother has spit up on the floor, rolling in it, kicking his hard shoes upon the newspaper. The headlines of which describe a recent commercial boom. Father, perhaps reading, perhaps not, blinks. The roof is stupendously heavy.

Our nights are static and lonely as ice gathers around the

perimeters of this family kitchen, this apothecary, this place in which even weak, leftover tea is as potent as methanol.

"Sonofabitch!" Mother screams maniacally from the rear bedroom, for she has misplaced her pendant.

Brother utters a chain of rough syllables into my hair.

If she is terrible, we say, the source of her anguish is a world beyond ours which we do not know, but which we can read like a stencil around her obfuscating yells and lies.

Is the cold northern angel a mere provocateur aiming to stir Brother and me to desire something, anything, in the way of solace and succulence? Our family is sad and does not live in a verdant place.

Distant snowaceous drifts, silhouettes of snow-burdened trees. The mountains which are ticking. We remain indoors; the little valley below our cabin being ceaselessly untouched.

Brother and I have an interview in the toilet. We must have it in our souls to relax—surely this is our atavistic right? but we are bound in a community tension and a stupendous threat the name of which only Mother knows. Unfortunately there are no other witnesses to this conundrum aside from the breeze which shoots vaporously from the table of snow. Perhaps the mountain itself.

The deep snow there which has intercepted our wills with its radar and produced in us a wish to topple the ideas upon which the world is founded.

Brother and I have known only Sweden.

He has comforted me with the unspeakably thin parchment of his chest. Because of our wounds, we each have grown permeable and have for example consoled one another at twilight. He babbles incurably gentle, ambiguous words that seal our complicity and this is true love, to which nothing else can compare.

Ruffled curtains of snow floating in the sky at dawn disguise all glare. Laughter and screams from the kitchen. We wish to flee, draw the weight of the weather to our breasts, interpolate the valley with our bitter knowledge, never be alone.

Beside me in the bathroom, brother seems to say that we must reason with them, try to talk. I am shocked; I violently disagree. We begin to struggle, grunting and slapping, bruising one another on the floor. Snow crusts drop from the window outside. Father hears, approaching with his hesitant curiosity. Then, the resoundingly loud footsteps of Mother.

That winter we learned that the snow incited our games and the desire to freeze away our mother's sickness and we grew angry.

There in the bathroom, we invented all sorts of people who adore the sun.

ACKNOWLEDGEMENTS

STEVE AYLETT for "Tusk." Copyright 1998 by Steve Aylett. By permission of the author.

DENNIS BARONE for "Day of Darkness, Day of Sorrow" and "The Substance." Copyright 1998 by Dennis Barone. By permission of the author.

MARCI BLACKMAN for "The Chokecherry Tree." Copyright 1998 by Marci Blackman. By permission of the author.

PAUL BOWLES and BLACK SPARROW PRESS for "Pages from *Cold Point*." Copyright 1947 by Paul Bowles. From *Collected Stories 1939–1976*, published by Black Sparrow Press, © 1979 by author and Black Sparrow. Reprinted by permission of Black Sparrow Press.

MICHAEL BRODSKY for "The Son, He Must Not Know." From *Southernmost and Other Stories*. Copyright 1996 by Michael Brodsky. By permission of the author and Four Walls Eight Windows.

THE CHARLES BUKOWSKI ESTATE and BLACK SPARROW PRESS for "Love for $17.50." Copyright 1973 by Charles Bukowski. From *South of No North*, published by Black Sparrow Press, © 1973, 1998 by Black Sparrow Press. Reprinted by permission of Black Sparrow Press.

GARRETT CAPLES for "Metempsychosis." Copyright 1998 by Garrett Caples. By permission of the author.

JEFF CLARK for "Sea Tang & Nino." Copyright 1998 by Jeff Clark. By permission of the author.

LYNN CRAWFORD for "Solow." Copyright 1995 by Lynn Crawford. From *Solow*, published by Hard Press, West Stockbridge, Massachusetts, © 1995 by Hard Press. Reprinted by permission of the author.

GUY DAVENPORT for "The Haile Selassie Funeral Train." From *Da Vinci's Bicycle*. Copyright © 1979 by Johns Hopkins University Press. Reprinted by permission of New Directions Publishing Corp.

RIKKI DUCORNET for "The Honk of M'Joob" and "Mandrake." Copyright 1998 by the author. By permission of the author.

JANICE EIDUS for "Snow White and the Seven Dicks." Copyright 1998 by the author. By permission of the author.

BRIAN EVENSON for "Body." Copyright 1998 by Brian Evenson. By permission of the author.

KENNETH GOLDSMITH for "Cunnilingus & Fellatio" and "Exhibitionism" and "Frigidity" and "Homosexuality." Copyright 1998 by Kenneth Goldsmith. By permission of the author.

JESSICA HAGEDORN for "F." Copyright 1998 by Jessica Hagedorn. By permission of the author.

SHELLEY JACKSON for "Jominy (An Art History)." Copyright 1998 by Shelley Jackson. By permission of the author.

LAURIE WEEKS for "Swallow." Copyright 1998 by Laurie Weeks. From *5 X 5 Singles*. By permission of the author.

JOHN YAU for "Tree Planting Ceremony" and "The Chinese Boy Who Lived Up to His Name." Copyright 1998 by John Yau. From *My Symptoms*, copyright © by Black Sparrow Press, Santa Rosa, California. By permission of the author.

STEVE AYLETT lives north of London. He is the author of *Slaughtermatic* (Four Walls Eight Windows, 1998), his first book to be published in the U.S. A collection of stories, *Toxicology*, is forthcoming from Four Walls Eight Windows in 1999.

DENNIS BARONE is the author of three books of fiction: *Abusing the Telephone* (1994), *The Returns* (1996), and *Echoes* (1997), which received the 1997 America Award for fiction. His novella *North Arrow* is forthcoming from Sun & Moon, and he is at work on a novel entitled *Temple of the Rat*. He teaches at Saint Joseph College in West Hartford, Connecticut.

MARCI BLACKMAN lives and writes in San Francisco, CA. Her first novel, *Po Man's Child*, is due out in the spring of 1999, from Manic D. Press.

PAUL BOWLES has lived for many years as an expatriate American in Tangier, Morocco. He is the author of four highly acclaimed novels: *The Sheltering Sky*, *Let It Come Down*, *The Spider's House*, and *Up Above the World*. In 1979 Black Sparrow Press published Bowles' *Collected Stories 1939-1976*. Also kept in print are *Midnight Mass* (stories) and *Next to Nothing: Collected Poems 1926-1977*.

MICHAEL BRODSKY lives in New York City. The translator of Samuel Beckett's *Eleuthéria*, he is the author of ten works of fiction and a number of plays and has received the Ernest Hemingway Citation of P.E.N. His latest book is *Southernmost and Other Stories* (Four Walls Eight Windows, 1996).

CHARLES BUKOWSKI published his first story in 1944 when he was twenty-four and began writing poetry at the age of thirty-five. He died in San Pedro, California on March 9, 1994 at the age of seventy-three, shortly after completing his last novel, *Pulp* (1994).

During his lifetime he published more than forty-five books of poetry and prose, including the novels *Post Office* (1971), *Factotum* (1975), *Women* (1978), *Ham on Rye* (1982), and *Hollywood* (1989). His most recent books are the posthumous editions of *Betting on the Muse: Poems & Stories* (1996), *Bone Palace Ballet: New Poems* (1997), and *The Captain Is Out To Lunch And The Sailors Have Taken Over The Ship* (1998) which is illustrated by Robert Crumb.

GARRETT CAPLES is a poet living in Berkeley, CA. He was born in 1972, ten years into the revolution that changed America (1962: invention of Pampers). He has published texts poetical (*The Dream of Curtains*, Angle), pornographical (pseudonymous), critical (reviews, liner notes), academical (on *Good Morning, Midnight* for *The Jean Rhys Review*), musical (on John Gilmore for *The Sun Ra Quarterly*), and hack (study guides, menus).

JEFF CLARK was born in 1971 in Matterhorn, California. His first book is *The Little Door Slides Back* (Sun & Moon).

LYNN CRAWFORD is the author of a book of short fiction, *Solow*, and a novel, *Blow* (both from Hard Press). She lives and works outside Detroit. Her reviews of art and literature have appeared in the *Detroit Metro Times*, *Art in America*, *American Ceramics*, and *Bookforum* (*Artforum*).

GUY DAVENPORT, a South Carolinian born in 1927, is a former Rhodes Scholar and MacArthur Fellow, and a current member of the American Academy of Arts and Sciences. He has published nine collections of short fiction, three of critical essays, and various books on art, as well as translations of Greek poetry.

RIKKI DUCORNET is a writer, artist, and editor. Her books include *The Complete Butcher's Tale*, *The Fountains of Neptune*, *The Jade Cabinet*, *The Stain*, and *The Cult of Seizure*. She lives in Denver.

JANICE EIDUS, winner of the O. Henry Prize for her short stories as well as a 1998 Pushcart Prize, is the author of four books: the short story collections *The Celibacy Club* and *Vito Loves Geraldine*, and the novels *Urban Bliss* and *Faithful Rebecca*. She is the co-editor of the anthology *It's Only Rock 'n' Roll: Rock 'n' Roll Short Stories*.

BRIAN EVENSON is the author of the recently published novel *Father of Lies* (Four Walls Eight Windows), and two books of stories, *Altmann's Tongue* and *The Din of Celestial Birds*. He teaches at Oklahoma State University.

KENNETH GOLDSMITH is the author of *73 Poems* (with Joan LaBarbara, Permanent Press, Brooklyn), *No. 111 2.7.93-10.20.96* (The Figures, Great Barrington MA), and *Fidget* (forthcoming from Maryland Institute, College of Art). In addition to being the editor of UbuWeb Visual, Concrete + Sound Poetry (ubu.com), he is a DJ at N.Y.C.-based freeform radio WFMU and a music critic for New York Press.

JESSICA HAGEDORN'S first novel, *Dogeaters*, was nominated for a National Book Award in 1990. Her second novel, *The Gangster of Love*, was published in 1996. A performance artist, poet, playwright, and screenwriter, she is also the author of *Danger and Beauty: Poetry and Prose*, as well as the editor of *Charlie Chan Is Dead: An Anthology of Contemporary Asian American Fiction*.

SHELLEY JACKSON holds an AB in studio art from Stanford University and an MFA on creative writing from Brown University. She is the author of the hypertext novel *Patchwork Girl* (Eastgate Systems 1995), the web-based multimedia project *My Body: a Wunderkammer* (Alt-X 1997). Her stories have appeared in various journals, including *Conjunctions*, *Gargoyle*, and *Fence*, and she has illustrated several children's books in addition to her own, *The Old Woman and the Wave* (DK Ink 1998).

Robert Kelly, poet, novelist, and short story writer, has published over fifty books. Recent publications include *Red Actions: Selected Poems 1960-1993* (1995). His fiction can be found in *Cat Scratch Fever* (1990), *Doctor of Silence* (1988), and *A Transparent Tree* (1985). He teaches at Bard College and lives in upstate New York.

Kevin Killian, born 1952, is a poet, novelist, critic and playwright. He has written a book of stories, *Little Men* (1996), two novels, *Shy* (1989) and Arctic Summer (1997), and a book of memoirs, *Bedrooms Have Windows* (1989). Recently published: a book of stories, *Little Men* (1996), which won the PEN Oakland award for fiction, and (with Lewis Ellingham) *Poet Be Like God: Jack Spicer and the San Francisco Renaissance* (1998), the first biography of the important U.S. poet. His first book of poetry, *Argento Series,* appeared in the autumn of 1997.

Cybele Knowles, who lives in the Bay Area, graduated with a Master's in English from UC Berkeley in 1998. Her poems have appeared in *Angle, Asian Pacific American Journal, Faucheuse*, and *The Prose Poem*.

Jonathan Lethem has recently published a novel *Girl In Landscape*. His earlier books are *Gun, With Occasional Music, Amnesia Moon*, and *As She Climbed Across the Table*. He's also published a story collection, called *The Wall of the Eye, The Wall of the Sky*. He lives in Brooklyn and is working on a new novel.

Stacey Levine is the author of *My Horse and Other Stories* and *Dra—*, both published by Sun & Moon Press. She lives in Seattle where she writes for *The Stranger*. She is at work on a novel, Frances Johnson, and likes to collect and read pulp nurse-romance novels.

Gordon Lish is the author of a number of works of fiction, among them *Dear Mr. Capote, What I Know So Far, Mourner at the Door, Peru, Extravaganza, My Romance, Zimzum, Selected Stories*, and *Epigraph*, all published by Four Walls Eight Windows. This body of work together with his activities as a teacher, founder and editor of *The Quarterly*, editor at Knopf, and fiction editor at *Esquire* have placed him at the forefront of the American literary scene. His newest work, *Arcade*, was released in fall 1998 by Four Walls.

Gary Lutz's *Stories in the Worst Way* was brought out by Knopf in 1996. He is a recent recipient of a fellowship from the National Endowment for the Arts and is at work on a second book.

Ben Marcus is the author of a book of fiction, *The Age of Wire and String*. His work has appeared in *Grand Street, The Iowa Review*, the *Pushcart Prize* anthology, *Conjunctions*, and other magazines. He edits the online magazine *Impossible Object* at Brown University, where he teaches writing.

Carole Maso is the author of six novels: *Ghost Dance, The Art Lover,*

AVA, Aureole, The American Woman in the Chinese Hat, and *Defiance*. The recipient of the Lannan Literary Fellowship for fiction, Maso is currently director of the Creative Writing Program and professor of English at Brown University.

Born in New York in 1930, HARRY MATHEWS settled in Europe in 1952 and has since then lived in Spain, Germany, Italy, and (chiefly) France. In 1978 he returned to the United States to teach for several years at Bennington College and Columbia University. When Mathews published his first poems in 1956, he was associated with the so-called New York School of poets, with three of whom (John Ashbery, Keneth Koch, James Schuyler) he founded the review *Locus Solus* in 1961. The author of five novels and several collections of poetry, he has since 1994 been preparing a comprehensive *Oulipo Compendium*, to be published by Atlas Press (London) next fall.

CRIS MAZZA is the author of eight books of fiction, including the PEN/Nelson Algren award-winning *How to Leave a Country* and, most recently, *Dog People* (novel) and *Former Virgin* (short stories). She was also the editor of the controversial anthologies *Chick-Lit* and *Chick-Lit 2*, which drew fire from a Congressional committee.

ALBERT MOBILIO has published two books of poetry, *Bendable Siege* and *The Geographics*. His poems have appeared in literary journals such as *Grand Street, Hambone, Talisman*, and *The Germ*. His reviews and essays appear in the *Village Voice, Harper's*, and *Salon*. The selection in this anthology is from a short story collection in progress titled *A Handbook of Phrenology*.

EILEEN MYLES' newest book of poems, *School of Fish* (Black Sparrow) just won a Lambda Book award. She is a frequent contributor to *The Nation, Art in America, Nest*, and *The Stranger*. "Poison Ivy" is an excerpt from her forthcoming novel, *Cool for You*.

BETH NUGENT teaches in the Writing Program at the Art Institute of Chicago. She is the author of a book of short stories *City of Boys* (1993) and a novel *Live Girls* (1997). She is currently working on a novel.

WANG PING, born in Shanghai, came to New York in 1985. Her publications include a book of short stories, *American Visa*; a novel, *Foreign Devil*; a book of poetry, *Of Flesh and Spirit* (all from Coffee House Press). She is writing a book on the fetish of footbinding.

JAMES PONIEWOZIK lives in Brooklyn. His fiction has appeared in *Mississippi Review* and *Indiana Review*; he has written nonfiction for magazines including *Salon, New York*, and *Fortune*.

A. G. RIZZOLI was born in 1896 in Marin County, California and moved with his family in 1915 to San Francisco, where he would spend the rest of his life. His arrival coincided with the opening of the Panama-Pacific International Exposition, a World's-Fair-like celebration whose symbol-laden, temporary structures—mixing a variety of architectural styles—would exert a lifelong influence on his work as a visionary artist. From 1935 until his paralyzing stroke in 1977, he made several series of drawings, combining allegorical representations of various people as buildings with elaborate textual glosses, the work for which he is best-known. But for approximately ten years prior, he conceived of himself primarily as writer, amassing a large body of unpublished novels, short stories, and verse in which he created many of the characters later to appear in his visual art. He died in 1981, having only ever shared his work with a handful of bewildered relatives and acquaintances. His work was discovered and promoted in the 1990s by Bonnie Grossman's Ames Gallery of Berkeley, CA. In 1997, the San Diego Museum of Art organized *A. G. Rizzoli: Architect of Magnificent Visions*, a complete retrospective of his visual art, which subsequently appeared at the High Museum of Art, the Museum of American Folk Art, and SFMOMA. A catalogue of the show was published by Abrams. This is his first published story.

RUDY RUCKER is known for his popular books *Infinity and the Mind* and *The Fourth Dimension* as well as for his ten science fiction novels, which include *White Light* and the classic cyberpunk series *Software, Wetware, Freeware*. Coming soon are Rucker's non-fiction futurology *Saucer Wisdom* from Tor Books, and Rucker's non-fiction anthology *Seek!* from Four Walls Eight Windows. More info can be found on his website www.mathcs.sjsu.edu/faculty/rucker.

LYNNE TILLMAN'S fiction includes the novels *Haunted Houses, Motion Sickness, Cast In Doubt*, and *No Lease On Life*, and two collections of short fiction, *Absence Makes the Heart* and *The Madame Realism Complex*. Her nonfiction includes *The Velvet Years: Warhol's Factory 1965-1967*, with photographs by Stephen Shore, and an essay collection, *The Broad Picture*. She is currently writing *Bookstore: The Life and Times of Jeanette Watson and Books & Co.*, to be published by Harcourt Brace in 1999.

LAURIE WEEKS is has had work appear in the Semiotext [e] anthology *The New Fuck You: Adventures in Lesbian Reading, Sulfur, Mirage/ Period [ical], 5 x 5 Singles, Reflex, The LA Weekly, The Austin Chronicle*, and *Out* magazine. Her play *Young Skulls II*, based on the true story of teenage lesbian thrillkillers in Indiana, was produced at the WOW Cafe in New York and The Lab in San Francisco. She teaches at The New School.

JOHN YAU'S recent books include a book of poems, *Forbidden Entries* (1996), a critical essay *The United States of Jasper Johns* (1996), and a book of short stories *My Symptoms* (1998). During the past year, he contributed essays to exhibition catalogs published by the Bonn

Kunstmuseum, Contemporary Art Museum (Tampa), IVAM Centre Julio Gonzalez (Valencia), Fundacio la Caixa (Barcelona), Jeu de Paume (Paris), and Staatliche Kunsthalle Karlsruhe. He teaches at the Maryland Institute, College of Art, where he also directs the poetry reading series. The recipient of a 1998-1999 NYFA Fellowship in fiction, he lives in New York.